Riley Parra
Season One

Geonn Cannon

Supposed Crimes LLC • Falls Church, Virginia

This book is a work of fiction. Names, characters, places, and incidents are products of the author's imagination or are used fictitiously. Any resemblance to actual events or locales or persons, living or dead, is entirely coincidental.

All Rights Reserved
Copyright © 2011 Geonn Cannon

Published in the United States.
Supposed Crimes LLC
Virginia

Second Edition

ISBN: 978-0-9828989-3-2

www.supposedcrimes.com

This book is typeset in Goudy Old Style, licensed by Ascender Corporation.

*This book is dedicated to everyone who kept reading,
and kept asking for more,
and turned it into the beast it's become.
I owe it to all of you!*

Better Angels	1
No Use Crying	115
Open and Shut, No. 1: Shades of Gray	163
Losing My Religion	177
Open and Shut, No. 2: All Mortal Flesh	229
Angels Would Fall	237
Open and Shut, No. 3: Beautiful Night	273
The Martyr	289
Open and Shut, No. 4: Heaven is Overrated	355
My Empire of Dirt	363
The Life of Riley	417
Ride Along	477
Maintenance	485

Better Angels

Chapter One

This far away from the center, the city began to reek. The tenements, the slums, the condemned buildings that still housed families unable to afford anything better, all combined to form the city's outer crust. Sometimes the elevated train still thundered through this part of town, lit from within like a shining bullet, giving the businesspeople aboard a look at what could have been. Many ignore it, some whisper a 'but for the grace' prayer, and then the train is gone again.

On street level, the stink was worse and more refined. Stinking plastic bags were stacked on the sidewalks because the garbage men couldn't be bothered to come here on a regular basis. Old Chinese food, various bodily fluids, and the underlying scent of decay. Patrolwoman Riley Parra entered the diner and felt the instantaneous shift of bodies on vinyl stools. Drug deals ceased, people stopped speaking mid-sentence, and every eye made a point to be somewhere other than the blue uniform that had just stepped through the door.

David Bowie wailed over the speaker system as she walked across the room to the counter. Riley was one of the few police in the city still willing to cross the imaginary line between the Good Side of the Tracks and the Bad Side. The general consensus was that if everyone on that side of town wanted to kill themselves, why not let them? Good riddance to bad rubbish, survival of the fittest and all that.

When questioned about why she bothered, Riley would simply put on her cap and slip the baton into her belt, shrug and say, "Call me an optimist."

She drummed her knuckles on the counter, and the owner reluctantly made his way over. He wiped his hands on a towel and showed his clean palms to her. "No crime here," he said.

"Glad to hear it, Leon," Riley said. "I need to know if you've heard about anything happening two streets over."

Leon pretended to think as David Bowie shouted about genocide through the speakers overhead.

Finally, Leon said, "Nope. Nothing."

"I'm parking my patrol car right there," she said, pointing to it through the window. "Anything happens to it, Leon... if a bird shits on my windshield. I'm coming after you. Understand me?"

Leon muttered his understanding and Riley turned to leave the bar. She stopped at the door and looked over the people who were being very careful not to watch her. Skells and drunks and junkies, all watching her from the corners of their eyes, their world on hold until she had moved out of their orbits. She pushed through the door, trading David Bowie's wail for the sound of sirens in the distance.

Riley sniffed as she stepped out onto the street. Her exchange with Leon pretty much summed up the police commissioner's feelings for this part of town; let the dregs kill each other off, thin out the herd, and then we can sweep in and clean the place up for whoever is left. Any effort Riley put into trying to protect these people was wasted, as far as the top brass was concerned. She rolled her shoulders and started walking.

She was investigating a call that came in from dispatch, a rather bored woman explaining that her kids hadn't been home in the last three nights. The woman gave their descriptions and said, "If you find 'em, keep 'em. Probably afford 'em better than I can, anyway."

Riley was accustomed to this kind of call. No one at the department cared if she looked, the parent didn't care if she looked, and she doubted the kids, when and if she found them, would be happy that she had stuck her nose in. She would take them home, kicking and screaming, deliver them to their disappointed mother, and return to the office to write a report that would most likely get shredded before it was read. So why bother?

"Because someone has to," she muttered. It was the real answer to the question her colleagues always asked. It was the reason she continued to patrol the area even though no one wanted her there. For the one kid who hid behind her bed while her parents fought, or while gunfire erupted next door. She stayed for herself, twenty years ago, crying and covering her ears and praying someone would come and help.

No one ever came for her.

The people on this side of town never really agreed on what to call their little slice of Hell. Some called it the Badlands, and the more poetic called it Satan's Shit Hole. The official name, in newspaper stories and on television, was No Man's Land. Riley, in her reports and in her mind, thought of it as just Old City. It was where she grew up, and what had made her who she was. Even though she was one of the few to make it out and start a life on the bright side of town, it didn't change who she was inside.

She knew that kids liked to hang out in burned shells of apartment buildings. She didn't bother checking every building; there were subtle themes to each gathering. One was drugs, identifiable by the scents wafting from within. Another was sex, an impromptu orgy of teenagers and adults that had, more likely than not, never met before. Riley bypassed each of these with regret; there was nothing she could do on her own, and back-up would never arrive. She would have to pick her battles. Besides, there was every chance that once she got the pictures from their mother, she would have to come back and find the missing kids among the "celebrants."

Riley was almost to the street where the missing kids lived when she heard a scream. She turned, now perfectly tuned in to her surroundings. She scanned the dark shadows between buildings, eyed the open or broken windows of the buildings, and put her hand on the butt of the weapon. She ran back the way she had come and turned down the alley from which she thought the scream had come.

Two dark shapes stood in the yellow sodium glow of a security light. One body was slumped, lifeless, held up by the other man's hands wrapped in the lapels of his coat. As Riley watched, the victor dropped his victim to the ground and stepped back.

"Police! Freeze!"

The man turned and looked at her, his face hidden by the hood he wore. He seemed to debate fight or flight, then dropped into a crouch. Riley thought he was going to lunge at her and drew her weapon. Instead, the man leapt up. He grabbed the bottom rung of a fire escape, yanked it down, and scrambled up onto the metal trellis. Riley stopped and said, "Freeze! I will shoot!" When the man continued his upward escape, Riley dropped down next to his victim. The man's eyes were still open, his features frozen in terror, but there was no doubt he was dead.

She looked up and saw her quarry was too far away and too protected by the fire escape for her to get a shot off. She dropped into a crouch, leapt, and just barely caught the bottom rung of the ladder. Her shoulders protested as she tried to haul herself up, kicking her feet as she tried to do a pull-up for the first time since the academy.

Finally, exhausted, she made it to the lowest level of the fire escape.

"Freeze!" she called again, but she had no hopes that the killer would listen to her. She took a deep breath and began the ascent. She was already dripping with sweat, panting as she climbed the metal ladder. There was something wet on the rungs and her feet kept threatening to slip out from underneath her. She lost her cap somewhere along the way, and her black hair waved around her head as it came loose from her bun.

When she reached the roof, she thought all her work had been for nothing. She stood, panting, and looked for any sign of the killer. Her head throbbed, and her heart felt like it was going to explode. There was a shack at the far end of the roof, plus a small wedge-shaped outcropping that she assumed led to the stairs. She moved to the stairwell door and found a thick padlock holding it shut. She kept her gun out, aimed at the ground as she moved toward the center of the roof. "All right, I know you didn't jump to the next building. Come on out."

Riley moved carefully, keeping her ears open for sounds of furtive movement. She reached the shack, braced herself, and stepped around the corner to face the back. She brought her gun up as she moved, ready to open fire, but it was unnecessary; no killer lurked, no length of pipe swung toward her head. She stepped away from the building and turned her attention to the roof. "All right, now, come on down. I've had enough of this."

"Pity," a voice said from right behind her.

Riley gasped and spun, but the man was too quick for her. He grabbed her gun hand, twisted, and popped the weapon from her grip. He tossed it across the roof with a flick of his wrist and closed his other hand around her neck. Riley suddenly couldn't breathe. She gasped and clawed at the man's hand as he lifted her off the tar of the roof. *God damn, how strong is this bastard?*

"You should have just let me go."

Moonlight and cast-off glow from the streetlights below gave her a look under his hood, and she felt something clench deep in her chest. The killer's face was hideous; a stretch of red, exposed muscle and yellow eyes. His mouth was the frozen grin of a skull, held together by thin rubber band tendons. Riley wanted to scream, wanted to faint, but she could only stare in terror as the man walked her to the edge of the building.

"Don't," she gasped.

The man tossed her without any apparent effort, and Riley went sailing over the edge of the roof. She fell in a slow, gentle arc, the wind cushioning her like a feather bed. She closed her eyes, anticipating the crushing, killing blow that would break every bone in her body and turn her into so much mush.

But the impact never came.

Riley opened her eyes some time later. She was flat on her back, spread out on the pavement. She could feel the sweat drying under her uniform, felt a painful throb in her back. But nothing seemed broken. She rolled onto her side and pressed her hand against the filthy concrete. She was hurt, but was undeniably alive and mobile. She coughed and rolled onto her hands and knees, then pushed herself up. Her head pounding and she squinted down the street. She was standing in front of the building she had... what? She had fallen. She must have fallen. There's no way she saw what she thought she saw. And no way anyone could have thrown her the way that... thing did.

She looked up at the building and counted the floors. Ten stories, about eight feet each. She had fallen eighty feet to the ground, maybe more, and all she had was a headache and a few sore bones. She checked her holster and found her service weapon was there, safe and sound. It must have been a hallucination. That's the only explanation.

Across the street, a man stood watching her. He wore a leather trenchcoat and blue slacks, his hands buried in the pockets of his coat. He dipped his chin to her, and Riley saluted with two fingers from her brow. The move made her remember that she had lost her cap, and she looked toward the alley where the chase began. When she looked back across the street, the man in the trenchcoat was gone.

Riley put her hand on the butt of her gun and walked to the alley to see if she could find her missing cap. She didn't want to have to requisition another one; she had no idea how she would even begin to fill out the paperwork.

Four years later

Blood-red flesh, eyes that burned with the fires of Hell. Riley felt the claws digging into her throat, the blood trickling down under her uniform blouse, and she knew this was it. The Thing stared at her, decayed teeth exposed in a snarl as it moved her to the edge of the building. When she was released, Riley knew she wasn't falling toward the street. Flames reached for her, the screams of the damned echoed all around her. The Thing on the Roof watched her fall, and his hood fell back to reveal two curled horns.

Riley shouted, lashed out, and her fist met soft flesh. Someone next to her said, "Ow, watch it," and Riley realized she had been in the dream again. She sat up in bed, panting as if the air had been sucked from the room. She was drenched in sweat, her tank top clinging to her chest as she slipped out from under the covers.

"Where are you going?"

"Bathroom," Riley said. Her voice was raspy, as if she had been screaming all night. Maybe she had been. A past lover had once revealed that Riley would open her mouth and silently scream for ten, twenty minutes at a time. It came out as a thin, raspy wheeze, and it always ended as suddenly as it began.

Riley turned on the bathroom light, squinted in the sudden brightness, and looked at her reflection in the mirror. Four years, and she still had the nightmare about the roof. No, not a nightmare. A terror. A psychological shriek. It had been so long that she no longer knew what the hell had happened that night. She told herself it was a regular, run of the mill killer and she was tripping off a contact high from one of the parties she had passed. That was the only logical explanation. It was the only explanation that kept her sane.

Someone appeared in the bathroom door, blurry in the dirty glass. The redhead, of course. Riley closed her eyes and pushed her hands through her dark hair. "Go back to bed. I'm sorry I hit you."

"It's okay. We all have nightmares." She stepped into the room and put her hand on Riley's shoulder. Riley had to resist the urge to pull away from the touch. The redhead pushed aside the strap of Riley's tank top and traced the tattoo on her shoulder. "Wow, this is awesome. Who did it for you?"

Riley did pull away from the woman this time, shrugging so that her shirt covered the tattoo again. "You should go."

"But... I thought we talked about breakfast. And..."

"No. You should go. I'm not feeling well."

The redhead looked disappointed, but took it like an adult. "All right. I'll get my things." She turned and went back into the bedroom. A few seconds later, she heard clothing being pulled on and items being shoved back into the bag they had come out of. Riley stepped to the bathtub, pushed aside the curtain, and turned on the hot water. She stripped out of her tank top and pushed her underwear down, hoping her guest would be gone by the time she got out of the shower.

Chapter Two

Riley didn't go back to bed after leaving the shower. She could never sleep so soon after having the Dream. So she dressed in sweats, went into the living room, and turned on the TV. There was a rerun of Family Feud on the Game Show Network, a Richard Dawson episode. Seeing it reminded her of being in Nana's apartment, the smell of cigarettes and butterscotches and hoping maybe this time Mommy wouldn't come home after all. Halfway through one of the rounds, Riley heard a shout from down the hall. A woman's voice starting high, ending low and then breaking off into a sob.

She stood up and walked casually to the front door. She was barefoot and unarmed, wearing plain gray sweats. She took a moment to assess the situation; the junk-head at the end of the hall was standing in his doorway, hand clasped around his "girlfriend's" upper arm, bent low to whisper something in her ear. He had to bend low because she was currently curled up against the wall, one hand covering her face as she shook with her tears.

The man looked up as Riley approached. He sneered and said, "What, you want round two?"

Riley didn't answer him. She got within arm's reach of him and swung her arm like a sword. The flat edge of her hand caught him in the throat, right at the Adam's apple, and he choked. Riley followed up by grabbing a handful of his greasy hair, yanking his head back, and rushing him toward the wall. Something - drywall, cartilage, she didn't care which - cracked when he hit, and the man went down.

Riley looked at the woman, who had a vivid red mark on her forearm. There was another mark, barely distinguishable from the older bruises, on her face. She was reed thin, and she lowered her chin in an attempt to cover her face with her black-and-white striped hair. "Are you okay?"

"I..."

"Get out before he gets up."

The girl looked at her boyfriend and decided to take Riley's advice. She scrambled to her feet, got to the stairs and disappeared in a flurry of footsteps pounding on the wooden steps. Riley turned back to the guy and hauled him to his feet. She pressed him against the wall and said, "I am a police officer. If you ever give me a reason to acknowledge your existence, so help me God, I will make you sorry. Do you understand me?"

"Yeah. Sure."

She released him and stepped back. His apartment door was open, and she could smell the combined reek of several drugs. She wrinkled her nose as she heard the familiar ring of her cell phone down the hall. She released the junkie and said, "Move. Out of the building. Tomorrow." She turned and went back to her apartment. She slammed the door, picked up her cell phone, and snapped it open. "What?"

"Whoa, testy. Did I wake you up?"

The voice belonged to Kara Sweet, Riley's partner. She sighed and sat on the edge of the couch. "We got a body," Riley said with a sigh.

"We got a body," Kara confirmed. "You're going to want your high-waters for this one."

Riley groaned. The day was getting off to a wonderful start. And the most horrible part was that it probably wouldn't even be her worst day that week. She got the specifics from Kara, then hung up and went to go get dressed.

The crime scene was at the so-called waterfront on the very edge of No Man's Land. Riley still hated the name, but the new mayor declared the moniker official during his inaugural address two years earlier. Since then, things in the bad part of town had only gotten worse. Rather than all the dregs of society dying off, they had grown stronger. People screwing anything and everything that moved bred new generations of leeches, and the leeches expanded inward. No Man's Land had nearly doubled in size since Riley first joined the force. Before long, the entire city would fall to decay. She wondered if anyone would be alive to mourn it, or sober enough to care.

The sun was just starting to rise when Riley arrived at the scene. Kara Sweet, also known as Sweet Kara by several men on the force, was standing just outside of the yellow police tape. She spotted Riley getting out of her car and walked over. Kara wore tight blue jeans, a baggy white peasant blouse, and a brown leather jacket. Her blonde hair was cut short and spiky. Riley looked her over and said, "Did we cut your date short?"

"Call it business casual," Kara said. She gestured toward the cliff. "Sewage pipes. We're always the lucky ones, aren't we?"

Riley sighed and ducked under the tape. As they approached, she caught a whiff of the unmistakable stench that came with sewage dumping. The ground was littered with orange juice cartons, Styrofoam containers, used condoms, used needles, diapers and take-out cartons, evidence that the people of No Man's Land didn't even bother to toss their trash into plastic bags before throwing it out. She wrinkled her nose and focused on the crime scene.

A group of forensic technicians were gathered around one of the pipes that jutted from the side of the cliff like stubs of broken finger bones. Kara took Riley's hand to help her descend without falling, Kara's red cowgirl boots digging in to the mud to give her better balance than Riley's sneakers afforded.

One of the technicians handed Riley a flashlight. "Don't touch anything," he warned.

"I've been doing this longer than you," she griped. She crouched in front of the pipe and shined the light inside.

The body was lying on its side, arms and legs crossed in front. The head was bent forward, so all they could see was thick blonde hair. She leaned to the left and saw that the man was either naked or wearing very skimpy underwear. Blood smeared the corrugated metal of the pipe, top and bottom. The middle of the man's back was flayed, as if an entire layer of skin had been excised. Riley made a face and said, "Figure that wound on the back is what killed him?"

"Don't know until we get him out of there," the tech said. "Of course, I haven't been doing this as long as you."

She handed him the flashlight and said, "Well, then, get him out of there." She brushed her hands on her jeans and joined Kara a few feet away.

Kara was looking up at the city, the lights glowing in the shattered buildings. She watched Riley approach and gestured. "You grew up around here, didn't you?"

"Close enough to smell the shit down here. Good place to hide a body. No one will smell it, no one will come down here to see it." She frowned. "How was it found, anyway?"

"Some guy's dog. Must have smelled the blood or something."

"We're lucky Fido didn't play fetch."

The technicians got the body out of the pipe and laid him out on a tarp. He was definitely naked, his porcelain white skin untouched by violence. No bruises, no cuts, no bullet wounds other than the obvious. The left side of his body was stained black and purple with livor mortis. Riley moved closer and said, "Give me some gloves." She snapped the rubber gloves on and pushed the body up so she could examine his back. One of the techs held the corpse up and Riley twisted her head to look at the wound.

"Nasty. What do you think, Kara? Blood loss? Shock?"

"Someone carved a hole in his back, so he decided to crawl into the pipe and die?"

"I don't see any other wounds." They let the body back down and Riley stood up. "Let me know as soon as you have a cause of death." To Kara, she said, "I guess there was no wallet lying around with a driver's license sitting in plain sight? So we'll have to wait for the fingerprints to come back before we know who this guy is."

"Yep. Care to join me in a door-to-door? See some of your old friends and neighbors?"

Riley eyed the buildings along the waterfront with distaste. "I never had any neighbors," she said. "And any friends, I left behind a long time ago."

Riley made the rounds in the nearest apartment buildings while Kara took the apartments further down. A few doors she knocked at revealed people who were wide awake, likely on their way to bed, while others revealed the bloodshot, wide eyes of paranoid druggies roused from their nightly comas. The only thing everyone had in common was that they were too caught up in whatever they were doing - sex, drugs, sleep - that no one had bothered to look out the window. Riley finished with the apartment on the top floor and trudged wearily down the stairs to the sidewalk.

She didn't see Kara, so she assumed she had a few seconds to herself. She moved to the edge of the sidewalk, folded her arms, and watched as the crime scene guys wandered across the waterfront. In an ordinary town, this would be a huge happening. The dawn was breaking, people would be getting ready to go to work, and everyone would gather outside the police tape with shocked expressions that something so terrible could happen on their doorstep.

Not here, though. In No Man's Land, life went on. People would come downstairs, see the crime tape and the flashing lights, and take alternate routes to wherever they needed to go. Not to work, most likely, unless that work involved standing on a street corner looking inconspicuous.

Riley saw her first dead body when she was five years old. He had been in her apartment stairwell, the needle still hanging from his emaciated arm. His eyes were open and he seemed to be staring at her, imploring her for help. She thought she would never get over it. But life had a funny way of trumping her worst nightmares, time and again.

"Got a smoke?"

Riley turned to see a woman exiting the building she had just canvassed. She reached into her jacket, found the pack of smokes she kept on hand for the ever-quitting Kara, and tapped one out. She held it out to the prostitute, who lit it using a match she produced from somewhere in her leather jacket. She took a deep drag, held it, then blew it from her nostrils in twin streams like a dragon. "Thanks. Had to get the taste out of my mouth."

"Long night?"

"Three apartments," the woman said. She took another drag. "You know what it's like trying to be just as fresh for Appointment Number Three as you were for Number One?"

"No one likes to know they were third in line."

The prostitute laughed gave a low, hoarse laugh. "Actually, some of them do."

Riley said, "What time did you get to Mister Three?"

"Honey, I don't know what time it is now."

The prostitute was staring across the street at the crime scene, but she didn't seem to be curious about it. Riley nodded. "You see anything happen over there?"

"Nothing I want to get involved with."

"Just between you and me, then," Riley said. "You give me information that helps me fill in some blanks, no one has to know where the information came from."

The prostitute hesitated for a moment, so Riley reached back into her pocket. She pulled out the pack of cigarettes and said, "Here. For later."

"Hmph. I cost way more than a pack of cigs, lady."

"All I want is to talk."

She took another drag, then took the pack. "That's what they all say, honey." She sighed, rolled her shoulders, and pointed across the street. "When I showed up, there were two guys standing on the rocks by the water. Like they were waiting for someone. It wasn't too cold, but they were both wearing big jackets. Like, um. Dick Tracy. Third guy comes walking down the street and he passed me, going down to the water."

"Anything unusual about him?"

"Sometimes, a guy will pull up in a car, and he'll ask you how much you charge. Sometimes you get in the car, go around the corner, and you get a little quick cash." Riley nodded. "Do this often enough, you know what cars not to get into. You get a sense. When this guy walked past me tonight, I wouldn't have gotten into his car for a million bucks. I've been with my share of assholes, got the bruises to prove it. But this guy made me want to run home and jump back into bed."

"Got a description?"

"Mm. He was wearing one of those hoodies pulled down over his face."

Riley felt like skeleton fingers were tracing up and down her spine. Not only impossible, but ridiculous. *The nightmare is getting to you.*

"When was that?"

"'Bout three hours ago."

Riley whistled. "What did you have up there, a marathon man?"

"Quickie followed by a nap followed by a hand job," she said. "Girl's gotta sleep."

"Yes, she does. Thanks for your help."

"Any time, sugar." She looked Riley up and down and said, "I have a police discount, you know. If you ever–"

"Thanks," Riley said again.

The prostitute lifted a shoulder and walked away. She passed Kara and they exchanged hellos. Kara was fiddling with a notepad as she approached Riley. "Hey. What were you talking to Ray about?"

Riley laughed. "Her name is Ray?"

Kara lifted her shoulder. "Ray can be a girl's name. What did she say?"

"I found out there were two guys, met by a third, standing down where we found our body."

"I got you one better," Kara said. "Two guys who met with a third, and one of them had a sword."

"A *what?*"

Kara nodded and motioned over her shoulder. "Landlord down there saw a guy climbing up the embankment with a sword."

Riley frowned at that. The wound she saw would have needed precision. She pictured the victim leaning forward, head bowed, while someone brought the sword down like a guillotine blade. The sword would have to have twisted to take out such a large chunk. It would be painful, sure, but would it be enough to cause death? She shook her head; that was for Gillian to answer. She checked her watch and said, "It'll take the ME some time to check out the body. Want some breakfast?"

"If you're paying."

"I just have to swing by my apartment and pick up some cash."

"You don't carry cash in No Man's Land anymore?"

Riley scoffed. "You're lucky I still carry my badge. I'm always afraid someone is going to steal the thing and melt it down."

Riley drove to her apartment while Kara went straight to the diner. Riley left her car running as she went inside, jogging up the stairs. When she reached her floor, she saw the black-and-white haired girl sitting on the floor outside her boyfriend's apartment. She looked up, recognized Riley, and had the decency to look ashamed of herself. She looked down at her hands, twisting the sleeves of her jacket between her fingers.

"You don't understand," the girl said.

Riley shook her head. "Thank God for that."

She walked past the girl without looking back, retrieved her wallet, and headed back downstairs for breakfast. She would have prayed that she wouldn't run into the girl again in a more professional capacity, but she was done with praying. Too many had gone unanswered.

Chapter Three

The Four-Ten Diner took up the ground floor of a run-down building that straddled the current line between the haves and have-nots, the bright from the dim, and No Man's Land from the 'good part of town.' A circular counter took up most of the space in the middle of the room, with stools all around it like satellites orbiting a planet. Several booths hugged the walls, for those diners who preferred the illusion of privacy.

Riley entered and spotted Kara sitting in the furthest booth from the door. She waved off the hostess and rounded the counter. Kara spotted her and said, "I already ordered you a coffee and the Big Time Breakfast."

"The kind with pancakes?"

"Mm-hmm."

Riley slid into the booth and shrugged out of her jacket. "Thanks."

"You look pissed off."

"Vicious cycle," Riley sighed. She folded her hands on top of the table and looked around the room. Few people from the good side of town risked coming this close to No Man's Land unless they had the protection of a badge. Conversely, no one from No Man's Land risked coming so close to the good side of town for fear of running afoul of the police. The Four-Ten, realizing they had to adjust or go broke, began catering exclusively to cops. At the moment, she and Kara had the place to themselves.

Riley sighed and leaned back. The vinyl of the booth cracked against her shoulders. "What do you think about our fellow with the sword?"

"Role-play gone wrong."

Riley shook her head. "The worst role-play I ever had, I ended up handcuffed to my bed minus a wallet and my TV. That's a far cry from getting part of my back hacked off."

"True," Kara said. "You never did thank me for letting you out of those handcuffs."

"It took you an hour to show up."

"I could have taken some pictures. Made you a legend at the department."

Riley rolled her eyes as their breakfast was delivered. Riley tapped the edge of her coffee cup and told the waitress, "Keep this coming." She poked at her eggs briefly before she dove in. It already felt like it had been an extremely long day, and it truly hadn't even started yet. She was going to need all the energy she could get just to make it to dusk.

Kara looked up as the front door of the diner opened. "Uh-oh. Gird your loins."

Riley tensed slightly and turned as someone came to a stop next to their table. She tried to hide the irritation on her face when she recognized Lieutenant Nina Hathaway's signature perfume. Hathaway put her hand on Riley's back, right under the collar of her blouse, and said, "Good morning, ladies. I heard you got an early start today."

"Yep," Kara said. "Body down on the waterfront."

"Well, close it quick. It's probably just another drug deal gone bad. We don't want to waste unnecessary resources on something like that. If either of you need to take off early today, let me know." She moved her hand to Riley's shoulder and squeezed. "I'll let you ladies get back to your breakfast. Good luck with the case." She backed away, but left her hand in place much longer than necessary.

When she was finally gone, Riley sighed and shook her head.

"You know what you need to do," Kara said. "You need to fuck her. And do it badly. Make her forget you ever existed."

Riley scoffed. "If only it was that easy."

"You saying you don't find her attractive?"

"Oh, she's attractive," Riley said. She turned and watched as Hathaway took a seat at the counter. Strong features, high cheekbones, and long dark hair that looked red in a certain light. She wore one of her navy blue business suits, with a black shirt and matching tie. Riley shook her head and went back to her breakfast. "She's just not my type. And she's my boss."

"All I'm saying is, the women you drag home with you, how would it be different than spending the night with Hathaway?"

"I never have to see those women again," Riley said. She was saved from further discussion by her pager going off. A moment later, Kara's sounded as well. She reached down and checked the number. "Dr. Hunt is ready for us." She pulled her wallet from her slacks, dropped enough money for the meal, and slid out of the booth.

Hathaway turned to watch them leave and said, "Be careful you two."

"We'll do our best," Kara said. "It's a dangerous old world out there."

The body that had been pulled out of the pipe was spread out facedown on one of the cold metal tables in the morgue. Two other new arrivals occupied the tables to either side, covered by stiff white sheets. Kara applied gel under her nostrils to keep the stink away, but Riley didn't bother. They pushed into the starkly lit room where Gillian Hunt, the medical examiner, stood waiting. She was a few years older than Riley, chestnut-colored hair pulled back in a ponytail. Her eyes were large and green, her thin lips pressed together as she leaned against the tile wall.

"Give us good news, Jill," Riley said as she walked into the morgue.

"Afraid I don't have much," Gillian said. Her voice was still dipped in the honey of the South, despite having moved from there in her teens. She pushed away from the wall and led the detectives to the table. "No wounds besides the obvious gouge on the back. Victim was a white male in good health, about twenty-five to thirty years old. No identifying marks or scars. Unusual lack of body hair. Not shaved, just... not there. He has hair on his head, eyelashes and eyebrows, so it's not alopecia universalis or chemo. I'll know more once I run some tests."

Riley looked down at the body. The missing piece of flesh and muscle looked like a diamond at this angle. The muscles that flanked the exposed spine looked like hamburger meat, but it had been a clean cut. The spine didn't appear damaged.

Gillian continued. "Also, I thought this was weird." She touched the skin just above the top curve of the wound. "These muscles here."

"What about them?"

"I have no idea what they are. I've never seen them before. They're extremely well developed. Whatever they are, they were cut completely in half."

Riley moved closer and examined the exposed musculature. The extraneous muscle began near the deltoid on each side, and stretched toward the spine. She frowned and shook her head. "That's weird. So how did he die?"

"At first glance, I would say he bled out. I'll know more once I finish the autopsy."

Riley stepped back and sighed. "Anything interesting on the type of blade?"

Gillian shook her head. "No such luck. It was a single, very sharp blade with nothing identifiable about it. You could find a couple dozen in novelty shops, I bet."

Kara said, "Hey, there's an idea." To Riley, she said, "I'll spring for the sword if there's anyone you want to frame."

"Let's give the case a full day before we start cheating," she said. "But I'll keep your offer in mind." She put her hand on Gillian's arm and said, "Thanks, Jill."

"Any time you need me to look at a body, you know where to find me."

Kara followed Riley out of the morgue and laughed as they approached the elevator. "The hunted has become the predator."

"What are you talking about?"

Kara nodded toward the morgue. "You and the Doc. Now that was flirting. I guess she is your type?"

The elevator doors opened and Riley stepped inside. "You don't know what you're talking about."

Kara pressed against Riley's side. "Any time you need me to... look at a body, Detective..." Her voice was thick Southern Belle, and she fluttered her eyelashes. "Why, you just call me right up and I'll be there right away."

Riley rolled her eyes. It was going to be a very long day.

They spent the next hour and a half calling shops in the area that might conceivably carry such a sword like the kind Kara's witness described. Riley was shocked to discover that there were a multitude of shops within walking distance that provided swords, maces, full-body knight armor, and everything else you could want to create your own medieval castle.

She dialed the next number and looked across her desk at Kara's workspace. Her desk was covered with little toys, knick knacks, and photos of family. A little girl with unbelievably large eyes smiled up at the photographer with a smile missing three teeth. Riley's desk, on the other hand, had one photo of herself at the police academy graduation, and various stacks of memos and reports waiting to be filed. Nothing more personal than a coffee mug with her name on the bottom. She sighed, closed her eyes as the phone was answered and began the spiel.

"Hello, sir. I'm Detective Riley Parra..."

One of the shops said they sold custom swords, but they didn't want to discuss customer information over the phone. Kara decided she would be the one to go, leaving Riley to man the phones and do the paperwork. Riley was in the middle of writing down the location of the body when someone across the bullpen called, "Parra! Line three."

She picked up the phone and pressed the flashing light. "Detective Parra."

"Are you the detective working on the waterfront murder?"

"I am," she said. She wondered if the report could have possibly hit the news yet. "Do you have any information on that?"

"Do not take things at face value. Nothing is what it seems. Have you looked into his eyes?"

"Whose eyes?"

"The eyes of the victim."

"Listen, if you want to…" There was a click, and she knew the call had been disconnected. She sighed, shook her head, and placed the phone back in the cradle. She got up, stretched, and looked around the bullpen. She saw Lieutenant Hathaway in her office, eyeing her through the blinds. She realized that, by stretching, she had stretched her blouse across her breasts and given the boss an eyeful. Hope you enjoyed the show you just got, she thought. It's as close as you'll ever get to the real thing.

Riley went into the break room still thinking about the call. She couldn't help wondering if she had, in fact, seen the victim's face. When the body was taken from the pipe, she was too busy looking for any other wounds to pay too much attention to what the man looked like. And then, in the morgue, Gillian - Dr. Hunt - had laid him out facedown so they could see the peculiar muscles in his back.

Ordinarily, it wouldn't have bothered Riley. She had investigated entire cases without knowing what the victim looked like. Disfigurement, beheadings, plain old negligence to look at a picture. But she knew that the phone call was going to bother her. And the body was right downstairs. It would only take thirty seconds to take a peek. Besides, it would give her a chance to (see Gillian again) put off paperwork for a while.

She got a cup of coffee and carried it to the elevator doors. The family of the victim would appreciate her effort, if they ever found his family. If he had a family to find. It was human decency. The strange phone call was entirely beside the point.

Riley arrived at the morgue to see all three bodies were covered and Gillian was nowhere to be seen. She ignored the middle table and walked to the office at the back of the area. Gillian was sitting at her desk with the crumbling remains of an egg sandwich on the desk in front of her. She was turned away from the door, going through an open filing cabinet drawer.

Riley stopped and considered Gillian with a critical eye. Sure, she was attractive. But any woman who could avoid looking like death warmed over after working under fluorescents all day, wearing little to no make-up and pea-green scrubs deserved praise. They flirted a bit, sure, but that didn't mean Riley wanted her. It didn't mean there was any underlying attraction that she was denying.

Gillian turned, spotted Riley out of the corner of her eye, and drew in a sharp breath. She coughed, pounded her chest, and shook her head. "God. Detective Parra. I didn't know anyone was down here."

"Sorry," Riley said. She wanted to pat Gillian's back, help her get the obstruction clear, but that would involve crossing the threshold of the office. It felt like a violation of privacy that she wasn't comfortable taking after spending so long ogling the woman. She waited until Gillian could breathe again and said, "I was wondering if I could take another look at the body."

"Sure." Gillian said. She stood up and Riley stepped aside to let her out of the office. "I was going to start the autopsy right after breakfast."

Riley gestured at the other covered bodies. "These guys don't take precedence?"

"Not for autopsy," Gillian said. "One person was shot in the face; the other was a hundred and three years old."

"A hundred and three?"

"Never even saw the bus."

Riley smirked as Gillian pulled back the sheet. "What did you want to look at?"

"The face."

The body was still lying facedown, so Gillian moved to one side and put one hand on his shoulder, the other in the middle of his back above the wound. She rolled the body until it was on its side and Riley stepped forward. She turned her head to the side and looked at the death mask of the man they pulled from the drain.

Plain features, pale eyebrows which were almost invisible against the bloodless face. His mouth hung slack. There was absolutely nothing remarkable about him, no reason for him to stand out in a crowd. But nonetheless...

It came back to her in a rush of memory. A man standing on a street corner, wearing a trenchcoat and staring at her. She had seen him moments after The Thing threw her off the roof of the building. It was the man she had seen the night she should have died.

"Riley?" Gillian said.

"Oh, my God. I know this man. Or... I've seen him."

"Where?"

Riley shook her head. "I think he saved my life."

Chapter Four

Riley and Gillian stood looking at the back of the dead man. Finally, Gillian broke the silence. "Are you going to remove yourself from the case?"

"There's no reason to. I only saw him for a moment, and we didn't even speak to one another. I'm not even sure he did anything. He was just there. No history. Nothing to compromise my professionalism." Not to mention the fact that if she handed the case off to someone else, it would likely be buried and forgotten within a matter of hours. For some reason, she couldn't let that happen. He had been present on one of the most unusual nights of Riley's life. He was proof that the night had happened. She felt she owed him.

She shook her head and looked at Gillian. "Do you have a picture of his face?"

"Yeah," Gillian said. She went to the file and withdrew a glossy photograph. It had been taken from overhead, the man's features washed out by the morgue lighting. "Are you sure you're okay?"

Riley nodded. "Fine. It was just a shock to the system when I saw him. We can keep this just between us, right?"

"Sure. Just take it easy. It looked like seeing his face took a lot out of you." She reached out and touched Riley's arm. "Take care of yourself. I don't want to see you down here unless you're upright and conscious."

"You and me both," Riley said. She took the picture and said, "Thanks, Doc."

"Any time, Detective."

Riley took the photo of the dead man up to the lab and gave it to an artist who could make the man look sort-of alive again. Now she at least knew he was from No Man's Land, or at least had a past there. Maybe he had friends, a family, people who would miss him. The artist said he would get it out as soon as possible and she left him to his work.

Upstairs, there was a report from AFIS waiting on her desk. No matches to the dead man's fingerprints. She put it aside and called the switchboard downstairs to get a trace on the number that had just called her. After a moment, the operator came back on the line. "I'm sorry, Detective Parra. No call has been put through to you in the past two hours."

Riley frowned, but she felt a twitch of unease at the news. "It may have come through the tip line," she said. The call hadn't come to her phone, after all. Someone had told her there was a call for her. She looked around the bullpen, but couldn't remember where the shout had come from. "Could you check all incoming calls during that period?"

There was a quiet sigh on the other end of the line as the operator did as she requested. "There were no calls."

"What?" Riley said. "No calls at all? We're talking a ten minute period."

"I can only tell you what the computer tells me, Detective. I'm sorry."

Riley pressed her lips together. "Fine. Sorry. Thank you for your help." She hung up and then stared at the phone.

She could explain away the fact there was no record of the call. If someone called any other phone in the office, and then asked for her phone. There were a multitude of things to be concerned about. First, how did the caller know she would recognize the body? How did he even know she was on the case? How could the call not only vanish from the records, how could the department have gone ten minutes without a call? Even now she could hear three or four phones ringing across the room.

The man from the pipe had no identity. And yet someone was already pulling strings to throw the investigation off the tracks. Why go through all this trouble when there was a very good chance they would hit a wall by the end of the shift? As much as Riley hated to admit it, the body could easily become just one of the many faceless buried in a Potter's Field. Unknown, not mourned, just forgotten.

She wished she had gone with Kara. Going from store to store might be dull and monotonous, but at this point, she would have preferred the boredom.

Kara returned just after noon with a package from the sub shop down the street. Riley, who had noticed her hunger ten minutes before her partner walked in the door, grabbed for the bag before Kara could even sit down. "Tuna, no tomatoes?" she said.

"Yep," Kara said. She took off her jacket and draped it over the back of her chair. "I figured my trip shouldn't be a complete bust. You wouldn't believe some of the people who hang out in these medieval gear shops."

"A lot of Dungeons and Dragons geeks?"

"Hey, I played D&D," Kara said. "But you're pretty close. Guys who are picking out codpieces like I picked out my last car."

Riley smirked. "Probably buying them all a few sizes too big." She took a bite of her sandwich and leaned back. "So no luck?"

"All the swords in all the stores are blunted, and every owner was offended by my implication that they could be sharpened and become a weapon. But I got a look at their customer list, and eighteen swords have been sold across the city in the last six months."

Riley shook her head. "Great. Armor piercing bullets aren't bad enough, now we have to worry about gang bangers swinging Excalibur at my head next time I go into a warehouse."

"They ain't never givin' up the Gat," Kara said with a bad mobster accent. She tore off a chunk of her sandwich and popped it into her mouth.

"Do you have the customer list?"

"Yeah, but I don't see what good it would do."

Riley shrugged. "Just because someone bought a blunt sword doesn't mean it stayed blunt. There are a lot of ways to sharpen a sword. It's worth looking into. And it's not like we have a boatload of leads in this case."

Kara raised her eyebrows and dipped her head. "True." She bent down and withdrew a few sheets of paper from her bag. She passed it across their desks and said, "The ones circled in red are regular customers. Unless you think our guy was killed by nineteen year old Scotty Bernstein, I don't think you'll find our guy on there."

"Can't hurt to look," Riley said as she scanned the list.

"If you say so. That's why you're the detective and I'm the eye candy."

Riley snorted and shook her head.

Kara decided tagging along on the interviews would be more productive than sitting in the office, so she offered to drive. They used the map in the glove compartment to narrow the list of possibilities from eighteen down to eight. People over the age of 75, addresses that weren't within walking distance of the waterfront, and women were considered unlikely and crossed out.

The first house on the list was a duplex on the north side of town. The neighborhood managed to present the togetherness of the good part of town while still shamefully exhibiting the worst parts of No Man's Land. The front yard of Martin Meade's house was ringed by a rusted chain link fence.

Riley scanned the yard for a dog, and saw only abandoned toys and a tall swing set that looked potentially fatal to any kid dumb enough to get onto it. Riley unlatched the gate and led the way across the dry, yellow grass. The porch had a washing machine and dryer parked on either side of the door, both of them looking older than the swing set. There were tools and car parts housed within the washing machine basin.

"I think I saw this place in Good Housekeeping," she said as she rang the doorbell.

Kara covered her mouth with her hand and pretended to scan the neighborhood.

The door opened and revealed a man in baggy sweatpants and a white T-shirt. His head was shaved and three hoop earrings ran along the outer shell of his ear. He looked between them and said, "What?"

"Martin Meade?"

"Yeah?"

They flashed their badges. "I'm Detective Parra, Detective Sweet. We'd like to ask you a few questions and then we'll be out of your hair."

"Questions?"

"You bought a sword about three months ago, is that correct?" He nodded. "We'd like to see it, if we may."

"Why?"

"We just need to confirm something."

He sighed and stepped back into the house. They waited and, a few seconds later, he reappeared with a sword. It was about four feet long and the blade caught the afternoon sun. Riley took the sword and immediately saw that the hilt had a thin layer of dust. The edge was, as reported, blunt. She turned the weapon around in her hand, but she was already discounting Meade as a suspect before she checked the list from the store. The sword in her hand matched the one on file.

She handed the sword back. "Thank you, Mr. Meade."

"Whatever."

"Could you do me a favor?" Kara asked.

Meade lifted his shoulder in a half-assed shrug.

"Can you say two words together?"

"What?"

"Humor me."

"Why?"

"Any two words."

Meade frowned at her, sure he was being mocked but unsure how. He looked between the two women and finally said, "We done?"

Kara smiled. "Thank you."

"Whatever." He pushed the door shut.

Riley brushed past Kara on the way to the car. "It's not polite to make fun of the mentally disabled," she said.

"You have your hobbies..." Kara said. She said, "Where to now, boss?"

"Lake Street. And then six more after that."

Kara sighed and rolled her eyes. "It's going to be a long day."

Kara pleaded exhaustion after five visitations and convinced Riley to call it a day after five houses. Kara drove Riley back to the station where her car was waiting in the underground parking. Kara leaned back and looked through the windshield. "So we'll tackle the other three places tomorrow?"

"Yeah. I'm going to come in late. Try to sleep in and make up for the early morning today. It's not like the body is going anywhere."

Kara nodded. "All right. So we'll skip breakfast. I'll meet you up at the office around ten. I doubt the last three will be any better than the first five. Maybe we could skip it completely."

"You just want to get out of knocking on doors. What, you got a new pair of shoes or something?" Kara shrugged. "Are you heading home?"

"The night is young," Kara said.

Riley nodded. "It may well be, but I'm not. Paint part of the town red for me."

Kara saluted as Riley got out of the car. Riley shut the door, stepped back, and watched until Kara's taillights disappeared around a row of cars. She sighed, rolled her shoulders, and pulled her keys from her pocket. She had just opened the driver's side door when the elevator bell sounded. Riley tossed her jacket into the car and casually glanced up to see who was coming out of the elevator.

Gillian's hair was down, and a long black coat covered her scrubs. She wore a pair of black-framed eyeglasses and looked like it was taking all her energy just to stay upright. Riley thought about ducking into her car, but she found herself waiting until Gillian noticed her. Gillian, though exhausted, mustered up a smile.

"Hello, Detective Parra. The Neanderthals had it right, huh?"

Riley was thrown. "Uh..."

"Walking with their knuckles dragging the ground. None of this staying upright crap." She leaned against the trunk of Riley's car and crossed her arms over her chest.

"Oh. Right. Well... imagine how bad their backs must have felt."

"Touché," Gillian said. "Calling it a day, then?"

Riley nodded. "Only so many doors my knuckles can knock in the course of one day."

"And only so many people you can stand speaking to." She smiled.

"Do you need a ride to your car?"

Gillian shook her head. "I'm right down here at the end of the row."

Riley nodded. "Okay." She didn't know what else to talk about, but she didn't want to end the conversation. "Did you get a chance to finish the autopsy on my guy?"

"Yeah. The report is on your desk. Basically it says what I thought originally. The guy wasn't beat up, didn't fight back, and died from bleeding out. He had been dead for about three hours when you pulled him from the pipe. Rigor mortis was just setting in."

"Good timing," Riley said. "Would've been hell to get him out of the pipe if he was literally a stiff."

Gillian smiled and pushed away from Riley's car. "Well, I've kept you long enough. Thanks for letting me rest for a moment."

"No problem."

"Good night, Detective."

"Good night, Doctor."

Riley got into her car and used the mirrors to watch Gillian walk away. She wondered if there really was an attraction there. There was admiration, and camaraderie. Riley impressed Gillian early on by entering the morgue without plugging her nose or appearing disgusted. Every other detective on the force relied on Vaseline or holding handkerchiefs in front of their faces, but Riley, in Gillian's words, was the first person to "look me in the eye and speak to me without a mask."

I'm not going to create a crush on a coworker, she swore to herself as she backed out of her space. I'm not going to sleep with a coworker. I am not going to put myself in a situation where I will have to work with a former lover.

Chapter Five

Riley was surprised to find the apartment at the top of the stairs was vacant when she got home. The door was open, revealing a quickly evacuated room. She stopped at the doorway and leaned into the room. She saw a few items that remained, dropped on the floor and forgotten. She suddenly recalled the scene that morning, the skunk-haired girl and her boyfriend. It felt like a lifetime ago. She felt a twinge of guilt about making the kid move, but she doubted he would have stuck around knowing a cop lived three apartments away from him.

She tossed her things onto her couch and closed the door behind her. Then she took the time to turn two locks and stretch the safety chain into place. *The only difference between us and the criminals is that we willingly lock ourselves into our cells.* The voice of her first partner echoed in her head as she turned and went into the kitchen. She hadn't thought about him in years, but now she longed for his guidance.

Donald Rafferty was one of the few cops who saw the decaying of the city and understood that it was only a matter of time before the entire place fell to the dogs like No Man's Land. He did his best to stop the decline, but there were times when he would shake his head and throw up his hands. "Like trying to catch every damn snowflake before it hits the ground. You might catch a couple, but before you know it, your boots are buried."

Raff died when some teenager decided he needed a new set of wheels. Raff stepped in and the kid panicked. All he had was a switchblade, but he made it work for him.

Because of Rafferty's death, Riley never got involved with a lot of the crimes she found off-duty. A kid dealing drugs outside of the restaurant where she was getting Chinese just gave her the hairy eyeball until she was back in her car. If she passed someone using a Slim Jim on a car, she would cross the street. But there were times when she just couldn't hold back. Times like that, she could be dangerous. She could break a guy's nose and kick him out of his home.

She took a beer from the fridge and went into the bedroom. She undressed out of what she considered her uniform and changed into a pair of shorts and a thick sweater. She wasn't lying when she told Kara she wasn't young anymore. She couldn't bear the thought of heading downtown, trying to decide which bar was on the "right" side of the street in the good part of town, and then setting up camp in the dim hopes that someone who was attractive to her as well as attracted to her would wander through.

Riley remembered the redhead from the night before. She was a witness in a previous case, and Riley had sensed the attraction immediately. As she and Kara were leaving, she handed over her card and said, "If you need anything, give me a call. Day or night." A week after the case closed, the phone rang. They met at a restaurant near Riley's apartment, and the woman slipped her hand onto Riley's thigh under the table.

They parted on good enough terms, she thought. Nightmare-induced punching aside. Maybe the woman would appreciate an apology. Riley picked up her phone and stared at the numbers. She knew the redhead's number. All she had to do was dial and talk to her, ask her to come over, and she could be wrapped around a warm, naked body within an hour. Faster than she could get Chinese food in this neighborhood.

She dropped the phone onto the couch beside her and stared past the TV to the window. She heard sirens outside, probably crisscrossing the streets in a vain attempt to keep the criminals from No Man's Land from gaining a foothold in the bright and shining city. Our boots are buried, she thought. We might not realize it yet, but it's true. We're all in No Man's Land. One day we're going to have to stop lying to ourselves about it.

Riley stood on the waterfront with a man in a long trenchcoat. She held a sword. It wasn't like any of the swords she handled earlier in the day, while they were interrogating people. She could tell this was the real deal just the way it felt in her hand. And it was heavy. She wondered what kind of strength it took to use a weapon like this. The waves were lapping at the shore, but she and her companion were standing on rocks and the water didn't touch them. She wrapped both hands around the hilt of the sword and held it up in front of her. The edge was too thin to see, and she felt it could cut her eye just by looking at it too closely. She lowered the sword and turned to face her companion.

It was the man from the street. He didn't look at her, but he smiled. He knew she was looking.

Riley lifted the sword again and rested it on his shoulders. One quick slice down. Like carving a turkey. She twisted the knife in her hands and the edge of the blade now pointed to the back of the man's neck. With one twist of her shoulders, his head would be in the water. She frowned. "Why did he cut a hole in your back?"

"Because it wasn't about my death."

"He didn't want you dead."

"He was unconcerned that death was a consequence."

Riley turned and saw the Hooded Man standing on the edge of the rocks. His back was to the apartments, and his hands hung limp by his sides. In the dim light, the fingers looked like they were tipped with deadly talons. Representatives of the sword he had used, she figured. It was the man from her dreams, the man - or whatever it was - that had thrown her from the roof. She couldn't see his face, but she knew what it looked like. Horrific. Unreal. So hideous she had never even bothered to put the description out onto the wires because she knew she would be labeled as a crackpot. She prayed he was just a holdover from the other dream; she couldn't handle it if he was really involved here.

The Hooded Man flexed his sharp fingers and backed away into the shadows and then he was gone. Riley lowered the sword and looked at the bright man again. "What happened to me that night? The night I fell off the roof. I should have died."

"You know what happened. Otherwise you would not expect a dream to tell you the answer."

"This isn't a dream," Riley said.

The man finally looked at her and the world seemed to flash with brightness. "Very astute of you, Detective." He smiled and Riley had to close her eyes against the light. She turned away from him as the glow continued to burn, warming her through her clothing. She realized she had dropped the sword and her hands shot out to grope for it.

Instead, she found herself groping for her alarm clock. It shrieked at her, half past six in the morning, and she cursed herself for forgetting to reset it before going to bed. She shut it off and sat up, rubbing her eyes with the heels of her hands. It was no use trying to go back to sleep now; once she was awake, she was awake. She pushed the blankets away and rolled out of bed. She was naked except for a pair of underwear and her apartment was cold. She heard thunder and knew a storm was moving in. The flash of light in her dream must have been lightning.

She could still feel the hilt of the sword in her hands, the intricate carvings in the gold. She wondered if she would recognize it when she found the actual murder weapon. If she found the actual murder weapon. If the rest of the names on Kara's list turned out to be nothing, then they would have gone twenty-four hours without a lead. Definitely a bad sign.

Riley went into the kitchen and searched the fridge for breakfast. She didn't want to close the case. She didn't want to give up on the man in the morgue for reasons that were beyond her. Maybe because some faceless entity was trying so hard to make her move on. She was reminded of the mysterious phone call as she poured herself a glass of milk. The killer cut off part of the victim's back, undressed him... unless he undressed the man first. Maybe it was a tryst gone wrong. She shook her head. Three men meeting for a tryst wasn't unheard of, but why would one of them bring a sword?

Unless the two men Ray saw had been meeting for a tryst and the Hooded Man stumbled across them. But why would the Hooded Man just happen to be carrying a sword? He had to have known what he would find and planned it out in advance.

She imagined someone standing at his apartment window, watching lovers meet on the waterfront. *If they ever show up again, I'll be ready. I'll make sure none of those fairies ever come here again.*

Riley shook her head. Using the murder as an example didn't work since the body had been hidden. If he wanted to keep others away, he would have left the body out in the open where everyone could see. And why only kill one person? Had the other man been lucky enough to escape? If so, where were the dead man's clothes? Why would the killer have taken them? Plus there were no waterfront addresses on the list of sword owners.

Riley rubbed the temple and finished off her milk. There were too many questions she would probably never have answers to. She knew the chance of the case turning into a nice, neat package she could wrap up with a bow was a fantasy. The most she could hope for was to find someone with a bloody sword. She couldn't even hope for a motive with this one.

She walked mostly naked across her apartment and searched her coat until she found the folded list of sword owners. There were only three left, and she was awake anyway. She decided she might as well cross the last three names off the list before going in to work. Kara would be grateful she had saved her the trouble. She carried the list into the bedroom to get dressed.

Riley handed the sword back to the man. He was a squat, toad-shaped man with thick Coke-bottle glasses. He took the sword and lifted his basset-hound eyes to her. "I certainly hope it wasn't used in the commission of a crime."

"No, sir," Riley said. "There were a few swords that were sold with sharp edges. We're just trying to make sure no one hurts themselves."

"Oh, oh, well that's very kind of you. Have a nice day, Detective."

She nodded and stepped back at the man closed the door. She reluctantly left the protection of his covered porch and flipped her collar up against the rain. The first person on the list for the morning wasn't home when she arrived, so she had to wait until he returned from his jog because his wife had no idea where he kept the sword. When he finally showed up forty-five minutes later, drenched and shivering, he asked if she could wait until he had taken a quick shower. She reluctantly agreed.

Now, with one sword left to check, she found herself losing hope. Of course, it would be her typical dumb luck that the killer was the last person on the list. Sometimes life just screwed with you that way. She climbed into the car as her phone began to ring. She checked the display screen and answered it. "Sweet Kara."

"Hey. I know I said we'd skip breakfast, but I thought I might bring something in. What's your pleasure?"

"Bagels. Any kind." She started the car.

Kara heard the engine over the phone. "Are you already on your way in?"

"No, actually, I'm saving you some legwork. Save you from knocking on doors in this rain. I'm getting the list out of the way."

"The list? The sword owners? But it's raining. And I thought we were going to do that this afternoon."

Riley pulled away from the curb. "I woke up early and decided we might as well get it out of the way. You can thank me later. Be sure to get me cream cheese."

"Yeah, sure. Riley, I should really be out there with you. What if one of these guys goes postal with his sword?"

"I'm fine. I only have one address left. Don't worry about it. Cream cheese," she said. She hung up before Kara could protest any further. She shook her head and checked the list for the last address. "See if I ever do her any more favors."

Chapter Six

Riley parked at the cracked curb and checked the map again. Either the address on the list was either wrong, out of date, or a fake. She looked through the swishing windshield wipers at the empty apartment building. Dark fins of soot marred every broken window, the lots on either side reduced to nothing but rubble. The building stood in the middle of a demolished block, the pathetic survivor of some holocaust or another.

The devastation had happened years ago, so she checked the date on the customer list. The buyer - someone named Nathan Overstreet - claimed to live in this building two short months ago. Riley doubted that, and figured he had just pulled the street name and number out of thin air when he created his false ID. But at least it meant they had some semblance of a lead in their dead end case. Still, she couldn't leave without giving the place at least a cursory once-over.

She got out of the car, having just started to dry out, and was immediately soaked again. She slammed the door and stalked to the trunk. Kara was going to owe her a week's worth of lunches after this. A month, maybe, depending on what she found in the building. She opened the trunk and withdrew her Kevlar vest. She was pulling the straps shut when a car pulled up behind her and flashed the headlights.

Riley turned, one hand on the butt of her gun, and squinted at the flooded windshield. It was Kara, already throwing open her door and stepping into the storm. She frowned and slammed the trunk lid. "Sweet Kara. I told you I would handle this."

"Look, there's no need. I recognized the address on the list when I got it. I swung by here, and I saw it was obviously fake. I just never took it off the list. I forgot. Come on, we're getting soaked. Let's get back to the office."

"We have to check it out, Kara," Riley said. "I offered to do it on my own. It's your own fault you're getting soaked."

She turned and started walking toward the building again.

"Riley, please stop!"

Riley turned. "What is your problem? If you checked this place out yesterday, why didn't you mention Overstreet was a fake name? Seems like a pretty strong lead to me. Just go to the office, Kara. I'll be there in half an hour."

"I can't let you go in there, Riley," Kara said. She pulled her gun from the holster and held it by her side, barrel pointed at the ground and trembling slightly.

Riley tensed and moved her hand to the butt of her own gun. "Sweet Kara, what are you doing?"

"I can't let you go in there," Kara said again. She brought her gun up and aimed it at Riley's head. "I'm sorry. Just get into your car and leave."

The rain was still pounding down on them, but Riley no longer felt the cold. Her heart was thumping, her hands trembling as she tried to make sense of what was happening. Kara wasn't wearing a coat, the rain soaking her lavender blouse. Her spiked hair was ruined, and she looked like a little kid.

"Why don't you just tell me what happened, okay? What did you find out?"

"He found me," Kara said. "I don't even know how he knew we were investigating, or who I was. But he came up to me in one of the shops. He gave me so much money, Riley. Enough for..." She closed her eyes and shook her head. "He just wanted this whole thing to go away. It doesn't matter anyway. One person. One person from No Man's Land who we are never going to identify. What does it matter?"

"It matters because he was a person," Riley said, moving closer to Kara. "It matters because we're cops."

"We're damage control," Kara snapped. "Nothing we do makes any difference. Every year No Man's Land is bigger and bigger and nothing we do is going to change that. So why not? Why not just let this one go? God, if it hadn't been for that man and his fucking dog, we wouldn't even have known about this body. He would have disappeared and no one would ever have known. Let's just let it be, please."

Our boots are buried, Riley thought, and felt a dark depression settling over her. "No," she said. "I can't accept that. I can't accept that, or I'm going to go home tonight and put my gun in my mouth."

"Riley, please."

It was hard to tell, but she thought Kara was crying now.

"Put the gun down. We can forget this ever happened."

"It's too late," Kara said. Her shoulders sagged and she slumped forward slightly.

Riley saw an opening and lunged forward. Kara saw her coming and instinctively pulled the trigger. Riley shouted as the bullet hit her mid-chest, the vest softening the impact so it felt as if she was broad-sided by a log instead of shot. She fell forward, wrapped her hand around Kara's, and forced the gun up and away from them. They grappled on the street, faces inches apart, and now Riley could definitely see the tears in Kara's eyes. They were both drenched, and Riley squeezed a pressure point. Kara shouted and dropped the gun.

Riley slackened her grip, and Kara suddenly shifted her weight. They fell together, and the back of Riley's head impacted the side mirror of her car. Stars danced in front of her eyes as she hit the ground. Kara pushed herself up and scrambled for her gun. Riley put her hand on the butt of her own gun, but something kept her from drawing down on her own partner. She just couldn't do it.

Kara got to the gun just as Riley got to her feet. She put a hand in the middle of her vest, trying to ease the pain from the first shot. She wrapped her arms around Kara's waist and pulled her down. Water erupted around them and Kara tried to twist out of Riley's grip. They scrambled together in the water, Riley's feet slipping as they tried to find traction, and Kara swung the gun up again. Riley grabbed Kara's hands and squeezed, praying it would keep her from pulling the trigger.

Riley was on top of Kara, the gun sticking up between them. "God damn it, Kara."

"I'm sorry, Riley," Kara said. "It was so much money. And it's not like it mattered."

"It always matters," Riley said. "Let go of the gun. Kara, please, let it go."

"I'm sorry." Kara pushed the gun forward and Riley felt the cold barrel brushing against her chin. She jerked instinctively away from it and braced for the sound of the shot. This close, the sound would deafen her. But the gun didn't go off. Praying the gun was waterlogged, Riley lifted her body and dropped her weight onto Kara's arms in an attempt to make her drop the weapon. Kara cried out, her arms pinned to her chest, and the gun went off like a nuclear explosion.

The last thing Riley remembered seeing was Kara's head whipping back and ricocheting off the asphalt. Then the world was white and red, filled with a high-pitched howling whistle. Riley shoved away from the sound, completely insensate, not even feeling the rain now. She suddenly realized she must have been shot, must have gotten the top of her head taken off, and now she was stumbling around like an idiot chicken.

She fell and felt the smooth metal of her car door. She searched for, found and pulled the handle, shoving herself into the warm, dry interior. She dripped on the driver's seat, rainwater and blood, and panted until she could hear the sound of her own blood rushing through her ears. Her eyes were wide but sightless, her mouth hanging wide open like a beached trout. She reached out and found her radio, pulling the mic from the cradle.

"Officer down," she rasped into the speaker. "Officer... involved shooting. Officer down. We need..." She looked down and saw, outlined in white, that her hand was covered in blood. "Oh, God. Oh, my God." She dropped the mic and slid out of the seat. The ground was hard and freezing under her ass, and she covered her face with both bloody hands.

Soon, the ringing faded into the sound of approaching sirens. She reached for her badge, but it wasn't there. She knew it had to have fallen off somewhere during the fight, but she didn't know where. She didn't want to look. Didn't have the strength to look. The top of her head was blown off anyway. She dropped her hands and rested her head - strange how it felt whole - against the door of her car.

Across the street, through the flashing red and blue lights, she saw a man in a hooded sweatshirt. His clothes didn't seem wet with the rain, but only because the raindrops seemed to evaporate before they touched him. His hands were in his pockets.

Someone grabbed Riley by the shoulder and hauled her forward. She was pressed face-forward to the ground and someone roughly began to frisk her. "I'm a cop," she said, returning to reality. "I'm a police officer. I lost my badge somewhere... somewhere around here. I'm a cop."

The rough hands stopped and someone conferred with another uniform nearby. While they were distracted, Riley lifted her head and looked across the street.

The Hooded Man was gone.

An hour later, Riley was in the back of a squad car with a thermos of coffee. Someone's jacket was wrapped around her shoulders. She could see and hear again, although there was an underlying whistle to every sound. The sun was rising, and the rain had been reduced to a steady drizzle. It gave the entire morning a fairytale quality. Unfortunately, there was no way for Riley to deny what really happened.

She was in the center of a maze of activity. The cops, armed with her badge number, had decided to take her at her word and trust her version of events for the time being. They found her badge behind the driver's side front tire of her car. They also took her gun, even though it was Kara's gun that did all the damage.

And what damage. Riley would never get Kara's ruined face out of her mind. It was going to be a fresh piece of her nightly terrors. The thought made her ill, and she closed her eyes against the encroaching headache. There were several layers of gauze wrapped around her head, but the wound where she impacted her car's mirror still throbbed.

My partner tried to kill me for money.

She wanted to sob, but she couldn't. She just kept running her thumb over her fingertips, making sure everything was still there.

Sweet Kara, what did you do?

She looked out the window as the crime scene guys swarmed the scene. The rain soaked their jumpsuits and made everyone look miserable. And there, amid all the activity, Kara lay sprawled in a puddle. She wanted to tell them to move her, because it looked like she was going to drown. But she knew that wasn't possible now. She closed her eyes and turned away.

Riley wasn't sure when she drifted off, but she jerked awake when someone knocked on the window. The movement caused her headache to flare, and she winced as she sat up in the seat. She was straightening herself as the door swung open and a few stray drops of rain hit her legs. Nina Hathaway ducked down into the car and invaded Riley's space. Oh, wonderful, Riley thought. "Lieutenant."

"Detective," Hathaway said. She looked at the gauze around Riley's head, then reached out and touched it. "How are you? Does it hurt very badly?"

"Feels like I died and forgot to stop moving."

Hathaway didn't even crack a smile. "What happened here?"

Riley closed her eyes and explained what she and Kara had been doing since the start of the case. The canvass and the sword hunt. She felt tears stinging her eyes when she explained what happened that morning. "She said someone paid her to keep me away. To drop the investigation."

Hathaway nodded and looked over her shoulder. "Move over." Riley reluctantly moved to give Hathaway room. She got into the car, shut the door, and turned in the seat to face Riley. The moment was far too intimate for comfort, and Riley tried to ignore how close the woman's body was to hers. I can't handle this today, she thought. Just back off.

"Someone should go through Kara's stuff. Find out if she wrote down anything about the money."

"Someone already did," Hathaway said. Her voice was low, as if she thought they might be overheard. Or maybe she just wanted Riley to lean in closer. Riley refused the bait and rested her aching head against the back of the seat. "I went through her desk as soon as I heard what happened. I wanted to know what I might be walking into."

"Did you find anything?"

"Yeah. She talked about the payoff and the bribe."

Riley sat up, despite the pain in her head. "That's great. Did she give a name?"

"Yeah," Hathaway said. "Yours."

Riley frowned.

"Kara said you were taking bribes. She said she was coming down here this morning to catch you in the act and turn you in." She opened the car door and stepped out into the rain. "You're going to have to ride with me back to the station."

Chapter Seven

Riley got out of the squad car and followed Hathaway across the street to her unmarked car. She got into the passenger side, once again soaked in clothes that had almost been dry, and stared ahead as Hathaway started the engine. They drove past the flashing lights and the absurdly bright yellow tarp that covered Kara's body. Riley closed her eyes so she wouldn't have to see it again, resting her head against the glass of the window.

"You should get checked out first."

"I'm fine. I don't want to go to the hospital."

"Someone needs to take a look at you."

Riley opened her eyes. "Gillian. Dr. Hunt." She was the only person Riley felt like seeing at the moment.

"The medical examiner?"

"Hey, if the fight had gone a little differently, I'd be seeing her anyway, right?"

Hathaway shrugged and faced forward. "Fine. It'll save me a trip."

They pulled into the parking garage and Riley followed Hathaway to the elevator. Hathaway pressed the button for the morgue and the elevator lurched into motion. "Am I under arrest?"

"No. See Gillian and then come up to my office after she's had a look at you."

"What if I run?"

The elevator doors opened. "We'll chase you," Hathaway said. "Don't be too long."

Riley stepped into the hall, and Hathaway disappeared behind the closing doors. Riley stood in the hallway for a moment, eyes closed, fluorescents light flickering above her head. The strobe made her feel like she was in a movie; everything felt false enough for her to believe it. She was freezing cold, her head throbbed, and she felt like curling up on the floor and sleeping until she died. But every time she closed her eyes, she saw Kara's head whipping back and hitting the pavement. All the blood.

Finally she walked into the morgue. Gillian was already moving toward the door and said, "Are you all right? They called and told me what happened. There was a shooting...?"

Riley said, "Kind of a brawl. I took a car mirror to the back of the head."

Gillian craned her neck and Riley leaned forward so she could see the injured area. Gillian nodded and said, "All right. Come on. Get on the table."

"It's that bad?"

Gillian managed a weak smile. "You can sit up if you'd like."

Riley moved to the table, put her hands on the edge, and grunted. She hung her head and said, "I don't... I don't think I can..."

"Here," Gillian said. She stepped closer and put her hands on Riley's hips. "Jump," she said softly, and Riley managed to give herself a bit of lift. Gillian took care of the rest, pushing her back until she was seated on the cold metal. "Okay. You hit your head. Were you hurt anywhere else?"

"Shot in the vest," Riley said.

"Okay. Take off your shirt, let me take a look."

Riley unbuttoned her blouse and shrugged out of it. She wore a tank top over her bra, but she still felt vaguely uncomfortable when Gillian began the examination. She touched a spot just above Riley's left breast and Riley hissed. "Ow. You found it."

"There's going to be a bad bruise there," Gillian said. "It's going to hurt like a bitch for a while."

Sweet Kara holding a gun on her. Pulling the trigger. Trying to kill her.

"It's going to hurt for a long time."

Gillian walked around the table to examine the head wound. She pushed Riley's hair out of the way and said, "The skin isn't broken. Going to be a nasty lump there for a while, though. I'll get you an ice pack." She moved her hands and looked down. She tilted her head to the side and said, "Oh, wow. I didn't know you had a tattoo." She pushed the straps of Riley's tank top and bra out of the way to see the entire ink. The tattoo was a small circle around two lines joined at the base. The flames looked more like red diamonds than flame. "What does it mean?"

"It's a symbol of protection," Riley said. She didn't know why she gave the real answer; she had always seen it as a private thing. Whenever a girlfriend or doctor asked in the past, she would say there were flaming chopsticks because MSG gave her heartburn, or wizard wands, or flaming drumsticks because a drummer broke her heart. But with Gillian, she wanted to tell the truth. "They're torches to ward off evil."

"Oh, I see. Because you're a protector?"

"Because I need protection," Riley said.

Gillian put her hand on Riley's shoulder, covering the tattoo with her palm. "Riley, if you need to talk about what happened... I want you to know I'm here for you."

"Thanks," Riley said. She leaned back, not wanting to break contact with Gillian's hand. "I should probably go upstairs. Hathaway probably wants to read me my rights."

"What? Why?"

Riley turned. "How much do you know about what happened today?"

Gillian shook her head. "Not much. There was a fight and a shootout. Sweet Kara is dead. I only know that much because they called and told me to be ready for her." Gillian took her hand away and crossed the room. She opened the freezer and filled a small blue bag with ice. She closed the top of the bag and carried it across the room. "Here."

Riley took the ice, picked up her shirt and slid off the table. "You're probably going to hear a lot more before the day is out. Don't judge me too harshly."

"I'll do my best," Gillian said. A buzzer sounded across the room and Gillian's head whipped toward it. Her eyes were pained, her voice a whisper, when she said, "That will be them." She looked back at Riley. "Are you sure you'll be all right?"

"Yeah. Do your job." She looked at the door through which men in blue jumpsuits would wheel Kara's body. "Say good-bye to her for me."

"I will," Gillian said softly.

Riley shrugged back into her shirt and went back to the elevator. She winced as she touched the ice to the back of her head and wished she had another pack for her chest. Of course then she would need three hands. She remembered one of her first cases with Kara, standing outside a Korean restaurant with a fresh bag of take-out in one hand and a Styrofoam cup in the other when it started to rain. Kara, holding only a drink, opened an umbrella and held it over both of their heads. "So I'll be your third hand," she said with a shrug.

Her eyes suddenly flooded and she sagged against the elevator wall, dropping the ice pack to her side. She felt utterly weak, drained and she didn't want to do anything, see anyone, or deal with what happened in the street. She wanted to walk into Hathaway's office, lay down her badge, and leave.

When the elevator doors opened, she forced herself out into the bullpen. Everyone stopped and looked in her direction, everyone aware of whose body was lying down in the morgue. She avoided their eyes, kept her head bowed and focused on the floor in front of her. Hathaway's office was across the room, so she had to do the walk of shame past every desk. She only stopped when she reached Sweet Kara's desk.

The purse Kara never carried was tucked in the knee space, and a half-eaten Danish was wrapped in a napkin next to her computer keyboard. Riley forced herself to keep moving forward, lifting her head to focus on the glass windows of Hathaway's office. The blinds were drawn, obviously to keep the firing or arrest or whatever was waiting private. Hathaway wasn't one for big theatrics when it came to doing her job.

Riley knocked and stepped into the office. "Boss."

"Come in, Riley. Shut the door." Hathaway was at her desk, signing a report. Riley shut the door behind her and stepped closer to the desk. She folded her hands in front of her and waited for whatever Hathaway threw at her. Hathaway glanced up and said, "Have a seat."

"I'd rather stand."

Hathaway shrugged, closed the file, and leaned back. "We have a bit of a problem here. After I received the call about what had happened, I decided I could take the time to look at your desks to see what you two were caught up in. I found this on Kara's desk." She pushed a different file closer to the edge of the desk and Riley picked it up. She flipped it open to find a typewritten affidavit.

'It's killing me to do this, but I don't think I have any choice. I need to have it down on paper what Riley Parra is up to so it doesn't come back and bite me in the ass. She's still my partner and I love her, but I can't afford to be taken down with her.'

What followed was an elaborate work of fantasy. Relationships with drug dealers, imaginary confidential informants, frame jobs, bribery. One instance of Riley shooting a suspect who tried to run and then leaving his body for, quote, "some other department to deal with," unquote. Kara claimed she watched everything from the passenger seat of their car, conflicted but certain that loyalty to her partner was more important than loyalty to the department.

The bottom of the page was marked with Kara's signature.

Riley felt her face burning, and her chest felt tight. It was hard to breathe. A woman she trusted with her life had written these words. A woman she had trusted more than any other woman in her life had betrayed her so totally. Riley wished Kara had just shot her in the back of the head. Quick, painless. None of this guilt and duplicity.

"It's..." she started, and she felt tears in her eyes and didn't trust herself to finish. She licked her bottom lip and tossed the paper onto the desk. "It's a lie."

Hathaway stood up and walked around the edge of the desk. "You've worked here a long time, Riley. I've seen a lot of cops come through here. Not one of them has cared as much or worked as hard as you do. None of them have half of your dedication. I know you're trying to clean up the town, however impossible that may seem. I admire that in you. But I also know that you draw the line. I know that you wouldn't be half as frustrated if you crossed that line and became some... vigilante hunting the streets."

Riley finally met Hathaway's eyes.

Hathaway was speaking softly now, like a friend. "If you were doing the shit Kara accused you of, the streets would be cleaner. Your case clearance rate would be much higher than it is. You would be a lot less frustrated. I don't know what happened to Kara Sweet, but I do know this entire thing is a work of fiction."

"Thank you, ma'am."

"No one outside of this room knows what I've found. And no one outside of this room has to know precisely what happened today. You found a suspect in the pipe job, you cornered him, and there was a firefight. Kara's gun accidentally went off. You did everything you could to save her, but there was no chance."

Riley just stood still, unable to believe what she was hearing.

"All your problems would go away, Riley. Kara would get her benefits. She would die a hero. There wouldn't have to be... ugliness. Her reputation wouldn't have to be tarnished."

"I understand."

"There is just one... issue. I'm taking a big risk covering all this up. If any of it, and I mean any of it gets out later, I'm the one who is going to hang. I'm willing to do it for you as a favor... but you have to ask me." She reached out and brushed her hand across Riley's cheek.

Riley frowned and said, "Lieutenant. W-will you—"

"No," Hathaway interrupted. Her voice was still soft, and she had moved closer to Riley. They were almost touching. "I want you to ask me for a favor, Detective Parra. I want you to ask properly." She touched Riley's cheek again and whispered, "Get on your knees."

Riley's eyes flared and it was all she could do not to pull away. Hathaway couldn't possibly be suggesting... She closed her eyes and remembered all the little touches, the looks, the comments about how Riley was dressed. She clenched her jaw and closed her eyes. It would make everything go away. The lies in Kara's letter, the stain on Kara's reputation. She had sisters, her parents were still alive, her little niece. They deserved her pension. She was a good cop who had gotten caught up in one very bad mistake.

"It all goes away?"

"Like it never existed."

Riley ran her hand over her face. She looked at the closed blinds, ran her tongue over her bottom lip, and slowly got onto her knees.

Chapter Eight

Riley bent over the bathroom sink and cupped her hands under the faucet again. She splashed her face, ran her fingers through her black hair, and winced as her hands ran over the bump on the back of her skull. She looked at her reflection, bright blue eyes staring out from a pale face. She supposed it could have been worse; it could have been a male boss. Still. It was what it was, and it was done. She wouldn't have to defend herself against a dead woman's accusations, and Kara wouldn't get her name dragged through the mud. All's well that ended well, wasn't that the saying?

She cupped her hands under the faucet and splashed her face again.

When she left the bathroom, her collar wet and the color still not back in her face, she found Detective Charles Timbale waiting for her. "Hey. Detective... um, Riley. I just wanted to let you know, we're all behind you on this. Everyone in the station, down to the uniformed officers. You need anything to track down this bastard, you let us know."

No need. I see the bastard every time I look in the mirror. "Thanks, Chuck," she said. "That means a lot."

"You just say the word. The full might of this police force will come down on the motherfucker so fast he won't know what hit him."

"Thank you. I should probably get back to work."

Timbale frowned. "You're kidding. Are you sure? I thought... I mean, I'd be taking a day to get my head straight."

"I'll take some time when I catch the bastards responsible," Riley said. "Thanks for the support, Chuck." She brushed past him and went to Kara's desk. She pulled the seat out and resisted a surge of sadness as her brain reminded her Kara would never again sit there. She took the seat for herself and scanned the top of the desk. Kara met the guy who bought her off at one of the sword shops. A quick search didn't show up the list Kara had used, so Riley checked her computer.

First he called me up and tried to throw me by playing Mr. Mysterious. At the exact same time, he was probably waiting for Kara to show up so he could pay her off. Who the hell was this guy? She had to give him credit, though. If he had come to her with a money offer, he would have been on the floor in handcuffs before he could even finish saying the words. Intimidation was better, relatively speaking. It scared her to think this guy could play them off each other so well.

Riley saw an email notification in the bottom corner of Kara's screen. Her head suddenly swam with the knowledge that Kara's family - the ones whose benefits Riley had just prostituted herself to protect - needed to be informed that she was dead. She wanted to be the one who told them, but she would give anything to hand the responsibility off. She moved the mouse and clicked on the email link, telling herself the blackmailer could have contacted Kara in that way.

One of the new emails was titled "Worse every day." Riley clicked on that and scanned the message.

"Melody is doing her best, putting on the brave face, but there's only so much an eight year old can take."

Riley couldn't look away from the screen. She read the rest of the email, and key words seemed to blaze out like neon signs. Malignant. Insurance won't cover... Eight-years-old.

Kara did it for her niece. She didn't decide to become crooked, she chose her sick niece over a nameless body in No Man's Land. Riley didn't show any emotion as she stood up, still staring at the flickering screen of the computer. She bent down, arm straight, and swept everything off the desk with one swift movement. The computer monitor teetered on the edge, and Riley gave it a shove. It hit the ground with a crack like a gunshot. Someone put their hands on her shoulders and she pulled violently away. "Don't you dare touch me."

"Detective Parra," Hathaway said from her office door.

Riley turned and stared at her from across the room. Hathaway's arms were crossed, the picture of professionalism. Riley was glad she didn't have her gun anymore.

"Take the day."

"I don't—"

"Take the fucking day," Hathaway repeated. "You've been through hell. Go home. Sleep it off." With that, she turned and walked back into her office.

Riley picked up the coffee cup from her own desk and twisted at the waist. She hurled the cup at the office door, watched the coffee splatter in a wide brown wave as the cup exploded. She rolled her shoulders and looked at the mess she had made. She looked up and saw Officer Yancy was the woman who had put her hands on her shoulders. "Sorry," she said. "Her... family might want some of this stuff."

Yancy nodded. "Okay."

Riley pushed a hand through her hair, hesitated for a moment as if unsure what to do or where to go, then walked to the elevators.

Riley sat on a bus bench and stared at the street light on the corner. There were no busses here, the benches a relic from a forsaken and forgotten age. They were colloquially called bum beds, and both ends were stained with drool, urine, blood, and other colors she didn't want to identify. She was sitting on an unfolded newspaper, her hands clasped between her knees, across the street from the building where she had been born.

Her father was a man named Benjamin Parra. When she was little, she thought her mother was a woman who changed appearance from day to day. One or two days, she would be a brunette with tiny, severe eyes. Then the next day she would have transformed into a blonde in a long Jack Daniel's T-shirt and nothing else. Riley didn't understand why she had to keep reminding her mother of her name every time she became someone else.

She was six when she finally figured out what was happening. She was twelve when one of her father's friends watched her cross the room and actually licked his lips. It was Riley's choice to go to bed with him, just to see what it was like, but she only remembered crying and wanting it to be over with as soon as possible. She fucked the boy at the corner store, too, and it wasn't so bad, but it was no fun, either.

Christine Lee was a puny little thing, hardly bigger than sixteen-year-old Riley, and a police officer. They met in a spotlight, just like in the movies, but this spotlight was on Christine's hood and their first embrace was Christine tackling the hooded shoplifter and pressing her face into the pavement. They talked while Christine drove Riley home, and soon Riley was crying and apologizing for every bad thing she had ever done.

They started to meet for coffee and lunch, and Christine would only pay if Riley proved she had been to school that day. The school had a prom, which was more of a joke than an actual party, and Riley nervously asked Christine to go with her. Christine said no, but politely. At the end of that night, they shared their first kiss. And the next morning, Riley woke up in her first strange bed.

Christine Lee died in a car accident five years later. Riley joined the police department in Christine's honor. It was Christine who, one night after they made love, inked the tattoo on Riley's right shoulder. They were both wet from the shower, Riley straddling a chair naked, and Christine on a stool behind her. Christine taught her that the world you inherited didn't have to be the world you left behind. Nothing was pre-determined. Not even No Man's Land.

Riley swallowed hard and looked down at her hands. Christine would roll over in her grave. To see how much No Man's Land had spread, like a cancer slowly overtaking the body. To see her protégé, for all her work and all her lessons, turning into a crooked cop. Regardless of her reasons, she had killed her partner and allowed everything to be neatly swept under the rug. There was no such thing as a good cop any more. No Man's Land was winning.

She stood up, hands in her pockets, and looked up at the building where she had started her life. There were nights she liked to pretend she was far away from those beginnings, but the building was never more than fifteen minutes away. Faster by elevated train. For all the lies she told herself, she was still in the same town and fighting battles that started decades before she was born. She tilted her head back and inhaled the scent of the town.

Riley always laughed when she heard that bullshit line, 'you can't go home again.' Home was the one place in this world you could never get away from.

She wandered the streets, thinking about the man in the drain pipe. Kara was dead because of him. She wanted to drop the case; it had already caused enough damage and pain, and they were no closer to knowing who he was than yesterday. On the other hand, stopping now would make Kara's death meaningless. They would never find out who gave her the money, or why he was so desperate to stop the investigation.

Besides, she wanted the bastard. She wanted this case closed so that the nameless man wouldn't haunt her dreams for the rest of her life. She already had enough demons taking up space in her brain, she didn't need another.

She finally found herself at her current apartment building, another distressing reminder of just how far she had actually managed to progress in life. She could go from the beginning to the end in just a matter of steps, walk it without breaking a sweat. The lobby was vacant and quiet as she entered, and she took the stairs to her floor. The apartment she had cleared out was still vacant, the door standing open like an invitation to squatters. Riley ignored it and started pulling off her jacket as she unlocked her front door.

The apartment was a mess.

Riley cursed her lack of a service weapon and moved to the table next to the door. She opened the top drawer, lifted the false bottom, and removed her spare. She checked the ammo and took in her surroundings. Her things had been tossed to the floor, her couch cushions tossed into one corner. The window to the fire escape was open and she could hear street sounds below. She avoided debris that lay on the ground and peered into the kitchen. Her dirty dishes seemed untouched, but the counter had been swept clean.

She heard a sound from the bedroom and moved in that direction. The door was slightly open, and somebody was moving around inside. She measured each step, making sure she didn't step on broken glass or any of the weak floorboards that would creak and give up her position. She was halfway to the door when it swung open and a blonde man stepped into her line of vision.

"Freeze!" she said. "Police officer."

The man brought his hands up and she saw a flash of something black in the left hand. God fuck it, not again, she thought as instinct took over, and she fired. The man grunted and fell back into her bedroom. Riley could already hear the sirens and the discussions. She saw her badge being taken from her. Two shootings in one day, for a case no one else believed was worth investigating. How on Earth could anyone spin that?

She stepped into her bedroom and saw the blonde man sitting with his back to the bed. His legs were spread in front of him, his head bowed and his left hand still clasped over his chest. He wore khakis, a light blue shirt, and - now that she saw him clearly - his hair was white, not blonde. The tail of his trenchcoat spread out underneath him like a cape. Riley was two steps away from him when he suddenly looked up at her.

She gasped and backed up, raising her gun again. "Don't move."

"You shot me."

The black object was next to his hand. Riley stepped forward and swept it away with her foot, seeing too late that it was just a wallet. She cursed under her breath and said, "I'm going to get you some medical attention."

The man said, "There's no need for that." He held out his hand to show that there was no blood. The hole in his shirt was also clean.

Riley frowned and kept her weapon trained on him. "What the hell?"

"May I stand?"

She nodded and stepped back, out of arm's reach as he used the bed to push himself up. He groaned and stretched. "God. It doesn't kill, but it hurts like a son of a bitch."

"Who are you? What are you doing in my apartment?"

"I'm here to tell you not to give up. As for who I am, well... that's a little more difficult to explain."

"Try."

"My name is Samael. I was on the waterfront two evenings ago when my friend perished."

Riley lowered her gun slightly. "Samuel?"

"Sam will do."

Your friend. You know his name?"

"Indeed I do. His name was Ridwan."

Riley raised an eyebrow. "Uh-huh. And the man you were meeting with?"

Samael stepped forward and Riley raised the gun again. He held his hands out and said, "I apologize. The man we were meeting with. I believe he is the reason you were brought into the investigation, Riley Parra. You know him. His name is Marchosias, and he was the man who threw you off a roof four years ago. And Ridwan was the man who saved your life."

"Ridwan, Marchosias... what are you guys, some kind of weird religious cult?"

Samael smiled and said, "Well. I suppose you could say that." He took off his trenchcoat and let it fall to the floor. Riley lowered her weapon and let it hang from slack fingers as she watched his wings spread out. They were enormous, ten feet from one end to the other.

"Marchosias is a demon," he said. "And Ridwan was an angel."

Riley dropped her gun and said, "Fuck."

Chapter Nine

Riley sat on the counter that separated her kitchen from the living room. Samael began cleaning up the mess of her apartment as he spoke, his wings once again concealed under his jacket. "Marchosias has ruled over the area which you call No Man's Land for several hundred years. Ridwan was charged as protector for the remaining area. For years, they've struggled to achieve balance."

"March was winning," Riley said.

"Marcho—"

"Yeah, I'm not going to remember that."

Samael considered it for a moment and then shrugged. "Very well. Yes, for the past several decades, March has gained a bit of a foothold. But this sort of thing can be fluid."

"Fluid. You mean in a hundred years or so, No Man's Land may not even exist."

"Correct."

"Bullshit."

Samael replaced the couch cushions and sighed. "Humans have very limited points of reference. Four hundred years ago, New York City was swampland. It became little more than a shantytown three hundred years ago. And now it is one of the greatest cities in the world. It might not see a renewal in your lifetime, but there is hope for this city. At least... there was."

"So after centuries of playing by the rules and treating this city like a giant chessboard, Ridwan just, what, got tired of it? Decided to skip to the end and kill his opponent?"

Samael looked away from her. "We were there for a meeting. Ridwan wished for an impartial third party to observe, so he requested I attend as well. Tempers flared."

"Wings," Riley said. She pictured the strange gouge in the corpse's back, the muscles Gillian couldn't identify. "Son of a bitch. March cut off Ridwan's wings."

Samael sighed. "He is probably displaying them as a trophy."

Riley nodded and then closed her eyes. "God damn it. I can't close the case. You've handed me everything I need, and my hands are tied. I can't walk up to my boss and tell her 'A demon did it.' Even if I did, how would we arrest him? Or incarcerate him? Forget the death penalty."

"You have fought for this case from the beginning, though no one else wanted you expending the time or the effort. You have fought to correct the sins in No Man's Land though you yourself admit it is impossible. Correct?"

Riley stared at him.

"Do both. Punish Marchosias for what he has done to Ridwan, and when he is gone, No Man's Land will experience a renaissance of life and hope and prosperity."

"You expect me to take down a demon?"

"I believe it is your destiny. You have fought him before and you won."

Riley laughed. "I was thrown from a building."

"When every other human being would have died of fright from a single look at Marchosias' face. You continued to fight. When dozens of detectives would have given up on this case within an hour, you continued to search. You were handed this case because it belongs to you. This is your fight. You must destroy Marchosias before he destroys this city once and for all. There is always a balance. Without Ridwan, you must become that balance."

Riley slipped off the counter. "You're full of shit."

"Please, Detective Parra. After everything this case has taken from you, do not give in now. You have his name. You know where to find him."

Riley stopped, her back turned to the room. She picked up her cell phone and dialed a number she knew by heart. "Hey. Yeah, it's Detective Parra. Listen, I'm... going to take a few days off. Yeah. Mental health. Thanks. I appreciate it." She hung up the phone and said, "The pipe man, uh, Ridwan's case has been passed over to another detective. I've got a few days to look into it myself, and that's it. All right?" She turned to see Samael's reaction, but the apartment was empty.

On the bright side, she thought, *at least he cleaned the apartment before he disappeared.*

Riley and Kara sat in a nearly-empty bar, nursing their latest glasses of whiskey. Kara picked hers up, downed the dregs, and pulled her top lip back against her teeth. "Ah, that's good." She ran her thumb along her bottom lip and tapped the bar with her knuckle. "Another, good barkeep."

The bartender was a broad shouldered, football player gone to seed type. He refilled Kara's glass, and Riley shook her head when he offered to do hers. When he left, Kara said, "All right. Tell you what." She fished a quarter from her pocket and placed it on the bar. "I'll flip you for him. Heads, I go, tails, you go."

"What are you talking about?"

"The bartender," Kara said. "He's giving both of us the eye, so we'll have to decide for him. Unless you're open to sharing."

Riley took the quarter and slipped it into her own pocket. "He's all yours, Sweet Kara."

"Aw, come on. Don't give up so easily."

"No, really," Riley said. "I'm more interested in..." She nodded at the end of the bar.

Kara turned and saw a blonde nursing a bottle of beer. Kara arched an eyebrow and said, "O-oh. Finding out all kinds of things about my new partner." She slipped off the stool.

Riley grabbed her arm. "Hey, wait. Where do you think you're going?"

"Jukebox," Kara said. "Don't be so paranoid."

Riley released her arm and Kara headed across the bar to the jukebox. Riley relaxed and went back to her drink. A few seconds later, the Rolling Stones began singing Let's Spend the Night Together. Riley looked over in time to see Kara stop next to the blonde at the end of the bar and lean down, whisper in her ear, and point at Riley. Riley groaned and shook her head, pressed her palm against her forehead, and said, "I'm going to kill her."

When Kara returned, she said, "She's waiting."

Riley looked at her.

"Your dance partner. Hurry, before the song ends."

Riley looked at the blonde, who was smiling in her direction. Riley hesitated and then slipped off her stool. "We're going to have to have a talk about this sort of thing."

"You can't control Sweet Kara. You can only hope to contain her."

The blonde slipped off her stool as she nervously approached the blonde. "Uh. Hi. Riley."

"Natalie. Your, um... friend said you wanted to dance with me."

"She's my partner," Riley said. "I mean... not... I mean, she's my partner on the force. Police force. I'm a... detective. A single detective, which is odd because I'm so good at talking to women in bars."

Natalie smiled. "All of that is very good to know. So. The dance?"

"Right." She put her hand in the small of Natalie's back and guided her onto the bar's small dance floor. As she put her hands on Natalie's hips, she looked across the room to where Kara sat flirting with the bartender. It was supposed to just be a drink after work, not a hook-up. She didn't want to take some woman home to her crappy apartment, she didn't want to get naked with someone new. All she wanted was a drink to get a feel for her new partner's personality. Well, mission accomplished, she supposed.

About a minute after they started dancing, the song ended. They were about to separate when another Stones song, Wild Horses, began to play. Riley started to pull away, but Natalie said, "No. Let's keep going."

"You sure? It's kind of a slow song."

"Slow songs are okay," Natalie said.

By the end of the song, Riley had her lips on Natalie's neck. By the time Kara's two-dollars worth of songs ended, Natalie's fingers were just under the waistband of Riley's pants. The final song faded and the bar fell silent, so they pulled slightly apart. Natalie looked at Riley's lips and then down at the undone buttons of Riley's blouse. She squared her shoulders and said, "Do you want to get out of here?"

"Yeah. I just have to tell Kara."

They parted and Riley went back to Kara. "I'm going to kill you. Tomorrow." She tossed a couple of bills on the bar and said, "The drinks are on me."

"You're welcome," Kara said.

"Do you need a ride?"

"Henry is taking care of that," Kara said. The bartender turned at the mention of his name and Kara winked at him.

Riley said, "You just wanted me out of the way so you could get laid."

"Hey, I was willing to do the threesome. But Option B works just as well." She and Riley both looked toward the door, where Natalie was waiting with her jacket. "Blondie just happened to be in the right place at the right time. Make it worth her while."

Riley rolled her eyes and left Kara at the bar. She grabbed Natalie's hand as she walked past and they headed for the door. Natalie looked over her shoulder and said, "So you guys work together? Is she a good partner?"

Riley smirked. "Yeah. I'd say she passed the test. Where is your car?"

Riley poured the last of the whiskey into the glass and set the bottle down hard enough to make the ice shift. She couldn't sleep because thoughts of Kara kept intruding on her mind. They were partners for two years. Two years of putting their lives in each other's hands. Walking up to unknown doorways, with unknown elements within, knowing that your life depended on the person standing just behind you. Her relationship with Kara was the longest and most rewarding relationship in her entire life.

Gone in a flash.

Kara pulled a gun on her. In what world did that make sense? And was it a world she wanted to live in?

Her spare gun sat on the bar, pointed toward the fridge instead of at her. If a bullet went into her tonight, she wanted it to be her choice. She stared at the liquor in front of her. Maybe she was insane. Maybe she was lying on the street with rain falling in her eyes and her brain was creating this fucked up world. Angels battling demons in the streets of No Man's Land was one thing. A Kara she couldn't trust? That was beyond the pale.

She picked up the gun and looked at it. Maybe the trick was to end the illusion with one big, drastic display and she would wake up in real life.

She put the gun down. Or maybe an angel had come into her apartment and told her that she was destined to kill a demon.

"What are you doing?" she whispered. She picked up the glass and pressed the edge against her bottom lip. Her chest still hurt, and the knot on the back of her head made it hard for her to lie down in bed. So why not stay up and drink? Finish all the liquor in the house and then go out and buy more, drink until the night made some sort of sense.

A demon ransacked my apartment, and an angel cleaned it up. What's so odd about that?

"Always knew you were special."

Riley jumped at the voice, but then she realized it was just her overtired imagination playing tricks on her. There was no way Kara was really sitting next to her. She closed her eyes, sucked her top lip and ran her finger over the rim of the glass. "Yay, me. I'd rather be a sheep."

Kara chuckled. "You know why I took the money, right?"

"Your niece." Tears burned her eyes. "I didn't know."

"I could have told you. Would you have turned your back on this case if you had known?"

Riley answered honestly. "I have no idea. I think if I knew all this would happen, yeah. I would have let it slide."

"You want to know something? The second I pulled my gun, I wanted a way out. I didn't want to kill you, Riley."

"You'd rather die yourself?"

"Yeah. You didn't compromise yourself. Not even when I asked you to. You're a good cop, Riley. Remember that. Believe in it." She leaned down and Riley felt ghostly breath on the side of her face. "And never, ever let the blonde at the end of the bar go without at least taking a chance." She brushed ghostly lips across Riley's cheek, and then she was gone.

After a while, Riley finished her glass and carried it to the sink. She poured out the ice, rinsed the glass and placed it on the drying rack. She turned, leaned against the counter, and looked out the window. Sirens were sounding, somewhere deep in the city. Maybe someone following a lead on the pipe man case, although not bloody likely.

Solving the case would, according to Samael, bring No Man's Land out of its downward spiral. She wouldn't be able to bring Marchosias in the usual way. But maybe, instead of bringing him to justice, she could find a way to bring justice to him. She turned off the light over the sink, casting the apartment into darkness before she went to bed.

Chapter Ten

Riley woke late and dressed with the feeling that she was playing hooky. The morning felt surreal and unusual, to be in her apartment so long after the sunrise was just wrong. While she dressed, she thought about her mysterious guest. She never checked out the guy's wings, she didn't actually see them coming out of his back. He could have been wearing a bulletproof vest to explain why he wasn't hurt by the gunshot.

Despite her rationalizations, she couldn't help but believe the man's story. She believed that Samael was an angel, and that pipe man had been killed by a demon. She wanted to go by the old 'if you hear hoof-beats' adage, but nothing added up as perfectly as Samael's story. Regardless of what the truth was, she wasn't going to find it in the good part of town. She was going to have to spend some quality time in No Man's Land. She put on a bulletproof vest under her blouse, shrugged into her jacket, and put her back-up gun into a shoulder holster.

Whether she called it muscle memory or just plain not thinking, Riley didn't realize the magnitude of what she did until it was too late. She left her apartment an hour before the train began boarding, so she decided to stop for breakfast. It wasn't until she stepped into the Four-Ten Diner that she realized her mistake.

The hostess looked up as she entered and gave her a smile. "Good morning, Detective. Is your partner joining you this morning?"

Riley felt like she had been punched in the throat. "Uh... no. I just... stopped in to see—"

"Detective Parra."

She closed her eyes. Shit. I would prefer the demon right now. She sighed and crossed the room to where Lieutenant Hathaway sat. "I was just having a late breakfast. Why don't you join me?"

"I was actually just going to grab a muffin to go," she said.

"Well, you're off, right? Taking a couple of days to process everything that happened? A couple of minutes won't kill you."

Riley gave her order to the waitress and slipped reluctantly onto the stool next to Hathaway. "How is this going to work?" she asked quietly, facing forward to avoid Hathaway's eyes. "Do you own my ass now? You say 'jump,' I say 'on what'?"

"That's a little uncalled for..."

Riley scoffed. "I'm just trying to figure out how much of me you bought yesterday. Are we even because I went down on you? Or is this going to be a regular thing? Are you going to make my life hell if I don't eat breakfast with you?"

Hathaway sipped her orange juice and waited a long moment before she replied. The waitress returned with her muffin, and Riley stared at it as she waited for a verdict.

Finally, Hathaway said, "Consider us even, Detective. Any relationship we have beyond this point will be your choice."

Riley stared at her. "You realize that you didn't seduce me yesterday. You raped me."

Hathaway's eyes flashed. "The situation was..."

Riley took her muffin and said, "Don't talk to me about the situation. You got what you wanted, and I was saved a lot of headaches, and Kara's family was protected from scandal. Everything came out fine. We'll close the book on that and forget it ever happened. From now on, our relationship is strictly professional. Have a good day, Lieutenant."

Hathaway continued to stare forward and nodded. "You, too. Keep your nose clean."

Riley left a dollar on the counter and left the diner. She was halfway to the el station when she changed her mind about her destination. No Man's Land could wait; she wanted to check out Kara's apartment before some other cop gave it the once-over.

Riley had Kara's spare key due to their habit of bailing each other out of dates gone wrong. Stepping into the apartment immediately reminded her of the times she arrived in the middle of the night to find Kara and some anonymous guy sprawled naked on the couch. Once, Riley arrived to find two naked men asleep in Kara's bed, but Kara was nowhere to be seen. A quick search of the apartment revealed her partner was on the fire escape, shuddering with a blanket wrapped around herself.

"They said they wanted a threesome," Kara said as Riley let her back in. "But they seemed more interested in each other. So I figured, why not, as long as I can watch. But then they wouldn't leave."

Riley kicked the guys out, claiming someone had called in a noise complaint. The guys dressed and left, and Riley spent the rest of the evening watching a movie with Kara on the couch.

The apartment looked exactly the same as always; a familiar controlled mess. The kitchen table was covered with magazines and open phone books. Riley went to the table and smiled when she saw the books were open to the map section. Kara pored over the maps like they were the Holy Grail, priding herself on knowing where every street in town was. She knew all the shortcuts, could tell how far one street was from another, and never hesitated when she headed out on a call.

Riley flipped the book shut and went to the stereo. She pressed play and a Missy Higgins album began. As the music filled the apartment and gave it some semblance of life, Riley began her search. She cleaned up the coffee table, stacking mail and placing it in a plastic bag after examining the return addresses. If anyone came in, she would just claim to be tidying up for her late partner. In reality, she wanted to find any evidence of Kara's bribe so Hathaway's blackmail wouldn't end up being useless.

She found a card and opened it to find a dark sea of tightly-packed penmanship. It took her a moment to figure out the hieroglyphs, but once she identified a few letters, the rest fell into place. The note was from Kara's sister, talking about her niece's illness. There was desperation in her words, a need to do whatever was necessary to save the little girl's life.

Riley closed the card and put it aside, disgusted with herself. How could she have not known what her partner was going through? Had Kara been that good at hiding her turmoil? Watching an eight-year-old die was hard on the soul. A good partner would have noticed. A good partner would have offered to help, and would have made a bribe unnecessary. But Riley was too caught up in her own shit to notice, and Kara was left to literally make a deal with the devil.

A shoebox on the top shelf of the closet held several packs of hundred dollar bills. She took the shoebox to the desk and found the card from Kara's sister. She made a note of the address; Kara had given her life for the money and Riley wasn't about to let it waste away in some evidence locker. She concealed the money with several layers of bubble wrap, and then covered it all with a brown paper bag.

She put the money into her coat pocket and continued to explore the apartment. She went into Kara's bedroom, the late morning light coming through the window and giving her enough light to search. The room had been redesigned since Riley's last visit, and the differences were for the worst, in her opinion. She had no idea how Kara managed to sleep with the new layout; the light would hit the pillows right after the sun rose. Maybe it was her version of an alarm clock.

Riley opened the closets and found a blue suit. She figured Kara wouldn't want to be buried in formal wear, so she removed the jacket and left the blouse and slacks on the foot of the bed. It would save her friends and family a little effort, and it would save Kara the embarrassment of being put to rest in the wrong thing.

She happened to glance at the floor and noticed grooves in the carpet. Drag lines that went from one wall and disappeared under the bed. She frowned and stepped back. Apparently the bed was moved recently, and its original position was better situated in regards to the window. Riley moved to the headboard and pushed it away from the wall. There was an electrical outlet with the face removed. Riley knelt down and felt inside the rough hole until she found a piece of paper. The paper was folded several times, and her name was written on the face.

"Riley Parra."

She unfolded it with trembling hands, afraid of discovering another skeleton in Kara's closet. But she sat with her back against the wall and rested her elbows against her knees as she read the note.

"Riley.

I don't know how to begin writing this. It was hell acting like nothing happened when I saw you in the station today. All our big talk, all our complaining about crooked cops, and now look at me. I guess you can never know whether you're a good cop or a bad cop until you take the true test. I took it, and I failed. I took the money. And when he told me to cover my ass by lying and saying you were crooked, well, I did that, too.

"I don't mind sacrificing my life or my career for Melody. But it tore me up to pull you down with me. I only hope you forgive me, Riley. I hope you find it in your heart to understand. If you're reading this, you've probably found out what happened and I'm sitting in prison somewhere. Please, come and find me and let me say this to your face. You mean everything to me, Riley. I love you, and I'm sorry if I caused you any strife.

"I'm going to hide this note somewhere the crime scene guys won't look (half-assed as they are) but I know you will. You're a good cop. A great cop. One of the last remaining out there, it seems. I wish I had been a better partner to you. The only problem is, the partner you deserve doesn't exist anymore. They would have to clone you.

"I really do love you, Riley, and I hope you accept this apology. Don't hold it against me. I was doing terrible things for the right reasons, but that doesn't excuse it. If you've busted me (and it will be you that slaps the cuffs on, I have no doubt), then I'll plead guilty. I'll do the time. I just hope you understand.

"Signed, Sweet Kara."

Riley covered her eyes with both hands and leaned forward. "Then why did you make me fight you, you stupid bitch? Why didn't you just put down the gun and walk the fuck away?" She pictured a scenario where Kara walked away, took the bribe money to her niece and disappeared into the sunset. Would Riley have been willing to live with the knowledge she let a crime happen?

For a little girl, she thought, you're damn right I would, too.

She sniffled and folded the note. "Sorry to disappoint you, Sweet Kara. But I don't think I'm the great cop you think I am. I would have let you go."

When her eyes were dry, she put the note in the pocket with the money. She pushed herself up, put the bed back into place, and made one last survey of the apartment. She turned off the stereo and looked to make sure the apartment was the same it was when she arrived. The phone book was closed, but that wouldn't matter to the crime scene guys. She left the apartment, locked the front door, and headed downstairs.

A lot of the people in Kara's neighborhood were unemployed, and the streets were livelier than she would have expected so close to afternoon. Down the street, an elementary school playground was filled with screaming, running kids. Riley stood on the sidewalk for a while and watched them, trying to remember when she had ever seen a playground without kids screaming and running. Were there designated kids who were assigned the job of circling everyone else, running and shouting? Or did it just happen spontaneously? She knew that if she ever saw one with kids playing quietly, she would feel uneasy.

She walked to the el station and bought a token. There was a train due in the next five minutes, which meant she would have to wait between ten and fifteen minutes before it arrived. She looked to her right, her view given the benefit of the station's elevation. She could see the edge of Kara's neighborhood, and the subtly grimier buildings on the other side of the line. The windows weren't as bright, and every surface had a subtle patina of decay. Somewhere in that warren of buildings, a demon was waiting. Pulling the strings to destroy what was left in the good part of town.

As the train pulled into the station, Riley thought of the kids in the playground, and of Kara's niece. She could do nothing, and let those kids inherit a world even shittier than hers. Or she could do something and try to make their worlds a little brighter.

The train doors opened and Riley stepped inside. She found a seat at the front of the train and, fifteen minutes later, she arrived in the heart of No Man's Land.

Chapter Eleven

Muse Skaggs leaned against a chain-link fence, drumming his hands on his thighs, snapping his fingers in tune to a beat only he could hear. He bobbed his head as he watched down the street, lips pursed, waiting for someone to come and give him some business. He didn't mind how long it took; he had all day. Ninety percent of business involved sitting and waiting and trying to avoid the rare boys in blue. Cops, though, were more of an urban legend than an actual threat. He liked to say he kept an eye out for the cops and the Sasquatch, but he wasn't scared of either since all the Bigfoot lived up north somewhere.

He didn't see her approach, but he suddenly found himself sharing a piece of sidewalk with Detective Riley Parra. He straightened and said, "Ah, the lovely lady cop."

"Don't waste my time, Muse. I need a hit."

"Got a big day planned?"

"Something like that." He reached into his pocket and she grabbed his wrist before he could pull his hand free. "What the hell are you doing? Gonna hand it to me right here on the street? What, you have cameras watching me?"

"Calm down," he sighed. "Ain't nobody care that you're getting juiced. But if you'd like to step into my office, pay my rent."

"Down here," she said, and led him around the chain link fence into the alley. They stopped halfway down, next to a dumpster, and Riley looked over her shoulder to make sure they were alone. She said, "Academy Award, here I come."

"You weren't that good," Muse said. He leaned against the wall. "I didn't call you."

Riley pulled a pair of twenty dollar bills from her pocket. She made sure he saw them both, folded them in half, and bent down to place them under a broken brick. "I was hoping you might want to earn a little spending money."

His eyes were locked on the brick as he spoke. "Stuff I know, only worth a little bit. What do you want to know?"

"Is there someone big in town? Someone who likes to keep his face out of sight but likes to pull the strings?"

Muse scoffed. "Every man out here is just a puppet. Most of the strings lead back to your part of town, though. You know that."

"I said I want someone big. Someone operating from No Man's Land. Might go by March or Marchosias."

Muse's expression changed instantly, his street patois fading. "You don't mess with someone like that, Detective. I don't care who you are, or what you have hanging off your belt."

"He got Sweet Kara killed."

Muse closed his eyes and backed up against the wall. He covered his face and shook his head. After a moment, he exhaled sharply and said, "So I guess we're down to one good cop in this godforsaken town."

Riley snorted at his choice of words. "March. Where is he? I'm going to make him pay for Kara."

Muse hesitated before taking an address book from the pocket of his coat. He flipped through and said, "The guy has his fingers in everything. Strings crisscrossing the city. Puppet master, Machiavellian, everything bad." He handed her an address. "This is where he hangs his hat. You go there, you better be protected. I mean for real, Detective."

"Is he dangerous?"

"Brainwasher. You walk in a regular old dope fiend, and you come out the Gordon Gekko of crime. Worse gets worse there. I don't want to find out that you got tainted by going there. I wouldn't be able to live with myself."

She could tell he was sincere, so she didn't mock him. "I'll do my best. Thanks for the info, Muse. Keep your nose clean."

"You know I don't sample my own stuff, woman. Now get outta here. Got business to attend." He pushed away from the wall, his swagger returning as the mask he put on for the world fell into place. Riley watched him go and wondered how many others in No Man's Land had to create an entirely new persona just to survive. She wondered how many of them started to believe the mask was real. Somewhere inside Muse was a smart kid who referenced Machiavelli and eighties movie characters in the same breath. She prayed that kid managed to survive, but she didn't hold out much hope.

She waited until Muse was back at his perch before she walked to the other end of the alley and disappeared.

Riley didn't believe buildings had auras. She knew a few cops who claimed they could tell 'bad' buildings just by looking at them, but that was sure it was mainly knowledge of who lived inside. She never believed someone could sense evil, but as she stepped out of the alley, she changed her mind. The building Muse sent her to was undeniably wrong. It didn't look much different than its neighbors, with the dirty windows and crumbling bricks that made up the rest of the neighborhood. But just looking at this particular structure made her eyes hurt. She wanted to scream, back away, run, but she couldn't.

She kept Kara's image at the back of her mind as she crossed the street and approached the front doors. Sweat erupted on her palms and trickled down her back. She was terrified, and she wasn't exactly sure why. Something evil was waiting for her. Nothing as simple as a junkie who needed his next fix or a bipolar maniac with a shotgun. That was just humanity. This was something more.

Riley put her hand under her jacket to touch her badge, hoping it would act as a talisman. She climbed the steps to the front door and looked up at the steel numbers on the portico: 842. She half expected 666, or something similar, but she assumed not everything was as easy or obvious as in the movies. She tried the doorknob and found it was open. She took a deep breath of cool, fresh air, braced herself, and stepped inside.

The lobby branched out on either side of her, leading to a vacant desk on one side and a pair of quietly-humming vending machines on the other. Riley pulled her gun from the holster and cleared the lobby to make sure she was alone before she moved to the stairs. "Hello, is anyone home? Police officer! I'd like to speak with you for a moment, if I could."

Silence from above. She reluctantly started up the stairs. The atmosphere of the building seemed heavier than outside. Her head felt wrapped in cotton, her vision swimming slightly as she climbed the stairs. At the first landing, she turned to the right and began checking the rooms. Every room was an apartment, fully-furnished, but none of the doors were closed. It was as if the residents had just packed up and left. Trash and dirty dishes lined every horizontal surface, and trash cans overflowed onto the floor.

Things that were once people occupied some of the rooms. Junkies in soiled underwear with a needle hanging from their arms, a naked couple clutching each other on a threadbare couch. And all around them, dark figures. Riley would have dismissed them as shadows, but they seemed to turn and follow her as she walked past the rooms. She felt eyes in the mist, and the hair on the back of her neck stood up. If Samael was telling the truth, then these rooms were flooded with demons.

"What are you doing here?"

The voice was deceptively calm, and Riley turned slowly to make sure the man saw her gun. He was standing on the top stair, blocking her retreat. He was immaculately dressed, well-groomed, and seemed utterly out of place in the festering ruins of the building. She had no idea where he had come from. He watched her, his eyes on her gun.

"I'm a police officer," she said. She pushed her jacket out of the way to show her badge. "Detective Riley Parra. I'm just here to talk to your boss. Is he here?"

"Police officers don't talk," the man said. He came closer and Riley smelled the reek of decay coming from him. "Police officers lie and obfuscate. Police officers are problematic."

She heard footsteps on the stairs; more people coming to see what all the fuss was about, no doubt. She moved closer to the wall, hoping to prevent anyone from sneaking up from behind. "You've had some bad experiences. I'm sorry to hear that. But maybe if you would just let me speak to your boss—"

"He doesn't wish to speak with you. Or any police officer. He wishes to be left alone."

Riley nodded. "I understand that, and I apologize for the inconvenience. But sometimes you have to do things you don't want to do."

The man was close enough now that she could see his eyes. They were completely red, not bloodshot but blood-filled, and his breath reeked of sulfur when he spoke. "You are about to make me do something I do not wish to do, Detective Riley Parra."

She knew the time for negotiating was done. He reached up to push her gun out of the way, and she pulled the trigger. The man yelped and pulled back, cradling his hand to his chest. Riley wanted to make a break for the stairs, but someone wrapped an arm around her waist and pulled her back. She struggled, but the grip was too tight. Something sharp pierced her side, just above the waistband of her jeans.

The man, or creature, holding her sniffed her hair. "I smell fear and pain. And loss. So much loss. I smell a woman who stepped over her own mother in the street and didn't realize who it was. So close to your mother at last, and you left her in the gutter to die. Just like your partner. Sweet, sweet Kara. Everyone around you dies, death surrounds you, seeped into your pores. I can smell it, and it smells..."

Riley lifted her gun and fired over her shoulder. The effect was deafening, but the creature fell back. Whatever he had held against her side jerked back with his body, and it tore through the thin material at the side of the bulletproof vest, cutting it like scissors through tissue paper. There was a white hot flash of simple pressure before the pain caught up with her brain and she realized her skin was being torn open. She shoved away from the creature and ran for the stairs just as the demons started to flow out of the rooms and descend from upstairs.

One of them grabbed her around the waist and Riley twisted to get away. The move opened the wound in her side and she cried out as she hit the ground. A demon was on top of her instantly, its horribly human face in hers. It parted its lips in a wild sneer, showing yellow teeth and a serpentine tongue. Riley rested her gun on the creature's tongue and pulled the trigger again. She was panicking, drenched with sweat and dripping blood as she scrambled to her feet.

A creature grabbed her again, shackle-strong hands closing around her wrists. "Do you wish to leave now, little girl?" It was the first demon, the one who had spoken to her. Her ears were still ringing, but she could hear him perfectly. She realized he was in her head, and she felt her grip on reality becoming loose. A wound on his forehead, where she had shot him, was quickly healing. She wanted to sob, she wanted to curl into a ball and weep, she just wanted it to stop.

"You can empty your gun on us, and we will keep coming. But all you need is one bullet to stop it all." He guided her hand up, and she pressed the barrel against her temple.

"Pain, pain, go away," another demon sang.

"Squeeze," a chorus of voices said inside her head. "Do it. One bullet."

Riley pressed her feet against the floor and bent her knees slightly. She leaned forward and then threw herself backward with all her strength. The demon was thrown off-guard and slammed into the plaster wall. His grip weakened and Riley shoved away from him before he could regain his bearings. The demons swarmed on the stairs and she knew she would never get past them. She didn't break stride when she reached the banister. She just grabbed the railing and hurled herself over into open air.

The demons howled as she fell, and every bone in her body trembled as she hit the ground. She rolled, praying she had saved her legs, and got back to her feet as fast as humanly possible. As she raced for the front door, she heard mocking laughter in her head, shrieking voices of the damned following her as she retreated.

She didn't stop until she was blocks away. She felt like she was high, her head still swimming whenever she tried to focus on anything. She touched her side and hissed as she felt the torn flesh and muscle through her useless bulletproof vest. Bulletproof, maybe, but apparently not demon-proof. Maybe the demon's knife had been drugged with something. She was achy, nauseated, and it was taking all her strength just to stand upright.

She took off her jacket and blouse, wincing as she twisted to get the vest off. She wadded up the blouse and pressed it hard against the wound on her side. A dark crimson trail ran down her left side and disappeared into her shoe. Riley scanned the street and tried to clear her head, tried to think of what to do next.

She didn't have anywhere to go. She was in No Man's Land on unofficial business, on a case her boss wanted to be closed by any means necessary. Her partner was dead. She was completely alone. The veins in her temple throbbed and she brought a bloody hand up to massage the pain away. She closed her eyes and stumbled forward, praying she wouldn't walk into a street and get hit by a bus.

"*Never even saw the bus.*"

She remembered Gillian's joke and realized she wasn't alone. There was one place she could go. It might push the limits of their relationship to show up like this, but it was either that or losing her life. She somehow found the strength and focus to climb the stairs to the el track, and dropped onto a bench. She closed her eyes and pictured Kara, six short months ago, showing an invitation to a housewarming.

"*That medical examiner, Dr. Hunt. She moved. I guess it's technically a, an apartment warming? Whatever, it's an excuse to get drunk and eat cake with people from work. I'm in.*"

Riley didn't go to the party. She thought it would be weird, but she wasn't entirely sure why. She had feelings for Gillian, she understood that now. The understanding was the last gift Kara gave to her. She was attracted to Gillian, and she didn't want that attraction to fade or become strained because of a romantic entanglement. If it grew into a full-blown crush, that would be the end of their working relationship.

The train arrived, and Riley stumbled on board. She dropped into the seat and looked out the window, shocked to see the sun setting behind the buildings of No Man's Land. Had she dozed on the bench? Could she possibly have slept through five or six hours of train arrivals? She reached down and touched her side. The wound was still seeping blood.

She prayed that she had lost consciousness, that she had slumped on the bench and gone undisturbed for the entire afternoon. Blood loss would do that to you, wouldn't it? And in No Man's Land, it was nobody's business if they saw you bleeding on a bench. They would just go on about their business.

Riley closed her eyes. She had just dozed on the bench for five hours. That was all that happened. Because the alternative was that somehow, she had lost most of the day in the hellish apartment building. And if she stopped to consider what had happened during the missing time, she would truly go mad.

Chapter Twelve

Riley nearly slept through the correct stop. She straightened in her seat and looked around the train car. A woman wrapped in what was probably every article of clothing she owned sat on the opposite bench, her hand wrapped around the metal bar like it was a lifeline. Riley stared at the homeless woman, who stared back. The woman didn't seem alarmed by the amount of blood on Riley's clothes, or the fact that Riley's hand looked like it had been dipped in red paint. Just another dreg of society on the late train.

Ancient speakers were valiantly attempting to announce the next station through a veil of static explosions. A man at the far end of the car was sitting with one arm draped over a boom box, Lou Reed's voice transformed into an eerie hiss through the crappy speakers.

The train lurched to a stop and Riley looked at the surrounded neighborhood. She pulled herself up, ignoring the horrendous pain in her side, and moved toward the doors. She stepped off the train and lost her footing, clinging to a trash can as she waited for her head to stop swimming. Lou Reed invited her to the wild side. She spent one afternoon in No Man's Land, and now she was limping through the streets waiting to die. She'd walked on the wild side enough for one life, she decided as she finally found her feet.

As she walked, she looked at her surroundings with a critical eye. The good part of town had its own problems. Drugs and violence, pain and misery. Apartment buildings had signs advertising vacancies, hardly a day went by when she didn't see a moving truck somewhere. People were taking the easy way out, leaving while the leaving was good. They knew it was only a matter of time before things went bad and stayed that way.

"What am I doing," she whispered. She was trying to single-handedly save a city that didn't want to be saved. Who would care if the place burned to the ground? Gather the ashes and let the wind take them. Why was she killing herself for this town?

When she reached Gillian's building, she climbed the front steps and looked at the call buttons. Most of the names were too faded or scrawled to read, so she just pressed one at random. A few seconds later, a loud buzz sounded and the front door opened when she tried the handle. Riley straightened as best she could, grunting as the skin pulled against the wound on her side, gritting her teeth as she walked through the lobby.

Someone was singing tunelessly on the other side of the lobby, an oldie about Buddy Holly dying in a plane crash. As she climbed the stairs as she recalled the end of that song about God and Jesus taking the last train to the coast, effectively abandoning humanity. Don McLean didn't know the half of it.

Her hand left red stains on the wood as she climbed, and she realized that she would probably fall over if she didn't keep hold. The weakness was shocking, frightening, and it made her wish she hadn't come. I don't want to die on Gillian's doorstep, she thought. But it was too late to turn back now.

"*Says Apartment 4-D,*" *Kara said, reading from the invitation.*

"*Forty?*" *Riley said.*

"*No, stupid. Four-dash-D. Are you coming?*"

Riley shook her head. "*Nah. I don't really do that kind of pointless gathering crap. You have fun, though.*"

Riley knocked on the door just under the gold numbers. She leaned against the wall and closed her eyes. She just wanted to sleep. Maybe if she slid down to the floor, she could close her eyes and rest until Gillian answered the door. She was just starting to slide when someone on the other side of the door said, "Who is it?"

"Detective Riley Parra," Riley said, "Badge number 2128. Four-ten precinct..."

The door opened before Riley could recite her social security number. Gillian's hair was mussed from sleep and she was wrapped in a sea-foam green robe. Her eyes widened and she out her hands out to steady Riley before she fell over. "Oh, my God. What happened to you?"

"They fought the law, and the law... got its ass kicked."

Gillian guided Riley into the apartment and pushed the door shut with her foot. Riley was surprised at the apartment's décor; it looked like something out of a fifties movie. Two lamps with brown-yellow shades flanked either side of the couch and Gillian turned one on as she passed. She gestured at the couch. "Sit down."

Riley looked at the ugly brown and tan couch. "I'm bloody."

"For God's sake," Gillian muttered. She grabbed an afghan off the back of a nearby armchair and tossed it onto the couch. "There. Bleed on that."

Riley sat down and nearly fell asleep on contact. Ugly though it may be, the couch was the most comfortable thing she had ever sat on. Gillian took off her coat and gently removed the blood-soaked blouse Riley had been using to staunch the blood. Riley leaned to the side as Gillian examined the cut through her tank top. "God. Weren't you wearing a vest?"

Riley lifted her head and looked around the room groggily. Where had she left her vest? "I was," she said. "It's... I don't know. I left it somewhere." She pictured the bench where she had dozed. The vest was probably already protecting the torso of some punk gangbanger. She dropped her head back against the back of the couch and said, "It's gone. Useless piece of shit." She ran her tongue over her dry lips and wondered if there was water.

"Let me guess, whoever did this had some connection to Kara's death?"

"Mm," Riley grunted.

Gillian sighed. She stood and went into the kitchen, and returned with a folded white towel. "Here. Use this to put pressure on the wound. I'm going to get some water and my medical kit." She disappeared back into the kitchen.

Riley looked at the towel in her hand. It was mostly white, with a stripe of blue along the bottom. A yellow duck was embroidered in the bottom right corner. Riley stared at the duck and then started to laugh. She turned the towel so she wouldn't bleed on the duck, and pressed the towel to her wound. Laughing hurt her side, but she couldn't help herself.

When Gillian returned with a bowl of water and a black bag tucked under her arm, she had put on her black-framed eyeglasses. She frowned and said, "What's so funny?"

"There's a duck on your towel."

"Yeah. I like ducks."

That made Riley laugh harder, and tears rolled down her cheeks from the pain. "This entire town is so fucking ugly. But you have ducks on your towels. I love that."

"Well, thank you," Gillian said. She eased Riley's tank top up, exposing her stomach. Riley looked down and all humor left her. The cut was ragged, running from her hip to the bottom of her rib cage. It was a bright and angry red, dark blood staining her skin around it. Gillian wet the towel and gently cleaned the wound. Riley closed her eyes and tried to keep her wincing to a minimum.

"This is going to need stitches. And you could probably use a transfusion."

"No," Riley said. "I don't want a hospital. Can you do the stitches?"

"I'm usually doing them on corpses," Gillian said. "We didn't exactly get points for neatness at my school."

Riley nodded. "It's okay."

Gillian was kneeling on the floor in front of her, and Riley couldn't help but notice the stretch of bare leg exposed by the open halves of Gillian's robe. Gillian was nearly finished cleaning up Riley's side when a door closed down the hall. Riley's eyes immediately shifted toward the other side of the apartment, but Gillian looked resigned. "I'll be right back. Keep pressure on that wound."

Gillian stood and pulled the two halves of her robe together. She went to the hallway just as a tall woman appeared. Gillian didn't step in her way, but she held her hands up. "Hey, can we talk for a second? Just wait." She moved the woman deeper into the hall, but Riley could still hear her hushed voice. "She's someone from work. She's hurt. I don't know. Just stay, all right? No, it—" She sighed and listened to what the other woman said, and then muttered, "Fine, all right, go."

The mystery woman walked through the living room without glancing toward the couch. She stepped into the hall and slammed the door behind her.

Gillian returned, her lips pressed together in anger. She knelt in front of Riley again and continued cleaning the wound. Riley said, "Damn, I'm sorry. I didn't... I didn't think that you might be..."

"Don't worry about it. That wasn't about you."

"Are you sure about that?"

Gillian nodded and chuckled without humor. "Oh, yeah. You're just her latest excuse. Her last excuse." She finished cleaning up the dried blood and reached down to open her bag. She hesitated and said, "Look, this is going to look like shit. You'll probably have a pretty nasty scar. You really should go to a hospital."

"I don't care about the scar. Please, Jill."

Gillian sighed, shook her head, and pulled out her kit. Riley closed her eyes - she didn't mind getting shots, but she hated to see the needle - and winced as she was injected. A soothing numbness spread through her midsection and she relaxed slightly. "Okay," Gillian said a moment later. "First living patient. Wish me luck."

"You don't exactly inspire confidence."

"You think my bedside manner is bad, wait until you get my bill."

Riley smiled and rested her head against the back of the couch. She could feel Gillian's fingers tugging at her, prodding the wound, but there was no pain. Riley relaxed and, in moments, felt herself drifting off to sleep.

"Riley?"

Riley was lying on the couch, and everything felt strange. At first, she thought it was aftereffects of the anesthesia, but then she realized she was no longer wearing her jeans. Or her socks. Her eyelids fluttered and she woke up, looking down at herself. Her bloody clothes had been replaced by a pair of blue scrubs. Her feet were bare. She touched her side and felt the bulky bandage under the crisp material of the scrub top. "What...?"

Gillian put her hands on Riley's shoulders to keep her from sitting up. "Whoa, hold it. Slow down. You need to give yourself some time to heal."

Riley grunted and fell back to the couch. She moved her hand and said, "Where are my clothes?"

"They're being washed."

"You undressed me?"

"You can trust me," Gillian said. "I'm practically a doctor."

Riley smiled.

"It's nothing I haven't seen before. Strictly professional."

Riley nodded. "It's okay if it wasn't. Strictly, I mean. You are still human."

This time Gillian smiled. "Well, someone has a high opinion of their beat-to-shit body." She pulled a blanket up over Riley's lower body and said, "Get some rest. You apparently went through a hell of a lot today. Your body needs time to catch up."

"Yeah," Riley said. She didn't want to think about everything that happened in No Man's Land, and she really didn't want to think about the note she had found in Kara's apartment. Her eyes snapped open and she tried to sit up. "Oh, shit," she said, and then winced as pain shot up her side. She covered the bandage with her hand and said, "My clothes. My jacket. It's..."

"I found the money," Gillian said from the hallway. "It's in a plastic bag, tucked between the kitchen counter and the fridge." She leaned against the wall and looked down at the ground. "I don't know what you and Kara were into, Riley. I don't want to know. I know you well enough to understand whatever it is, I shouldn't be worried about IAB coming and knocking on my door. Get some rest, Riley."

Riley settled back against the couch and nodded. "I'm sorry for ruining your night."

"Don't worry about it. Good night. If that's possible for you."

Riley looked away. "I'll try."

Gillian disappeared down the hall and Riley stared at the ceiling. She heard Gillian's bedroom door close, and looked around the living room. It was a beautifully quaint room. In the weak lamplight, she could see pictures hanging in frames on the wall. An old-fashioned rotary phone stood on the end table, next to a cell phone resting in a charger. She plucked at the afghan covering her and knew it was handmade, probably the work of some relative.

She realized this apartment was the answer to her earlier question. People like Gillian were why she fought. People who made a life in this city and weren't willing to turn their backs on it. She was fighting for all the people who were hoping for a brighter day. If she didn't, no one would. She couldn't give up. But it was so damn hard fighting by herself.

She pushed the afghan away and carefully rose from the couch. She held her side, hoping to keep the stitches from popping, and shambled down the hallway. All the doors were open except for one. She saw a bathroom, some sort of office, and she passed them without a thought. She paused at the closed door and twisted the knob.

The bedroom was dark, and she listened hard for the sound of snoring. A second later, Gillian said, "Riley?"

Riley opened the door the rest of the way. Gillian was sitting up in bed, blankets gathered around her waist. She wore a nightgown with lace shoulder straps, her hair down on her shoulders. Her glasses rested on the table next to the bed, along with a bottle of pills and an alarm clock. Riley wasn't sure why she had come down the hallway and she looked at her hand on the knob. "I should have knocked."

"That's okay."

"Can I... can..."

Gillian pushed down the blanket on the opposite side of the bed. "Come on."

Riley stepped into the bedroom and closed the door behind her. She crossed the room, climbed into bed, and settled down against the pillows.

Gillian lay down next to her and turned her head. "You deserve a soft bed after a hard day."

Riley closed her eyes and, without warning, began to cry. Gillian moved close to her and cradled her head to her chest.

Chapter Thirteen

The demons claw at her, pulling her away from the stairs. Their voices are a sibilant hiss in her head, threats and nightmares, winding around her head like snakes. There is no escape from them, their claws tear through her clothes and pierce her flesh. She feels blood seeping underneath her clothes and she falls to the ground with a shout and a scream as she is dragged back into the darkness. One presses his lips to her ear and hisses, "What makes you think you really got out of this building alive?"

The others laugh and Riley screams because she knows it's true, she knows the demon is telling the truth. Everything after - the train and Gillian - was an elaborate fantasy created by her brain to keep her sanity. But now she knew the truth and she couldn't run away again, and she screams louder and longer than she knew was possible as they begin to tear her apart.

She never got out, she will never get out, not even through death. She screams as the demons devour her, because she knows it will never, ever stop.

Riley was jerked from the nightmare by Debbie Harry telling her that the "The tide is hi-igh!" She pushed herself up and immediately remembered the tear in her side. She winced and clutched her side, staying still until the pain subsided. She rolled onto her back and stared at the bedroom. The closet was open, revealing a row of green scrubs alongside casual outfits. She could hear the shower running in the next room and she turned to put her feet on the floor. There was a fat, stuffed duck sitting on the floor in front of the nightstand, and Riley stared at the tiny unseeing brown eyes.

She wasn't sure when she finally fell asleep, but she was pretty sure she was in Gillian's arms. She covered her face and rested her elbows on her knees. What the hell had she been thinking, getting into bed with Gillian? She would never be able to show her face in the morgue again. The list of places where she would feel comfortable showing her face was already painfully short, and she hated Gillian's domain being taken off the list.

The shower shut off, and Riley tried to push herself up. She grunted as she shuffled across the bedroom floor, one hand on her side. She was almost to the door when Gillian came out of the bathroom. "Hey, what do you think you're doing?"

Riley didn't turn to look at her. Whether Gillian was in a towel or a robe, she was more than likely closer to naked than Riley had ever seen her. She said, "I was just going to see if I could find my clothes. Get out of your hair."

"You're still recovering. Crash on my couch today."

"No, you've done enough."

Gillian put her hands on Riley's shoulder, and Riley nearly jumped out of her skin. "I'm the closest thing you have to a doctor right now, and I'm saying rest. I do not want to have to re-stitch your wound." Gillian began to massage Riley's shoulders. Riley closed her eyes; it felt so good. "You nearly got your head taken off in that fight, some asshole shot you..."

"Kara shot me."

Gillian's hands froze. "What?"

"I shot Kara." She took a deep breath and turned to face Gillian. She was in the same robe she had worn the night before, her hair slicked back against her head and darkened from the shower. Riley closed her eyes and explained everything that had happened since discovering the body in the drain pipe, leaving out only the part of Samael entering her apartment and revealing the existence of angels and demons. She told about Kara's false affidavit, and Hathaway's offer to cover it up in return for a "favor."

When she finished, she felt physically lighter. She opened her eyes and looked at Gillian, expecting to see revulsion or horror. Instead, she saw understanding. "Sounds like you've had a rough couple of days."

Riley scoffed. "Yeah, you could say that."

"So stay here. Sleep on the couch, watch some crappy game shows. Get your energy back. Get your feet back underneath you. You're not going to do anyone any good going out like this. I don't want to see you get hurt. Well, any more hurt than you already are." She smiled and moved her hands to Riley's cheeks.

Riley's smile faded as Gillian leaned in. She said, "Wait," just as Gillian's lips met hers.

Riley put her hands on Gillian's shoulders to push her away, but instead she closed her eyes. She parted her lips, and moaned as Gillian's tongue touched hers. She moved her hands to Gillian's hips and was very aware that there was nothing underneath. They parted, and Gillian gave her a quick kiss on the cheek before pulling back. "Do you remember the junkie who blew his head off down on Sonomala?"

South No Man's Land, Riley immediately translated. She vaguely remembered the apartment, the blood painting one window bright red. She and Kara walked in and the medical examiner stood up and extended her hand over the corpse.

"It's where we met," Riley said.

"I've wanted to do that right then and there. But it seemed inappropriate at a crime scene."

"Good call."

Gillian smiled. "And after that, we only seemed to meet when there was a corpse around. So there was never a really opportune time."

"You could have come up to my office some slow afternoon."

"That would have involved taking the first step."

"You didn't seem to have a problem with that just now."

Gillian shrugged. "I spent last night watching you sleep. I didn't think there would be any better time."

Riley felt herself blushing. "You watched me sleep?"

"All night," Gillian said softly.

She remembered the nightmares and flinched. "Did I..."

"You made some noise," Gillian admitted. "But I managed to calm you down."

"You should have tried to sleep."

Gillian shook her head. "I couldn't. I had to make sure you were safe."

Riley touched Gillian's bottom lip and leaned in for another kiss. Gillian moved to put her hands on Riley's hips, but her hand brushed the still-sensitive wound on her side instead. Riley hissed through clenched teeth and pulled back. Gillian said, "Shit. I'm sorry. Are you okay?"

"Yeah. Just a little sensitive." She looked at Gillian and said, "Maybe when I've had a chance to heal a little more."

Gillian's eyes sparkled. "Yeah?"

Riley nodded. She kissed Gillian, taking the time to really appreciate the feel of the other woman's body pressed against hers. They finally pulled apart, and Gillian forced herself to take a step back. She messed with the tie of her robe and said, "That woman, last night. She wasn't... I mean, you don't have to worry about breaking us up or anything. She and I were just..."

"I understand."

"We just help each other out sometimes. It's just been a little more frustrating lately." She scratched her forehead and wrinkled her nose. A strand of hair fell forward and hung in front of her face. "I should... stop talking and get ready for work."

Riley reached up and brushed the strand of hair away. Gillian looked up, green eyes wide. Riley said, "Who knows. Maybe something good can come out of this whole damned mess."

Gillian smiled. "I would really like that."

Riley leaned in and kissed Gillian's cheek. "I'll go see if I can muster up the strength to cook you breakfast."

"I'll take Pop Tarts. But you, I'll cook you something. You need to get your strength up after the day you had yesterday."

"Okay. I'll get out of your room so you can change." She stopped at the threshold. "Unless you need a hand with something."

Gillian put a hand on Riley's shoulder and gently pushed her out of the way so she could shut the door. Just before the door latched, Gillian said, "All in good time."

Gillian made oatmeal and sausages, ordering Riley to eat both of them. "Lots of iron," she said. "Make up for your blood loss."

"Is that so?" Riley said.

"Hell if I know. You're the only patient I've ever had who was alive the day after I worked on 'em."

Riley said, "I wouldn't put that in your ads."

"Who needs ads? The wounded hunt me down in the middle of the night." She added another pair of sausage links to Riley's plate. She finally abandoned the stove and sat down next to Riley at the dining room table. "All right, I know you're not going to just sit around the apartment all day. What are you planning?"

"Nothing strenuous," Riley said. "I barely managed to get my foot in the door last time before I got taken down. I need a better battle plan."

"Planning sounds safe." Riley nodded. Gillian put her hand on top of Riley's and said, "Promise me you won't go back into No Man's Land. In your condition, you would definitely not make it home again."

Riley looked into Gillian's eyes and saw the anxiety and fear behind them. She quickly looked away and said, "I haven't had anyone waiting at home to worry about me in... a really long time. If ever. I haven't had anyone who cared."

Gillian stood up and moved next to Riley's chair. "Look at me." Riley lifted her eyes and Gillian cupped her face. "At the risk of sounding corny, I care. I didn't finally share my bed with you just to have you disappear before I get to see you naked. Do you hear me?"

"You saw me naked last night."

"Shut up," Gillian said. "Promise me."

"I promise."

Gillian bent down and kissed Riley's lips, holding the position for a long moment before she backed away. "All right. I'm going to go. Be safe."

"I will."

She turned in her chair and watched Gillian gather her things for work. She slipped her horn-rimmed glasses on, checked to make sure her cell phone was in her pocket, and said, "Okay. I'll be back around six. Try not to have any more wounds by then."

Riley waved good-bye and turned back to her breakfast.

Riley decided to take a bath when she finished her breakfast. She usually preferred showers, but every now and then she just wanted to sit and relax. Unfortunately, the huge fresh wound in her side would hamper that, so she was going to take whatever she could get. She went into the bathroom, trying to shake off the unease at being alone in such an intimate area of Gillian's apartment. "You've been in her bed," she told herself, "and she would probably tell you to do this if she was here. Get over yourself."

She reached over her head and grabbed the back collar of her scrub top, bending forward to pull the shirt off without stretching her wound any more than necessary. She turned to the mirror and lifted her arm. She carefully peeled away the bandage and winced when she saw the extent of the damage. The wound would definitely leave a nasty scar. It scared her that she didn't even know what the demon had used to cut her open. A knife? The sword used to cut off Ridwan's wings? She remembered several of them had clawed, animal hands. Maybe it had been his fingernail.

Riley shuddered and put those thoughts out of her mind. She sat on the edge of the tub and turned on the hot water. As the tub filled, she took a quick moment to snoop. Evidence of Gillian's newly-exposed duck fetish was everywhere; a duck-shaped bottle of liquid soap, pale ducks on a blue background dancing over the shower curtain, and a small porcelain duck standing next to the sink.

When the bath was full, Riley turned and lowered her feet into the water. She wet a washrag and then swept it up her arm. She hissed as the water touched her myriad of bruises, cuts and scrapes. She washed her chest and stomach, avoiding the wound on her side. She would have to clean it eventually, but she didn't want to see it any more than necessary. Instead, she looked at the white marble tile that made up the tub's alcove.

Her side already felt marginally better. She wondered if Gillian slipped some painkillers into her oatmeal. She also wondered if there were any more pills in the house. Maybe she would still try to save the city. Maybe she would go after Marchosias like Samael wanted. But whatever she decided, it could wait until she finished with her bath.

Chapter Fourteen

When Riley finished her sponge bath, she risked a naked walk through Gillian's apartment to retrieve her clothes from the dryer. When she stepped into the dining room, she gasped when she realized someone was already there. She brought one hand up to cover her breasts before the man turned and she realized who he was. "Shit. Samael. Don't you knock?"

"No," he said. "Most people never realize I'm here." He tilted a small white cookie jar - surprisingly not duck-shaped - and withdrew an Oreo.

Riley stopped the pretense of covering herself and continued to the laundry room. She retrieved her clothes and stood in the doorway to dress. "What are you doing here now?"

"I wanted to apologize for your ordeal at Marchosias' apartment building. I had no idea that would happen."

"Yeah, demons. You never know what they're up to." She winced as she pulled her tank top on. There was a rust-colored stain on the left side, and she doubted it would ever completely come out. "I could have used your help there. Maybe kept my head clear."

Samael looked down at his cookie. "I do not believe I would have been effective against Marchosias' forces."

Riley rolled her eyes. "You know, if you picked me as some sort of champion, I think you guys might want your deposit back. I don't know how you expect me to fight a guy I can't even get close to."

"You'll have to come up with a way."

Riley slapped the counter and lifted her arm. "Maybe you missed what his minions did to me yesterday. I didn't have a chance."

Samael sighed. "There is always a way to overcome."

"Yeah, well, maybe you should have picked a smarter human."

Samael took a few more cookies from the jar and walked around the counter. "You will find a way to stop Marchosias because of what is at stake. Your honor, Kara Sweet's memory, your city. The promise of a relationship with Gillian. Everything you hold dear hangs upon Marchosias being defeated. This city can be returned to its former glory."

"What if the city needs a sacrifice? What if that is my role in all of this?"

Samael shrugged as he walked past her. He put his hand on her right shoulder and quickly pulled it away before she could break his wrist. "Then you will die for a cause greater than yourself. An admirable death."

"Yeah," Riley scoffed. "Maybe for you." She looked over her shoulder and saw that Samael had disappeared again. She sighed and shook her head, then took the rest of her clothes from the dryer.

Riley chanced leaving the apartment later that morning. By the time she reached the train station, she felt like someone was digging their fingers into her side. She rode all the way to her apartment and managed to disembark, walk to her front door, and get into her apartment without keeling over. She immediately went to her medicine cabinet and dry-swallowed a handful of pain pills. She leaned against the sink and looked at her reflection.

Gillian kissed you this morning.

The smile that spread across her face caught her off-guard. She chuckled, looked down at the sink and shook her head. She pushed her hair out of her face and went into the bedroom to find some clean clothes.

Her bed was a cinder.

She stood in the doorway and stared at the remnants of her mattress. The blaze seemed to have been contained around the bed, a near perfect circle of ash surrounding the bed frame. The window was closed, nothing else in the room seemed to have been affected. She pictured crime scene techs surrounding the room and throwing out theories of spontaneous human combustion. "Parra ever smoke in bed? Well, there ya go." But she knew the truth. Marchosias sent someone to finish the job. They thought she would crawl home and climb into bed. Had they looked to make sure she was there before they lit the torch? Or was it just a blind job? Had they reached out from No Man's Land and tried to kill her from miles away?

Riley realized her hands were shaking and she stuffed them into her pockets. She took a deep breath, ignored the bed, and went to the closet. Instead of just changing clothes as she planned, she filled a duffel bag with enough things to get her through the week, and slung the strap over her shoulder. She figured that would be enough. If Marchosias was still around in seven days, odds were that she wouldn't be.

She left her apartment and headed downstairs. She stopped on the sidewalk and looked up at her window from the street. There were no scorch marks, no claw marks on the windowsill where some gargoyle hunkered and sent a fireball at her bed. But she knew without a doubt that one of Marchosias' demons was at fault. So the options are die trying to save the city, or die to make sure I won't be a problem in the future.

Riley shook her head and crossed the street. The girl who had been to a grand total of one church service in her entire life, and that was on protection detail for the mayor's grandmother, was now caught up in some holy war between angels and demons. Damned if she did, truly damned if she didn't.

"Maybe I should have gone to church once or twice," she muttered.

Riley didn't want to go inside. The building was imposing from the outside, so she could only imagine what the inside was like. All polished oak, stained glass windows casting rainbow shadows on the floor. Great big wooden guy nailed to a cross at the front of the room. What kind of morbid decoration was that, anyway? Wake up Sunday morning, put on your best clothes, ride the train with the junkies and the hookers, then take a seat and look up at a blood-stained, half-naked guilt trip.

Riley finally mustered up the courage and climbed the stairs. A black sign declared that Sunday services would begin at 10:30, and a soup kitchen was open every night at six. The heavy wooden doors creaked as Riley stepped inside, and - as in the demon fort - she felt as if she had entered another world. She tried to walk slowly, very aware of how her footsteps echoed, and happened to look to her left to see what was apparently a bird bath.

She frowned at it. Did churches have birds? She walked over, dipped her fingers into the water, and flicked them. What the hell was the thing?

"Holy water."

Riley jumped back a step and spun around. A stout black man in a cassock was approaching from the far side of the sanctuary. He smiled and said, "I apologize, I didn't mean to startle you."

"It's all right. I've just had a lot of people jumping out at me lately."

He nodded as if he understood and gestured at the water. "Holy water. Some of our parishioners like to cross themselves with it." He dipped two fingers in the water and demonstrated. "You're not a regular churchgoer, I take it?"

"No," she said. She pulled the strap of her bag higher on her shoulder and looked at the crucifix at the front of the room. To her surprise, Jesus was black. She was about to comment when she realized the priest was black, too. "Oh. This isn't a black church, is it? I could leave..."

The priest laughed. "Don't be ridiculous. You obviously have questions, and answers aren't easy to come by no matter what your skin color. My name is Jacob."

"Riley."

"What can I do for you, Riley?"

If you can't trust a priest, she thought. She said, "Do you believe there are angels and demons in the world?"

"Oh, yes. There are legions, I'm certain. And I don't mean Legion." His chuckled died off when he noticed her blank look. "Boy, it has been a while since you were in a church. The short answer is yes, I believe they walk among us. The long answer is more complicated. I believe humanity is influenced by these entities, rather than the angels or demons truly interacting with our affairs."

"Tell that to my side," she muttered.

He frowned. "I'm sorry?"

"Nothing. Never mind. What about an exorcism? If someone is possessed by a demon. Would that work if no one was possessed? Like if the demon was just... around?"

Jacob shook his head. "I'm not sure what... my dear, just what is it you're dealing with? Do you believe someone in your life is a demon?"

She sighed. "Let's skip the psychoanalyzing, okay? Just tell me what someone should do if they come face to face with a demon. The horned one. Whatever." She gestured at the sanctuary. "Don't you have weapons? Holy water, crucifixes, silver bullets. Anything to ward off evil spirits."

Jacob took a deep breath and folded his hands in front of him. "I'm afraid there's a slight problem with your request. If one of the church members came to me with this problem, yes, I would suggest several things. Prayer, crucifixes, yes. Holy water. But those items only work if you have faith in the power they represent. Wielded by an unbeliever, a crucifix is no more effective than a common piece of wood. I take it you are... not a believer, Riley."

"No. Not for a long time."

Jacob reached out and touched her arm. "I can see you're in pain. I know whatever trial you are facing right now, it weighs on you. And platitudes aren't worth the paper they're written on to you. But have faith. Trust in God to help you, and he may surprise you. You may even come out the other side of this as a believer."

"Somehow I doubt that, Father."

He smiled. "I'm sorry I couldn't be of more assistance to you."

"Right. Don't sweat it." She turned and started walking down the aisle to the front doors. When she was almost there, she stopped and turned. "Father." Jacob turned to face her. She pointed at the crucifix and said, "You're saying that is just a piece of wood without the strength of a belief behind it."

"That's right. Belief is strong enough to change the world. To turn an ordinary word carving into something that can push back the darkness."

Riley nodded slowly. "Thank you, Father. You've actually been a really big help."

She thought over her predicament at length before she finally made a decision. She found a phone book in one of the city's few remaining pay phone booths - although the receiver had been cut off and taken who-knows-where. She found a shop on the reputable part of town, a building she had passed countless times without ever giving it a second thought. She knew a lot of cops used the place, though, so she decided it was trustworthy. She made a note of the address and dialed her cell phone as she walked.

"City morgue."

"What are you wearing?"

Gillian chuckled. "Nothing but a surgical mask."

"That's more creepy than sexy."

"I know. I just pictured it. What's up?"

Riley didn't know how to answer that question. She didn't have any official news, she didn't want to tell Gillian her plan until she knew it would work, so why in the hell had she called? She finally realized she had just wanted to hear her voice. "I just... wanted to call you. And say how much I appreciated last night."

"It was my pleasure. How is your side?"

"It's been getting better all day. I may be full strength tomorrow."

"Heaven forbid," Gillian said. "I may have to tie you to the bedposts before I leave for work."

Riley nearly tripped over her feet. She looked around to see if anyone was eavesdropping and said, "Really?"

Gillian laughed. "I need to get back to work. I'll call you when I have some more time."

"Okay. Jill..."

"Hmm?"

For some reason, she wanted to say something she had never said outside of the heat of the moment. She didn't doubt it was true, but she was terrified of how true it was. She said, "I, um... I don't know."

"I don't know, too," Gillian said.

Riley smiled and hung up without saying goodbye.

The bell over the door chimed as Riley entered. Security cameras peered down from every angle at the interior of the store. Riley crossed the room to the man waiting at the cash register. "Good evening, ma'am. How can I help you?"

Riley dropped her duffel bag on the glass case that displayed various guns with price tags tied to the trigger guards. "You can make custom bullets, right?"

"Yes, ma'am."

"Can you make them out of bronze and brass with copper tips?" He rubbed his chin and she added, "I have the material. I just need to know if you can do it."

He nodded. "Oh, sure."

Riley unhooked her badge from her belt and dropped it on the counter. He raised an eyebrow and Riley showed him her police ID to confirm it was hers. "I need you to melt that down and make me some bullets."

"Out of your badge?"

"Yeah."

"That's—"

"Crazy. I know." It was her shield, an emblem of power and protection. It was a symbol of the one thing she still believed in, despite all of its flaws. She was a police officer, this was her shield, and she believed it would kill demons. "Will you do it?"

The man rubbed his chin. "I suppose."

"I'll give you an extra hundred bucks to have them ready for me tomorrow morning."

"Tomo—" He scoffed and ran a hand through his hair. "I'll do my best."

"Tomorrow morning, no later than ten, or no deal."

The man looked at her badge and then finally held out his hand. "We have a deal."

Riley shook his hand. One way or another, everything was going to get settled before the sun set tomorrow.

Chapter Fifteen

Riley wasn't exactly sure why, but she returned to Gillian's apartment rather than risk going to her own. On the surface, she could claim fear that the demons would return and take another whack at her when they discovered they missed her the first time. She went up the stairs, let herself in using the spare key, and tried to ignore the feeling of strangeness as she walked into someone else's apartment.

It was an unusual trait for a cop, especially for a homicide detective, but she always felt awkward in stranger's homes. She was an intrusion, something that didn't belong, and she never knew the lay of the land. Once, as a rookie, she had nearly screamed when what she thought was a cat statue suddenly stood, stretched, and jumped down from its perch. She used that as a lesson to never take anything for granted. A closed door might be a closet or it could hide a stairwell leading to a torture chamber.

She went to the stereo and picked out a CD so the apartment wouldn't be quiet. She couldn't stand silence for long periods, plus it gave her a chance to check out Gillian's music collection. She found a Leonard Cohen CD and let it play when she went into the bathroom. She lifted her shirt to inspect the dressing on her side. Fortunately running around all day didn't seem to have caused any further damage.

Leonard Cohen sang in a rough, beaten voice from the radio and Riley hummed along as she went into the kitchen. She found herself distracted by a series of framed photographs on the wall separating the dining room from the rest of the apartment.

There were photos of Gillian as a much younger woman, maybe fresh out of high school, with a woman who must have been her mother. Gillian stood alone in front of a waist-high brick wall, gesturing at the hills behind her.

Riley shook her head and examined each picture. She had no idea what she was doing in the apartment. She and Gillian were coworkers. Even if they did try to make something, they were destined for disappointment. She didn't want to have to avoid the morgue just because it would be awkward. Besides, Gillian wasn't even her type. Too old, although she was only a few years older than Riley, too straight-laced. Riley went for the women in tight jeans and loose blouses. She didn't want someone this... stable.

So why are you in her apartment? Why was she the only one you thought of when you thought you were dying?

She went into the kitchen and hoped to silence the voices in her head by any means necessary. Even if that meant taking drastic measures.

When Gillian arrived home two hours later, she paused in the doorway and sniffed. "Riley? Are you cooking something?"

"Yeah. In the kitchen."

Gillian dumped her bag and took off her coat as she crossed the room. "Well, if you're going to cook in my apartment, I would prefer you do it there." She went into the kitchen and couldn't help laughing.

Riley looked up at the laugh and looked down at herself. She realized she was standing in a kitchen wearing a red-and-white checkered apron. Her black hair was tangled in a sloppy ponytail, her blouse open at the collar. Her sleeves were rolled up, and a dried red sauce clung to her forearm. Gillian covered her mouth and looked around. "What are you doing?"

"Making spaghetti."

"Uh-huh. Where did the dishes go?"

"Washed and dried."

Gillian nodded. "Okay. How is your side?"

Riley waved her off. "Fine. It's good." She sighed and said, "I just needed to do something productive. I couldn't sit around and sulk all day."

"I understand. I'd still like to take a look."

"Okay. After dinner."

Gillian moved closer to the stove and looked into the pan. She put her hand in the small of Riley's back and Riley tried not to tense at the touch. It was a good touch. A very good touch. Gillian said, "Looks good. You're an excellent chef." She smiled at Riley and seemed to realize how close they were standing. Riley swallowed, her eyes drifting from Gillian's lips to the v-neck of her scrub top to the pan on the stove. Gillian sensed the tension and said, "Riley..."

Riley turned and suddenly kissed Gillian's lips. Gillian kept her eyes open through her kiss, her hands resting lightly on Riley's hips with high awareness of the wound. Riley turned away from the stove and pressed herself against Gillian for a moment before she broke the kiss. Riley sagged against Gillian and said, "I'm sorry."

"Don't be sorry," Gillian said. She put her hands in the small of Riley's back. "It was good."

Riley looked at the stove and said, "I'm not even really that hungry."

"And I had a big lunch."

Riley looked up at Gillian. There was desire in her eyes, and Riley suddenly realized how wanted she was. It was disconcerting, flattering, frightening. She stepped back long enough to lift the pan of spaghetti off the stove, move it to another burner and turn off the heat. Then she turned and kissed Gillian again. Gillian was a few inches taller than her, and still wearing shoes, so Riley had to stretch a bit. She winced as her stitches pulled, but Gillian soon made her forget about the pain.

When they parted, Gillian said, "With your wound, you're going to have to be on the bottom. I get the feeling you're not... quite used to that."

Riley smirked. "Never let it be said I turned down new experiences."

Gillian kissed Riley again and started backing out of the kitchen. Riley followed, moving her lips to Gillian's jaw and throat. When they reached the hall, Gillian moved Riley until her back was to the wall, then leaned back to look into Riley's eyes. She stepped out of her sneakers, kicking them toward the living room to even the playing field up a bit. Riley ran her hands over the crisp material of Gillian's scrub top, her hands trembling as they cupped her breasts.

Gillian placed her hand over Riley's shirt, covering the bandage on Riley's side with her palm. She looked down and ran her hand gently over the cotton. "I'll be gentle with you, Riley."

Riley pushed away from the wall and wrapped her arms around Gillian. They managed to make it down the hallway, Gillian reaching out blindly to open the bedroom door. Riley stopped at the foot of the bed they had shared the night before and sat down, spreading her legs as Gillian stepped forward. Gillian bent down and kissed Riley, easing her down onto the mattress.

As she traced Riley's lips with her tongue, her hand trailed over Riley's body. She cupped her breast, ran the back of her hand over Riley's stomach, and toyed with her belt buckle. She climbed onto the bed, straddling Riley's lap, and leaned back to begin undoing the buttons of her blouse. Riley watched as her shirt was unbuttoned, the two halves pushed aside, and then looked up to gauge Gillian's reaction.

Gillian ignored the rectangular gauze on the left size of Riley's midsection and put her hands on Riley's belly. The warmth of her palms spread across her whole stomach, and Riley groaned. Gillian let out a shaky breath and whispered, "I've thought a lot about this, you know. As long as I've known you, I've wanted you. I never thought I would be lucky enough to... to be with you like this."

She moved her hands up and cupped Riley's breasts through her bra. She chuckled and shook her head. "I'm a little nervous."

"It's okay," Riley whispered. She arched her back and reached back to unhook her bra. Gillian curled her fingers around the straps and gently pulled it up and off. Gillian looked down, eyes wide and staring. She parted her lips and touched the corner of her mouth with the tip of her tongue. After a moment, she bowed her head and kissed between Riley's small breasts. She brought both hands up, cupping them and brushing her thumbs over the nipples. Riley closed her eyes and bit her bottom lip, arching her back as Gillian's lips moved higher. She brushed her tongue over the bruise left by Kara's bullet and Riley barely contained a shout. She wasn't sure if it was pain or pleasure, but she decided it was somewhere in between.

Gillian lifted her head and kissed Riley's chin. "Tell me if I hurt you."

"It's okay," Riley whispered again.

Gillian moved her hand to Riley's cheek, cradling the smooth line of her jaw. "You're gorgeous with your hair down. Such pale skin, beautiful features. My God, you don't even know."

Riley closed her eyes and leaned into Gillian's caress. She kissed Gillian's hand, just below her thumb, and reached down to undo her own pants. Her hands tangled with Gillian's, and a moment later, her jeans were being pushed down and off. Gillian lay next to her and reached down, running her hand up the inside of Riley's leg. She moved slowly, moving her fingers against the soft flesh behind Riley's knee, her thumb running in circles over her thigh. By the time her hand finally cupped Riley through her underwear, Riley could barely breathe.

"Please," she said.

Gillian kissed her way down Riley's body. She paused to swirl her tongue in Riley's navel, then moved off the bed. She settled between Riley's legs and pulled her close. She slipped her arms under Riley's legs, moving them onto her shoulders. Gillian met Riley's eyes, wet her lips, and bowed her head.

Riley pressed the back of her head into the mattress, a dull throb spreading from the knot where she had hit the rearview mirror a few days earlier.

She brought both arms up and pressed her fists against her temples, focusing on nothing but Gillian's lips and tongue. She whimpered when Gillian pushed aside her underwear, and Gillian softly asked, "Are you okay?"

"Yeah," Riley grunted. "Keep going."

Gillian's tongue touched her, and Riley bit her bottom lip to contain the shout building in her chest. Gillian moved her hands up, lacing her fingers together on Riley's stomach. Gillian moved her tongue slowly, an excruciating exploration that was driving Riley right to the edge. Right before she let herself fall, Gillian lifted her head and placed a kiss on each of Riley's thighs.

"You have to let me come," Riley gasped. "Gillian..."

"Shh," Gillian whispered. She stood up and quickly shed her scrubs. She dumped them on the floor, her bra and boy-shorts following in short order. Riley skimmed her eyes down Gillian's body; slender and lean, average breasts with dark nipples, and a thin patch of copper-colored hair between her legs. She climbed onto the bed, straddling Riley's right leg as she pulled Riley up for another kiss. She put hand on Riley's side and said, "Are you okay," against Riley's lips.

"Yeah," Riley said. She pushed herself down until she felt Gillian's thigh pressing tight against her. She put her hands on Gillian's hips, raised her own thigh, and then rocked her hips forward. "Oh, God..."

"Go slow," Gillian whispered breathlessly. She had one hand on the back of Riley's head and the other on her breast. They rocked against each other slowly, Gillian doing most of the work because of Riley's side. Riley leaned forward and kissed Gillian's breasts, resting her face between them to inhale the scent of Gillian's sweat.

Riley moved her head up, tentatively licking Gillian's neck. Gillian sighed and Riley closed her teeth around her earlobe. Gillian gasped and curled her fingers in Riley's hair. "Oh, God, Riley..." At the sound of Gillian saying her name, Riley arched her back and came. She bit her bottom lip, and Gillian said, "You can cry out... if you want..."

Riley released a tortured, shattered groan, and then sagged against Gillian's body. She moved her hand between their bodies, found Gillian's clit, and gently circled it until Gillian came as well. She watched Gillian's face - eyes closed, chin lifted, lips slightly parted - until the orgasm washed over her. And then, finally, she cupped Riley's face and whispered, "Riley..."

They kissed, still wrapped around each other, and Riley fell back. Gillian fell with her, covering Riley's body with her own. She ran her hands over

Riley's body while peppering her face with lazy kisses. Gillian groaned and looked down. "Is your side...?"

"Sh. It's fine."

Gillian said, "Is it all right if I lay on you for a little while?"

Riley nodded.

Gillian ran her fingers over Riley's face, starting at her hairline and moving down to her chin. Riley closed her eyes and allowed the exploration. "You're so gorgeous, Riley. You better get used to me saying it." Riley pressed her lips together, but then relaxed. She hated her chin; she always felt it was a weak, little girl's chin. Her lips were too wide. Her eyebrows were too full. She was attractive, but she didn't think anyone had ever described her as cute. But now, for the moment, under Gillian's touch, she let herself believe she was.

Chapter Sixteen

Riley knew she should sleep, but it wouldn't happen. They broke their lovemaking into two rounds, taking a quick break for dinner. They wore robes into the dining room and made quick work of the final dinner preparations. When they finished, they returned to the bedroom and explored each other again. When Gillian finally suggested they get some rest, Riley agreed and spooned against Gillian from behind. But she didn't sleep.

She stared at the window and thought of the war happening in the streets of her town. It seemed like so much work and wrath for such an inconsequential piece of real estate. She didn't understand why Ridwan and his fellow angels were willing to give their lives to protect it. A quiet voice at the back of her brain asked, "Isn't that precisely what you've been doing your whole life? You've never been in love. You've focused everything on being a cop. This city is all that matters in your life."

Riley kissed Gillian's shoulder and smiled when she murmured in her sleep. The city was all that mattered in her life, at one point. Not anymore. The thought scared her. Her entire life, she had only had one person to care about; herself. That changed slightly when Kara Sweet became her partner, and Kara's safety became as paramount as her own, but that was different. She knew that whatever happened the next morning at Marchosias' apartment building, she was going to work like hell to survive, for Gillian's sake.

An hour or so before dawn, Riley slipped out of bed and took a shower. She went into the living room, pausing to make sure Gillian was still asleep, and sat down at the desk behind the couch. She found stationary and a pen, then hesitated before she began writing.

"*Gillian.*

Tonight has meant everything to me. I don't want you to think my leaving means anything bad. I just have something I need to do. One last case needs to be closed. I may not come back from it alive, and I apologize if that's the case. I would hate to think we started something tonight that can't be finished. Thank you for giving me something beautiful tonight. If you don't hear from me by tomorrow night, you should probably assume the worst. There's nothing the police will be able to do. Just know I tried my best to do the right thing. Not for the city, or for myself, or for Kara, but for you. You deserve better than what we have. So I'm going to try my damnedest to give you a better world."

Riley stared at the note and drummed her pen on the edge of the desk. She lifted her head and stared at the wall and then, before she could change her mind, scrawled, "I love you," at the bottom of the note.

She signed it, folded it, and carried it into the bedroom. She rested it on the nightstand where Gillian was sure to see it, then bent over the bed and lightly kissed Gillian's lips. "I love you."

Gillian stirred, but didn't wake. She sighed and said, "Riley..."

Riley closed her eyes and brushed Gillian's hair. She didn't want to say good-bye, and she didn't want to leave with a promise she couldn't keep. So she simply said, "I'll never forget tonight." She backed out of the bedroom, still talking herself in to what she had to do. She took her bag off the chair as she crossed the living room and left the apartment before she could change her mind.

Riley stopped at an ATM before she went to the gun shop. The cost of the custom bullets, plus the extra fee for having them ready for her so quickly, nearly wiped out her bank account. It was a problem she would deal with if she survived the coming attack, which was so unlikely that she didn't want to think about it. She drove to the shop and arrived just as the owner was flipping the sign on the door over to 'open.'

She could tell the owner hadn't slept. He still wore his clothes from her previous visit, and he hadn't shaved. "Just got 'em done," he said as she followed him through the shop. "I managed to get you twelve rounds. I'm not sure..."

"That'll be fine," she said. She prayed to God it would be.

He picked up a box and flipped open the top. The bullets were perfect and silver, with rings of copper and bronze on the tips. Riley took one out and twisted it to watch the shell catch the light. This was her badge, her totem, the symbol of her one true belief. That despite some of the people involved in it, the police department was her god and this was her crucifix. It would have to work.

She paid the man, took her bullets, and went out to her car. She sat behind the wheel and realized the sun was rising. It was captured between two buildings, framed as if on a movie screen, and she froze to watch it. If it was going to be her last sunrise, she wasn't going to waste it. As the sun tracked higher, the sky changed colors. Orange and yellow, bright, sweeping colors. Sunrises, she thought, were always better than sunsets. They were the exact same thing, albeit from different directions, but a rising sun always seemed brighter than a setting one.

When the sun disappeared behind a building, she got to work. She dumped the bullets from her gun into a coat pocket and loaded the weapon with the custom-made ammunition. Concrete Blonde was on the radio and Johnette Napolitano growled, "God is a bullet, have mercy on us everyone."

Riley slipped the gun into the holster and muttered, "You said it, sister."

Riley drove into No Man's Land rather than taking the train. If she survived, she figured she would want to make a quick getaway. If she didn't, well, it didn't matter what happened to the car. Driving allowed her to see, once again, that the line between No Man's Land and so-called respectable society was more blurred than ever. A few businesses that were in business a year ago were now closed, standing empty and forlorn. Apartment buildings grew less and less desirable the closer they were to No Man's Land, which caused a domino effect on the neighbors.

No one person can ever fix this. Not even a cop. Not even if that cop kills one demon. This is not the work of one person, and it can't be fixed by one person.

Riley shook her head and silenced the voice. She focused on the memory of Kara. "Got a smoke?" Riley giving her the eye as she handed over a cigarette. "Thanks. Quitting is hell."

Trying to finish her paperwork while Kara recounted the latest bar conquest. "Six foot five and covered in denim and tattoos. Looked like the Marlboro Man, hung like Mr. Ed."

She remembered a crime scene their first year as partners. Two little kids were found dead in their beds. Their mother, their killer, was on the couch when the cops arrived. She gestured at the bedroom with her cigarette but didn't look away from the TV until she was thrown to the ground for the handcuffs. They were looking over the scene when Riley noticed Kara was missing and went looking for her.

She found her in the alley, hugging herself, sobbing uncontrollably.

Kara never explained why she was hit so hard, and Riley never asked. She leaned against the wall next to her partner, lit up a cigarette despite the fact she didn't smoke, and gave it to Kara. Kara smoked until the tears dried up and then finally said, "It's just shit, you know. Sometimes..."

"Yeah, I know," Riley said. "You want me to handle it?"

"No," Kara said. She knocked her fist against Riley's shoulder and said, "But thanks, partner."

Kara's head jerking back as Riley pulled the trigger.

Riley punched the steering wheel.

"I could bring her back."

Her hands tightened on the steering wheel and she focused on the road. She knew what that voice was. Marchosias. He knew she was coming, and he was scared. Her heart pounded and she tried to push him away, but he was too strong.

"Do you think it's outside of my abilities? I could make it like this never happened. Send you back a few days. You'd never even see that crime scene. Wouldn't you be so much happier? Wouldn't everyone be so much happier?"

She pictured Gillian sprawled in her bed, the taste of her lips.

"No," she whispered. "You're scared. You should be. Because I'm coming."

The demon laughed in her head, and then his voice faded. Riley wanted to scream, wanted to jump from the car and run for the hills, but she couldn't. If she ever wanted to erase the image of Kara's death from her memory, she had to see this through to the end. No matter what it cost, she had to kill Marchosias.

Riley parked a block away from the apartment building. She held the gun with one hand and admired the sleek, sharp lines. She didn't even know if the damned bullets would work. She prayed they would, and had faith they would, but she couldn't remember the last time she had put any stock in faith. Everything she was supposed to have faith in - family, the church, her superiors - always let her down and left her behind.

But the department had always been there. They always stood behind her, gave her the faith to walk in dark places. She lifted the gun and rested the barrel against her forehead. The smell of oil and gunpowder was comforting, and she breathed deep. It didn't occur to her until a minute had passed that she was praying. She asked for a blessing - how could it hurt? -

and lowered the gun.

The street was empty, but she couldn't help feeling as if she was in a western. She could feel eyes on her, people hiding behind curtains and lurking in the shadows, waiting for her. She had a vision of herself standing in the middle of the street, feet apart, gun slung low on her hips as she called Marchosias out. It would never work; she looked ridiculous in cowboy boots.

Riley opened the door and climbed out of the car. She knew she should have holstered the gun, but she didn't want to. It took a couple of seconds to draw the gun, and she might not have the luxury of time. She kept the gun down against her thigh and watched the buildings as she walked. There were no tell-tale signs she was being observed, but these were demons she was dealing with. Who knew how many eyes they had?

She was almost to the front door of Marchosias' building when movement on the opposite side of the street caught her eye. She tightened her grip on her gun, turned, and groaned when she recognized Samael.

He was dressed as he had been in her apartment; business casual. His wings were again folded and hidden by a trenchcoat, but she could see the bulge they made near his shoulders. He crossed the street and fell into step next to her. "What's wrong?" she said. "Did you suddenly grow a conscience? Get embarrassed about having a human do your dirty work for you?"

"Every human deserves a guardian angel," he said. "I fear you don't know what you're getting into with Marchosias."

"Well, if I don't, then it's your bad. Everything I need to know about March, I learned from you, Sam I Am."

He pressed his lips together in displeasure. "I can't do anything once we're inside," he said. "Do you understand? I can't raise my hand against the demons in their sanctuary."

"So basically you're as useless as you are out here."

"I'm trying to make sure you understand—"

She spun on him. "You're the one who told me I was destined to do this. You're the one who told me all of this shit and told me I couldn't back down. Stop trying to hedge your bets." She checked her gun, glared at him, and said, "It's too late to second guess. I'm going in there and I'm going to do what you should have done on the waterfront that night. It would have saved everyone a hell of a lot of trouble."

She didn't wait for his reaction. She turned, opened the front door of the building, and stepped into the demons' lair.

Chapter Seventeen

The lobby was unchanged, but Riley felt a surge of apprehension as she stepped into the darkness. She had a vivid memory of herself running from the building, the demons she wasted bullets on rising and rejoining the attack. Goosebumps rose on her arms and she felt a trickle of sweat in the small of her back. She closed her eyes and focused on the knowledge that, only a few hours before, Gillian's tongue had traced along her spine. She was protected. She opened her eyes and walked deeper into the lobby.

She heard quiet, hissing whispers coming from the floors above. "I know you bastards are up there. Come on out. There's no use hiding."

They seemed to peel away from the woodwork, sliding from the shadows and into the light. Their eyes were dark, smoldering, and she looked at their lips to avoid being entranced by them. One of the demons started down the stairs, smiling brightly at her. He was bald, with broad shoulders that strained the material of his shirt. He laughed, a sound like rocks scraping against each other, and said, "Well. Look who has come back for round tw—"

Riley's bullet hit him in the middle of his broad forehead. His entire body jerked with the impact and his hand tightened on the banister. Black spider webs spread out across the dome of his head and thick black smoke rose like a ribbon from the hole as he collapsed. The echo of the gunshot filled the lobby, echoing off the walls. None of the demons moved as their point man crumpled to the ground. They looked at his body, then turned to face Riley. Their hisses and growls grew louder.

"He's not getting up," Riley said, keeping the smoking barrel of her gun as steady as possible. "We can wait as long as you want, but he's down. I have enough bullets for all of you." Providing they all went down with a single bullet. Even then it was questionable. "All I want is your boss. I can either mow you guys down until I find him, or you can let me pass and everyone here moves a step up the corporate ladder." She looked at the dead demon. "Or two steps, depending on how low that guy was."

The demons didn't speak, but she got the feeling they were conferring. She waited. Eventually, they began to back up and fold themselves back into the darkness. One by one, they vanished until the stairs were clear. Riley moved to the stairs and finally let out the breath she had been holding. Samael entered and eyed the dead demon. "Impressive. Bullets dipped in holy water?"

"No," Riley said. She started up the stairs, taking care to step carefully around the demon's body. Samael followed her. She didn't stop at the first floor; too many bad memories, and she knew Marchosias wouldn't bother with an office there. She felt comforted having Samael behind her; she wished she didn't, wished she could tell him to take a hike. But knowing he was there kept her moving forward.

The second and third floors made her skin crawl. They looked normal, if dark, but she found she couldn't focus on any surface for very long without shuddering and looking away. There was something there, a presence, and she wanted to be away from it before it permanently scarred her. She never once let herself think about leaving the building, didn't allow her brain to rationalize that everything she passed, she would see again when she left. Would the demons who were so easily cowed by her demonstration allow her to go free when she had killed their boss?

She took her right hand from her gun and wiped it on her jeans, then repeated the move with her left hand.

"Perhaps you should request back-up."

"I'm not a cop anymore," she said. She suddenly realized it was true. She had no badge, and she was using her back-up gun. "Besides, what would I say? Officer needs assistance, demon infestation in progress?"

The stairs ended at the top floor, and Riley looked down the hall at a row of closed office doors. She didn't relish the idea of checking them all, but something besides fear made her turn away from them. She went around a small outcropping and found a fire exit. She leaned on the press-bar and let a burst of sunlight into the narrow hallway. She felt a surge of fear and realized this was it; this was where Marchosias was hiding.

Riley stepped out onto the roof and squinted into the sun. The wind picked up her hair and whipped it around her head. It didn't take long to find what she was looking for.

Directly ahead of the stairwell door, was an office. The windows hung in mid-air, curtains motionless despite the breeze. There were two potted plants marking the far corners of the office, and a huge oak desk in the center of the space. Marchosias, the demon who had thrown her off another roof so many years ago, sat behind the desk with his feet up. He smiled as Riley and Samael stepped out onto the roof. The door swung shut behind them and locked with a loud click. Riley suddenly wished she had melted more badges. Like every badge on the force.

Riley started across the roof toward the desk. She felt a gust of wind against her back and turned to see Samael's coat dropping to the ground, his wings unfurling out to either side of his body. Riley felt comforted by the sight, and hated that she felt comforted. She turned away and continued forward. "I assume you're Marchosias."

"Indeed I am, Detective Parra." He wore a black suit and a red tie, his hands folded on his stomach. His face wasn't quite the death mask she remembered. She wondered if her memory was faulty, or if he had been putting on some kind of performance for her. This time, he had skin. His lips pulled back over yellow teeth, and his eyes - now crimson and shining - wrinkled when he smiled. "It is so nice to see you again."

"Yeah, I just bet it is. Show me your hands."

Marchosias widened his eyes, and would have raised his eyebrows if he had them. "Do you believe I would need a weapon to harm you?"

"Humor me."

He sighed and showed her his hands. "What now? Are you going to handcuff me? Read me my rights?" He laughed. "Are you going to arrest me for a crime I didn't commit?"

Riley smirked. "Right. I have a witness who places you at the scene."

"I'm sure you do. I was there."

Riley flashed back to that night, standing with Ray the Hooker on the street. She saw Ray staring at the water, a haunted expression on her face, and she said, "This guy made me want to run home and jump back into bed." Her gun wavered and she had a sudden, horrible realization. "She was scared of you. But she didn't know why."

Marchosias gestured at himself. "Does she really need a reason, dear?"

"No," Riley said. She was talking more to herself than to Marchosias now. Her hands shook as she put it all together. "No, but she would have known why she was scared if you were carrying a huge fucking sword. Where was the sword?"

Marchosias opened his suit jacket and looked at the inside pocket as if seeking a misplaced wallet. "What sword?" he asked.

"The sword you used to hack off Ridwan's wings. And what did you do with the wings after you chopped them off?"

"You know, I would really like to help you, Detective. I would."

"I know," she said. She brought her gun back up and turned around, aiming it at Samael's head. "You, on the other hand. You had that nice, big coat that could have concealed a sword. What did you do with the wings?"

Samael stared at the gun for a long moment and then his shoulders sagged a bit. He lowered his wings and said, "I emptied garbage bags that were nearby and placed the wings inside. I sent them out to sea. They're... they're gone."

"Why?" Riley asked. It was nearly a hiss.

The answer came from behind her. "Because Ridwan was suggesting a truce. He wanted to come up with a plan where we wouldn't have to fight any more. He would get part of the town, and I would pull back and keep a portion of No Man's Land. We were meeting to discuss particulars of the deal on neutral ground. The waterfront is... is... well, for lack of a better term, it is a no man's land. Neither of us had any power there."

Riley said, "You weren't there as a moderator. You were there to talk Ridwan out of it. You wanted to stop him from making the deal."

"He was making a deal with a demon," Samael hissed. "He was not in his right mind. He was giving up. Surrendering. Showing weakness."

Riley shook her head, tears burning in her eyes. "He would have given people hope. If No Man's Land stopped spreading, people would see that. They would see that they didn't have to give in to the inevitable. Maybe things would have changed. Maybe No Man's Land would start to shrink. Right, March? If people made the decision, if people changed the town for the better, that wouldn't have affected your deal with Ridwan."

"I suppose so. Free will, and all that. But if they decided to keep on the way they were, and No Man's Land continued to spread, well. Nothing Ridwan could have done about that, either. We were just taking ourselves out of the equation a bit. Seeing how the mere mortals dealt with being masters of their own destiny for a change."

"Humans don't change," Samael sneered. "Humans never change. Ridwan would have sacrificed everything, and this city would have crumbled. Within years, it would have been nothing but a shameful memory. And Ridwan would have been a shell of himself. I couldn't bear to see that happen."

"So you murdered him," Riley said. "And mutilated his corpse?"

She pictured it; two angels standing in the darkness, one carrying a sword. Had it been flaming, like the angel protecting the Garden of Eden?

She pictured Ridwan dropping to his knees and bowing his head in supplication. Accepting his fate and allowing his fellow angel to slaughter him.

"I thought... if his body was found, the police would merely drop the case. I removed his clothing so it would look like a tryst gone awry. I thought he would be buried and forgotten." He looked at Riley. "I never would have dreamed your dedication, or your connection to us."

Riley scoffed. "You thought Ridwan was giving up."

"Your predicament remains the same, Detective Parra," Marchosias said. "How does one arrest an angel?"

Before Riley could answer, the sky darkened. All three people on the roof - representatives of three vastly different species - looked to the sky and saw large black clouds from horizon to horizon. Thunder roared, shaking the building under their feet.

Marchosias gasped. "Oh, pardon me, Detective. I'm afraid you have an entirely new set of problems."

"No," Samael said. His voice was barely above a whisper, his head tilted back to expose his throat. "No! I did it for the right reasons! Don't do this!" He trembled and his wings curled around him. Riley stepped back and bumped into Marchosias, recoiling away from him as she brought her free hand up to cover her eyes. Samael was consumed by red and black flames, his screams piercing her eardrums. She tried to turn away, but she couldn't move, couldn't think. After what felt like years, the flames died down and Samael stumbled to his knees.

The angel wept, his charred and black wings arching out of his back like limbs of a dead tree. His entire body trembled with his sobs.

"That is the sound," Marchosias said, "of an angel falling. Detective, I would suggest you flee."

Riley looked at him, but he was gone. His office was gone. If she were a betting woman, she would say that the entire building below them was empty as well. Samael pushed himself up and looked at her. His eyes were red, his teeth clenched. Other than his scorched wings and the fact his shirt had burned away, he was physically unchanged, but looking at him made Riley feel sick with dread. His skin, pale before, was now the color of wax. His hair was dead and slack.

Samael spoke, and his voice was like tires on gravel. "Why didn't you just destroy him? Why didn't you put one of your damned bullets in his head? Why didn't you end this?" He leaped, his ruined wings carrying him across the roof to Riley.

She fired and missed, one of her precious bullets flying uselessly into the void.

Samael was on top of her then, his face a fright mask inches from hers. She could see the burst veins in his eyes, the blue irises turned deep blood red. His flesh looked diseased from this distance, and Riley was sickened at the thought of him touching her with those corpse fingers. He choked her, tears streaming down his face as he tried to force her to her knees. "Don't..." she gasped, and pressed the gun against his stomach.

Samael released her throat to swat the gun aside, then he slammed his fist into her side. Riley howled and doubled over, dropping her gun from sheer shock. Samael didn't let up. He extended his fingers and she felt the bandage burning away, felt her flesh starting to burn. Her wound opened and fresh blood soaked the side of her shirt. Riley's eyes flooded and she bit the inside of her cheek to keep from crying out. "I'll destroy you," Samael hissed.

"I'm the last chance this city has," Riley managed to say.

Samael grabbed the front of her shirt and shoved her back. She stumbled and fell to her ass, staring up at him as he advanced on her. "This city can rot," he said, his voice like the slithering of a horde of rats running through the sewer. "Sodom. Gomorrah. Cities fall. Cities of the damned. This city has destroyed two angels, it will not destroy another."

Riley swung her foot out when he was close enough and made contact with the side of his knee. Samael dropped, but she knew he wouldn't be down long. She put a hand to her side, hoping to staunch the bleeding as she scrambled to her feet. She saw the gun lying a few feet away and she lurched toward it.

"Don't you see?" Samael taunted. "It's over. This city has gone to hell."

Riley jumped and covered the gun with both hands just as Samael descended on her. *No fucking fair. If he can fly, I should be able to fly, too.*

He grabbed her shoulder to haul her up and howled in pain. He flew back, and Riley rolled over to look up at him. She could see something burnt into the flesh of his palm, but she couldn't make out the shape. She remembered him touching her yesterday in Gillian's apartment, remembered he pulled his hand back quickly as if burned. It was the same spot he had just touched now; her right shoulder.

He had touched her tattoo. Protection. Riley reached up and tugged on her blouse until it hung open to expose her tattoo. She rolled her shoulder forward and tried to look at it. The lines were glowing, the black ink transformed into deep crevasses. She drew strength from it and realized that her badge and the police weren't the only things she had faith in. She turned and looked at Samael as he alighted on the far side of the roof. He turned and looked at her. "It doesn't have to hurt," he said.

Riley brought the gun up and fired. The tiny piece of metal from her badge hit Samael high in the left shoulder and he reared back, baring his teeth in a primal scream. She took advantage of his distraction and ran across the roof toward him. By the time he recovered from the searing pain of the bullet, she was on top of him. He put an arm up to ward her off, but it was too late. She slammed into him and they both toppled.

She felt her shoulder throbbing, a steady, burning pain. But it was a good pain. It was protection. They rolled, limbs twisting together as the momentum of Riley's charge pushed them toward the edge of the roof. Riley managed to dig her heels into the roof and rose into a crouch as she watched Samael dig his fingers into the sticky tar and stop himself just before he went over the edge. He staggered to his feet, black blood seeping from the wound in his shoulder. Thin spider webs, like the ones on the bald man downstairs, spread away from the wound like bolts of black lightning.

Riley flexed her fingers on the gun and Samael met her eyes. There was no emotion in them; red had become black, inhuman. He sneered at her and rose to his full height. His ruined wings spread out to either side of him and they shook in the breeze like shreds of a scorched curtain. "This city will be completely unprotected."

"No," she said. "It won't."

She fired all but one of the remaining bullets into his chest. Samael's body glowed, the dark light flaring as each bullet entered him. When she was finished, his chest was smoking like a refinery, black smoke billowing around his head. Riley said, "I know you won't die. I know you'll just... go somewhere else. So just go. And don't come back." She fired the last bullet into his chest, and Samael rolled back with the force of the impact. Flames licked around his arms and legs, rising around his torso until he was engulfed. The wind lifted the flames into the air until they became embers, then faded.

As soon as he was gone, the dark clouds began dumping rain on her as if trying to wash away evidence of what had happened. And, the adrenaline seeping from her system, every pain Samael had inflicted upon her began to throb, then ache. She dropped to her knees and let the rain wash over her. She looked down at her side and saw a wide blossom of bright red blood staining her shirt, and it was still spreading. Some part of her realized she was losing massive quantities of blood, again, but she just watched it swirl around her in the pools of rainwater.

Her head hurt. If she was wrong and there were demons downstairs, she was unarmed. And they would know it.

She closed her eyes and tilted her head back. The rain washed over her face.

In a few minutes, she would go downstairs and pray the demons really did leave with their boss.

Maybe when the rain stopped, she would go look.

Maybe.

Epilogue

Riley opened her eyes when the music began to play. She turned and looked out the window of her car, where the black-clad legions were gathering. Every cop in the city was here, decked out in their dress uniforms to pay respect for a fallen colleague. Riley looked away and rested her gloved hands on the steering wheel. Her presence was the height of hypocrisy. She was the one who pulled the trigger. If not for her, Kara would still be alive.

She sighed and opened the car door. She straightened her uniform jacket, settled her cap, and put on a pair of sunglasses. She felt like a limo driver, probably didn't look much different from one, either. She hated the uniform; it was one of the reasons she took the detective's exam as early as she did. She rolled her shoulders, a tug on her side reminding her of the fresh stitches in her wound.

Riley barely remembered leaving Marchosias' apartment building. She remembered flashes of going downstairs and the empty rooms all around her. She was grateful for that; it wouldn't have taken a demon to kill her as weak as she was at that point. The next clear memory she had was Gillian's voice on the cell phone, and a blurry, half-conscious arrival at the hospital. A fresh batch of stitches, a blood transfusion, and Riley was well on the way to feeling human again.

The fresh, bright, antiseptic light of the hospital also had the side effect of making the battle on the roof seem too surreal to have actually happened. But she knew it was real. She would never be able to forget what happened to her there. And she was never going to forget what happened in the hospital, either. She woke up after the first blood transfusion, her first awakening since being sure she was going to die, and found Gillian asleep in the chair next to the bed. She'd refused to go home until she knew Riley was going to be safe.

Riley spotted Gillian in the crowd of mourners and made her way over to her. She whispered apologies to people she passed and took her position at Gillian's right. Gillian wore a black and purple dress, her hair done up and her eyes hidden behind dark sunglasses. Gillian glanced over and slipped her hand into Riley's. Riley accepted the touch and squeezed.

They listened to the priest's words and bowed their heads for the prayer. Riley closed her eyes and pictured Sweet Kara, her bright eyes and knowing smile. She thought about the way Kara could read people with just a glance, and the way she could cheer someone up at the drop of a hat. Kara was always hit hard by cases involving children, her rare tender side coming out when she had to hold the hand of a kid who'd been abused. Riley had lost a partner, a friend, and a sister. At the end of the prayer, she whispered, "I'm sorry, Kara."

Gillian pressed gently against Riley's side, a comforting weight, and Riley briefly returned the weight as a thank you.

When the priest dismissed them, Riley kept her hand in Gillian's and led her to the aisle. She scanned the crowd until she found faces familiar to her from Kara's desk. "Jill. There's something I have to do... Will you come with me?"

"Of course."

Riley slipped through the crowd and approached the family. An eight-year-old girl, Melody, sat quietly in one of the folding chairs as her parents tried to fend off a group of well-wishers. Dawn, Kara's sister and Melody's mother, glanced at Riley and then looked away to finish a conversation. She thanked whoever she had been talking to, let them walk away, and then broke away from the group. She walked up to Riley and said, "You were Kara's partner, aren't you?"

"Yes, ma'am. Riley Parra. I just wanted to say how sorry I am for your loss."

"It's your loss, too," Dawn said. "Kara absolutely loved working with you."

Riley looked down at the ground, grateful for Gillian's hand in hers. It gave her strength. She swallowed the tears that threatened to fall and said, "There's something Kara wanted you to have." She reached into the pocket of her uniform jacket and withdrew a slim wooden box. Inside was all the money Kara received from her bribe. "Don't open it until you get home. But it's something Kara sacrificed a lot to get."

Riley looked at the little girl, who looked completely wiped out despite the fact it was still before noon. She smiled. "We used to call your aunt Sweet Kara. I'll bet she called you Sweet Melody."

The girl smiled shyly and looked away.

Dawn held the box to her chest and said, "Thank you, Riley."

Riley nodded and excused herself. She let Gillian lead the way across the lawn to the cars. In a group near the trees, Riley spotted Lieutenant Hathaway and tensed slightly. Gillian caught the look and said, "Are you going to be able to work with her?"

"I'm going to have to," Riley said. She hadn't been back to work since their confrontation in the diner, but Hathaway had called several times just to check up on her. "We need you back on the streets." Riley decided to take the olive branch at face value. Whatever happened in Hathaway's office was in the past, and it would stay there.

During her recuperation, Riley told Gillian everything. Angels, demons, the entire story from start to finish. In hindsight, she realized that it was obvious Samael was the one who gave Kara the bribe. There was too much compassion in the bribe to have been a demon, in her opinion. She didn't worry about sounding insane, she just wanted to tell one person exactly what had happened to her the past couple of days. And if she couldn't trust Gillian with that, what chance did they have?

When she finished the story, Gillian took a sip of her tea and said, "When I was eighteen, I went mountain-climbing. I lost my grip and I started to fall. And... I don't know. I felt like someone was holding me up while I focused on a handhold and grabbed it."

"So you believe me."

Gillian didn't flinch. "Every word."

The difficult part was filling out a report on the body in the pipe. She was a terrible fiction writer. But she finally managed, with Gillian's help, to write something that at least seemed feasible. A drifter named Samuel (no known last name) killed a fellow drifter named Rick Wan. Riley and Kara were involved in a shoot-out with Samuel at the abandoned building, during which Kara was fatally shot. Riley tracked Samuel down to No Man's Land and, in the process of the investigation, lost her badge. She filled out the appropriate paperwork and now had a brand-new badge. Ridwan was buried in the potter's field, the file was shuffled away to some store room, and the case was closed. It was like the pipe man case had never happened.

They stopped near Gillian's car and Riley turned to face her. Gillian said, "Do you want to come over?"

"Yeah." She leaned in and kissed Gillian's lips. "I'll follow you."

Gillian nodded.

Riley reluctantly let go of Gillian's hands and turned to walk back to her car. Something near the trees caught her eye, and she spotted a man standing away from the rest of the mourners. He wore a dark suit with a white tie, his long blond hair slicked back out of his face. He smiled when he realized he had been seen, and lifted a hand in greeting. He joined the crowd of mourners leaving the graves, and Riley tilted her head to get a better look.

There was a bulge in the back, just between the shoulder blades. The tail of his jacket flipped up when he walked, she saw the white feathers of his wings.

She smirked and let the man disappear into the crowd. She unlocked her car door and took one last look at the city that surrounded the cemetery. She was going to have to ask Gillian for an early night; she had a lot of work to do in the morning.

She had a whole city to fight for.

No Use Crying

Chapter One

Riley's bed was still a charred remnant, and the spot where the headboard met the wall still smelled of brimstone.

She dumped her duffel bag on the bed with the mouth gaping open so she could just toss clothes inside. She didn't bother folding. It wasn't that she was scared to be in her own apartment, she was just anxious to get out before anyone came to see if she was there. She was trying to avoid landlords and demons alike. The fire that destroyed her bed hadn't burnt anything else in the apartment, but the smoke was a different story. Smoke alarms on all four floors had gone off and sprinklers drenched every apartment. Her mailbox was full of notices and warnings that she could be held responsible for paying the building's insurance premium.

Riley didn't want to fight it, even though she was pretty sure she would win. She just didn't want the hassle.

Riley emptied clothes out three drawers, stuffing them into her bag before turning to start on the closet. As she was turning, something in the center of her charcoal mattress caught her eye. It was a threadbare rabbit, with eyes made of brown buttons and floppy ears brushed back over the top of its head. The thing wore faded blue overalls and had oversized feet spread out to either side, fingerless paws hanging down in front of it.

"Do you like it?"

Riley tensed and moved her hand to the butt of her gun.

"It's just something I found lying around."

Marchosias stepped into her line of sight and picked up the rabbit. He swept his blood-red hand over the top of its head, and then he tossed it back onto the bed. The skin of his face was stretched tight over his skull, his yellow eyes buried deep in shadowed sockets. He wore a crimson dress shirt underneath a black hoodie. He put his hands in his pockets and smiled at her. "Hello again, Detective Parra. How have you been since our last meeting?"

Riley didn't answer him. She bent to pick up her duffel bag and turned to the closet. "You could kill me any time, March. Either do it or leave me alone."

"Aw," Marchosias said. "Are you leaving, Detective? That makes me feel so bad. I'm sorry to run you from your home."

"Not much of a home, now was it?" she muttered. She shoved a jacket into the duffel bag and yanked the zipper closed. "Don't forget to take your March hare with you when you go." She gave him a wide berth as she slung the bag over her shoulder, holding her breath until she was past him and into the hallway.

Marchosias laughed. "Clever." He followed her from the bedroom. "Am I to presume you are moving in with the lovely Dr. Hunt?"

Riley tried not to show her tension at the demon casually saying her new lover's name.

"It's good. I wish you nothing but the best. Of course, coming from me..."

Riley stopped at the front door and looked over her shoulder at the demon. Marchosias was holding the rabbit again, staring down into its eyes. Riley looked at the rabbit and tried to figure out what the significance was. She'd never had a rabbit like that, or a toy even similar to it, growing up. It did look familiar, though. Maybe she'd seen one in a store. Or maybe it was supposed to signify her lost childhood. Finally she sighed and said, "All right, you win. What's with the rabbit?"

"Oh, this?" he said. He held it with both hands, turning the face toward her. He made one of the paws wave with his index finger. "This is Chekov's gun. In reverse."

"Right." Riley's cell phone rang and she fished it out of her pocket. She looked at the Caller ID, and then looked up to find Marchosias and his damn rabbit had disappeared. She flipped the phone open and stepped out of her apartment. "This is Parra."

"Detective Parra," a familiar voice from dispatch said. "I got a crime scene for you, if you're not too busy."

"You have perfect timing," she said. She checked the door to make sure it was locked, not that it would make much difference to her myriad of enemies, and started down the stairs. "Where is it?"

There was a pause. "Well, that kind of depends on where you are, Detective."

Riley frowned as she stepped into the sun. "What's that supposed to mean?" She opened the back door of her car and tossed the bag inside.

Riley climbed to the top of the elevated train platform and looked both ways down the vacant tracks. Tall metal arches rose around the tracks, framing the train when it was in the station. They were supposed to make the platform seem elegant, Victorian, but they were covered with too much bird crap for that. A few of them had tattered nests tucked into any available openings. Riley couldn't imagine any birds ever being born there.

A uniformed officer was leaning against the route map, arms crossed over his chest. Riley looked at his name tag and said, "Tell me they're joking, Baines."

Baines held his hands out and shook his head.

"They didn't even bother to stop the train?"

"People gotta get to work."

She stepped to the edge of the platform and leaned out to look down the track. Buildings hugged the edge of the track, just close enough for the dust to be blown off the bricks when the train went by. She shook her head and checked her watch. "Where are they now?"

Baines took his radio and said, "This is 4-4 Delta. Detective is on the scene at Third Station, requests ETA."

There a burst of static followed by a disembodied voice. "We just passed Second Station. We'll be there in about five minutes, give or take."

Riley sighed and put her hands on her hips. She rolled her neck and said, "Who is with the body?"

"Bodies," Baines corrected. "My partner stayed on the car, making sure no one disturbed the crime scene before you could show up and take a looksee. The medical examiner got on about three stops back. I've been playing catch-up waiting until you got here so I can get back on. I've been to three different stations waiting for a detective."

"Give me a break," Riley grumbled. "I just barely missed it at the last two stops." She had spent the last twenty minutes racing the train, driving through the streets like Gene Hackman in The French Connection, trying to get to the next station before the train departed. She wasted time stopping at each one, running up to the platform, and cursing as she watched the train pull away just as she arrived. She finally got smart and jumped ahead three stops, following dispatch's directions.

Finally, the train rounded the corner and slowed to a stop at their station. The doors slid open and passengers disembarked as if it was any other day. Riley sighed and finally snapped, "All right, come on, folks. Not like there's a dead body on this train. Let's move, please." The last passenger got off in no particular hurry, and Riley boarded the train with Baines. She looked toward the front, where the engineer was stationed. "Go get him. I want to talk to him."

Baines headed off, and Riley moved toward the back of the train. A second uniformed officer was blocking the door to the last car of the train, thumbs hooked in his belt. Riley showed him her badge. "Officer Otero," she said, reading his name from the tag. "Been waiting long?"

"Beats being in the room with the body, Detective." He stepped aside and held the door open for her.

Riley stepped inside and let the door close behind her. She stood with her back to the wall for a moment, taking in the scene. To her left and right were eight orange bucket seats, four facing the front, four facing the back. Beyond them, two long bench seats hugged the wall. The bodies were on the benches, one on the left and the other across from him on the right. The kid to her left was dressed in baggy jeans, stylishly torn at the knee, and a sweatshirt Riley suspected was deceptively cheap-looking. The other body was wearing what seemed to be a red robe.

Gillian was crouched in front of the slumming rich boy, examining the bloody flower blooming on his chest. Two technicians in jumpsuits were taking photographs, eyeing the floor in case a random bit of trash turned out to be the case-breaker.

Riley couldn't help feeling claustrophobic in the tight space. She moved forward and crouched next to Gillian. "When I was a kid, you had to be dirt poor to dress this badly."

"The times they are a-changing," Gillian said.

"What have we got?"

Gillian's hair was swept back out of her face and held with a brown and black plastic clip. She glanced over her shoulder and said, "Two victims, one shot each. Estimate their ages to be twenty for this one, about twenty-five for the other. No one saw anything. Bodies were first reported at five-thirty this morning, right when the morning commute was getting under way. Not sure how long they could have been riding back here before someone stumbled in."

Riley looked at the rich kid's body, the blood obscuring whatever logo had once been written across the chest. She sighed and looked at the rest of the car. "Didn't the last car on a train used to be called the caboose?"

"On a rail train, not an el," Gillian said. "The caboose used to be crew quarters. Conductor had a little desk where he could do paperwork."

"You're making that up."

Gillian smirked.

"All right. So I guess we have no witnesses. Either of these guys have ID?"

Gillian gestured at the technicians. "I've already bagged the wallets. This one is Keith Wakefield, but the other one is a bit of a mystery. He had a wallet, but no ID whatsoever. Eighteen dollars, a couple of pictures of people I guess are his parents, a generic library card, but no driver's license."

"Naturally. Well, we can have the library scan the card and tell us who it belonged to."

The uniform guarding the door, Otero, stepped inside. "Detective. The engineer asked if he can talk to you after his shift."

"Sure," Riley said. Otero remained as Riley turned and squatted in front of the other victim. He was the older of the two, dressed in layers despite the warm weather of the past few days. The outer layer was a bright red robe cinched tight with a belt. His head was covered by a brimless hat, pushed down to his eyebrows. His chin rested on his chest.

Something gold glittered next to him on the seat and Riley craned her neck to see what it was. "Pocket watch. A nice one, considering how he's... oh, hell." She knelt in front of the man and pushed his head up so she could see his face. "Oh, goddamn it."

"What?" Gillian asked, joining Riley in front of the man.

"This is the Crier."

"Get out of here," Otero said. "I just took care of him the other night."

Riley sighed and shook her head. "It's definitely him."

Gillian shook her head. "Who is the Crier?"

Riley stood up and put her hands on her hips. "He's this guy who used to wander up and down the streets all night. I always assumed he was homeless. He walks down the middle of the street and he announces like they used to all the time. You know, 'Two o'clock and all is well, three o'clock and all is well.' He wasn't completely right in the head, but he was harmless. I think he got the idea from a book. People called all the time with noise complaints—"

"They still do," Otero said.

"I answered more than my share back when I was on patrol. We'd take him to a diner or something, get him a cup of coffee, then tell him to give it a rest. And he would give it up for the rest of the night. And the next day, he would be right out there again, doing the same thing." She looked around the floor and asked the technicians, "Did you find a bell? He carried a little gold bell with him."

"Nothing but fast food garbage."

Riley sighed and looked at the other body. "I doubt a murderer just happened across two people he had grudges against in a vacant train car. We need to figure out which one of these guys was just in the wrong place at the wrong time. Killing the Crier was a big mistake."

"Why?" Gillian asked.

"Town criers were protected by the ruling monarchy. To injure or harm one was considered as an act of treason."

Gillian said, "And you mock me for knowing about cabooses."

Riley smiled at her. "Okay. So how are we going to get these guys out of here?"

Gillian took a police radio from her pocket and held it up. "Danny, you still keeping up with the train?"

"Yes, Dr. Hunt. Sure could use a siren next time."

"Hopefully we'll never have to do this again, Danny. You're doing great. We're coming up on the Fifth Street stop. We'll have the bodies ready for transport then. We'll ask the conductor to give us a little extra time so we can unload them." She released the button and raised an eyebrow at Riley. "We're done, right?"

"Yeah. Load 'em up, move 'em out. I'll never again take a stationary crime scene for granted."

While Gillian and the techs dealt with getting Keith Wakefield into a body bag, Riley looked at the Crier again. The guy was harmless. A bit of a nuisance, maybe, but nobody worth killing. She was sure he was the one in the wrong place and the wrong time. Unfortunately, the entire city seemed to be the wrong place, and no time was very good. She sighed and stepped back to let Gillian do her job.

Officer Otero drove Riley back to her car, and from there she went straight to the library. The building always depressed her; she loved books when she was younger, but she couldn't remember the last time she'd had time to sit down and read. From the looks of the library, not many other people in the city bothered with books, either. The stairs were cracked, and the flower bed in front of the building was overgrown with weeds.

The woman behind the counter looked up as Riley entered, surprise and then boredom registering in her eyes. "How can I help you?"

Riley showed her badge and placed the library card on the counter. "Detective Parra. I was wondering if you could scan this card and tell me who it belongs to."

"You're a lost and found cop?"

"Just run the card, please."

The librarian sighed and scanned the card. Her demeanor immediately changed when she read the information on her screen. "Oh. This is Stevie C's card. Steven Cabrera. There isn't a current home address listed. I would be happy to give it to him when he comes in."

"That won't be necessary, ma'am," The card was found on his body. He was killed sometime last night.

The librarian's eyes widened and her lower lip began to quake. "He's dead? Oh, no. Oh, dear, that can't be. He was always so sweet!" She groped for a chair and pulled it out, dropping into it as she covered her mouth with one hand.

"Did he come in often?"

"No. Well, sometimes. I mean, he would come in if it was cold or raining, and he'd sit for hours. I always just assumed he was homeless. We never asked, because if he had confirmed it, we would have had to revoke his card. So we just kept his parent's address on the file and looked the other way. He took such care of his books..."

"What did he do on the cold or rainy days?"

She pointed to the back of the main room. "He would take encyclopedia and newspaper back issues, and just go through them. Front to back, taking notes in his little journal. He only checked out the books on local history or biographies of local people. I thought it was nice. A little bit of information about your own city. So many people don't bother."

Riley said, "I'm sorry I had to break the news to you. Is there anyone else here who can sit with you?"

"Yeah, yes, um. Martin is in the back..." She perched on the edge of her chair and handed the library card back to Riley. "Detective... Paris?"

"Parra."

The librarian put the card in Riley's hand and folded her fingers over it. "Get justice for him. He might have been a nobody, but he was a kind human being."

"He wasn't a nobody," Riley said. "He was the Crier."

The librarian's eyes brightened and she said, "Yes, yes he was."

Riley thanked her again and left the library. The sky was overcast, but it seemed like it always was lately. She sniffed the air, trying to see if rain was in the future, but she didn't pick up any hint of ozone. Maybe a surprise storm would sneak up and surprise her later that day.

Riley parked in the station's garage and headed upstairs. The elevator was a cramped shoebox, the light overhead flickering as she rode it up to her floor. She stared at it, watching the bulb flash and dim until the doors opened. "Is anyone going to fix that damn elevator light?" she asked the man in the maintenance jumpsuit. "It's sending me into fits every time I come in to work."

"So stop coming to work," the maintenance man said.

She dumped her jacket on the back of her chair and was about to go in search of coffee when Lieutenant Nina Hathaway appeared. Riley tensed at the sight of her and quickly looked away before the bad memories could resurface. Riley wasn't sure she would call what had happened between them rape, but it certainly wasn't something worth writing home about. Hathaway said, "Detective, I need to speak with you for a moment."

"Sorry, boss," Riley said. She already knew what the conversation would be about. "Need to get started on this train murder."

"It'll only take a second," Hathaway said. "Caitlin Priest. She's transferring from the Three-Six. She knows the city, and she knows No Man's Land. Congratulations, you have a new partner."

"I don't need a new partner," Riley said. She peered past Hathaway and squinted through the window of the break room. "Has anyone made coffee?"

"Peterson."

Riley wrinkled her nose and decided she didn't need caffeine that badly. She pulled out her chair and took a seat. "I'm doing just fine on my own."

"You've been out of the hospital for a week, Riley," Hathaway said, sitting on the edge of Riley's desk. Riley looked at Hathaway's slacks and had a flashback. "I want you to ask me for a favor, Detective Parra. I want you to ask properly. Get on your knees." In the present, Hathaway said, "You might think you're going to do okay on your own, but you need someone watching your back. I want someone watching your back. This is non-negotiable."

Riley said, "I just started the case, and I already have a list of suspects."

She picked up the phone book and held it up. "I just have to narrow it down a bit."

Hathaway didn't even smile. "Funny." She dropped Caitlin Priest's file on top of Riley's keyboard. "Get to know her. You're going to be spending a lot of time together."

Riley glared at Hathaway's retreating back as she picked up the file. "Priest. Great. I have such a great track record with them." And an even worse track record with partners. She shook her head and put the file aside to deal with it later. She stared at her computer for a long moment before she got up and headed for the break room. Peterson's coffee might be swill, but it was better than nothing.

Chapter Two

The Crier always made his rounds in the same general area. The neighborhood was on the very edge of No Man's Land, basically straddling the line of the haves and have-nots. Crappy cup of coffee in hand, Riley requested a tape of the nuisance reports from the night before to see if the Crier had bothered anyone more than usual. On her way back to her desk, she stopped by Sweet Kara's old desk and went through the drawers. Someone would have to clear her stuff out soon, but Riley didn't have the heart and no one else was dumb enough to take the job from her. She finally found the street map in the top right-hand drawer and carried it back to her desk.

The first call came from Eighth Street at 12:43 in the morning. "Yeah, that moron with the bell is at it again. I gotta be up at four damn thirty in the morning and he keeps on ringing that damn thing."

Fifteen minutes later, on Ninth Street, another caller: "I don't know if anyone's called you yet, but this guy has been ringing his bell for almost half an hour and he's screaming at the top of his lungs. I don't want to get anyone in trouble, but seriously, I need my sleep."

Almost a half hour later, the Crier was about three blocks away on Jefferson Street. "Shut the fucking asshole up before I go down in the fucking street and shove his fucking bell down his goddamn throat! He woke me up and I can't get back to sleep with all-a that ruckus."

Riley listened to enough of the calls to get an idea of where the Crier had been before he was shot. She wrote down the addresses of the complainants and marked them on the map. The last call came in at a quarter past four in the morning, from someone who lived on Downing Street. She knew the neighborhood; it probably hadn't been the Prime Minister.

She found the el station nearest to the final call. If the Crier was on Downing, then he probably boarded the el train at half past four in the morning from the Lory Street station. His body was then found an hour later. She would have to see if Gillian could narrow the time of death down any further.

She tapped her pen against the edge of the desk and decided to go out and canvas the neighborhood to give the good doctor time to do the autopsy before she dropped in.

Riley stopped by the train station to pick up a schedule. The train did indeed stop at Lory Street at 4:30 in the morning. Had the Crier boarded the train with his killer? Was his fellow victim already on the train when he got there? And what were they doing in the last car? The train couldn't possibly have been full at that hour. Riley put the schedule on the sun visor in her car and decided to retrace the Crier's steps going backward. The most likely solution was that the person who made the last complaint followed the Crier down to the station, boarded, shot and killed him. She hoped the case would be that open and shut, but experience didn't make her hopeful.

Riley found the Downing Street address and knocked. After a few minutes, a small window set at eye-level on the door opened. A man peered out at her and she held up her badge. "I just have a few questions."

The window closed, and the door opened. The man was pudgy, dressed in sweats and a ratty robe despite the fact it was closer to lunch than breakfast. There was a dried, discolored splotch of something on the shoulder of his robe. "What's going on?"

"Mr. Paul Gentry?" He nodded. "I'm Detective Riley Parra. I'd like to talk to you about that complaint you made last night."

He grunted and rubbed his face. "Look, it was four in the damn morning, you know? This retard is out there ringing his bell and yelling. He does it all the time. 'Four o'clock and all is well.' Well, thank you very fucking much, ass wipe. I almost slept through nothing happening." He sighed and held his hands out. "That was no cause for me to be rude on the phone, but... it was the middle of the night."

"You obviously had to be up for an important business meeting," Riley said.

Gentry didn't flinch. "I have an eight month old girl. You ever tried getting a baby to sleep? Try doing it at four in the morning. My baby was crying, I was pissed off, and I lost my cool. I apologize. But that guy does it all the time. All the damn time. I was just, I was finally sick of it."

"I'm sorry," Riley said. "I shouldn't have..." She shook her head. "Do you own a gun, Mr. Gentry?"

He was taken aback by the question and shook his head. "No. Never even held a gun. What does that have to do with the asshole?"

"He's dead, Mr. Gentry."

Gentry sagged against the door and his shoulders slumped. "Ah, Christ. I didn't... I mean, I just thought you were... the guy..." He shook his head. "Look, I was mad, but I wasn't that mad. You know? If I'm going to kill anyone, I got plenty of other people higher on the list than that guy. He was a nuisance, but that's it."

Riley nodded. She decided the man's gruff demeanor was due to a lack of sleep and gave him a pass. "I understand, Mr. Gentry. I'm sorry I disturbed you. Thank you for your time."

"Yeah, sure."

When Riley got to the street, she tried to picture it at night. She had seen the Crier at work enough to picture him strutting down the middle of the street ringing his bell. She remembered how many times he had irritated her with that 'all is well' spiel. What was well? Just a block away, store owners were paying protection money to drug dealers who were using the money to bribe cops to look the other way while they slowly destroyed the neighborhood. What was 'well' about that?

She remembered one of the complaints she'd responded to when she was a patrol cop. A woman called in crying, and said the Crier woke her up. "And on top of waking me," the woman said, "the motherfucker is lying."

Riley stopped at a diner to have lunch before returning to the station. Her desk upstairs beckoned, but instead she traveled down to the morgue. Most cops tried to avoid the long, sterile corridors, but Riley had never minded it much. It was peaceful, ordered. She was sure the presence of Gillian Hunt helped her appreciate the morgue's fine points, but she had liked the place even before they started dating.

The main autopsy theatre was a long, narrow room with five steel beds running down the middle. Gillian's office was at the far end, its light reflecting off the cold storage drawers. Riley went through the swinging doors and saw Gillian hunched over a corpse, one of her guests. Riley crossed the room and put her hand in the small of Gillian's back, pushing her hand up along her spine until Gillian straightened. "You'll develop a stoop."

"Not if you keep rubbing out my kinks." Gillian straightened, her face concealed behind goggles and a surgical mask. Since Gillian's mask precluded a kiss, Riley settled for squeezing the back of Gillian's neck in a gentle massage.

Riley gestured at the body. "What have you found out, Jill?"

"They hadn't been dead long before they were found. I figure less than an hour."

"We got a complaint from someone on Downing Street at four-fifteen. I think the Crier boarded the train about fifteen minutes later." She shook her head. "I don't understand why. He walked everywhere. Why did he suddenly decide to take the train?"

Gillian shook her head. "No idea. The other guy, Keith Wakefield. Typical high school honor student with a drug habit. We have track marks all over, some healed and some new. I figure there was a break somewhere in the middle of a rehab or two. Didn't stick. He had drugs in him when he died."

"At least he died with a buzz on," Riley muttered.

"His parents have been contacted. They're coming down to identify the body."

"Do I need to be here for that?"

Gillian said, "No. I'll let you know if they say it's not him, but the driver's license picture doesn't lie."

Riley nodded. "Okay. I'm going to see if I can find anything to connect him with the Crier. Maybe they were meeting on the train for a reason."

Gillian tilted her head and pushed a stray hair away from her face. "You think maybe the Crier bought or provided drugs to Wakefield?"

"I hope not. The Crier was the only person in this town with a consistently positive outlook. I'd hate to think it was just because he was stoned out of his mind."

There was an Asian man sitting at Riley's desk when she finally made it upstairs. He was leaning forward, elbows on his knees, a baseball cap hooked on long knobby fingers. Riley approached from a direction where he would be sure to see her. He straightened as she approached and she said, "I'm Detective Parra. Can I help you?"

He rose and tucked the cap into the back pocket of his jeans. "Oh. I was expectin'..." He shook his head. "I'm Joshua Ly. I was running the train where those two... the men were, ah... Thank you for letting me put this off until the end of my shift."

"No problem, Mr. Ly. Please, sit down." He reclaimed his seat and Riley sat as well. "Did you have any idea what had happened on your train this morning?"

"Not until that fella came running and banging on the door. I thought he was a nutcase or something, but sure enough..." He exhaled sharply and shook his head. "For the record, I wanted to stop and give you all some time to work. But the boss told me I couldn't hold up a bunch of people who needed to get where they were going..."

Riley held up a hand to stop him. "It's all right. It all worked out." She found the case file lying in her inbox and opened it to find pictures of the two victims. Thank you, Jill. She turned the file around so Ly could see them. "Did either of the victims ride your train regularly?"

Ly looked at the pictures. "I don't get to see the passengers very often, understand. And even if I do, I'm not very good with faces." He pointed at the Crier and said, "Him, though. I remember him because of his hat and that little bell. He was always standing in the station with a big goofy smile on his face. He acted like he was coming home from a day at the office, only he loved his job. Unlike a lot of people I pick up."

Riley nodded. "But you've never seen the Wakefield boy before?"

Ly shook his head. "Couldn't say either way. He looks like a lot of kids who ride the train down to the bad parts of town in the middle of the night, you know? Strung out, eager for a fix. I think the first time they just want a thrill, or something, but pretty soon they can't stop. Then they're stuck."

Riley knew the story all too well. "How many other passengers got onto the train at the Lory Street station last night?"

"Just that young fella with the bell. He was all alone on the platform, because I remember seeing him wave his bell when I rolled up. If someone else had been there, they'd have told him to stop. Or tried to force him to."

"Right," Riley said. "How many other passengers were riding the train this morning?"

Ly rubbed his chin. "Less than half a dozen, but that's all I can say for sure. That time of night I'm half asleep myself, you know."

Riley leaned forward. "Yeah, I know. How did you feel about the Crier? The young guy with the bell."

Ly looked down at the picture and sighed. He shook his head sadly. "He was all right. Wasn't hurting anybody. Kept quiet on the train, so that's all I cared about, really. It's going to be strange not seeing him anymore."

"So he rode the train every night? Where would he usually get off?"

"Um... he always got off at the same place. The Green Street station."

Riley looked down at her desk blotter. Why did that name sound so familiar? She went through the pages of the file one at a time, aware that Ly was staring at her. Then she found it. Keith Wakefield lived with his parents at 3144 Green Street. It could have been a coincidence; it made sense they were going to the same place seeing as they were both on the same train at the same time. The fact they were both murdered, however, made it seem like a very important clue.

"Do you remember where Keith Wakefield got on the train? Which station?"

"He got on at the station right after Mister... um..."

"Cabrera," Riley provided.

Ly nodded. "It's about an hour from Lory Street to Green. I was about to pull into the Green Street station when the guy who found 'em came and started making a ruckus." He looked down at the pictures. "It's a shame."

"What?"

"Nothing," Mr. Ly said. "It just... it seems so wrong."

Riley nodded and picked the photos up again. "Yeah. It does."

Chapter Three

Riley considered going down to the morgue to question Wakefield's parents, but she didn't want to intrude on their mourning. She decided the conversation could wait until the morning. She transcribed her notes from the door to door interviews, as well as the talk she had with Joshua Ly. By the time she finished, it was nearly five o'clock. Officially quitting time in some jurisdictions, and close enough for her.

She shut down her computer and took her coat off the back of her chair. As she was heading for the stairs, Hathaway came out of her office. "Parra."

"Just on my way out, boss. Can it wait?"

"Priest will be here tomorrow."

"I'll be sure to have a nice long list of confessions for him."

Hathaway rolled her eyes. "Caitlin Priest. Your new partner."

Riley shook her head. "I'm in the middle of a case. I can't just catch some newbie up on—"

Hathaway interrupted with a swift cut of her hand. "She's just going to be support on this one. She'll do all the heavy lifting, or any footwork you need done. It'll give you a chance to see what she's good at. And it'll give you both a chance to feel each other out before your lives are on the line. You're getting a new partner, Parra. Deal with it."

Riley sighed and held her hands up in surrender. She went downstairs and took a detour to check in with Gillian. The main hall was dark and the morgue glowed like a beacon at the end of the hall. Riley pushed through the swinging doors and eyed the empty tables in the middle of the room. Jon Bon Jovi was singing in Gillian's office, announcing that he was a cowboy riding on a steel horse. Riley stepped into the doorway and admired Gillian for a moment. Her hair was coming loose from the black-and-brown catch, wisps hanging down in her face as she signed a report. Her feet were crossed at the ankles, toes of her sneakers pointed toward the ground under her chair. Riley announced herself by singing along with the end of the chorus. "I'm wanted, dead or alive."

"Dead or ali-ive," Gillian agreed. She leaned back in her chair and laced her fingers over her stomach. "Hey, Detective. Heading home already?"

"Yep. We convinced all the murderers to start keeping banker hours. How about you? I noticed all your customers were safely stored."

Gillian nodded. "Yeah, but I still have a lot of paperwork to do. I've probably got another hour here. You go ahead, I'll catch up."

Riley hesitated. "That's all right. I could hang out here for a bit..."

Gillian chuckled and pushed away from the desk. She stood up and put her hands on Riley's hips, lifting one white sneaker to push the door close behind her. "Honey, I know you still feel awkward being alone in my apartment. But you've been out of the hospital for a week. I know you don't want to go home because of... well, you know. And I'm happy to have you there. But you need to get used to thinking of it as home."

"It's just a mental block."

Gillian said, "I understand. But your only other option is to go back to the apartment where demons blew up your bed."

Riley smiled and put her hands in the small of Gillian's back. "Live with you, or risk getting killed by demons. Is there a third choice?"

"Nope. Pick up some Chinese on the way home. I'll be there soon." She leaned in and brushed Riley's lips with hers, their hips pressed together.

Riley ran her hands over Gillian's back and was very aware that she was only wearing a black T-shirt under her scrub top, and a pair of very thin panties under the bottoms. Riley broke the kiss and said, "We could have sex on your desk..."

Gillian moved her hands to Riley's belt and kissed her neck. "Mm, then I would be running even later. And what I have planned for tonight may have to be delayed."

"You have plans for tonight? Am I involved in these plans?"

"You're a main character," Gillian promised. She slid her hands lower and squeezed Riley's ass before pulling out of the hug. "Go on. You'll be fine."

Riley sighed and opened the door to the office. "Chinese?"

"Yeah. You know what I like."

"Well, I hope so," Riley said. "See you later."

Riley rode the elevator down to the parking garage, surprised to see the janitor had, in fact, changed the light bulb. When she stepped out into the concrete maze of the garage, she regretted putting her jacket on. The night was clammy, residual heat of the day rising from the asphalt and turning the garage into a giant oven. She moved quickly toward her car, already imagining the blissful air conditioning. As she moved, she spotted a man out of the corner of her eye. He was leaning against one of the concrete pillars, arms crossed over his chest, the picture of innocence.

Riley didn't want to overreact and draw her gun, but she swung her key ring around and pinched the longest key between her index and middle finger. She faked a sigh, rolled her shoulders, and flipped her head as if to get the hair out of her eyes. She took the chance to get a closer look at him. He was tall, blonde, fair-skinned, and was already moving toward her. Riley ignored him until he was within arms reach.

"Detective Parra?" he said, reaching out for her shoulder.

His hand never landed. Riley rolled forward on the balls of her feet, spinning at the waist. She brought her fist up and punched the man in the wrist, the key digging into the soft flesh below the heel of his hand. His face twisted into a grimace of pain, and he shouted as he twisted the key against the raw flesh. Riley shifted her weight to her left foot and swung her right leg around to sweep his feet out from underneath him. Riley pulled her hand back and pushed him to the ground, a knee planted in the middle of his chest, her gun aimed at the center of his forehead. "What was the plan, asshole?" she asked.

The man's eyes crossed trying to keep the barrel of the gun in his sight. "I just... wanted to speak with you."

"Quite the conversation starter, isn't it?" she said, gesturing with the gun. "Gets right to the point, and it can end the conversation very quickly if I don't like what you have to say."

"I am the one who felled Samael."

Riley flinched. She rose off his chest, lowering the gun but not holstering it. "What do you mean?"

"I am Raguel. It was my responsibility to—"

"You're another angel and you smacked down the bad seed."

"I am the vengeance of the Lord," Raguel said. "It's my duty to strike down those who break God's laws. Samael transgressed and I dealt with him appropriately."

Riley said, "So he's dead?"

"No. He is Fallen."

Riley finally holstered her gun. Whether Raguel was an angel or a demon, regular bullets weren't going to have any effect on him. "Stand up," she said. He got to his feet, and she saw a hint of feathers underneath his long jacket. "Is everyone who wears one of these coats an angel?"

"Not necessarily. Not all angels like the fashion statement it makes."

Riley sighed and walked toward her car, letting him follow her if he wished. "So. Samael isn't dead. Are you here to warn me he's gunning for me?"

"No."

She unlocked the car and pointed to the passenger side door. "Get in if you're getting in."

Raguel opened the door and peered inside. There were files and papers all over the passenger seat. Riley grabbed them and dumped them in the backseat. "I have some catching up to do. Recuperation is a bitch."

"Yes. How is your side?"

"Why are you here, Rags?"

Raguel sighed and shifted in his seat. Wings obviously weren't conducive to sitting. "I am here to tell you that you will not be alone in protecting this city."

"You going to step up?"

"No. Zerachiel will be taking Samael's place."

Riley rolled her eyes. "You guys seriously need to think about rebranding yourselves. Normal names. Regular, every day person names."

"Like Parra?"

"That's like Smith compared to you guys. All right. Zerachiel. When will I meet him?"

Raguel looked at her. "What makes you think the two of you will meet? You could have gone your entire life without meeting Samael. The only reason he showed himself was in an attempt to deceive you. All you have to know is that you haven't been abandoned, Riley Parra. You're not alone."

Surprisingly, Riley found herself relieved by that. She sighed and said, "All right. Thanks for the heads up, Rags. Can I drop you somewhere?"

He smiled. "No. I have my own means of transportation."

Riley watched as he got out of the car. He walked across the garage, weaving between the concrete pylons until, finally, Riley lost sight of him. "Nice to know I'll have back-up," she muttered. She started the engine and said, "Maybe you could send him a partner. Get me off the hook. Think about it. Get back to me." She sighed and tried to remember where the closest Chinese take-out was.

Riley hated the Happy Panda Restaurant, but it was on her way to Gillian's, cheap, and the food was decent. She waited in the red and gold atrium, staring at the red-topped candy dispensing machines as the clerk got her food. Only a handful of customers filled tables near the back of the restaurant, and the blinds over the window were cockeyed and twisted around themselves. It was hardly four-star dining.

The waiter, an emaciated Chinese man in a white tuxedo shirt and a black bow tie, carried the brown paper bag with her order out from the kitchen. The smile was pasted on his face, his eyebrows raised in a permanent expression of hope. He placed the bag next to the cash register and Riley paid him.

Outside, the businesses all around the Happy Panda were shut down, windows boarded over and doors standing askew. Riley put the food in the passenger seat, securing it with the seatbelt, and drove out to Gillian's apartment building. She could actually track the neighborhoods getting better, the chain link fences stopped sagging, the cracked sidewalks mended, and the streetlights were mostly lit. It was like watching a time-lapse video in reverse.

Riley parked in front of the building and carried the food upstairs. It was still difficult to walk up the stairs without remembering her first trip up them, bleeding from a multitude of wounds, sure she was about to die. She ignored the painful memories and used the temporary key Gillian had given her to unlock the apartment door.

She left the food on the kitchen counter and quickly went through every room in the apartment. She made sure all the windows were secure, that there was no lingering scent of sulfur on the drapes, and that none of the furniture had mysteriously burst into flames since the last time she had been there. Finding everything in place, she divided the food into two bowls. She placed one bowl in the microwave and carried the other into the living room.

The nature of their jobs meant that she and Gillian would often be eating dinner separately, so they made a pact that neither had to wait for the other to eat. Neither of them liked the idea of the other one starving because she had paperwork. Riley began to eat, but she planned to save her egg roll until Gillian was there. It was technically breaking the rules, but that didn't matter.

She sat on the couch and put the food on the coffee table, looking over the newspaper as she ate. She read the stories differently after her encounter with Marchosias in No Man's Land. She connected the dots, stunned to find that most of the crime in the city could be linked back to him in some way. A crime boss named Dupre was well-known by the police, but Riley could now see the puppet strings connected to his arms. According to the paper, he was connected to a bribery scandal that got the last mayor kicked out of office. Unfortunately, there was no way to connect him to anything criminal.

"What else is new," Riley muttered, and flipped the page. She skimmed the terrible and depressing stories, made herself even more depressed realizing how many smaller stories never made it into the paper, and forced herself to continue. She found a brief article about the two men found shot on the train, but no details were available to the press at the time. Riley was glad for that; the one good thing about being a cop in this hellhole of a town was that they seemed to have the press reigned in pretty tight.

She plucked at the rice with her chopsticks and thought about Wakefield and the Crier. Two completely different kids from two completely different backgrounds, ended up on the same train at the same time, both of them most likely trying to go home. Then someone showed up with a gun and ended them both. But which had been the target? She supposed she had to consider the possibility that neither was the target; random joy-killings weren't unheard of in that part of town. Maybe it was just a gang initiation. Two bodies were double points, for all she knew.

Riley heard the key in the lock and checked her watch. By the time Gillian got inside, Riley was on her way into the kitchen. "Hey, you're early."

"I couldn't bear the thought of you sitting all alone in my apartment," Gillian said.

Riley retrieved Gillian's dinner from the microwave and brought it out to her. Gillian took the bowl and kissed Riley hello. They let the kiss linger, pressing against each other now that they didn't have to worry about someone seeing them. "Did you get the sauce?"

"Yeah," Riley said. She took some sauce from the bag and handed it over as they sat next to each other on the couch. Gillian looked over the newspaper, and Riley looked over Gillian. She hadn't bothered to change out of her scrubs before coming home, and her chestnut-colored hair was hanging sloppy from three different ponytails. Riley slid her hand under the loose strands, cupping her hand over the back of Gillian's neck.

Gillian's eyes closed and she moved her body with each squeeze of Riley's fingers. "Mm. You're going to have to stop that."

Riley leaned in and kissed Gillian's neck. "Make me."

Gillian shivered and put her bowl down on the coffee table. She turned to face Riley, pulling her close. Riley shifted on the couch, pushing her weight against Gillian to make her lie down. Gillian brought one leg up and onto the couch, giving Riley a chance to slip between her legs. Their lips met, and Riley slipped her hands under Gillian's scrub top. Gillian bent her leg and pressed her thigh upward.

They assaulted each other for a long moment before Gillian began working the buttons of Riley's top. She gasped as Riley's hands cupped her breasts through her bra, then slid down over her stomach. "Riley," Gillian whispered. Riley pushed one hand under the waistband of Gillian's scrub pants, over her underwear and between her legs.

Gillian moved her head to Riley's neck and began to suck, lick and bite, moving against Riley's hand while pressing her thigh harder between Riley's legs. Soon, they were both panting against each other's shoulders, Riley biting her lip to keep from shouting out. Gillian came with a quiet, "Riley, now," and Riley slipped her wet fingers free. They kissed, and Riley pushed her tongue into Gillian's mouth.

A moment later, the kiss broke and Gillian said, "Ugh, sweet and sour pork..."

Riley laughed and licked Gillian's cheek, gripping her hips for balance as she began to rock hard against her. "Come for me," Gillian whispered, her hair mussed and crossing her eyes like a veil. Riley's toes curled inside her shoes as she arched her back and did as Gillian commanded. She swallowed her cries, the veins in her throat throbbing madly.

Riley finally collapsed and kissed Gillian's lips again. Gillian flipped them so that Riley was on the bottom, pinning her to the mattress. "There," Gillian said, sweeping her hair out of her face with the back of her hand. "May I please eat my dinner now?"

"No," Riley said. "But I can feed it to you." She stretched one arm out, plucked a piece of chicken from the bowl, and held it out.

Gillian wrapped smiling lips around Riley's fingers and plucked the chicken free with her teeth. She chewed thoughtfully, then said, "Hm. There's a peculiar aftertaste to this particular batch..."

Riley realized which hand she had used to offer the food. "Oh, damn," she chuckled. "Sorry."

"Don't be," Gillian said. She sucked the excess sauce from Riley's thumb and said, "I think I have a new favorite dipping sauce. Of course, I can think of a sauce I would like better..." She slid her hand down Riley's body and cupped her between her legs.

Riley wriggled against the cushions and kissed Gillian as she was stroked. She cupped the sides of Gillian's head and tried to think of the last time she had felt happier, or more fulfilled. With Gillian, she could face demons or angels or whatever Hell threw at her.

Chapter Four

Riley woke the next morning with a renewed belief that sleeping on the couch was a very bad idea. Gillian was exhausted, and went to bed before the late news ended. Riley wanted to stay up for a little while longer and get lost in the idiot box. Unfortunately, she hadn't lasted very long. She grunted as she sat up, putting both hands in the small of her back and stretching her tired muscles back into their usual shape.

She searched the living room for Gillian, and then noticed the sound of running water in the bathroom. She had just enough time to think about water conservation when her cell phone chirped. She sighed. "Naturally." She flipped the phone open without checking the Caller ID. "Detective Parra."

"Detective. Did I wake you?" Riley groaned. Lieutenant Hathaway was not the person she wanted to hear first thing in the morning.

"No, I was up," Riley said. "What's going on?"

"Keith Wakefield's parents are here. They want to speak to you about their son's murder."

"Great," Riley said, quickly waking up. "I want to talk to them, too. Are they in the office?" She reached down and hooked her fingers in her shoes, pulling them closer.

"Waiting at your desk as we speak."

"Give me twenty minutes."

She hung up and went into the bedroom to make a quick change of clothes. She glanced at the closed bathroom door and wondered if she could resist temptation long enough to bathe. The mental image of Gillian's naked body under the flow of warm water was enough to convince her that she wouldn't be able to restrain herself. She changed out of her day-old outfit, threw on the first clothes she found, and slipped into the bathroom.

The mirror was steamed, so she wrote her note there. "Had to go in to work. I'll see you there, or later. XO. Riley."

She frowned at the "XO." She had never done anything like that, such a high school thing. But she couldn't wipe it away without being obvious. So instead, she slipped out of the bathroom and hoped Gillian wouldn't hold it against her.

She drove to the station and parked in the garage. There were no angels waiting to ambush her, and she reached the elevator without incident. When the elevator doors parted, she saw Hathaway standing at her desk. The lieutenant frowned, checked her watch, and said, "You couldn't possibly have made it here from your apartment so quickly."

"You're right," Riley said. "The parents waiting at my desk?"

"I moved them to interrogation room two, actually," Hathaway said, falling into step next to Riley. She headed off Riley's shocked look. "It was their choice. They didn't want to spend anymore time than necessary 'surrounded by the dregs of society.'"

"I thought Talbot had the day off."

"Ha," Hathaway said. She said, "Be nice to them, Riley."

Riley knocked on the interrogation room door before she slipped inside. Keith Wakefield's father was a large man, broad in the shoulders and tapered at the waist. His hair was cut in a military style, his eyes blue and fierce. The mother was just as intimidating, blouse perfectly ironed and bright white hair cut short. Riley was suddenly extremely aware of how badly she had to reek.

"Mr. and Mrs. Wakefield? I'm Riley Parra. I'm the detective investigating your son's death."

Mr. Wakefield stood and extended a hand. "Eugene. This is my wife, Hattie. I want to apologize for the trouble our boy has caused you."

Riley hesitated before lowering herself into the seat. "Trouble...? Did Lieutenant Hathaway explain..."

"She explained everything quite clearly," Hattie Wakefield said. "Our son was involved in a criminal enterprise. It got him and some other young man killed yesterday morning. It's hardly worth your time."

Riley was stunned. She noted on to the mother's way of speaking and said, "I take it you're military."

"Both of us," Eugene said. "It's where we met."

Riley nodded. "And Keith didn't quite live up to the doctrine."

Hattie sighed as if this was a conversation she'd had many times before and didn't quite enjoy it. "Don't misunderstand. We loved our son. We gave him every opportunity. He chose to squander it for a life of drugs and thievery."

"Right," Riley said. "I just want to find out who killed your son and Steven Cabrera—"

"Who?"

"The man who was found with your son's body."

Eugene nodded. "Oh. The homeless man. Forgive me for asking, Detective Parra, but... who cares? I know that sounds incredibly harsh, but who does care that one homeless man has been removed from the world? He was a bit of a public nuisance, if what I'm told is correct."

Riley stared at him. She couldn't believe how callous he was being. "The man was a human being. He deserved to be treated with respect in life and in death. Sir, you and your wife have basically told me your son didn't deserve to live and the other victim wasn't worthy of being considered human." She decided she was done playing nice with the family. "Mr. Wakefield, I assume you own a gun?"

He narrowed his eyes at her. "What does that—"

"Where were you yesterday morning between 4:30 and 5:30?"

Eugene leaned back in his chair and placed his hands on the table. "I did not kill my son."

"Sir, please just answer the question."

"I was jogging. I wake up every morning at five and jog. My wife exercises in the house using one of those video things. I didn't get home until six, so I guess neither one of us has an alibi for you."

"Pity," Riley said. "You never said, sir. Do you own a gun?"

"Yes, I do. I own nine," Eugene snapped. "I just told you, I'm military, you sanctimonious bitch. I ought to..."

Riley raised an eyebrow. She gathered her papers and pushed away from the table. "Mr. and Mrs. Wakefield, it's been a soul-sucking experience speaking with you. Don't leave town. A uniformed officer will accompany you home to examine your weapons. Thank you for waiting for me so we could have this chat."

"Now just wait a damn—"

Riley was out of the room before Eugene Wakefield could say anything else. She slammed the door behind her and nearly collided with a blonde woman lurking outside the room. Riley backpedaled and said, "Watch where you're standing, damn it."

The woman was a few inches taller than Riley with straight blonde hair that hung to her shoulders. She wore a gray vest over white dress shirt and red tie. "Detective Parra, I presume?" she said, offering a hesitant smile.

"I don't talk to reporters," Riley muttered, trying to push past the woman.

"That's a good philosophy. I don't talk to them either."

"Glad we're..." Riley stopped walking and hung her head. "Oh, shit, no."

"Hello. I'm Caitlin Priest. I'm your new partner."

Riley turned and examined the woman more closely. She was not much older than thirty, with clear skin and bright blue eyes. She looked eager to please, but there was a hardness in her eyes that told Riley she'd taken her punches. Based on the first impression, she decided that working with Priest might not be a total disaster. Still, anyone trying to replace Sweet Kara was bound to be a disappointment. She sighed. "Riley Parra. I drive, except in the case of an extreme emergency. Like I have broken arms and my legs don't work. Or if I get shot in the head with a nail gun."

"Does that happen often?"

"Lately, I wouldn't be surprised," Riley said. She started toward her desk. "What do I call you? Kate? Caitlin? If you say Katie, I'll shoot you right now."

"Priest is fine."

Riley pointed at the desk that was once occupied by Kara Sweet. "That's where you sit. But not right now. I need you to take Mr. and Mrs. Wakefield home. Get a uniform and a crime scene tech to gather any and all handguns you find."

"Do we have a warrant?"

"Hm," Riley said. "They never mentioned we would need one."

Priest raised an eyebrow. "Ah, so that's how things work."

"Don't get into the habit of that. Rules aren't made to be broken," Riley said. "Unless they need to be bent. Those people really pissed me off."

"Gotcha." Priest sketched off a salute and headed to the interrogation room.

Riley watched her go and shook her head as she examined the memos on her desk. A case she'd been working for almost six months had been closed by another detective whose case overlapped with it. Fine by her, one less open case on her books. There was a call from a law firm regarding Marchosias' stronghold in No Man's Land. It was the place Riley had nearly died twice, and the last place she'd seen Samael. She was hoping for an owner's name, some link she could follow back. Unfortunately, the lawyers claimed the building was condemned and, as far as they knew, unoccupied.

She tossed the memos aside as Hathaway approached the desk. "Did she find you?"

"I hate her."

"Sweet Kara hated you when you first met."

Riley shook her head. "I don't need a partner, Lieutenant."

"And I say you do," Hathaway said. "Do you know why that's such a good argument? Because I'm the boss and you can't punch me."

"Anything's possible to those willing to face the consequences," Riley muttered as Hathaway walked back to her office.

While Priest took care of the Wakefield weapons, Riley decided to do a little investigation of the Crier. She did a computer search for any and all reports filed on Steven Cabrera. The first mention of him in their records was six years earlier, when he would have been nineteen. He was brought into the station on a public nuisance charge. The arresting officer let him sit in a jail cell overnight and let him go in the morning with a stern warning.

A few days later, there was another complaint filed and another officer went to quiet him down. It took a few weeks before it became evident nothing they did would dissuade him, so the cops started the tradition of sitting him down and getting him a hot meal. Riley leaned back in her chair and spotted Talbot a few desks away. "Hey, Talbot. Did you ever pick up the Crier?"

"Couple of times when I was in uniform," Talbot said, not looking up from his work.

"What was your impression of him?"

Talbot shrugged. "I don't know. He was a loony. But he was polite and kind. And clean. He never threw up in my cruiser." He leaned back in his chair. "Kind of sad he's gone. Haven't thought about him in ages."

"Yeah," Riley said. "Me either."

She ran her thumb over her bottom lip and stared at the list of complaints. There were hundreds of them, people disturbed by the Crier and wondering what the cops were going to do about it. She wondered why he kept doing it. What possible good did it do to walk the streets and say all was well? Even the most self-delusional citizen knew the best days of the city were behind them.

Of course, she was one to talk. She saw angels and grappled with demons.

She also wondered how many thousands of dollars had been spent feeding the poor kid. Riley herself had sat down across from him countless times. She and her partner both appreciated the break in the shift, and they could fool themselves into thinking they were actually helping someone. Prison would break the Crier, not help him. It was half an hour out of the day, and a couple of dollars every couple of shifts. It was the least they could do.

She remembered their breakfasts together. She would sip a cup of coffee while the Crier told her about things he read in the paper and in history books. She had always nodded and pretended to pay attention, but mostly she spent the time looking out the window or listening for a call to come in over the radio. She wished she had treated him better.

She figured she could make up for it now, by finding out who had murdered him. She still didn't know which victim was the intended target. Once was a nuisance and the other was a disgrace. Had a drug dealer come after Wakefield and decided to get rid of the only witness? Or had someone decided enough was enough and silenced the Crier for good?

Riley rubbed her face and rested her elbows on the edge of the desk.

Where was the bell?

She opened her eyes and looked at the top of her desk. The Crier's bell was missing. He always carried a little hand bell that barely made a 'tink' sound, but he waved it like it was the Liberty Bell. He was never without it, at least when he was on his rounds. If Wakefield had been the target, why would the killer have taken the bell? Riley was about to call the crime scene unit to see if they found any sign of the bell in the Crier's personal effects when her phone rang.

"Parra."

"Riley, it's Gillian. I need you to come down here. There's something interesting with the Crier's body."

Riley was out of her seat before the phone was completely in the cradle. First one clue dropped into her lap, maybe there was a chance Gillian was going to offer her a second one. Maybe she was going to be able to close this case after all.

The elevator seemed impossibly slow, but she finally arrived in the morgue. Gillian wore her scrubs, as usual, and a crisp blue apron over it. The Crier lay naked on one of her tables, a sheet draped over his midsection. He was much heavier than Riley would have guessed, and his torso was almost pink compared to the brown of his arms. Riley pulled on a pair of rubber gloves and said, "Tell me you found something good."

"I'll let you be the judge of that," Gillian said. She stepped to the side and pointed at the body. "Do you see anything right there?"

Riley leaned in. "Where?"

Gillian stepped close, pressing against Riley's side. She aimed her finger at the body again, this time resting her arm on Riley's shoulder. "There."

Riley turned her head slightly, breathing in Gillian's scent. "I'm not sure I see it. Maybe you should come closer."

Gillian did a poor job concealing her smile. Her free hand came up and swatted Riley's hip. "Murder investigation," she whispered.

"Right," Riley whispered. She looked back at the body and focused. She saw a splotch of red on the Crier's throat. "Blood spatter."

"That's what I thought. It's consistent with the wound," she said, pulling away from Riley and going to the top of the bed. She lifted the shirt the Crier had been wearing. "But you'll see there's no blood anywhere near the collar."

"So he was hunched forward, trying to protect himself."

Gillian shook her head. "The blood was odd enough, and I'm curious enough, that I took a sample. It's not the Crier's DNA."

"Wakefield's?" Riley asked, but she knew Gillian wouldn't call her down here for anything less than amazing.

"No. Wakefield and the Crier were the same blood type. AB. This blood came from someone who was A-positive. I looked at Wakefield's clothes and, surprise, surprise, the same blood was on the cuffs of his shirtsleeves." She looked down at the body. "I think they were both at another crime scene that night."

Chapter Five

Riley drew a diagram of the train car on her pad, staring at it and waiting for inspiration to strike. She had every detail marked; bits of trash, each individual bucket seat. She drew an X where the murderer had to have stood. She couldn't picture someone walking onto the train, pulling a gun, and killing Keith Wakefield and Steven Cabrera in cold blood. Neither had put up a fight. Neither had tried to run.

Caitlin Priest returned and stood next to the desk for a long minute. Riley was aware of her presence, but refused to break her silence. Finally, Priest gave up and went to Sweet Kara's old desk. "Gathered up all the Wakefield's guns. Only two of them matched the bullets Dr. Hunt took out of our victims. What have you been up to?"

"Trying to figure this shit out," Riley said. She turned the pad around and held it out to Priest. "Here. See if you can make any sense of this."

Priest took the pad and looked over it. "So what do I call you? Parra? Or just Riley? Calling you Detective might get a little old, but I'm willing to give it a try."

"Riley's fine," she muttered. She rested her chin on her hand and tried to fit all the pieces of the puzzle together in her head. "I still don't understand the bell being taken."

"Bell?"

"The Crier always carried a bell. When we used to take him into diners to keep him off the streets, he treated the thing like it was alive. It was a treasure to him. But there was no bell on him or in the train car when he was found. Why the hell would someone take it?"

"Maybe it was an antique?"

"It was a shitty little thrift shop bell. It barely even made a sound." Riley sighed and rubbed her eyes. "He had eighteen dollars in his wallet. If it was a robbery, why not take that?"

Priest pointed at the drawing. "Why did the other one sit there?"

"Sit where?"

Priest turned the pad around to show her. "They're sitting across from each other. They both died where they sat. So someone shot one of the guys, and then turned around and shot the other one. Whoever was shot second had to sit there while the other guy got killed."

Riley sat up and frowned at the diagram. She supposed the killer could have stood between the victims, a gun in each hand, and shot them at the same time. But this wasn't some cheesy action movie. Someone quick enough could have done it. Pop, spin around, pop. If the Wakefield kid was the second victim, his reflexes may have been slowed by too many drugs. If the Crier was the second victim, he may not have realized his life was in danger until it was too late to move.

"That still doesn't explain the fucking bell being gone."

"Maybe the kid dropped it."

"He's the Crier. He treated that bell like it was the most precious thing in the world." Her phone rang and she answered it with a sigh. "Parra."

"Detective. We found Steven Cabrera's mother."

Riley grabbed a pen. "It's about time. Where does she live?"

"I've got an address here," the officer said, "but it looks like no one's been there in a long time. I finally got a-hold of the landlord. He recognized the picture from Cabrera's wallet, and he told me where I could find Mrs. Cabrera."

"If you say the name of a cemetery, I swear to God..."

"No, not a cemetery," the officer said. "Close."

Riley sighed and braced herself for bad news.

Riley was surprised it had taken so long to find the family, but the surprise diminished when she was introduced to the mother. She looked ancient, but Riley knew she couldn't have been more than fifty. Her clothes looked like they hadn't been laundered in quite a while, her face devoid of make-up. The lights of the hospital room didn't do her any favors, but Riley knew the woman was having a tough decade.

Riley tried to avoid looking at the man in the bed between them; he wasn't easy to look at. "I take it you weren't home when the officers did the canvas," she said.

"I haven't been 'home' for about a week, Detective," Ana Cabrera said. "And our real home... well, it's been even longer. A lifetime." She looked at the man lying in the bed between them. "Since Ernesto's accident, I've been here as often as possible."

Riley nodded and suppressed a shiver. She'd had her fill of hospitals in the past few weeks. She waited until Steven's mother pushed herself out of the seat and said, "It's about time for me to do my walk. I need to get up and move around a bit every day so these old joints don't lock up on me. We can talk and walk at the same time, can't we?"

"Of course."

Ana slipped past Riley, and Riley looked at the young man lying in bed. She guessed he was a few years younger than Steven, tubes running in and out of his body in every possible place. According to the doctor's, he hadn't moved in almost seven years. His friend had been driving and the car went off the road, wrapped around a tree. The driver died, but Ernesto Cabrera had been thrown into a coma. It wasn't long after that the first nuisance calls started coming in, and the Crier was born.

Riley turned and followed Ana into the corridor. "I'm sorry to be the one to tell you about Steven, Mrs. Cabrera."

She shook her head. "I knew. When he didn't come back to the hospital yesterday, I knew. I've just been dreading the news." She exhaled a shaky breath and said, "But murdered. I never would have... I never imagined."

"He must have really loved his brother."

Ana laughed. "They were inseparable. After the accident, Steven was despondent for so long. I don't know what finally pulled him out of his funk, but he found a way to get out of his bedroom. That's all I cared about at the time. Then police officers started bringing him home." She sighed. "His whole deal was wishful thinking. He just wanted to believe that if he said everything was all right, then maybe it would be. And though the people who complained might not want to admit it, whenever they heard him outside, they would know they were safe. That if a robber was outside, or a murderer, or a rapist, they would have either shut him up or ran away. My boy was a laughingstock, I know, but he did help people. Even if no one is willing to admit it."

Riley nodded. "I answered a few calls about your son myself. He was a good kid. I liked him a lot. I... was under the impression he was homeless."

Ana sniffled and dabbed at her eyes with a Kleenex. "Yes, I suppose he was. Ernesto's bills are astronomical. We lost the apartment and both cars. I found a tiny apartment where I could stay, but there was only one bedroom. There was hardly enough room for one person to live, let alone two. Steven told me it was all right, said he had a place to stay. I knew he was lying, but I couldn't..." She shook her head.

"It's all right, Mrs. Cabrera."

"No, it's not all right! I gave up everything for one of my sons while I ignored the other. I lived in a shoebox to pay for this son's bed, while my other son slept on a train every night. That's not a good mother." Fresh tears rolled down her face. "I should have let Ernesto go."

Riley wasn't listening to Ana anymore. She stopped and put a hand on Ana's shoulder. "Steven slept on the train?"

"In the last car. The train hardly ever filled up, so he didn't get disturbed very often."

Riley thought back to the diagram. Maybe someone shot Wakefield, and the noise woke the Crier up. He sat up, confused and disoriented, and the shooter killed him. That explained the shooting order; Wakefield had to have been the intended victim and the Crier was just in the wrong place at the wrong time. But if that was true...

"Why did Mr. Ly say that Steven always got off the train at the Green Street station?"

Ana lifted her head and stared at Riley. "Did you just say 'Mystery'?"

"No. The engineer of the train was Mr. Joshua Ly."

"Detective, my son was terrified of someone named... someone I thought he was calling Mystery. He said the man harassed him. Called him a vagrant, tried to kick him off the train all the time. I just thought it was a made-up person. But if..."

Riley was already nodding. "I think I'm going to be having another talk with Mr. Ly very soon, Mrs. Cabrera."

When Riley got back to her car, she called Priest. "I need you to do something for me."

"Anything, boss. I live to serve."

Riley ignored the jab. "There's a number on my desk blotter for a Joshua Ly. He's the conductor of the train where the two men were shot yesterday morning. When I hang up, I want you to call and make sure he's at home. I don't care what you tell him, just don't tell him you're a cop. And I want you to find his address."

"Okay. What did this guy do?"

"He lied to me."

"Didn't know that was a capital crime."

"Good thing you learned it early," Riley said.

Priest fumbled with the phone and said, "All right, I have his address right here. Got a pen?"

"Just give it to me." Priest gave her the address and Riley wished Kara were around with her encyclopedic knowledge of the city streets. "I'm on Hayes Street now. How far away is that?"

"About ten minutes, give or take. You need back-up?"

"No."

"All you have to do is ask, Riley."

Riley hung up and muttered, "Yeah, yeah." She shoved the phone into her pocket and gripped the wheel with both hands.

She had a lot more of the puzzle in front of her now; the Crier slept on the train, and Mr. Ly wasn't exactly understanding about it. Things got a little out of hand, Ly pulled a gun, Crier got shot. But that didn't make sense. She had just decided Wakefield was the first victim. And what about the blood on the Crier's neck? Where had that come from? Ly? She didn't remember any wounds on the man, but maybe the Crier punched him and caused a bloody nose.

No. There were no signs of a struggle on the train.

"Damn it," Riley said. "This damn case..."

"I could tell you what happened."

Riley jumped and nearly swerved the car onto the sidewalk. She looked in the rearview mirror and saw Marchosias lounging in the backseat. "No thanks," she said.

"Ah, come on." He slid to the edge of the seat and leaned over her shoulder. His breath, rotten and sickly sweet, washed over her face. "I know every little detail. All I'd have to do is whisper it in your ear..."

"And then I would owe you one teensy favor. And the next time I get stuck on a case, I would think, 'well, hell, I already owe him one favor...'"

Marchosias laughed. "I bet you never turn the newspaper over and peek at the crossword answers, either."

Riley looked in the side mirror, double-checked the rearview, and slammed on her brakes. Marchosias slammed against the front seat and then crumpled in the floorboards. Riley twisted in her seat and said, "Out of the car, March. Now."

Marchosias pulled himself back up onto the seat. "All you had to do was ask nicely, Detective." He coughed, straightened his jacket, and said,

"Good luck figuring it out." He winked and then Riley's vision twisted. She blinked to clear it and, when she looked again, Marchosias was gone. She shook her head and turned to face forward again. "Damn demons."

Chapter Six

Riley managed to find Ly's house without any problem. The mailbox was shaped like an old fashioned steam train, the façade of the house made up to look like an old fashioned depot. She parked in the driveway behind Ly's truck and pulled her badge as she approached the front door. She knocked and stepped back, ready to badge whoever answered. Even if it was Ly himself, he would know it wasn't a social call.

The door opened and an Asian woman about Ly's age peered out at her. "Hello," she said, her eyes flicking from Riley's face to the badge. "How can I help you?"

"Mrs. Ly?"

"I just have a few follow-up questions for your husband. Is he in?"

The woman clung to the door and shook her head. "No, I... h-he said he had to go in to work even though he's not scheduled."

Riley resisted the urge to curse. "Thank you, Mrs. Ly. Do you know which train he's working today?"

"The B train," she said. "I know, he told me specifically when he left. 'Gonna take the old B train.'" She smiled and said, "He's... not in any trouble, is he?"

"Why would you say that?"

She shook her head. "I don't know. Since the murders, he's been so distraught. I think if you're able to close the case quickly, it would do him a world of good."

Riley nodded curtly. "I hope so, ma'am. Excuse me."

She turned and hurried off the porch, fishing her cell phone free as she went. She dialed Priest's number as she got back into her car. "Priest, it's me. I need you to call the train station and find out when the B train left. Joshua Ly is the engineer. I'm not sure what he's planning, but I doubt it'll be anything good. I need the schedule so I can find out where to intercept it."

"Got it. You need back-up? Come on, Riley, might as well get it over with."

Riley growled and said, "Fine. Call me back when you know where I can get onboard."

She flipped the phone shut and pictured Joshua Ly as the shooter. It made sense that the conductor of a train going through No Man's Land in the dead of night would carry a gun. But why would he choose that night to kill the Crier? Ly didn't seem to think the kid was a nuisance. Maybe all of his complaints were addressed to his bosses rather than the police department.

Overhead, Riley saw a train streak by on elevated tracks. She hoped it wasn't the B train.

Riley thought back to the list of complaints delivered the night the Crier was killed. There was nothing out of the ordinary to them. Well, nothing except... she frowned and thought about the map she had drawn. People were complaining because the Crier had been yelling for half an hour. But that wasn't his way. He walked, he meandered through neighborhoods. Maybe he would cross his own path every now and then, but crying in one spot for over thirty minutes?

Her phone rang and Riley flipped it open. "I want you to check open cases from the night the Crier was killed," she said. "Anything in that general area."

Priest was thrown. "Um. Okay. I have the stations. You need to get to Adams Street in the next four minutes or, barring that, Quincy Street in the next twelve."

"Got it. Get me those open cases."

"Yes, ma'am."

Riley made a sharp turn and raced down Adams Street. She figured she would just barely make it in time to catch the train. Her mind raced with the pieces of the puzzle. She thought about the Crier remaining stationary, and why he would have stopped moving. She wished she had asked the complainants about what he was yelling. Maybe he had seen something. The spot of blood on his neck, the blood that didn't seem to have come from anywhere. The Crier had been at another crime scene that morning.

She parked illegally at the train station and raced up the stairs. She flashed her badge at the station agent as she ran across the platform, the doors standing open like an invitation. She jumped onto the train just as the doors were closing; cutting it tight enough that she thought her shirt was caught between the two doors.

She paused to catch her breath and her phone rang again. She answered it, returning the stares of the commuters all around her. They were representatives of the few respectable businessmen and women in the city, and she was wearing yesterday's clothes and reeking of sweat. A few people nearby wrinkled their noses and stepped away. She wanted to flip them off, but instead she focused on Priest. "What do you have?"

"Do you ever say hello on the phone?"

"Priest..." She started toward the front of the train.

"Dead body found in the alley on Ninth Street. Drugs and paraphernalia in his pockets. No ID. It's in No Man's Land, so the cops barely gave it the old once-over."

"That's all I needed to know. Thanks, Priest."

Priest said, "I'm on the move now. I'll catch the train at Madison."

"Take your time," Riley said. She hung up and slipped the phone into her pocket.

The Crier saw something. Something very bad, like a drug deal going south. Keith Wakefield maybe deciding he wasn't going to pay this time. Maybe he couldn't pay and needed the hit. Whatever had happened, there was a fight and the dealer was killed. The Crier saw it and couldn't claim "all is well." So he tried to tell people. That was what a crier did, after all.

She pictured the Crier, a sweet innocent kid who just wanted to believe everything would be all right, being chased through the streets by Wakefield. Wakefield would have caught up to him at the train station. Maybe he tried to intimidate the Crier into keeping quiet. She could very clearly see Wakefield grabbing the bell and tossing it onto the tracks. Ly would have seen what was happening on the platform. The Crier and Wakefield boarded the train and the fight continued. Ly grabbed his gun and probably just meant to threaten the kid with it. Things got out of hand. Ly was probably just trying to protect the Crier at first.

Riley reached the engineer's station, a small closet at the front of the train. There was an egg-shaped window in the door, and she could see Ly staring blindly out at the tracks ahead. She knocked on the glass with her badge, and he turned to look at her with sad eyes. Riley mimed opening the door, and Ly stood up like a man expecting a hangman's noose.

"Mr. Ly," she said once the door was open. "Maybe you'd like to tell me what really happened that night."

He closed the door behind him and said, "I was just trying to shut the kid up. I kept saying I didn't mean to shoot him. I said it over and over again. But that kid was so annoying, with his goddamn fucking bell. I was sick of him. I pushed him down in the seat, but he kept callin' me a murderer." He rubbed his face with his hands. "I just wanted to scare him into shutting up. I didn't mean to pull the trigger."

Riley saw Ly pulling Wakefield off the Crier. Jostling around on a train, it wouldn't be hard for the gun to go off accidentally. Wakefield fell into the seat, gun went boom.

"Doesn't this train have a dead man's switch?"

Ly nodded. "I have a way to jerry-rig it. In case I need to go to the bathroom or deal with an unruly passenger or something."

Riley looked out the front of the train and saw that they were fast-approaching Madison Street. She hoped Priest was already there waiting for her. "Here's what's going to happen, Mr. Ly. You're going to stop the train, and you're going to let my partner and I take you in."

Ly looked out the window and shook his head. Riley followed his line of sight and watched the train whip past the station without stopping.

She tensed and looked at the door to the engineer's cabin. He had a way to jerry-rig the dead man's switch so the train wouldn't stop. Riley felt a chill and said, "Mr. Ly, open the door."

"Door's locked."

Riley shoved him out of the way and tried the handle. It wouldn't budge. She peered through the glass and saw a long stick with a wedge-shaped foot pressing against the pedal. The stick extended back underneath Ly's chair, braced against the back wall of the cabin. The train wouldn't be able to stop and, without Ly to maneuver it around the curves, they were going to turn into a runaway train. If they were lucky. If they weren't, the first turn in the track would turn them into a silver bullet.

Riley tried to break the glass with her badge, but all she managed was scratching the surface. She pulled her gun and hammered the butt against it. Still nothing. She didn't want to try firing her weapon in such an enclosed space; it would deafen everyone in the car. But she didn't think she had a choice. She pulled her handcuffs off her belt and turned to Ly. "Unlock the door right now."

"I can't."

Riley growled and dragged Ly away from the door. She shoved him into a seat and cuffed him to one of the security bars. "Stay here."

She turned to face the crowd of commuters, dread sinking in as she realized the enormity of what was about to happen. Mothers, fathers, all of them with someone waiting for them on the outside. She whistled to get their attention and held her badge over her head. "Everybody listen to me! This is a police emergency. I need everyone to move to the back of the train right now. Keep it orderly and safe. There's no need to panic. Thank you for your cooperation."

Riley waited until they began evacuating before she aimed the gun at the glass. "Even if you get in, you have no idea how to drive a train. The ricochet will probably do more harm than good. God, Parra, you're..."

The train began to slow.

Riley looked out the window and saw that they were indeed coming up on a turn, but the train was rapidly losing speed. They would be stopped before they reached it. She lowered her gun and moved to the glass, peering out to see if something on the tracks could have stopped them. Behind her, Ly said, "What did you do? What happened?"

"Shut up," Riley said.

There were footsteps on the ceiling of the train car. A pair of shoes suddenly dangled in front of the window and Riley stepped back, gripping her gun in case things had just gone from bad to worse. *If this is Marchosias, I swear to God...* The person dropped from the roof of the train, slowly enough that Riley saw flesh-toned hands sticking out of the dress-shirt sleeves. As the person fell, a pair of pristine white wings spread out to either side of their body, catching the wind and slowing the descent.

Riley recognized their savior's suit and her shoulders sagged. "Oh, you're fucking kidding me."

Caitlin Priest dusted herself off, turned to face the tracks, and folded her wings against her back. She spotted Riley in the glass and waved to her. Riley pointed to the side of the train and Priest stepped onto the track to walk around to the side. Riley holstered her weapon, the adrenaline seeping from her as she turned to walk back to Ly. "Sorry, Mr. Ly. You don't get to martyr yourself today."

"I just wanted to make amends," he whispered.

"By killing dozens more. Couldn't wait until tonight when the train was empty to off yourself? Had to make a big splash in rush hour? Just say 'thank you, Detective Parra, for letting me live to see my wife again.'"

Ly hung his head and wept.

The doors opened and Priest stepped onto the train. Her suit was immaculate, and her wings were nowhere to be seen.

"I thought your name was Zerachiel," Riley said.

Priest shrugged. "You're the one who said we should get new names."

Riley gestured at her own back. "What happened to the, uh...?"

"We don't have to show them if we don't want to."

"Raguel and Samael wore big coats to cover them up."

"Boys. Such show-offs."

"Speaking of, I thought you were also supposed to be a guy."

Priest shrugged. "I can take any form I deem necessary. I decided you would respond better to a woman."

"And a blonde to boot," Riley muttered. She looked down at Ly, who had apparently ignored their conversation. She decided to leave him to weep. "Come on, angel. Help me evacuate these people."

Epilogue

Riley went into Gillian's apartment, dumped her things on the couch, and dropped down next to them. She bent to untie her shoes and peel them off her feet before stretching out on the cushions. She had spent all afternoon talking to newspaper and radio reporters, telling them over and over again that the train "miraculously came to a stop on its own when the brace Joshua Ly set up was knocked askew by the vibrations of the train." By morning, her name and picture would be all over the damn city. She was cursing the decision not to take a shower that morning.

Her evening was filled taking Ly's statement. He confessed to killing the Wakefield boy in defense of the Crier, killing the Crier accidentally, and attempting to kill all of his passengers along with a police officer when he crashed the train. There was debate about whether he could get off with the insanity defense, but Riley was sick and tired of listening to it all. She finally filed her report and slipped out before Priest found her.

She was about to fall asleep fully dressed when the bedroom door opened. She managed to open her eyes and watch Gillian walk into the living room. She wore a lilac nightgown and the matching robe was hanging off one shoulder. Riley smiled. "There's something worth coming home for," she said. She held her hand out and Gillian walked over, curling up on the couch next to her. They kissed, and Riley said, "Hey."

"Hey yourself." She undid the top two buttons on Riley's blouse. "Come to bed."

"In a minute. I just needed a break from being upright."

Gillian nodded and leaned down. She pushed apart the collar of Riley's shirt and kissed the flat part of her chest. Riley put her hand in Gillian's hair and closed her eyes.

"I almost lost you today. Again."

"Sorry."

Gillian kissed Riley's neck. "I know. So how did the train get stopped?"

"My new partner is an angel."

Gillian leaned back and looked for signs Riley was joking. "Seriously? Caitlin Priest?"

Riley shrugged.

"Wow. I guess I can relax knowing an actual angel has your back." She curled against Riley's side and played with her fingers. "You did very good work today."

"Thank you."

"But now it is time for you to go to bed." She kissed Riley's cheek and moved to the edge of the couch. "Come on." She wrapped her hands around Riley's and pulled her up. Riley grunted and let Gillian lead her out of the living room. Riley put one arm around Gillian's waist and said, "I should probably take a shower first."

"Probably should," Gillian said.

Riley released Gillian and went to the bathroom under her own power. She undressed and quickly bathed, feeling the life seep back into her as the hot water seeped into her pores. She ran a hand through her hair, scrubbed to make sure she got every last bit of sticky, stinky sweat off of her, and toweled off. She put on one of Gillian's big fluffy robes and went into the bedroom.

Gillian was sitting on top of the blankets reading the newspaper. She looked up and smiled when Riley came into the bedroom. "Already a far sight better."

"Yeah," Riley said, flipping her hair onto the collar of the robe. "I clean up well."

"Ya clean up reeeal good," Gillian drawled. She put the newspaper aside and said, "C'mere, darlin'. Let me show ya how we do thangs down south."

Riley shed the robe and climbed onto the mattress. Gillian parted her legs, the nightgown riding up her thighs. Riley settled between her legs, pushing the nightgown higher, and kissed her lips. Gillian ran her hands down Riley's naked body, pausing at her breasts to tease her nipples. Riley moaned and put her hand on Gillian's hip, resting her weight against the crux of Gillian's legs. Gillian gasped and wrapped her arms around Riley's waist. She kissed Riley's chin and jaw, then began a slow trail down her throat.

Riley turned her head to give Gillian some more room, and opened her eyes to see the dresser in the back corner of the room.

A rabbit in blue overalls sat in front of the mirror.

Riley's chest constricted and she wheezed, trying to draw air into lungs frozen stiff with fright. She pushed away from Gillian, her desire fading as she looked at the stuffed toy. "This is Chekhov's gun. In reverse." Marchosias. That was what he said when he showed her the rabbit the day before. Riley was aware of Gillian questioning her, but she couldn't register the words. Instead, she pointed across the room. "Where the hell did that thing come from?"

Gillian frowned and looked. "Gravy?"

"What?"

"Gravy the Rabbit. My grandmother made that for me when I was eight."

"Has it... always been here?"

Gillian nodded. "Yeah. He's been there since I moved in."

"You never noticed him missing?"

"No... Riley, it's okay. You don't have to notice everything—"

She shook her head. "No, you're right. You're right." She closed her eyes and pushed thoughts of the demon out of her mind. She turned back to Gillian and kissed her once, then again, pushing her down to the mattress and forcing herself to focus on making love rather than what the rabbit in the corner meant.

The rabbit in the corner meant that Marchosias had been in the apartment and took something.

It meant he had gotten back in, undetected, and put the rabbit back.

It meant that Marchosias could get to Gillian whenever he damn well pleased.

Gillian brushed her hand over Riley's cheek and said, "Sweetheart. You're crying."

Riley closed her eyes and buried her face in the curve of Gillian's neck. "I'm just so happy, Jill. That's all."

Open and Shut, No.1:
Shades of Gray

Riley had never realized there were so many churches in town. She parked at the curb in front of the First Baptist Church of the Savior, looking at the businesses that flanked it. The church was a narrow storefront of cream-colored brick wedged between a pizza parlor and a pawn shop. The single window of the church was completely filled by an eight-by-ten painting of Jesus, and the glass front door had a sign inviting passersby to "come worship with us!" Riley could hear live music coming from within and wondered how an organ could fit into the tiny space, not to mention worshippers.

An exterior stairway was draped with wet laundry, various pieces of garbage caught in the railings. Riley walked upstairs to the plain green door and knocked. She stepped back as she waited for a response, using her tongue to work out whatever was caught in her teeth. Bacon, she thought. She smiled, still surprised that Gillian had gone to the trouble to cook her breakfast.

"Better get used to it," she had said. "Organic food is the best. None of that greasy stuff from the diner. Did you know their eggs come in a milk carton? All goop-ified. It's really alarming." She had punctuated her argument by cracking another brown egg on the side of the bowl and saying, "Seconds?"

Breakfast had been nice, it was normal, it was almost enough to make her forget about Marchosias and his threat against Gillian's safety. Almost. Riley pushed thoughts of the demon out of her mind and focused on getting her partner out of bed so they could actually go to work. Riley waited a few more seconds before trying the knob. The door was unlocked, and she felt a twinge of unease. Would Marchosias go after Priest? Could he? She stepped inside. "Priest? Everything okay... in here...? Wow."

To call the apartment spartan would be an understatement. An empty bookcase separated the foyer from the living room, and she could see the rest of the apartment through the wooden boards. She stepped around the bookcase to the empty living room, and raised her eyebrows when she saw what was on the floor. She took off her sunglasses and said, "I could come back if this is a bad time."

Priest was lying spread-eagle on the floor, naked except for a half-slip over her lower body. Her wings were extended, lying beneath her like a pillow. She shook her head in answer to Riley's question and said, "No. It's fine. They're almost done." The corners of her lips curled up and she twisted her body against the floor. "Early morning mass. Their praise rises through the floor and washes over this entire apartment. It's... invigorating."

"I'll bet," Riley said. Priest's breasts were flat at the moment, due to her position, her nipples plain, pink, barely distinguishable from the rest of her skin. Riley was surprised to find that, for the first time in her adult life, she was looking at a half-naked woman and feeling absolutely nothing. She spotted a shirt on the floor and bent down, tossing it to Priest with a flick of her fingers. "Going to have to cut the sponging short this morning. We got a call."

Priest sighed and pushed herself up off the floor. She took the shirt Riley had tossed her and stood up. "I'll dress quickly." She turned to walk away, and Riley watched as the large white wings folded in on themselves. The feathers seemed to mold against Priest's back and rearranged themselves until they faded from view.

"Freaky," Riley muttered. She went to the window and leaned against the sill, checking out her new partner's view. She could see the elevated train track two buildings over, and wondered how loud it got when the train went by. It would make the people in the church worship louder, and that would make Priest buzz like a bug zapper. Win-win. A handful of windows in the building across the street were still dark, and she could see vague shapes of people moving within. She was in the middle of making up stories for each of the residents when Priest returned.

She wore a knee-length tweed skirt and a button-down dress shirt. She was rolling up the sleeves when she came back into the living room. Riley gestured at the empty floor and said, "You need furniture? I know a guy."

"That's not necessary."

Riley shrugged. "Suit yourself. Come on." They left the apartment and Priest followed Riley down the stairs. "We have a body on Talbot. Hathaway called me in the middle of breakfast." Actually, the call had come just after Gillian, robe held aside to show her legs, had settled in her lap for a little replay of the night before. She tried to keep the frustration from her voice as she walked to her car. "You up for your first full-blown investigation?"

"No time like the present," Priest said. She opened the passenger door and looked toward the church again. She smiled and said, "Maybe I should drop in sometime. Put some money in the collection plate."

"Couldn't hurt," Riley said. She put her sunglasses back on and said, "C'mon. Body isn't getting any deader, but we kind of have a time crunch."

Priest nodded. "First forty-eight hours of a homicide are the most important."

"You been reading up on the police handbook?"

"Crime novels."

Riley nodded and got into the car. "Well, don't let them fool you. Those things are nothing like real life."

"Oh?"

"Yeah," Riley said. She pulled away from the curb and said, "Real life is worse."

The apartment building was a few blocks away from the decay of No Man's Land, one of the few buildings that seemed to be doing whatever it could to hold off its own decline. As Riley got out of the car, she looked up at the apartment windows and counted four flower boxes and the majority of the windows were actually washed and clean. There was no garbage piled on the sidewalk, and the door was protected by a well-maintained buzzer system. Every occupied apartment had a clearly-written tenant name next to the button.

Riley pressed the button for apartment 2-B and said, "Or not to be..."

"What's that?"

Riley glanced over her shoulder at Priest. "Soliloquy by Hamlet. Shakespeare."

Priest nodded. "Oh. I'm not very up on pop culture."

A man's voice came through the tinny speaker. "Who is it?"

"Detectives Parra and Priest."

The door buzzed, and Riley pulled the door open. She ushered Priest inside and said, "Five hundred years ago is not pop culture. It's ancient history."

"Says you," Priest said.

The lobby was tidy, but not clean. There was evidence of water damage on the ceiling and walls, and the floor tile had definitely seen better days. Leaves that had blown in through the front door congregated under the stairs. Riley led the way upstairs and stopped on the second floor landing. Every apartment door was open, and a black man wearing a rumpled fedora stood before Apartment 2-A like a sentry. His needle-thin arms were crossed over his chest, his chin thrust forward as if in challenge. "I saw everything," he said. "You need an eyewitness, I'll testify, you bet."

"Thank you, sir," Riley said. "For right now, please go back into your apartment. Okay?"

The man reluctantly left his station, turning toward 2-B as he backed up. "You go easy on her, hear?"

"Yes, sir."

Riley stopped at the threshold of 2-B and knocked on the freshly-painted doorframe. The kitchen stood to her right, and a short hallway to the left most likely went to the bedrooms. Straight ahead was the living room, where two uniformed officers were standing guard. One of them saw Riley and nodded as she stepped into the apartment. "Officer. Is Mrs. Post...?"

A woman came out of the kitchen, wiping her hands on a towel. She wore a turtleneck and a pair of old blue jeans rolled up to mid-calf. Her feet were bare, toes unpainted. Her entire body seemed to be shaking. "Hi. Are you the detectives? Please come in." She touched the back of her hand to her lips and disappeared back into the kitchen.

Riley watched Mrs. Post return to the sink, which was filled with frothy white bubbles. She lifted a plate from the water, looked at it, then returned it to the sink. "I don't know what I'm doing. I just wandered in here and started doing the dishes."

"It's all right," Riley said. She looked at the rack of dirty dishes and then smiled. "I'm Detective Parra, and this is my partner, Detective Priest. Why don't you tell us what happened?"

The woman said, "I'm Anna Post. I... I was still in the bedroom. I heard someone come into the apartment and start shouting. And..." She swallowed hard and began to shake, wrapping her arms around herself.

"It's all right," Riley said. "We'll get the rest of the information from the officers. Priest, will you stay with her?"

"Yes, of course."

Riley went into the living room where the other policemen were waiting. She took in the scene. A man lay facedown on the floor between the couch and coffee table, his hand stretched toward the TV in the corner. He wore sweatpants and a white T-shirt, blood staining the carpet around him. A handful of framed pictures flanked the only window in the room. The wall next to the TV had piles of old magazines and newspapers stacked against it. Some of the newspaper stacks had empty beer cans standing on top of them. The coffee table had two plates, the remnants of breakfast cooling upon them.

Riley smelled sausage and pancake syrup and was very aware that organic food had nothing on greasy hash browns from the diner. Of course, the service at home was second to none. She glanced at the officer closest to her and said, "What's the story?"

The officer, a man named Cooley, said, "Woman says she heard people screaming and came out of the bedroom in time to see someone stab her hubby. She screamed, guy panicked and ran out of the apartment. She was too shocked to try and chase him."

"Anyone get a description?"

"Old guy next door. We were about to go take his statement."

"Go ahead."

They left Riley alone in the living room and she walked around to get a better view of the dead man. She knelt next to his outstretched hand, eyeing his knuckles without touching anything. The skin was raw, broken, and she wondered if he'd had time to fight the robber before the knife came out. The couch was in full view of the front door, which meant Mr. Post would have seen the burglar coming into the house. So why did he stay at the couch? A big guy like this wouldn't just stand back and let someone come into his home. All the burglar would have to do is step to his left and he would have been in the bedroom where the wife was.

So why had Mr. Post stayed on the couch while someone broke into his apartment?

Riley walked back to the door and eyed the frame. It was pristine. Maybe Mr. Post unlocked it when he went to get the newspaper. She turned to the kitchen to ask Anna if they subscribed to the daily paper. Priest was sitting at the dining room table, holding a tiny white teacup with both hands. Anna was, at the moment Riley looked, bending over to place something in the recycling bin. When she leaned forward, her sweater rode higher on her torso to reveal the small of her back.

Three purple blotches shaped like purple diamonds marred her skin just above her belt.

Riley looked at the mountain of dish soap in the sink and retreated to the living room. She looked at the framed pictures on the wall and noticed a pattern; the man always had his hand on his wife's shoulder, and she was always leaning slightly away from him with a forced smile. In every photo, the man was obviously the focus. His wife, if she was in the picture at all, stood at his side like a prop.

The table next to the couch had a stack of magazines - sports and fishing, mainly, with one dedicated to guns and ammo - and the remote control. On the opposite side of the couch was a single crossword puzzle book. Riley picked it up and eyed the entries. Tiny letters, drawn with a gentle hand, filled the boxes. She was no handwriting expert, but she doubted the woman who had finished the puzzles would be able to take down a man of Mr. Post's size.

At least, not without a damn good motivation.

The officers returned from interviewing the neighbor. Cooley stopped in the living room doorway and read off his notepad. "Black male, average height, average weight. White T-shirt and black track pants. Shouldn't be too hard to find him."

"Shouldn't be too hard to find ten of him," the other officer said.

Riley nodded and the downstairs buzzer sounded again. Cooley pressed the button. "Name, please?"

"Gillian Hunt, ME."

"Come on up."

Riley glanced at the body again. "You guys ever been to this apartment before?"

"Not us personally," the one who wasn't Cooley replied. "It's pretty well known around the station, though. A lot of loud 'disagreements.' The neighbors sometimes complained about the guy yelling and going on tirades. Mr. Winston next door said that people tried to avoid him on the stairs and in the laundry room."

"People claim he stole their laundry." Riley and the officers turned toward the kitchen door. Anna stood, looking at her husband's body, one hand pressed against her cheek. "He didn't. He just sometimes... he would switch stuff. He would put one person's shirt in someone else's washer. As a joke. He... thought it was funny."

Riley put her hand on Anna's shoulder and the woman flinched slightly. "It's okay, Anna." To Cooley, she said, "Why don't you take her outside for some fresh air?"

"Yeah, sure."

"This is Officer Cooley," Riley said. "He's going to make sure no one bothers you while you're outside refreshing yourself, okay? Take as long as you need."

The officer led Anna out of the room as Gillian and her assistant arrived. Gillian wore her street clothes, a dark blue windbreaker zipped up over her blouse. She barely glanced at Riley as she entered the apartment and went toward the crime scene. "Detective Parra."

"Dr. Hunt," Riley said. They walked to the body together. Gillian put down her bag and knelt next to the man, craning her neck to look at his face. Riley examined the man herself, trying to see what Gillian saw. Mr. Post - she wasn't even sure of his first name - had a bit of a jowl, scruffy growth of beard on his cheeks and chin. His hair was shaggy and hung over his eyes. Riley figured he must have been quite the stud twenty years and a hundred pounds ago.

Gillian's gaze had moved to the hands. "Oh, we've seen knuckles like these before..."

"Yep," Riley said. She looked around the living room and said, "I'll be right back. I want to check something."

"Take your time."

Riley went down the hallway to the bedroom. The bed was made, and fresh flowers stood in a green vase next to the bed. Dirty clothes littered the floor around a tall white hamper, but Riley could tell where Anna had tried to make the place presentable. The room smelled of air freshener, obviously sprayed around the time of the phone call to police. Even in her current condition, she didn't want people to see a dirty apartment.

Riley looked at the wall behind the door, stretched to look behind the dresser, lifted every painting to see if it covered a hole in the drywall. A quick survey of the rest of the apartment told her that the walls weren't the source of his bruised knuckles. She returned to the bedroom and looked in the dresser on the rumpled side of the bed. She wrinkled her nose as she gave a cursory examination of the items inside.

Lots of couples used toys, and she was sure a lot of them had paddles like this in their bedrooms. She took a rubber glove from her pocket and used it to pick the paddle up. She turned it over and saw the domed heads of four screws drilled into the face. She shuddered and put it back down. That was not good clean fun no matter who you were. She pushed the drawer back in and wondered just how much of Anna Post's body was covered with hard-to-see bruises.

"Riley." She turned around to see Priest standing in the doorway. "There was no intruder."

"No."

Priest nodded and said, "I think she was on the verge of confessing to me. Perhaps if we were to speak to her at the station..."

"She's not going to the station," Riley hissed. She grabbed Priest's arm, hauling her into the room as she pushed the bedroom door closed. "Listen to me, Caitlin. This guy abused her. He treated her like shit. I don't know what set her off this morning. Maybe he just happened to hit her when she was in arm's length of a knife. Whatever it is, it's not our problem."

"She murdered a man, Riley."

"Oh, for..." Riley paced toward the bed. She pointed at the drawer. "There are sex toys in that dresser. At least, that's what they appear to be on the surface. To me, they look more like torture devices. Even having sex with her was like a kind of abuse. He got off on causing her pain. She was barely a person in her own house."

Priest said, "That doesn't give her the right to murder a man."

"Yes, it does. We call it self-defense."

"I don't know..."

"What is our job description?"

Priest frowned. "To enforce the law."

"To catch bad guys. To stop them from breaking the law. What happens if we go out there and arrest that woman? She would have to spend time in jail overnight, most likely, until she's arraigned. And if the judge doesn't buy the self-defense angle, I doubt she could afford the bail, so she's going back to her cell until trial. Who knows when that will be, or if she'll survive. Then if and when she does finally get out, odds are that she'll be hooked on one drug or another."

She sighed and paced the short distance to the wall. "Our job is to serve and protect. We haven't done either for this woman. We couldn't stop her husband from beating her, so she took care of it herself. The least we can do, the very least, is make sure that it ends here."

"Are you sure about this, Riley?"

Riley nodded. "Absolutely positive. We'll put out the neighbor's description, and we'll do whatever we can to close the case."

"Looking for a suspect we know doesn't exist."

"Anna Post will probably never commit another crime in her entire life. Putting her in prison won't solve a damn thing. Putting her on trial won't help anyone. It's one of those rare situations when doing the wrong thing is to do the right thing."

"Does this sort of thing come up often?"

"Too damn often," Riley said. "Remember what I told you about crime novels and real life? Well, sometimes real life can be tricky. It's up to us to decide, sometimes at the drop of a hat, what we're going to do in a certain situation. People's lives depend on us making the right decision. I think this is the right thing to do. If you don't agree, then maybe you should wait in the car."

Priest shook her head. "No. I trust your judgment."

"Glad to hear it." Riley stepped around Priest and opened the bedroom door. They arrived in the living room just as Gillian stood up and pulled her gloves off.

Gillian glanced at Priest and said, "I don't believe we've met. Dr. Gillian Hunt."

"Caitlin Priest."

They shook hands, and Gillian glanced at Riley. "Detective Parra. Could I have a word with you in private?"

"No," Riley said.

Gillian blinked. "Um... it's about the victim. I really think—"

"That Detective Priest and I need to get the neighbor's description out as soon as possible. Make sure whoever did this doesn't get away. Good thought, Jill. It's just what I was thinking."

They stared at each other for a moment and then Gillian nodded. "Right. The suspect." She glanced at Priest and said, "I'll get the body taken care of and see you guys at the office. Case seems pretty open and shut to me, though. The... intruder stabbed the guy three times in the chest. He fell and bled out."

Riley walked back into the living room. "He fell where he was standing?"

"Mm-hmm."

"And how long did it take him to bleed out?"

"About fifteen minutes. The wounds were big and nasty. He went fast."

Riley went to the coffee table and stood where the killer would have been. She mimed stabbing someone three times, then looked at the ground. There was a bloody wedge-shaped mark on the carpet. The killer dropped the knife. And then... Riley turned and looked at the wall behind her. The newspapers and magazines had been disturbed.

The truth of what had happened played in her mind like a movie. Mr. Post said something to his wife, maybe started beating on her again. She had a knife with her, for breakfast, and she probably didn't even think before she started stabbing. Then she dropped the knife and backpedaled, probably sat on the stack of newspapers in shock and watched her husband bleed to death. The only pity Riley felt was for Anna. But even if everything had happened exactly as she imagined, she couldn't picture Anna Post coming up with the fake suspect all on her own. Then it dawned on her.

"I wonder who actually called 911."

Priest shook her head.

Riley figured it was the neighbor, Mr. Winston. Anna had probably either screamed or started crying, and Winston came over to see what happened. The cover-up was his idea.

The officer returned with Anna Post. She looked at the body bag, and sniffled, the sleeves of her sweater pulled down over her hands. "I just... came to get some things. The officer told me I would probably want to spend a few nights somewhere else."

"Do you have somewhere to go?" Riley asked.

Anna nodded. "I have a friend."

"I'm glad to hear it. Dr. Hunt, are you...?"

"We're done here. We just need to move the body."

Riley nodded. "We'll leave you to that." She walked over to Anna, put a hand on her shoulder, and said, "We're going to do everything in our power to find the person who murdered your husband. No matter how long it takes. But you have to prepare yourself. We may never find him. Do you understand?"

Anna frowned and finally, for the first time, met Riley's eyes.

"Do you understand?"

"Yeah," Anna finally managed. "I-I understand."

Riley nodded and said, "Come on, Priest. Let's get the killer's description out there."

"You got it, boss."

They left the apartment, and Mr. Winston came out of his apartment. "Well, you goin' make an arrest?"

"Yes, sir," Riley said, not breaking stride as she went past him. "Just as soon as we find the young man you describe. Might be hard without a better description, but we'll do our best."

Winston seemed to relax. "Well, all right. Guess we can't ask much more of you than that."

"We'll let you know if we make any progress, sir."

Priest remained silent until they reached the street. "So this is it?"

"No, we'll put the description out on the wire. We'll get about a hundred calls by the end of the day by people swearing up and down they saw the kid. We may follow up on a couple of them. Just to have something to do. But none of them will lead anywhere. This time next week, Hathaway will tell us to put it into the cold file and move on."

"You'll have an unsolved case on your record."

"I have a couple already. And they haunt me." She looked up at the building with its flower boxes and polished windows, the desperate attempt to have something nice in a world that was doing its best to pull everyone down into the mud. She admired the effort, and she was going to do everything in her power to reward it. "This one won't."

Gillian was helping her assistant lead the gurney out of the building, Mr. Post's body filling a black rubber bag on top of the mattress. She met Riley's eyes across the street and nodded once. That single nod contained understanding, acceptance, and the full knowledge of what Riley had done. Riley returned the nod, then opened her car door. "Come on. Let's get something for breakfast. My treat."

"Oh, yeah? Where are we going?"

"Let's try and find a place that serves organic food."

Priest shrugged. "Sounds good to me."

Riley pulled away from the curb, passing Gillian at the back of the Medical Examiner's van. She lifted her hand as she passed, and Gillian mimicked the move. When they got to the curb, Riley looked in the rearview mirror and saw Anna Post coming out of the building. Officer Cooley led her to his car, but she still looked dazed.

Anna had a whole new life standing in front of her. A life without the man who had made a sport out of slapping her down. Riley prayed she made it, but her job was done. She pulled away from the stop sign, turning the corner and leaving Anna Post and her new life behind her.

Losing My Religion

Chapter One

The church smelled of incense smoke. Sandalwood and something else underlying that Riley couldn't place. The old man she had met during her first visit to the church was moving slowly along the pews. He was humming quietly to himself as he took a handful of red-covered books from a box on the pew. He glanced up at the sound of Riley entering the church and smiled as he turned away. He slid the books into slots on the back of the pew.

When Riley was halfway down the aisle, Father Jacob said, "You know, we tend to do this on Sundays. A whole group of people come in and I just take care of them all at once. Kind of a bulk deal. You should try it one of these weeks."

"No, thanks," Riley said. She took one of the books from its slot and read the gold leaf on the cover. "What's a hymnal?"

The stooped black man raised his eyes to see if she was joking. "A book of worship songs." He smiled. "It has been a while for you, hasn't it?"

Riley returned the book to the slot. "I need your help. I need to learn how to protect someone from demons."

He sighed and said, "Like I told you before—"

"Right, I know," Riley said. "You have to believe in the talismans or they won't be effective. I understand that. But there has to be some kind of... barrier spell, right?"

"We're not witches," Jacob said. "There's a Wiccan church a few blocks down the street if you want spells and charms and such."

"It's not for me. A demon has threatened someone I care about. I want to make sure she's protected in case..."

"In case a demon comes after her?" Jacob said. He groaned as he lowered himself into the pew, gripping the back of the pew in front of him to keep from falling over. He put the hymnals in his lap and gestured at the seat next to him. "Sit down, please." Riley did. "Did you tell me your name when you were here last, or did I forget it? My age, it could be either."

"Detective Riley Parra."

Jacob arched his eyebrows. "Detective. Well, you're certainly bull-headed enough for it." He leaned back and scratched his chin. "I don't believe the spiritual world works quite the way you think it does, Detective Parra. I believe there is good and evil, but they're mostly indifferent to the things we, as humans, do on this world. We're simply below their caring. I believe there is an afterlife, a heaven and a hell. But as for angels and demons actively taking part in the affairs of humans..."

"It's true," Riley said. "I have the scars to prove it. I just... I need something to make sure she stays safe."

Jacob sighed and rubbed his hands together. "Is she a believer?"

"I'm not going to tell her what I'm doing."

Jacob frowned. "Does she even know she's in danger?"

Riley pushed up from the pew and said, "I'm sorry I bothered you with this. I'll find some other way to protect her. Thank you for your time." She turned and walked down the aisle toward the door. She was almost there when Jacob called her name. She turned and he was turned in the pew, his head bowed to look at the hymnals.

"You may say you don't believe in the rites of the believers who come here every Sunday. And yet you've been here twice looking for help. Maybe you believe more than you think." He shrugged his shoulders and said, "It couldn't hurt to have your friend's home blessed by a priest. You can sprinkle holy water. Make it a sacred place, and demons will avoid it like the plague." He shook his head and pressed his lips together. "I cannot believe I'm even entertaining the idea."

"Believe it, Father," Riley said. "You may have just saved someone's life."

She turned and walked the rest of the way to the door, pausing by the font that stood at the head of the aisle. After a moment, she dipped her fingers into the water and used it to cross herself. She wasn't sure what she hoped to accomplish, and she doubted it would do anything but make her skin wet. But she also didn't think it would hurt.

Gillian turned on the light as she entered the morgue, focused on the file in her hand. Four bodies had come in overnight, one of them important enough for the coroner to call her in the middle of the night and ask her to come in early. The light switch next to the door turned on several fluorescent lights throughout the room, illuminating the bodies lying covered on the steel tables in the middle of the room.

She looked up from the file and noticed the corners of the room seemed darker than usual. She eyed the fluorescent bulbs to see if they were dying, and made a note to talk to maintenance about the problem. They tended to avoid the morgue as often as possible. Her sneakers squeaked as she went to her locker and quickly donned her light blue scrubs. She put her hair up, washed her hands, and pulled on a pair of rubber gloves before returning to the first table.

Gillian reached above her head and switched on the microphone to the recording device. Every bed had a microphone hanging down over the head of the deceased, and Gillian always imagined it looked like they were trying to let the dead have one last word before they went.

She sighed and laid the report on the bed as she drew back the white sheet. "Medical Examiner's Report, Dr. Gillian Hunt. May 8. Subject is a thirty-four year old Caucasian woman, cause of death is a gunshot wound to the right temple. Police on the scene determined suicide." She lifted the woman's hand to inspect the fingers. It was surprising how many 'suicides' came into the morgue with scratches on their trigger finger and broken nails. She called those 'involuntary suicides' and handed it off to homicide to figure out.

"No sign of cutting on the finger. No indication suicide was forced."

She moved to the second body to begin the initial examination. "Second subject is an eighty-one year old woman found enclosed in her apartment. Believed to have been dead for two months. The cause of death, while not readily apparent, is thought to be—"

"Dr. Hunt."

Gillian lifted her head and turned toward the voice. The morgue seemed empty. "Danny?" she asked. She looked at the watch on the inside of her right wrist and moved toward the office. She had no idea why Danny would have come in so early, unless the coroner had called him, too. The office light was off, and a quick look through the open door revealed the room was empty.

She frowned and walked back to the second table. She could hear the hiss of the tape recorder, and decided her sleep-addled brain had just confused her into thinking she heard someone speak. She picked up the scalpel and hesitated before making the first cut. If she was tired enough to confuse a dream with reality, then maybe she needed another cup of coffee before she got to work.

She had just started to turn away from the table when the dead woman's hand shot up and grabbed her wrist.

Gillian couldn't even draw breath to scream, could do nothing but stare wide-eyed as the cold, adipocerous fingers wrapped around her bare wrist. She flicked her eyes toward the woman's head and saw blood-red eyes staring at her. She wanted to drop the scalpel, but her brain didn't seem able to get signals past that horrific hand.

"Doc. Torhu. Nnnnt."

The voice came from behind her now, and snapped her back to reality. She yanked her hand back, trying to free herself from the monster's grip, but the fingers wouldn't give. The elderly woman, lips pulled back in a dying grimace, rolled to the edge of the table and started to fall. Gillian shrieked as her sneakers slipped on the floor, and she went down, pulling the dead woman along with her. She hit the floor, mouth still open in a silent scream, and tried to ignore the fact that a dead body was on top of her.

The hand finally released, and Gillian - no longer thinking about respect for the dead - kicked the woman away from her. She rolled onto her hands and knees, already justifying what had happened in her head. Just a death twitch, a bizarre muscle spasm. That was all, nothing sinister or supernatural. She was halfway to the door when a determined voice howled, "Doctor Hunt!"

The voice echoed off the metal drawers, filling the room with its anger. Gillian's hands came up and clamped over her ears, but the words still reverberated through her skull. She was almost to the door when something grabbed her from behind. Something phenomenally strong pulled her back, swung her like a rag doll, and hurled her toward the cooler. She slammed into the cold metal drawers and pushed back, staring at her own reflection.

Behind her, she saw the blurry images of the three dead bodies starting to sit up on their tables. Something huge was approaching her from behind. It didn't seem so much dark as it was an absence of light. Darker than any night she had ever experienced, seeming to draw her vision toward and into it.

"No," she murmured. "No, no, no, no... please, no."

"Doctor Hunt," the voice said again, and she closed her eyes and began to scream.

Riley was halfway to the precinct when her cell phone rang. The personalized ring tone was Sarah McLachlan singing, "In the arms of the an—" Riley flipped the phone open mid-word without bothering to look at the screen. "What's up, Priest?"

Her new partner's voice was unusually hesitant. "I'm not sure. Maybe nothing. Where are you?"

"I'm about ten minutes from the precinct. I was going to call and see if you wanted breakfast. Do you eat breakfast? Angels, I mean."

There was a pause. "What? Oh, right. Uh, yeah, we do. I do, anyway. But no, I'm not hungry. Listen, Riley, you need to get here fast."

Riley instinctively stepped on the gas. "What's going on?"

"I don't know. Maybe nothing. I just… I have a very bad feeling that something very bad is going to happen here today. And I feel like time is of the essence."

"Get these feelings a lot, do you?"

"No. Not really."

"When was the last time?"

"The day Samael fell."

Riley hung up and tossed the phone onto the passenger seat. "Shit." She fumbled in the glove compartment and placed the revolving red light on the dashboard. As it began to rotate, she stood on the gas and whipped around the other cars on the road as if they were standing still.

When she pulled into the parking garage underneath the 410 precinct building, she spotted Priest pacing between two concrete pillars. She wore a white blouse under a red sweater, her hands in the back pockets of her black jeans. She watched Riley approach and moved to meet up with her at the parking spot. When Riley got out of the car, she checked her gun to make sure she was good to go. She looked up at Priest, her new partner and the latest angel to enter her life. "Any more clues on what's happening?"

"No. Just a sinking sensation in the pit of my stomach." She looked toward the elevators. "I think we need to hurry."

Riley led the way across the garage and jabbed the elevator button with two fingers. "You always get feelings about bad stuff that's going to happen? Because that could be handy."

Priest shook her head. "No. It hardly ever happens. But when it does, I know not to ignore it." They stepped into the car, and Priest reached out and punched a button.

Riley looked at the lit button for a long moment as the doors closed. "The morgue?"

Priest looked at the button and said, "Did I hit that?"

Riley pulled her gun again and pressed her palm tightly against the grip. "Fuck," she whispered. She rolled her shoulders and stepped through the doors as soon as they opened. She ran down the hall, Priest's footsteps echoing on the floor behind her. The lights were low, still operating at half-power before the official start of the day. She knew Gillian liked to keep the ambiance as long as possible; she said she wanted to give the passed souls a comforting last memory.

Riley pushed the morgue door open with her shoulder and took a moment to take in every detail. Three bodies lay covered on the tables in the middle of the room, the dark office directly ahead of her. Other than the quiet sound of the cooler motor, the room was, to coin a phrase, deathly quiet. Gillian was nowhere to be seen.

"Go back to sleep," Gillian said, bending over the bed and kissing Riley's lips. "I have to get in early today. Bigwig bit the dust."

"Rich or poor, it doesn't matter who you are," Riley murmured.

"We each owe a death," Gillian said.

So why wasn't she there? Riley crossed the floor and said, "Jill? You in here?"

Priest started to follow, but stopped short at the threshold. She drew a shuddering breath, arms out to balance herself. She hunched her shoulders and said, "Riley, get out of there."

Riley ignored her. "Jill, are you here? I thought you were supposed to come in early." She looked at the covered bodies on the table. A dreadful thought occurred to her, but two bodies were the wrong shape for Gillian, and the other was either a male or a female with a small-chest. Either way, not Gillian.

"Dr. Hunt?" Priest tried, finally braving the room when she decided Riley wasn't going to play it safe. "Dr. Hunt, are you here?"

They both heard the shriek. It was strange, as if coming from the far end of a tunnel. Priest was closest to the drawers and said, "Dr. Hunt?"

"Stop it!" Gillian said. "Stop it, please!"

Riley holstered her weapon and ran to the drawers. She yanked one open and then another, searching frantically. "Gillian, it's me. It's Riley. Where are you? Gillian, talk to me."

"Riley?"

She moved toward the voice and tugged the handle up. Gillian was inside, curled in the fetal position. Unlike the other bodies, Gillian appeared to have crawled in head-first. Riley grabbed the back edge of the tray and pulled the slab out of the drawer. Gillian rolled onto her back and looked up at Riley, eyes streaked with tears.

Gillian sat up and looked around the room. "They were here. They were alive." She wrapped her arms around Riley's neck and held on for dear life. She was freezing cold, and Riley immediately began rubbing her back through the thin scrub top she wore. "They were going to kill me. Oh, my God, Riley, they were going to kill me."

"It's okay," Riley said. "It's okay. Nobody is going to hurt you anymore." She looked past Gillian to Priest, who was lurking through the autopsy theater like a jungle cat. She met Riley's eyes and shuddered, then shook her head. "It's okay. I'm here now. You're safe."

Gillian clung to Riley's jacket and sobbed, her body shaking with the force of her fear.

Chapter Two

Riley helped Gillian into the office, and eased her into her seat. Priest got a blanket from Gillian's locker and wrapped it around her shoulders. Riley knelt in front of her lover, rubbing her thighs through her scrubs. Gillian finally stopped hyperventilating, but her hands were still shaking as Priest handed her a cup of water. She drank it all at once, started to wipe her lips against her wrist, and recoiled. She shuddered violently and two fresh tears rolled down her cheeks.

Riley reached up and brushed the tears away with her thumb. "Jill, tell me what happened."

Gillian shook her head and looked at Priest, then closed her eyes. "I can't."

"It's okay," Priest said. "Whatever happened, we'll believe you."

Gillian looked down into the empty Dixie cup and said, "The bodies on the table. They came to life. And there was... something else. Grabbing at me. I opened one of the empty drawers and got inside. The thing shut the door on me. I thought he'd locked it. I could hear him laughing outside." She shuddered and drew her knees together, hugging herself and leaning forward. "It was freezing. When I heard you saying my name, I thought it was them again."

Riley resisted the urge to push away from the chair and go searching for something to shoot. Gillian needed her to be there. She took Gillian's hands, squeezed, and brought one to her lips. She kissed the knuckles and said, "I'm so sorry."

Priest glanced at Riley and said, "I'm going to check on the bodies. See if there's any residual energy. Be well, Gillian." She touched the top of Gillian's head with her fingers before she turned and left the office. Gillian swallowed hard and watched her go and then said, "Put on some music, please."

Riley stood and went to the CD player sitting on Gillian's filing cabinet.

She pressed play, and Bon Jovi began to sing. "Do you want a different disc?"

"No. Track five."

Riley hit the button until the display read '5,' and returned to Gillian. "I'm so sorry I wasn't here. If anything had happened..."

"Something did happen," Gillian said.

Riley flinched. "Right. I know. I'm sorry. I just meant that if you had been..." She closed her eyes and shook her head. "It could have been so much worse, Jill. You were so smart jumping into that drawer."

"It was terrifying," Gillian whispered. "I thought I would never get out." She burrowed deeper into the blanket, clutching it with shaking hands. "I-I can't get warm."

Riley pulled off her blazer and draped it over Gillian's shoulders. She rubbed Gillian's arms and said, "When you feel up to it, I'll take you home. I'll call your boss and tell him to send a replacement for the day."

"I think it's going to take more than a day, Riley," Gillian said. "Someone came after me. Some thing came after me. I crawled into one of those drawers certain I would either never get out, or that I would be dragged out and killed. Do you have any idea..." She swallowed hard again and bit her bottom lip. "I think I'm going to take a leave of absence."

Riley nodded. "Of course."

Gillian took a deep breath and exhaled slowly. The Bon Jovi ballad filled the silence between them. Outside in the theater, Riley heard Priest talking to herself about the bodies. Finally, Gillian pushed her hair out of her face and said, "I think I can walk. Can you please take me home?"

"Yeah. Come on, let me help you up."

Riley helped Gillian stand, put an arm around her, and helped her out of the office. Priest looked up when they appeared, pausing in the act of raising the sheet from one body. Riley motioned for her to drop it, and Priest complied. Riley said, "Tell Hathaway there was an incident down here. I'm taking Gillian home. I may not be back until afternoon."

"I'll cover for you."

Riley guided Gillian out of the room, aware that Gillian refused to lift her head until they were past the dead bodies. When they reached the elevator, Gillian pulled away from Riley and rubbed her arms furiously. She shook her head and said, "I don't think I can be around dead bodies anymore."

"Just take it a day at a time," Riley said. "It'll be fine. You're strong. You'll get through this."

Gillian nodded slowly, and let Riley guide her onto the elevator. As

Riley pressed the button for the garage level, she risked a glance at Gillian. She was pale, withdrawn into herself, and she kept rolling her shoulders and her neck. She worried her bottom lip with her teeth and absently touched her hair. Riley said, "Jill, if you need to talk... I've been there. Crowded by demons, sure they were going to tear me apart."

"How'd you get through it?"

"I found you."

Gillian finally met Riley's eyes and said, "Yeah."

Riley stepped forward and lightly kissed Gillian's lips. She pressed close, her lips pressing against Gillian's until they felt warm again. When she backed away, Gillian touched her lips and closed her eyes. Riley said, "I'll help you through this. I promise."

Gillian took Riley's hand and squeezed the fingers.

Riley didn't bother turning on the lights when they got to the apartment. Gillian hadn't spoken during the drive; she just pulled her feet up into the seat, hugged her knees, and watched the city go by through the window. Riley led Gillian into the bedroom and sat her down on the mattress. Gillian said, "I'm sorry I'm acting like a five-year-old."

"You're not. You're fine." She untied Gillian's sneakers and pulled them off. She peeled away the socks and gently massaged the arches. "This is all my fault. If I hadn't gotten involved with this whole damn mess..."

"Shh," Gillian whispered. "It's nobody's fault."

"Marchosias warned me," Riley said quietly. She looked up into Gillian's eyes. "He warned me with your toy rabbit. He wanted to show me that he could get to you whenever he wanted. I didn't learn the lesson well enough."

Gillian leaned forward and kissed Riley's forehead. Riley closed her eyes, glad that Gillian's body warmth seemed to have returned. Gillian slid her lips across Riley's right eyebrow and said, "I don't blame you for this, Riley."

Riley wrapped her arms around Gillian's waist and pulled her close for a hug. Gillian returned the embrace, gently at first but slowly growing stronger. When they finally parted, Riley pushed Gillian's hair out of her face and said, "Do you want me to stay here with you?"

"No," Gillian said. "I just need some time to process everything. Thank you for getting me home, though. I finally feel safe for the first time all day."

Riley said, "I'm glad. I'm going to go back to work and see what Priest has found out."

"Yeah. I'm going to take a hot bath."

"Let me get the water running before I go." She stood up and kissed Gillian's lips. "I'm so glad you're okay, Jill. I don't know what I do…" She touched Gillian's hair and didn't finish the thought. She smiled and said, "Okay. I'm going to go start the bath. I'll see you later. And I'll call to check up on you through the day, okay?"

Gillian nodded, and Riley went into the bathroom. She looked under the sink and found a small bottle of Epsom Salt. She had done a bit of reading on the preparation of holy water, and she found that salt was an essential ingredient. She sat on the edge of the tub and started the water, pouring a bit of the salt under the flow so it would spread throughout the entire bath.

She closed her eyes and whispered, "Okay, God. I know I'm not your number one fan. You and I haven't exactly been close. But Gillian deserves better protection than just me. She needs someone watching out for her, and I guess that might as well be you. Protect her. Keep her safe while I'm away." She wiped away her tears and stopped the water.

Riley stayed until Gillian was undressed and safely delivered into the bath. She made the rounds of the apartment, locking windows and making sure no one was lurking on the fire escape before she felt comfortable leaving. She knew things like locks and security systems weren't a deterrent to demons, but it gave her peace of mind. By the time she got back to her car, her concern transformed into anger.

Her hands gripped the steering wheel until her knuckles turned white, her teeth grinding together loud enough that she turned on the radio to drown it out. Alice Cooper howled, "No more Mr. Nice Guy," and Riley sang along, getting out some of her anger through the lyrics. She pictured Marchosias in her mind, his blood-red hand petting the head of Gillian's toy rabbit.

Mess with me, that's fine, she thought. *But you crossed the line, March. Gloves are off, no holds barred.*

On the radio, Alice Cooper sang that he wasn't going to be Mr. Nice Guy anymore.

"Damn right, Alice," she growled, banging her hand against the steering wheel again for good measure. The next song on the classic rock station was

Thin Lizzy singing Whiskey in a Jar. Riley drove to the police station with the guitars vibrating the glass in the windows of her car. She spotted Priest standing on the sidewalk and slowed just enough to let her jump in.

"What did you find out?"

"Not much," Priest said. She turned down the radio so she wouldn't have to shout over the song. "The bodies were definitely animated by some kind of demonic force, and it sounds kind of like something Marchosias would order. I don't think he was actually there. He would have sent one of his foot soldiers."

"Any idea which one?"

Priest thought for a long moment and then said, "I can narrow it down to three."

"Give me their names and tell me where I can find them."

Priest shook her head. "Do you remember what happened last time you went into No Man's Land without a plan?"

"Yeah, one of your buddies turned on me and nearly killed me. It's a very vivid memory, believe me."

"I meant the first time," Priest said quietly. "You walked into a demon's stronghold and you barely got out with your life. I don't suppose you melted your badge down again so you'll be armed?"

Riley said, "Maybe this time my partner will step up and cover my back."

Priest shook her head and said, "This is ridiculous, Riley. You know why Gillian was attacked. This is exactly what Marchosias wants."

"It's exactly what I want, too."

"You're not going to be a very good protector for the city if you're dead."

"He has to learn what's off limits."

"Nothing is off limits to a demon."

"Gillian is!" Riley shouted. Her shout was loud enough that Priest recoiled, the car filled with Phil Lynott's singing. Riley tried to steady her nerves and slow her breathing. Finally, in a much more subdued voice, she said, "Tell me where to find the three demons you think might have done this." Priest didn't answer immediately, so Riley said, "If you don't tell me, I'll kick you out of my car and go try to find them on my own."

Priest's shoulders sagged in defeat and she looked out the window for a long time before she answered. "Alistair Call is the first one. Ethan Winn, and then another one just called the Duchess. I suggest you begin with Alistair. He's the one with the most to gain by doing this. He wants to get into Marchosias' good graces."

"How does killing Gillian accomplish that?" Riley asked, nearly spitting the words.

"He didn't want to kill her," Priest said. "You should understand that. If they truly wanted to kill her, she would be dead. What Marchosias wants is this, right here. Gillian is out of commission for the time being, and you're racing straight into Marchosias' home turf completely unprepared. You're going to let him win."

Riley ignored her and slowed at an intersection. The area of the city around them was just beginning to decay, evidence of the steady advance of No Man's Land. To her left was a boarded up hardware store, the awning hanging loose over the door like a funeral veil. Riley could see faded letters in the window where a name had once been. She looked away from the abandoned business and looked toward Marchosias' domain.

"Which way?" Riley said.

Priest frowned and stared at Riley. "That's what you want, isn't it? You want to give Marchosias what he's after so he'll leave Gillian alone."

"I'm not suicidal," Riley said. She looked into Priest's eyes and said, "Which way?"

Priest pursed her lips and finally pointed. "Straight ahead until you get to Marquis Street. There's an old fire station on the right side of the street. I'm pretty sure you'll find Alistair and the Duchess there. Maybe we'll get lucky and Ethan Winn will be there, too. Three demons for the price of one. You'd like that, wouldn't you?"

Riley nodded and pulled away from the stop sign.

"Promise me, Riley," Priest said. "Promise me that if things get bad, you'll get the hell out of there. Don't let them kill you."

Riley stared straight ahead through the glass, watching for the street sign where she was supposed to turn. "No promises," she said.

Chapter Three

"YET FROM THOSE FLAMES," was written in black paint above the windows in the firehouse's garage door. "NO LIGHT BUT RATHER DARKNESS, VISIBLE" was written underneath. The letters were long and thin, long dripping lines trailing from each letter down to the pavement. Riley parked across the driveway to prevent anyone from trying to escape before she had a chance to talk to them. She got out of the car and looked down the street, watching for signs that they were being watched.

"Just accept they're there," Priest said. "You won't be able to see them."

"I want them to know I know," Riley said. She slammed the car door and looked at the building. She wore the reflective sunglasses that had served her well ever since her foot patrol days, willing to take any amount of intimidation she could get. She considered going to the trunk to get her bulletproof vest, but she knew it wouldn't do any good. So she walked up the door in her plain blouse and jeans. She hung her badge around her neck and let it dangle, the gold catching the light.

The fire station seemed alive compared to the businesses on either side. The wide red garage door was crowned by a Gothic carving, gargoyles sneering down at the street. Black iron sconces hung on either side of the door, the lanterns missing the glass. Riley avoided looking at the gargoyles, sure that their eyes would follow her, and approached the man-sized door tucked to one side. She glanced back to make sure Priest was following her and saw the angel staring at the words written on the door.

"You recognize that?"

"Yes. John Milton, Paradise Lost."

"I might have to read that one of these days, given the company I've been keeping." Riley pounded on the door. "Police. Open the door, please." She rested her other hand on the butt of her gun and waited for a response. After a moment, she pounded again. "This is the police. Open the door."

Finally, there was a sound of movement inside; feet shuffling against concrete, and then a rough cough. The door opened and a tall, emaciated man stepped into the space. He pulled the door tight against his shoulders and eyed both women before he focused on Riley. "What?"

"Are you a member of the volunteer fire department?"

"Mebbe," the guy slurred. He turned and looked at Priest. "What's the angel doing here?"

"We're just here to talk," Priest said. "Alistair, the Duchess, and Ethan Winn. Are they in?"

The guy screeched, "Nobody sees the wizard. No how, no way, nuh-uh," and slammed the door in their face.

Riley and Priest exchanged a look, and Riley pounded on the door again. When the guy opened the door again, she had her gun out and aimed between his eyes. "What do I need, ruby slippers? I can make my shoes red in about five seconds. You probably won't be around to see it, though. Open the damn door and step back."

"Okay, okay. No need to get vi-o-lent." He stepped back and pushed the door wide open. Riley gave her eyes a moment to adjust to the gloom before she stepped into the doorway. The interior of the former firehouse stank like a charnel house, and Riley could detect the copper scent of blood and the off-putting scent of bodily waste. Bags of trash lined the walls, falling against each other and spilling open across the floor.

The main floor was dark, but light spilled down a flight of wooden stairs standing at the back of the room. From above, Riley heard the sounds of people moaning but couldn't decide if they were in pleasure or pain. Riley stepped into the building and Priest followed, trembling hard enough that her clothes made quiet rustling sounds. The angel whispered a prayer under her breath and crossed herself.

"Welcome to the madhouse, babies," the doorman said. He strutted past them and walked across the floor to the ruins of a fire truck. Water dripped from the back of the truck, evidence of a leak in the tank. The equipment compartment had been ripped apart, the tools scattered on the concrete floor all around. There were pools of dark liquid near the ax and the Halligen; a part of Riley suddenly knew that the tools had been used for torture.

The doorman saw her staring toward the truck and pointed his middle finger at it. "Burnin' building collapsed on it." He mimicked an explosion sound. "They were just pullin' up and, boom. Every last one became a crispy critter. They came back here to haunt, I guess. They're fun." He smiled and walked toward the stairs.

Riley looked at Priest, whose face was deathly pale. "Are you all right?"

Priest nodded distractedly. "I do not like it here," she said, her voice rough and thin. She swallowed hard and said, "Let's... please... make... this quick."

The doorman pointed upstairs. "Mr. Call is upstairs. The Duchess is probably with him." He looked Riley up and down and winked. "She'll like you."

Riley led the way upstairs without hesitation. She kept her gun drawn and looked back frequently to make sure Priest was following her. Despite the pallor of her skin, she seemed determined to back Riley up. She met Riley's gaze and nodded, then pressed her lips together and swallowed hard as they reached the second story.

What once served as the firefighter's bunk room had been turned into a den of iniquity. A semicircle of plush couches stood in the center of the room, draped with furs. A fat man wearing a soiled business suit sat on the edge of one divan, his head in his hands, his shoulders racked with sobs. Riley watched him as she approached, then turned her attention to the man and woman holding court in the center of the room.

Alistair Call stood at least six foot eight, his bald pate gleaming even in the dim light. His suit was impeccable, but he was standing barefoot to one side of the couches watching the businessman weep. He turned casually toward Riley and Priest and then looked back at the subject of his apparent concern. His brow was furrowed, his lips slightly pursed. He put a hand on top of the man's head. "It hurts, doesn't it?"

The man looked up with red rimmed eyes. He looked at Riley for a long moment, eyed the badge hanging between her breasts. Finally, he shook his head and pushed to his feet. "I should go... I shouldn't be here."

"That's right." Alistair moved his hand on the man's shoulder and said, "All your problems will work themselves out. The solution is much easier than you think." He grinned and said, "All right. Very well. Go and take care of business. Thank you for coming to me, Mr. Davidson."

The man wiped his eyes and shuffled toward Riley. Priest said, "Sir, wait..." Mr. Davidson waved her off, moving to one side so she wouldn't be able to touch him. Priest watched him walk down the stairs and then turned back to Alistair.

The demon wiped his hands on a handkerchief and smiled at Riley. "Hello, Detective Parra. And Zerachiel. Always a pleasure. You look a bit drained, Zerachiel. Would you like something to drink?"

"She finds this place repulsive."

Riley jumped away from the sound of the woman's voice. The Duchess was standing close enough that Riley felt the breath of her voice against her cheek. Riley had an instant impression of bright green eyes and red hair before her attention was drawn away. Ruby red lips parting in a smile seemed burned on her retinas, and she blinked to erase it as she spoke to Alistair. "Did Marchosias order the attack on Gillian Hunt?"

"I'm not aware of any decree. Perhaps someone chose to have a bit of fun with the good doctor." He walked to the divan and dropped himself onto the cushions, stretching his arms out over the back to either side. "I hope she wasn't hurt."

Something caused goosebumps to rise on Riley's arms, and she thought she felt a breeze ruffling her hair. She rolled her shoulders trying to get rid of the awkward sensation, focusing on Alistair. She was beginning to regret coming into this place without a solid plan. Her usual questions - where were you this morning, can anyone corroborate your story? - wouldn't work on something like this.

"Get off of her," Priest muttered, but Riley didn't understand the context and didn't seek an explanation. She was too focused on Alistair to care what Priest meant.

Alistair simply smiled. "Detective Parra, please. I've heard all about your impressive solo raid on Marchosias' stronghold. Trust me, we were all very impressed. But your fifteen minutes are running out. Our admiration at the sheer bulk of your balls is going to fade and be replaced with the realization that you may be more trouble than you're worth. We're a patient bunch. And we admire tenacity. But there will come a time when you have pushed us too far and... measures will be taken. When that day comes, if you're still in this city causing problems, you will be dealt with. You won't be able to fight back. You won't see it coming. I know you struck down Samael and decided to take up the mantle of this city's protector. Again, admirable. But what do you hope to accomplish? A simple mortal? When all I have to do is snap my fingers and you'll be ended."

A sharp hiss sounded next to Riley's ear and she jerked away. Her head swam as if she had stood up too fast, and the room spun. She brought her gun up, aiming at nothing in particular as she tried to make sense of everything that was suddenly happening all around her. She stumbled, nearly fell, and righted herself before she hit her knees.

Her blouse was open, the right shoulder pulled down to expose the strap of her tank top. Her belt was undone. Priest was sagging against the back wall, wings extended, her head hanging as if in exhaustion. Standing between Riley and Priest was the most beautiful woman she had ever seen. She wore a white blouse and a flowing tan dress, her feet obscured by the lace hem. Her right hand was wrapped around her left wrist, cradling it to her chest as she raised her eyes to Riley's. The beauty vanished, replaced with something so hideous Riley could barely contain the scream that rose in her throat.

"The bitch burned me," the formerly beautiful thing hissed.

Riley spun around and saw Alistair rising off the couch. All the humor was gone from his face. "The tattoo on your back. Where did you acquire it?"

"Stay back," Riley said, wishing she sounded more confident than she was. Suddenly she felt exhausted, as if she had been up for days. How much of her conversation with Alistair had been in her head? "I'll shoot."

"I'd prefer you didn't. I like this shirt." He grabbed Riley's right shoulder, well away from the exposed tattoo on her back, and twisted her to look at the design. "Well, well. It's been a while since I've seen this."

"Give her to me," the Duchess growled.

Riley realized she had again forgotten the woman was there. She pulled away from Alistair and stepped back, hoping to keep both demons in her line of sight. She was sweating, and her arms hurt. She flexed her fingers, tightening the grip on her gun, and said, "Gillian Hunt. Who ordered the attack on her? Marchosias?"

"The misconception is that you're thinking too much like a human," Alistair said as he moved to stand next to the Duchess. "There are no edicts or assignments. Marchosias is the Grand Marquis of Hell, but he's more of a hands-off sort of supervisor. If a random demon thought it would be fun to drive your little girlfriend crazy, then they would go ahead and do that. Odds are, you'll never find out who it was."

Priest pushed away from the wall and said, "Riley, we have to leave this place."

Riley dipped her chin toward Priest in acknowledgement and buckled her belt. She shrugged her blouse back onto her shoulder, raised her gun to Alistair, and tried to tamp down the fear that she was in way over her head. "You could find out. You're going to ask around, and you're going to tell me who did it. You're going to deliver them to me."

"Why would I do that?"

Riley said, "Because you don't want to end up like the Duchess."

Before Alistair or the Duchess had time to question what she meant, the Duchess howled in pain. Priest had approached the demons from behind and managed to take the Duchess' burned hand. Light seeped between Priest's fingers, her face dark and determined as she poured energy through the burn from Riley's tattoo.

The Duchess howled, her voice inhuman as she dropped to her knees. Black spider webs tracked down her arm until the flesh was black all the way to her elbow. Priest finally released her hand and stepped back, stumbling a bit over her own feet as she retreated. The Duchess stared at her hand with a mixture of disbelief and fury, her lips pulling back over the needle-sharp teeth of a piranha.

Riley tried to appear unmoved as the reek of burning flesh filled the room. "All I want is the name, Alistair. Give me the name, and I leave you alone. For now. Priest, you all right?"

"Yeah." The voice was barely audible, with no strength behind it.

Riley moved toward the door, keeping her eyes on the demons. Alistair's friendly manner evaporated, his eyes turning into embers as he tracked her retreat. When she reached the top of the stairs, Riley said, "You have twenty-four hours, or I come back and finish what I started."

Priest released the Duchess, who fell to the floor. She looked up and narrowed her gaze at Riley. "You will suffer."

"Sure," Riley said. "Par for the course." She waited for Priest to start down the stairs before she finally turned her back and followed.

They hurried down the stairs, their footsteps echoing hollow in the main garage of the former firehouse. Priest hit the floor running, wings tucked in against her back so they wouldn't slow her down. Riley kept her eyes straight ahead, ignoring the way the shadows moved in her periphery. Priest threw open the front door and lurched out into the sunshine. Riley followed two steps behind, squinting at the brightness of the day.

It took her a moment to realize the street was full of activity. Priest was bent over next to the car, spitting into the gutter after apparently throwing up. Her wings were no longer in sight, her hand trembling against the hood of Riley's car. But the main show was in the middle of the street. A garbage truck stood idle a few feet away, at the end of the block, and two police cars were blocking off traffic. A man in a business suit was lying in the street, a spray of blood spreading out from his head.

Riley recognized the man's suit and knew he was the man they had seen leaving Alistair's office.

"Insurance," Priest said, touching the cuff of her shirtsleeve to her lips. "He needed money and Alistair told him the insurance would pay enough to cover his debts if he... in the case of an accidental death."

Riley said, "Why?"

Priest shook her head. "The guy came to Alistair for help."

"So Alistair made him kill himself? Why?"

"He didn't make the man kill himself," Priest said. "He just planted the seed. The decision was all his." She nodded at the body in the street. "As for why..." Priest shrugged. "Maybe he was just bored."

Riley looked away and walked toward her car. "Are you feeling better?"

"A little every minute we're out of that place," Priest said. She breathed deeply a few times and said, "I know you want to try to find Ethan Winn, but I don't think I'll be able to stand it. Maybe we take a quick breather."

Riley didn't even try to argue. "Okay. We'll retreat for the time being. I want to see Gillian anyway. It'll give Alistair a chance to look for us. Maybe we'll get lucky."

Priest shook her head. "Waiting is not going to do any good. Alistair will simply alert Ethan - not to mention every other demon within hearing distance - that you're on the warpath."

"So they'll know I'm coming."

"And they will kill you."

Riley climbed into the car and didn't answer until Priest climbed into the other side. "I don't care. If they don't know that Gillian is protected, then I don't care if they kill me. When I'm dead, they'll have no reason to go after her."

"My Lord," Priest said. "Is that actually your plan?"

"No," Riley said. "It's the back-up plan."

Priest seemed to relax. "What's your main plan?"

Riley pulled away from the curb, eyeing the police officers dealing with the death behind her. "I'll let you know when I come up with it."

Chapter Four

At the first church they passed after crossing the border of No Man's Land, Priest said, "Drop me off here."

Riley pulled to the curb and looked at the dark stained-glass windows. "I think they're closed."

Priest unfastened her seatbelt and opened the door. "They'll let me in. Riley, I want you to think about what you're doing here. The forces you're up against are so much bigger than you. You saw what happened to me at that firehouse. If an angel can barely stand up against them, what hope do you possibly have?"

"I didn't ask for this job, Priest," Riley said. "Believe me, if I thought I could get out of it, I would be out of here in a heartbeat. But I can't just turn my back. You heard Alistair. He wants me to leave this town and forget it ever existed. I can't do that. And not because of what Samael said, and not because I feel obligated. I'm staying because this is my city. I was born here, and I've bled here, and I'm not giving up on it just because a demon is trying to scare me. I'm willing to die for the cause, but I am not going to let someone hurt Gillian because of my crusade."

Priest sighed and shook her head. "Raguel told me you were stubborn when I took this assignment. I should have listened to him."

"Are you going to be all right in there?"

"Oh, yeah," Priest said. "I'll be right as rain. I just need a little first aid. Take care of yourself, and of Gillian. Do not go back into No Man's Land without me."

Riley nodded and Priest finally got out of the car. Riley watched until Priest disappeared around the back corner of the church, swallowed by shadows, and then pulled away from the curb. She still felt ghostly fingers on her skin, shivers running through her body as she started to remember the Duchess touching her. It terrified her to think that the demon had been able to move around her, touch her, undo her clothing, without her even noticing. If she couldn't even prevent her own near-rape, then what did she hope to accomplish running into buildings waving her gun and badge around like they meant anything?

Riley thought about her position throughout the drive back to Gillian's apartment. She parked at the curb and jogged across the street, letting herself into the building as if she'd lived there for years. The lobby was empty, but she could hear the rattle of the Coke machine from the laundry room down the hall. It felt like home. More like a home than anywhere else she had stayed in her life.

Gillian's apartment door was locked, and Riley took the key from her wallet to get inside. The living room was middle-of-the-day dark, and she could hear music from the bedroom. She recognized Vienna Teng's voice, but not the song. The main part of the apartment was dark and still, and Riley quietly went to the back hallway. The bedroom door was open and she saw the light of Gillian's bedside lamp against the wall.

She stopped in the doorway and looked at Gillian, curled up in the bed. She was clutching Gravy the Rabbit, the toy Marchosias used to threaten Gillian's safety. Gillian had changed into a pair of white pajamas, her knees drawn up to her chest and her feet crossed at the ankles. She looked so innocent, at least thirty years too young, and Riley felt a pang in her chest at the sight. "I'm sorry, Jill," she whispered from the doorway. "I'm sorry I brought this into your life."

Gillian stirred at the sound of Riley's voice and looked around blindly for a moment. She saw Riley in the doorway and breathed in, a quick gasp that was quickly stifled as her brain recognized who it was. She covered the gasp by yawning and put Gravy the Rabbit aside. She said, "Riley. Are you okay?"

"I'm fine. I just wanted to take a quick shower. How are you holding up?"

Gillian shrugged. "Hurry back."

Riley nodded and went into the bathroom. She stripped down to her underwear, turned on the extra lights that Gillian used to put on her makeup, and examined her body carefully. The demon could have done any number of things while Riley was blinded, could have done anything before touching her shoulder and breaking the spell. She checked her breasts and stomach, turned around to make sure the small of her back was unmarred. She was about to consider herself unharmed when she noticed the change to her tattoo.

The design was two torches joined at the base, surrounded by a yellow circle. The woman who gave it to her, Officer Christine Lee, told her that it was a symbol of power. She was sure it was the reason she wasn't completely fooled by the Duchess, but she wasn't sure how it truly worked or what its origins were. And now, both torches and the surrounding circle had changed color from sunset yellow to a deep, dark red.

She reached back and touched the edge of the circle. It didn't hurt, but the color made it look like a wound. As she watched, the color faded to a less violent shade, and she decided it was residue from direct contact with a demon. She shuddered and turned to face the mirror so she wouldn't have to look at it anymore.

She got into the shower and scrubbed away the encounter, trying to push the questions out of her mind. When she got out of the shower, she dressed in the same clothes she'd been wearing earlier and went back into the bedroom. She sat on the edge of Gillian's side of the bed and took her hand. "How are you doing?"

"Coping. Trying to get those voices out of my head." She took a deep breath and looked Riley over. "What happened to you? You looked like five miles of bad road earlier."

"And now?"

Gillian smiled weakly. "A little better."

"Just two miles, then?" Riley leaned in and kissed Gillian's lips. When she pulled back, she said, "I was trying to find the people who did this to you."

"Riley, don't. Just leave it alone."

Riley frowned. "Gillian, look at what they did to you. I can't just let that go. They came after you because of me. They have to know I won't allow that."

Gillian closed her eyes. "I love that you're ready and willing to do that. But getting yourself killed won't solve anything."

"Either I teach them a lesson, or they take me down. Either way you're out of the line of fire."

"Do you honestly think I want that? To be alive without you?"

"What other choice is there?"

Gillian said, "This town has angels for all its demons, right? There's no need for you to stay here and get tossed around. They're treating you like a plaything, Riley. You need to get out of here. We both do."

Riley frowned and thought back to her conversation with Alistair.

"That's it. That's what they're trying to do."

Gillian looked up. "What?"

Riley said, "They want to get me out of town. They're scared."

Gillian reached up and put her hand in the middle of Riley's back. She let her fingers slide down Riley's shirt and come to rest on the mattress.

Riley arched her back to the touch, but didn't let it distract her. "It's why they just scared you. They wanted me to run."

"I want you to run," Gillian said. "Is that their plan? Then fine. I'm all for it."

Riley turned and said, "I told Priest that I won't run. I refuse to turn my back on this city."

"Why? It's killing you, Riley." Gillian sat up and put her arm around Riley's shoulders. "Do you think that will count as a win? If you end up thrown off another roof, or if you get ambushed again, what do you really think it will accomplish?"

Riley pressed the heels of her hands against her eyes. She focused on the warmth of Gillian's body next to her, the strong pressure of Gillian's hand against her back. She was sitting in the bed she was just beginning to get used to sharing with the woman she loved. Was she really willing to risk all of this for a city that had done nothing but stomp on her again and again?

Gillian moved her hand up to Riley's shoulder and squeezed. "You know I'm right, Riley. We should just get out while we can, before this place takes any more pieces out of us. Forget about angels and demons."

Riley rolled her shoulders, lifting them against Gillian's impromptu massage. "I can't," she said quietly.

Gillian leaned in and rested her head on Riley's shoulder.

"Were you born here?"

"No," Gillian said. "Georgia. My family moved here for Daddy's job when I was sixteen."

Riley put her hand on Gillian's hip and rubbed in slow circles. "This city can get into you. I was born here. I spent my teenage years in No Man's Land stealing from convenience stores. I spent a couple of nights a week sleeping on the streets. This city is like my home. And I don't want to walk away if there's a chance I can fix it."

Gillian continued her massage for a long time, moving her hand from one shoulder to the other. Riley closed her eyes and pulled her legs up, resting her chin on her knees.

"Can you stay?"

"I should check in at work."

"Okay."

Riley turned her head and looked at Gillian. "Do you need me to stay?"

Gillian said, "No. I'll just nap some more when you go."

Riley nodded. "I should probably go soon." She touched Gillian's cheek and pulled her close for a kiss.

When they parted, Gillian gripped Riley's collar and held her in place. "I'm serious, Riley. I want to go. I don't think I could stand living in this place very much longer after... what happened."

Riley reached up and covered Gillian's hand with her own. Every time she closed her eyes, she pictured Gillian curled up in the morgue drawer, the terror in her voice when she shrieked for them to go away. Riley was responsible for that terror. She kissed the back of Gillian's hand and said, "We'll go."

"Yeah?"

Riley nodded. "Yeah. You're more important to me than anything else. I love you."

The corners of Gillian's mouth curled. "You've never said that to me out loud."

"Yeah, I have," Riley said, picturing herself bent over a sleeping Gillian and brushing the hair out of her face. "But this time you can hear it."

Gillian kissed the corner of Riley's mouth and said, "I love you, too, Riley. Come home soon, please."

"And in one piece."

"Preferably."

Riley smiled at that and gently eased Gillian down onto the mattress. She propped herself up on one arm and said, "Close your eyes. I'll go when you're asleep."

"It may take awhile," Gillian said, her eyelids already drooping.

Riley touched Gillian's cheek. "I can wait."

Riley walked into the bullpen to find Priest was already at her desk. Riley was almost to her desk when Hathaway stepped into her office doorway and said, "Detective Parra. A minute?"

Riley stifled a groan and adjusted her path. She passed Priest's desk and whispered, "How are you doing?"

"Much better. Thank you."

Riley nodded and continued into Hathaway's office. Hathaway closed the door and stepped around Riley to lean against the corner of her desk. Riley had a flashback to the horrible night Kara died, but forced her mind back to the present. "What can I do for you, ma'am?"

"I heard there was an incident in the morgue today. Is Dr. Hunt all right?"

"Yeah, she's fine. She just needed a little time to get over the whole... thing."

Hathaway nodded. "What exactly was the thing? Priest was pretty vague about it all. She only said that Dr. Hunt had a disarming experience with one of the bodies. Is there something the replacement ME should know about?"

"No, ma'am," Riley said. "Who did you get to replace her?"

"Dr. Mill Herron," Hathaway said. She crossed her arms and said, "Riley, where were you this morning?"

Riley shrugged. "Following a lead on an open case."

Hathaway nodded toward the bullpen. "Are you sure that will follow what Priest claimed you two were doing?"

"I assume she would only have told you the truth, lieutenant, so I'm not terribly worried. We were in No Man's Land questioning a person of interest."

"What case?"

Riley sighed. "I'm not going to tell you."

Hathaway raised an eyebrow. "Excuse me?"

"I'm not going to detail every single step-by-step of my investigations. I don't have to justify my police work to you, lieutenant. Detective Priest and I were in No Man's Land following a lead, talking to someone who had information pertinent to the case in question. If the information goes anywhere, I'll fill you in. I promise. Is that all?"

"No, it's not all." Hathaway pushed off the desk and stepped forward. "If something happened in my morgue this morning, I want to know. I don't want you playing vigilante. I don't want you dragging Caitlin Priest down along with you. Have I made myself clear?"

"Perfectly," Riley said. "May I be excused now, ma'am?"

Hathaway waited a breath before she nodded and stepped back. "Go on."

Riley turned and left the office. When she was safely at her desk, she glanced across the room to make sure Hathaway's office door was closed before she leaned forward. "Priest. What did you say to Hathaway about this morning?"

"We were following a lead on a case," Priest said. "I don't think she believed me. I still looked pretty rough when I got back."

"The church didn't help?"

Priest made a so-so gesture with her hand. "It was still bad enough that she noticed. We're going to have to be careful if we go after Ethan Winn."

"When we go after him," Riley corrected. She leaned back in her chair and squeezed the bridge of her nose. She remembered her promise to Gillian, their plan to just run away and let the city sort itself out. But she had to finish this one last thing just to show the demons they had messed with the wrong cop.

Chapter Five

Riley used the database to pull up a record for Alistair Call. The few cops who had run up against him in the past believed he ran several street gangs in No Man's Land, organizing them and keeping them stocked in weapons and drugs. He'd been dragged in several different times for a variety of offenses, the most popular of which seemed to be the corruption of a minor, but nothing ever stuck to him. He was one of many such figureheads on No Man's Land, one of the reasons so many cops had just given up on the place.

There were no records of any associate using the moniker "the Duchess," but Riley wasn't surprised. She was still unnerved by how easily the demon managed to slip under her radar. She was in a hostile environment, well aware of the two demons sharing the space with her, and somehow the Duchess just... slipped out. She was going to have to pay special attention the next time their paths crossed.

Ethan Winn was another story. There were no files on him, no arrests, no record he had ever been brought in for questioning. She logged onto the internet and did a search for the name and came up with nothing. Praying he wasn't another trickster like the Duchess, she said, "Priest. What's the story on Winn?"

Priest glanced around to make sure no one was close enough to overhear and shrugged. "He's a puppet master. He likes to stay hidden. He's pretty much equal to Alistair, but he doesn't get hassled as much because so few people know to look for him."

Riley went back to the database and said, "How many others are there? I mean, in total. Just so I'll know what I'm dealing with."

"Marchosias commands thirty lieutenants throughout No Man's Land."

"Thirty isn't so bad."

"Each one commands a smaller group of underlings."

Riley said, "Naturally. How many underlings?"

"Figure at least fifty for each demon. More if they're higher up on the totem pole."

Riley groaned and rubbed her face with both hands. She remembered the scene in Marchosias' lobby. She couldn't remember how many demons there had been, but she was sure it was less than fifty. She tried to imagine thirty demons each with a legion doing their bidding, and she felt all their weight dropping onto her shoulders. "God, what have I gotten myself into?"

She rested her hands on the desk and stared at her computer screen. Thirty demonic leaders, each with a horde of their own. Every fiber of her being wanted to drive into No Man's Land that minute, exterminate each and every one of them, and damn the cost. But she knew that plan would only get her killed. She just felt so helpless every time she pictured Gillian at home in bed, holding that damn toy rabbit.

"What would happen if I killed Marchosias?"

Priest lifted her head. "For one thing, I don't think you could. No offense."

"Humor me. Would the others just go away?"

Priest leaned back in her chair and considered it. "No. They would all start jockeying for position. They would try to take over as Grand Marquis of No Man's Land. Some of them would get killed in the power struggle, but then the strongest would take Marchosias' place at the top of the hill. You might cause enough confusion for them to stop focusing on humanity for a few years, but it would just be a temporary fix."

"Long enough to get away unnoticed," Riley muttered.

Priest stood up and walked to Riley's desk. She next to Riley's chair and said, "Look at me, Riley. I don't know what you're thinking here. You cannot run. Do you understand me?"

"Why can't I? Fuck this city. All I want is Gillian. I have her. All I have to do is take her and run. Forget about Marchosias and all the demons coming after us. We can forget this town even existed."

"Can you really turn your back on your home?"

"What do you think I would possibly miss? My coworkers? The boss who forced me to have sex with her? My father, if he's even still alive. As long as I have Gillian, this city can go to hell for all I care."

"It would, Riley. Literally. This city would be consumed from the inside out. Marchosias would have free reign and then what would be standing in the way of spreading to the next town? Across the state? The country?"

Riley lashed out and swept the open files off her desk. They hit the floor with a clatter, drawing the attention of everyone in the room. Riley shot to her feet and stared down at Priest. "Why does it have to be me? Find some other patsy to take my place when I'm gone. I'm sure it wouldn't be hard for you guys. There are millionaire televangelists on TV every night getting senior citizens to send in their last five bucks. Should be easy for you to find some other idiot willing to lay down their life for a lost cause." She stormed toward the stairs and Priest followed. "Get yourself a new partner, Priest. I'm out once I finish this."

She made it to the stairwell before Priest grabbed her arm and pulled her back. Priest waited until the door was closed before she spoke. "We can't just get another champion, all right? It doesn't work like that. This city was protected by angels for centuries. Ridwan, and before him, Haniel. When Samael killed Ridwan, things were a bit traumatic to say the least. There had never been a situation like that. With the establishment in disarray, the city was unprotected. No one was assigned to it. Until someone took the mantle upon herself."

Riley groaned. "Oh, don't tell me."

"You declared yourself this city's protector when you killed Samael. If you shirk those duties, the city will be left wholly unprotected again."

"What about you? Raguel?"

Priest shook her head. "Not our department. Raguel is kind of like a manager. He keeps angels from going off the tracks. He's the Vengeance of God, so he's not going to dirty his hands with mortal affairs."

"And you?"

"I'm your guardian angel, Riley," Priest said.

Riley let the words echo in the stairwell for a moment, letting them soak in. Finally, she shook her head and said, "You're what?"

"I was sent here to keep an eye on you. Because even though you made a stupid mistake going up against Marchosias, the declaration was binding. So I was sent to make sure you didn't get struck down immediately. But I'm also here to make sure you don't try to renege on your promise. This is your job now, Riley. Keeping Marchosias from solidifying his power."

"So because I said one thing in the heat of the moment, you guys own my ass for the rest of my life?"

"We're not that arbitrary, or cruel. You're special, Riley. And don't ask me why, I'm not privy to the details. But that tattoo on your back... you have to know that's not an ordinary piece of artwork. You saw what happened with the Duchess' hand. That kind of power doesn't happen accidentally."

The door opened and a uniformed officer stuck his head in. He looked at the two of them and said, "Uh, Detective Parra? You have a call."

"Who is it?"

"He just said, 'Call for Parra.'"

Riley glanced at Priest. "Send it to my desk."

The officer nodded and said, "Line six."

Riley led the way out of the stairs, following the officer across the room. She lifted the phone as she sat down, waiting until Priest was at her own desk before pressing the six button. "Detective Parra. To whom am I speaking?"

"That was a nifty trick with the tattoo. I fully expected you to have an ace up your sleeve, but nothing of that caliber. The Duchess may lose that hand. I hope you're happy."

"Thrilled, Mr. Call." Riley picked up her pen. "So why don't you keep my happy mood going and tell me what I want to know. Who sent the demons after Gillian?"

"If I give you an answer, you'll owe me, Detective. We'll be sort of like partners. Won't that be fun?"

"This isn't a quid pro quo situation, Ali. This is a 'you tell me what you want, you get to live another day' sort of thing. So why don't you go ahead and give me that name before you crawl back into your hole?"

Alistair sighed. "Fine. Although I'm sure your lovely partner has already told you what name I'm going to say. And how is Zerachiel? Listening in, I assume. Quite a nice change, seeing you as a female. Interesting choice." He sighed, getting back on topic. "The name is Ethan Winn. Your partner will know how to find him. It has been a pleasure speaking with you, Detective Parra. I'm sure we'll soon get a chance to discuss that tattoo at length. Goodbye for now, Riley."

Riley hung up the phone and looked across the room at Priest. "We're going to have to come up with a lie to tell Hathaway."

"You let me take care of that," Priest said. "I'll be right back."

Riley watched her go, and picked up the phone to dial Gillian's cell phone. After a handful of rings, she was about to give up when Gillian answered. "Hey, don't hang up. I'm here."

"Hey. Were you sleeping?"

"Dozing," Gillian said. "It's all right. I was dreaming about you."

Riley smiled and leaned back in her seat. "Oh, yeah?"

Gillian chuckled. "I was thinking about what we were going to do when we get out of this place. I got an offer from a hospital in New York. They could probably always use cops out there, so you would have a place to work."

"Yeah," Riley said. "Jill..."

"Uh-oh. What's going on?"

"Nothing. I promise. It's just that there's something I have to do. A case I'm working on. I'm not sure when I'll get home tonight. I may miss dinner."

Gillian's voice hardened. "I know we haven't been together very long, but I do know that tone. You're lying to me. You're going after whoever tried to attack me this morning."

Riley looked down at her fingers, ashamed that she was so transparent while proud that Gillian loved her enough to read her so well. "Jill, I can't just ignore what they did to you."

"I'm not asking you to. I'm just asking you not to exchange your life for mine. I'm in one piece, I'm alive. There's no need for another Riley Parra Suicide Mission."

Riley looked across the room at Hathaway's closed door. "They need to know. They need to know I won't lie down."

"Why? Why does it matter if we're leaving, Riley?"

Riley reached up and touched her shoulder. She could almost feel the tattoo burning under her shirt. "Sweetheart..."

"No, Riley, no." Gillian sighed, and her breath carried across the receiver like broken waves. Riley closed her eyes before the sound made her cry, too. "We'll talk about it tonight, because I know nothing I say now will keep you from running off like a chicken with her head cut off. But be safe. Come back to me."

"I will," Riley said. "I love you."

"I love you, too."

They hung up and Riley took a moment to compose herself. She took her gun from the drawer, slipped it into the holster, and went to Hathaway's office. She knocked lightly before she opened the door and stepped inside. "Priest? You about ready... to go...?" She frowned at the sight that greeted her.

Priest stood behind Hathaway's desk, her hands on Hathaway's shoulders. Hathaway's eyes were closed, her head rolled forward as if she were asleep. Priest said, "Hello, Detective Parra. Say hello, Nina."

Hathaway slurred, "Hello."

Priest squeezed, and Hathaway sat up straighter.

"Nina? Detective Parra and I are going into No Man's Land on assignment from you. Do you remember that, Nina?"

"Mm-hmm."

"What was the assignment?"

Hathaway frowned as if the question was unexpectedly difficult, then focused on Riley. She pressed her lips together and cleared her throat. "Detective Parra. I'm glad you're here. I need you and Detective Priest to go into No Man's Land. Your confidential informant, Muse, called with a tip relating to the Harmon case. I want you to get out there as soon as possible and see what he has to say." She swallowed, frowned, and moved her lips as if there was suddenly a bad taste in her mouth. She focused on Riley, and then turned to look over her shoulder at Priest. "What...?"

"Feeling better, lieutenant?"

"Yes. I... I, uh..." She shook her head as Priest walked around to the front of the desk. She straightened her shoulders and said, "Did I call you both in here?"

"Yes, ma'am," Priest said. "You gave us the assignment to check out Muse's information."

Hathaway nodded. "Oh, of course. Yes." She checked her watch and said, "You better hurry. You know he doesn't like to be kept waiting."

"No, he doesn't," Riley agreed. "We'll be back as soon as we can." She turned and followed Priest out of the office, closing the door behind her. They were halfway down the stairs before curiosity got the better of her. "Why can't we use that on everyone?"

"Because it's not a parlor trick. I know how big a deal this is to you. I knew that you would have gone into No Man's Land with or without permission. I figure this way, you get the option of back-up."

"Still. A stubborn eyewitness, a suspect who doesn't want to cooperate..."

Priest grabbed Riley's shoulder and pressed her against the wall. "I will not use it unless absolutely necessary, in the event of an absolute crisis. The things it does to the human mind... it's not pretty. Lieutenant Hathaway will probably be feeling the effects of it for weeks, but she won't know quite what's wrong. Every time I do it, I feel like I'm raping the person. So do not ever, ever ask me to do it just to make your job a little easier, am I understood?"

"Yeah," Riley said. "Sure. Whatever."

Priest backed up and rolled her shoulders. She smoothed down her hair, took a few calming breaths, and said, "Sorry. I just... I hate the feeling. Let's go."

Riley led Priest lead the way down the stairs. She had been partners with Caitlin Priest for almost a month, but she was starting to think she still hadn't truly met Zerachiel. She dreaded the situation where Priest would let her true nature take over completely. Riley straightened her shirt and headed downstairs behind her partner.

Chapter Six

"Alistair said you would know where to find Winn. You got a feeling?"

Priest nodded slowly. "Riley, you have to understand this is a trap."

"I would expect nothing less from a demon. Just point me where I need to go."

"They'll be at the firehouse. I'm sure Winn showed up there five minutes after we left. He and Alistair will have taken good use of their time to prepare for you coming back."

"Can I count on you as back-up?"

Priest pressed her lips together and looked out the window. "I don't know. I will be slightly better prepared than I was the first time, but it took a lot out of me to take down the Duchess. And I only managed to temporarily take her out of the equation. There's a chance she'll be back to full power already."

Riley shuddered. The thought of that woman slinking around in the shadows without being seen gave her the creeps. "Is there any way you can make me immune to whatever she does to block herself from my sight?"

"No. I couldn't see her myself, not in the way you're thinking about. There was a concentration of dark forces all around you. All I could do was focus on it. And then she touched your tattoo and the spell shattered."

Riley nodded and thought back to Alistair's reaction to the artwork. "Do you know anything about the tat?"

"I've never seen anything like it. The design or its effect."

"Samael had the same problem with it," Riley said. "His hand burned even though he touched it through my shirt. It's the only reason I survived our fight."

Priest nodded and frowned as Riley turned right at the intersection. "I thought we were going into No Man's Land."

"We are. I just have to make a stop first."

She drove until she found a Catholic church and she parked in front of the steps. "Come on in. Juice yourself up before the big fight."

Priest shrugged and got out of the car. She followed Riley into the building, pausing to take a knee as she crossed the threshold. The interior of the church was lit with flickering candles. Riley expected music or at least conversation, but was greeted instead by a weighted silence. She walked directly to the holy water font and cupped her hands. She pushed her hands under the water, soaking the cuffs of her shirt, and closed her eyes. "Priest, you want to help me out with this? I'm kind of a heathen here."

"What is it you want me to do?"

"I don't know," Riley said. "Pray? Bless the water?"

"The water is already blessed. But without faith..."

"I know, I know, it's just water. But if I have faith it'll work, then that should count for something, right?"

Priest looked at the water and then put her arm around Riley. She rested her palm over Riley's tattoo and closed her eyes. Riley self-consciously scanned the church, trying to see if anyone was watching their little ritual. Priest's hand grew warm on her back and she shifted uncomfortably until the heat went away.

"Amen," Priest said.

Riley pulled her hands from the water and, without thinking, dumped her handfuls of water over her head. She soaked her shirt, spluttered and wiped the water from her eyes. She smoothed her hair down with her palm, her long hair plastered to her head. "What the hell?" Riley said to Priest. "Couldn't hurt, right?"

"I suppose," Priest said. She dipped two fingers into the water and crossed herself. "Are we ready to go now?"

"Yeah," Riley said. She looked toward the front of the church. They also had a crucifix hanging over the pulpit, a white Jesus as opposed to Father Jacob's church, staring mournfully down at the sinners congregating before him. The statue made Riley uneasy; the constant guilt trip hanging in front of you every week, the knowledge that no matter how many pews you sat in or how many times you hit your knees and sang a little song, you would never pay back what you owed. She didn't know how people could live that way.

"Yeah," she said again. "We're ready. Let's get out of here."

Riley parked across the driveway of the firehouse again. As she climbed from the car, she looked at the sky and watched heavy clouds rolling in.

"Well, that's kind of cliché," she said. "Convenient mood lighting."

"It's the demons inside," Priest said. "They're drawing their power. It causes all kinds of atmospheric disturbances. Rain, hurricanes... you remember what happened when Samael fell."

"Vaguely. Angels cause storms, too?"

"Thousands every day across the world," Priest said. She looked warily up at the firehouse door and pulled her gun from the holster and examined it closely. "I was hoping I could masquerade as a cop without having to use this thing. I heard most cops go their entire career without drawing their weapon once."

"A lot of cops say that," Riley said as she walked toward the door. "None of those cops work No Man's Land. You do know how to use it, though?"

"Yeah," Priest said. "I'm not sure whether I hope it will do any good or not. I don't fancy the idea of shooting any living thing, even if it is a demon."

"You'll get over that once they start shooting at you."

Riley walked up to the man-sized door and tried the knob. It was unlocked, so she turned and shrugged at Priest. "Looks like they were maybe expecting us." She stepped to one side and pushed the door open with her foot, leading with her gun as she stepped inside. The garage was just as dark as that morning, and Riley could hear whispering voices in the darkness. Her mind flashed back to the time in the lobby of Marchosias' building when the demons first overwhelmed her, flooding her mind and senses as they tried to drag her inside.

"Stay calm, Riley," Priest said from behind her. "I have your back."

Most of the holy water had evaporated during their drive to the firehouse, but she could feel some of it dripping from her hair and pooling under her collar. She wasn't sure if it was completely a mental component, but she actually did feel calmer. She kept both hands on her weapon, resisting the urge to wipe the water away from her face. The garage seemed deserted, but she wasn't about to take that at face value after what happened last time.

"Mr. Call," Riley shouted. Her voice echoed against the bare concrete. "Mr. Winn? I thought we could have a nice conversation about what happened this morning."

"Riley," Priest whispered. Riley glanced back and saw Priest nod toward the ravaged fire truck. A thin person wearing a football jersey was perched on top of the cabin, watching her with a wide smile on his face. When he knew she had seen him, he flipped around on his hands and knees and scurried out of sight like a cockroach under the glare of a kitchen light. "I saw two others," Priest said.

"Call off your boys, Alistair," Riley said. "We're just going to have a nice chat."

"You reek of holy," Alistair said, his voice coming from everywhere around them.

Riley lifted a shoulder as she moved closer to the foot of the stairs. "Yeah, well, you hang around with angels long enough..."

"It's just a simple talk, Alistair," Priest said. "Don't make it more than it is."

"Zerachiel!" Alistair said. "Winn was so hoping you would come back this time. He was so envious of the fun we had with you last time."

Priest said, "Yeah, I'm sure the Duchess can't wait to see me again."

"Unfortunately, the Duchess is still mending from your little attack. Worshippers aren't what they used to be. It's taking the poor dear a while to gain enough power to properly heal."

"My heart weeps," Riley said. She reached the bottom of the stairs and pressed her back to the wall, dropping into a crouch so she could see the floor above. "Is Mr. Winn actually here? I would love to talk with him about what happened this morning. Of course, if he's not willing to talk with me directly..."

"I am here, Detective Parra."

The voice was like thick velvet, the voice of a late-night disc-jockey on a blues station. Each word was clipped as if it was carved from stone before spoken.

Riley said, "Why don't you come down here where we can speak like civilized people."

"That is unlikely. I am a demon and you are a police officer. How can evil incarnate and a thug with a gun hope to emulate civilization?"

Riley rolled her eyes. She looked back toward Priest and saw that she was looking back and forth across the garage, her gun lowering as if she was focused on something else. Riley watched her while she spoke. "You threatened my girlfriend. Why? A power play to oust Marchosias? Trying to earn brownie points?"

"You are a small thing," Winn said. "You are a mortal. This morning was merely a demonstration of what you are getting yourself into. I am merely a lieutenant of Marchosias. Imagine the kind of power he has. Imagine attempting to stop that when all you have is a puny gun and the lifespan of a human being. Quit now while you are still in one piece."

"Riley," Priest whispered. She moved closer and said, "There are windows in here."

Riley frowned and whispered, "Yeah, I noticed the architecture. I want to do my living room like th—" She stopped when she realized what Priest meant. The sky overhead was filled with storm clouds, but it was still early afternoon. There should have been some light. Riley pushed away from the wall and looked toward the ceiling. "How did Gillian describe the creature in the morgue?"

"Darkness," Priest said. "Absence of light."

"Shit," Riley said. She straightened, realizing it was stupid to try and find cover when the person they were after was already surrounding them. "Ethan Winn, I presume."

The smoke coalesced in the middle of the room, taking on a vaguely human shape. Priest stepped back from it, her lips pressed tightly together.

"You okay?" Riley said.

"I'm nauseated," Priest managed. She swallowed hard and shook her head. "It'll be fine. I'll be fine."

Alistair came down the stairs, hands in his pockets. He still wore the self-righteous smirk. "I was hoping to have fun with you for a while longer, Detective Parra," he said. "I applaud you on your ingenuity. Looks like it won't be as easy to fool you as it was the first time we met. Marchosias asked me to give you something." He took his hand from his pocket and reached into his jacket. He fished around and then smiled. "Ah, here it is. Catch."

He tossed something at Riley, and she stepped out of its trajectory. She kept her gun steady on him and glanced at the object out of the corner of her eye.

It was a thin, laminated card with a metal clip on one end. It landed face down, but Riley knew exactly what it was. She had pulled the clip off of Gillian's scrub top enough to recognize the morgue ID. She focused on Alistair and tried to control her breathing. "Where is she?"

"Oh, my Lord," Priest gasped.

"What is it?" Riley said. Her voice was raw, tears burning the corners of her eyes.

"We burnt the Duchess. If she doesn't have enough worshippers to heal, then she'll go to plan B. Demons don't allow themselves be crippled for long."

Riley frowned. "Plan B?"

"Possession, my dear detective," said a woman disgustingly smooth, seductive voice. A familiar purr underlined the words. Riley's blood went cold and she finally lowered her gun.

Gillian stood at the base of the stairs, wearing a white blouse and a flowing tan gown. Her hair was wet and smoothed down against her skull, her teeth showing as she crossed the floor toward Alistair. "The last thing you said to each other was a declaration of love," the Duchess said with Gillian's voice. "You should be grateful. So few get that opportunity."

"Let her go," Riley growled. Her voice was feral, her teeth clenched hard enough to hurt.

The Duchess laughed. "That won't be happening, dear. Did you really think you could call down a demon for a chat? Did you think you would punish him for what he did to sweet Gillian Eleanor Hunt? That is not what this meeting is about, Riley Parra."

Priest suddenly groaned and clutched her stomach. Riley couldn't tear her eyes from the blasphemy of Gillian's face to check on her. Priest hit one knee and her wings spread out from her back, reaching out to their full span. "Riley..."

"You wanted to ensure no one ever hurt Gillian again," the Duchess said. "You wanted to be together with her, and to be safe. We're prepared to offer that to you."

Riley saw Ethan Winn moving closer to her.

"Possession," Priest gasped.

"We'll be together forever. Nothing will hurt us. All you have to do is accept him."

Something cold and clammy touched the back of Riley's neck and she hunched her shoulders to get away from it.

"Just relax," the Duchess said in a soothing whisper, far too like Gillian's voice for comfort. "It will be over before you know it. And you and Gillian will be together forever."

Riley closed her eyes and felt tears rolling down her face. She felt Ethan Winn's approach, a skip in her heartbeat as he moved within arm's reach of her. All it would take was a moment. She prayed she wouldn't be conscious for the depravity. She parted her lips to let him in.

Chapter Seven

The Duchess tightened her grip on the back of Riley's neck, her smile widening as Ethan Winn's lips touched Riley's. Riley released her gun and brought up her right hand, moving slowly, letting both demons distract themselves on her imminent conversion. Right before Ethan completed the kiss, Riley shoved her hand upward. Her palm, which had been pressed against the grip of her rifle, was sweaty and still wet from being dipped in holy water. Her fist passed through Ethan's "head," and he recoiled with a god-awful screech.

The Duchess' eyes widened and Riley turned and slapped her across the face. It tore out a piece of her to watch her hand hit Gillian, and she resisted the urge to drop to her knees and beg forgiveness. The demons backed off and Riley retreated, dropping down next to Priest. "Are you all right?"

"No," Priest said. She looked at the demons, eyes red and watering, and said, "Focus on them. Ethan Winn can—"

A sudden gust of wind knocked Riley and Priest off their feet. Riley sprawled, and Priest went flying like a piece of paper on the breeze. Her wings caught the gust and carried her all the way across the room until she was enveloped in shadows. Ethan moved forward, his form a little less composed. "Bitch!" he howled as he stalked toward Riley.

"Why didn't I soak my bullets?" Riley muttered. She got to her feet and prayed she had enough holy water on her head and shoulders to make what she was about to do count. She ran forward, her head bowed as she charged. Ethan stepped to one side to avoid her, as she figured he would, and she waited until she was next to him to throw her body to the side.

She passed through the mist, as could be expected, and a part of his gossamer body passed across her right shoulder.

Ethan howled again as the tattoo burned a trail through his body. Riley came out the other side deathly pale, shuddering as if she had just gone for a walk in Antarctica in her pajamas. She stumbled and turned to find the

Duchess walking casually toward her. "You will watch your heart beat in your girlfriend's hands," she swore. "You will die knowing that I used her body to kill you."

"Okay. And then what are you going to do about her?"

The Duchess started to move forward, but Priest was too fast for her. She wrapped her wings around the Duchess and white light began to pour from them both. The Duchess screamed in Gillian's voice, and a rusty nail tore through Riley's heart. She bit the inside of her cheek to keep from screaming at Priest to stop hurting her. She rolled onto her front and pushed herself up, wiping the back of her sleeve across her lips. She could still taste whatever made up Ethan's darkness as if they'd been brushed by a rotten banana peel.

"How long can you hold her?"

"I don't want to push it. Riley, Ethan resurrects the dead. Not as they were, as they are. He did it to the bodies in Gillian's morgue and the firemen..."

"Right," Riley said.

Priest suddenly cried out, and her light wavered. Riley turned away, knowing there was nothing she could do, and focused on Ethan and Alistair. Both had vanished into the shadows. Riley ran across the garage, her shoes echoing on the concrete, and scanned for any kind of movement. She reached the fire truck and climbed onto the side runner, peering in through the broken windows. The seats were torn apart, the dashboard gutted of the radio and other niceties. The steering column was intact, however, and a key ring decorated with a rabbit's foot hung from the ignition. The floor was filled with fetid ooze.

Ethan Winn said, "You're only making this difficult on yourself, Detective Parra. You'll never get out of this building alive."

"People keep telling me that," Riley whispered.

Something grabbed her from behind, and she found herself hauled down off the truck and tossed to the concrete floor. She yanked the gun from the holster and brought it up as she fell, firing blindly behind her. She saw only a glimpse of the dead fireman's face before it rocked back with the impact of the bullet. Riley was moving as soon as she hit the floor, pushing with her feet to get away from the truck and the horrific dead man. Across the room, the Duchess and Priest were still entangled in a column of light.

Three firemen corpses stood between Riley and the stairs. She was sure Alistair had disappeared to the upper level, but she didn't relish the idea of trying to get past the zombies. They still wore their turnout jackets and helmets, their faces a charred horror story behind the glass masks. One of them carried an axe in a glove that wrinkled as if it was empty, but she knew it was simply skeletal.

Riley moved along the edge of the truck, and the remnants tracked her movements. "Don't worry, guys," she said as she climbed back onto the runner. "Don't mind me." She saw the fireman who she shot in the head lurking to her right near the front of the vehicle. She fumbled over the side of the truck until she found the controls. She remembered the story the demon told her; the fireman died on their way to a fire. She prayed that meant their tanks were full, and the water hadn't evaporated as she twisted the knob.

She heard the rush of water in the mechanism and moved to the back of the truck. The firemen saw what she was doing and rushed her, making quiet hissing sounds low in their throats as they moved. Riley saw one of them stumble, his leg apparently breaking inside of his pants, and grabbed the hose from the back of the truck. She tucked the hose against her side, aimed the nozzle at her pursuers, and pressed the heel of her hand against the lever on the handle.

The water shot out in a clear, solid blast. She hit the first body mid-chest and knocked him off his feet, then swung the hose around to hit the other three. She continued firing until they had all been pushed to the far side of the room, then she dropped the hose and made a break for it. The zombies didn't get up; she figured every remaining bone they had was now broken.

She didn't think of anything as she raced up the stairs; all she could see was Gillian's beautiful smile, her self-conscious smirk when Riley caught her singing along with the radio. The way she ruffled her hair after pulling a T-shirt over her head, and the way she covered her mouth with her fingers when she yawned. The way she said Riley's name at work compared to how she whispered it at home.

When she reached the top of the stairs, she spotted Alistair standing among the velvet sofas. "That was rather impressive, Detective Parra. I've never seen a human stand up to something like that and maintain their sanity."

Riley fired twice, and Alistair's body jerked with the impacts. He grunted, shook his head and said, "Honestly. Haven't you learned anything yet?"

"Bullets don't kill you," Riley said. "But they make you bleed." She slammed into him and reached into her hair, running her fingers through the strands. They came back wet.

"What are you—"

Riley shoved Alistair down onto the couch, straddling him like a lover. She pressed her hand against one of his wounds and the moisture seemed to be sucked into his body.

Alistair's body went rigid, his eyes wide as the holy water seeped into his blood. "No, no, no! You bitch! You bitch!"

Riley pressed harder, perched on her knees so she could bring her full weight against his chest. Blood and water mixed together on her palm and Alistair's body went into spasms. "You messed with the wrong fucking bitch," she growled. "You and all of your kind will pay for what you did to Gillian. Because I believe in holy water. I believe it will fuck you up."

Alistair's shriek became too piercing for Riley to bear, and she jerked away from him. The damage was done. As she stumbled away, she saw his flesh began to blacken and blister. The couch underneath him burst into flames and he was engulfed by them. Alistair stopped shouting curses at her and convulsed, his body eaten from within by the holy fire.

Riley finally managed to turn away from the disgusting site and ran for the stairs. Her shoes pounded the stairs, which she belatedly noticed were wooden. The first was already spreading across Alistair's den of iniquity and would soon engulf the entire structure. "Not good, not good at all."

When she reached the bottom of the stairs, she saw Priest kneeling over Gillian's prone body. The splinters in Riley's heart twisted and she dropped to her knees next to her limp girlfriend. She pulled Gillian's head into her lap and stroked her wet hair. "Caitlin. Please, don't tell me..." She looked up at Priest and barely kept herself from recoiling.

The angel's features were drawn, her face a death mask. She swallowed with great difficulty and rasped, "She is alive. Barely."

"So are you." Riley knelt and gathered the limp, but still warm, body into her arms. She looked at the face and realized the truth. The Duchess was gone. She cradled Gillian to her chest and said, "We have to get out of here."

"That won't be so easy," Priest said. Her voice sounded like wind blown through torn sheets. Riley wondered how she was still standing. "We have company."

The sound of fire was coming down the stairs, and Riley knew it was only a matter of time before the garage was ablaze. But her main concerns were the dark gremlins lining the exterior walls. They were bunched together near every exit. "Shit," Riley said. She doubted the holy water trick would work again, let alone whether she would be able to pull it on all of them. "They won't let us pass just because their boss is dead, will they?"

"No. The one who kills you will become the new leader."

Riley looked at the fire truck and said, "Think God is getting sick of saving my ass?"

"What are you thinking?"

"The ghost truck had water. Maybe it'll drive."

"Not a chance in hell."

Riley shrugged and ran to the driver's side. The demons, wary of a distraction meant to draw them from the doors, stayed put and watched. Priest climbed into the truck, keeping her feet away from whatever was flowing on the floor, and Riley gently transferred Gillian to her arms. She pulled herself up and gripped the ignition. "If you have any pull with the guy upstairs, I suggest you use it now."

"I'm calling in every favor I've ever had right now."

Riley closed her eyes, turned the keys, and felt her heart stop.

The engine roared to life.

Riley yanked the door closed as the demons realized her plan. They surged toward the fire truck as Riley slammed her foot down on the gas. The fire truck lurched forward and Priest said, "Wait, Riley, slow down, where did—"

The truck crashed through the ancient garage door, splintering it around the truck's block face. A moment later, it slammed into Riley's car and demolished the passenger side.

"Where did you park," Priest muttered.

"Whoops," Riley said. The storm that was brewing when they first arrived pelted the truck with fat, quarter-sized drops of rain. She swung the wheel around, taking them out onto the main street. "We got any hitchhikers?"

Priest looked in the long, thin side mirror and then leaned out the window to look back with her own eyes. "No, no one." She reached over and clicked the windshield wipers on and off to clear the windshield, but nothing happened. She shook her head and said, "Looks like we used up all of our prayers."

"You better hope we haven't," Riley said. She looked down at Gillian, her head lying in Priest's lap, and tried to ignore how lifeless she looked. She bit the inside of her cheek and stood on the gas pedal, driving the ancient fire truck through the streets of No Man's Land as the rain pounded down all around them.

Epilogue

Riley helped Priest down the aisle, Priest's arm tight around her shoulder. She felt as if she weighed ten pounds, nothing but skin and bone under her clothes. Riley walked her to one of the back aisles and sat her down, kneeling next to her to make sure she was going to stay upright. "We should have brought you here first."

"No. Gillian needed the hospital worse." She licked her lips and swallowed. "I'll be fine. You go be with her."

Riley said, "The Duchess...?"

Priest shook her head.

"Exorcised?"

"No," Priest said with a quiet chuckle. "That would have been easy. But there was no guarantee it would have stuck. I had to make sure the Duchess really left and wasn't just... pretending."

Riley nodded. "So Gillian is Gillian."

"Yes." She sighed and tried to lie down in the pew.

Riley winced at the way Priest moved, her body twitching now and then with some new pain. She waited until Priest was lying down and said, "Is there anything I can do for you?"

"Pray."

"Yeah," Riley said.

She stood up, and Priest said, "Riley... this was a battle. A small battle. We killed three out of thirty, and Marchosias is still out there somewhere. We only won a battle. The war hasn't even started yet."

"I know," Riley said.

"I'm just telling you. You should be prepared."

"For what?"

Priest looked away and closed her eyes. "Casualties."

Riley winced and looked away, focusing on the altar at the front of the church. When she looked back down, Priest appeared to be asleep. She slipped out of the pew and walked down the aisle toward the doors. She hated leaving Priest there, but she couldn't bear to be away from Gillian longer than necessary. The doctors were competent, and she was sure they were doing everything they could, but she felt that if she wasn't physically at Gillian's side, then something terrible was going to happen. As bad as she felt leaving Priest on her own, she couldn't be in two places at once.

At the front of the sanctuary, Riley paused next to the holy water font. She stepped over to it and thought of Alistair's anguish as he died. She thought of Gillian's pain, and the death they had planned for her and Priest. Maybe there was something to the stuff after all.

She dipped her fingers into the water and crossed herself. "Caitlin Priest." She repeated the move. "Riley Parra." And once more, this time pressing the fingers hard against her body. "Gillian Eleanor Hunt."

Riley didn't want the bed offered by a kind-hearted nurse. She didn't want coffee or dinner. She sat in the uncomfortable blue armchair next to Gillian's bed until dawn, then walked the halls just to clear her mind. She couldn't stop shaking. She couldn't stop worrying that Gillian's heart monitor would suddenly flatline, or that her eyes would open and she would speak in that horrible Duchess voice.

The doctors had no idea what had caused Gillian's comatose state; there was nothing physically wrong with her. For all they could tell, she was simply asleep. She just wasn't waking up. There was nothing they could do but monitor her condition.

Late on the second day of Riley's vigil, Lieutenant Hathaway arrived. She looked at Gillian and then nodded to Riley and said, "As long as you need, Detective."

After three days, Riley was physically weak. She refused to sleep, although she did doze with her head resting on Gillian's chest. She wanted to be close in case Gillian woke up. She finally relented and let the nurses bring her food, but she ended up only picking at the meals. On the fourth day, it started to rain. Riley went to the window and pressed her forehead against the cold glass. The rain cascaded down the other side of the window and she closed her eyes, hoping the rain would wash away all the crap in No Man's Land. Just clean everything up and wash it down to the river.

Her eyes were closed, her lips moving soundlessly through a prayer, when she heard something moving behind her. She turned and saw Gillian shifting under the blankets, her hand coming up to touch her forehead. She murmured, "Riley, have you showered yet? You have to go to work."

Riley moved to the bed and took Gillian's hands. "Hey. Hey, baby. Nice to see you awake."

Gillian looked around the room and seemed to realize where she was. "How long was I away?"

"A couple of days." She kissed Gillian's knuckles.

Gillian shook her head. "I meant... how long was I... h-her?"

Riley said, "No more than an hour or two."

Gillian closed her eyes and then squeezed them shut tighter. "I keep hearing her in my head. Awful things she said, and showed me... trying to make me shut down."

"She's gone now. Priest saved you."

"I remember. She is so beautiful, Riley."

Riley smiled.

Gillian's smile faded. "Is she dead?"

"I don't know. I don't think so." She brushed Gillian's hair and said, "I'm going to be here every night until they let you go home. Then I'll take some time off, wait on you hand and foot at home. We're going to get through this together."

Gillian brushed Riley's palm with her thumb. "I know you want that. But I also know it's not possible. So I'm going to stay with my mother for a few days."

"Your mother... in Georgia?"

"Yeah. I have to get away from this city, Riley. They're going to keep coming after me just to get to you. I'm not strong like you. I can't deal with all of this."

"I'll leave with you, Jill."

Gillian rolled her head against the pillow and said, "Riley, I know I was pushing for that. And I love that you're willing, but it's not possible. So just listen to what I have to say, and accept it. All right? For some reason, you've been chosen. You're going to bring this city back from the brink. And I know I should be there to help you, but I can't. I'm an anchor. I'm your weakness. You'll never do what you need to do if you're worried about me."

"This city doesn't mean jack to me if you're not here," Riley said. "You're the only reason I give a damn."

Gillian touched Riley's cheek and said, "No. It's not. There's something special about you, Riley. It's why you were chosen. You need to stay here.

And I need to go."

Riley pressed Gillian's hand against her forehead and let out a strangled sob.

Gillian put her hand on top of Riley's head and shushed her. "It's okay, Riley. It's not forever. I'll be back."

"Promise?"

"I swear," Gillian said.

The door opened and Riley heard the squeak of a nurse's shoes. Gillian said, "Could we have a moment, please?" The door closed again, and Riley turned Gillian's hand over. She kissed the palm, and then the tip of each finger.

"Do what you have to do," Riley said, barely keeping her voice steady.

Gillian nodded. "Same to you, Riley."

Riley put her head back down, this time on Gillian's stomach, and closed her eyes. Gillian stroked Riley's hair and turned her head, watching the rain streak down the windows.

Open and Shut, No. 2:
All Mortal Flesh

The church was an ancient affair, or as ancient as things got in America. Probably built in the late 1800s, reminiscent of old churches in Europe and England. The windows were stained glass, discretely lit by tiny spotlights, and candles flickered in covered sconces. She could hear people deep in the back of the church, voices and laughter, but she knew no one would disturb her. She waited until Riley left before she let the true pain of her ordeal show. Being in the demon's den took a lot out of her, more than she was prepared to admit, and destroying the Duchess nearly took the rest.

The pain was a shock, a revelation, and a part of her brain refused to believe she would ever feel normal again. She had never known pain, never thought of what it would be like. Her entire existence had been spent as an angel. Even when there were wounds, they were different than what humans would recognize. Spiritual wounds, tears in the fabric of faith, enough to cause sorrow, but nothing like what she was experiencing now.

Worship helped. Churches were the closest approximation humanity had to what she was used to. Voices singing praise echoed the heavenly host, filled her with light and gave her strength to mend her wounds. She closed her eyes and breathed deep, letting the consecrated air wash over her.

Another pain she hadn't expected was the pain of dislocation. When Samael fell, Zerachiel felt the shockwaves in her bones. It was the deepest ache she had ever felt, throwing her to her knees as she prayed for the surcease of her agony. And then a hand touched her forehead, brushed her tears away, and an offer was whispered to her. She replied without hesitation, and she became another being. She felt bound, her body twisted and molded to take an unnatural shape.

When her mind stopped reeling, when her senses returned, she found herself in a church. She was kneeling at an altar, head bowed, and raised her eyes to the statue of Christ on the cross hanging before her. She bowed her head again, whispered a prayer of thanksgiving, and pushed to her feet. She went outside and breathed air into new lungs, felt the wind brush through her hair. She was female, and human. The name Caitlin floated at the front of her mind, an Irish name that meant 'pure.' It was a good name, and she felt it was appropriate for her.

The first person she saw was a priest. He was crossing the street, a bag of groceries in his arms. He smiled when he saw her, inclined his head, and said, "Blessings, my child."

Priest merely smiled, nodded a greeting, and took her new name from him. Caitlin Priest.

She spent the rest of the night walking, getting accustomed to her new world. Earth was so much noisier than she thought, dirtier, and somehow larger and more claustrophobic at the same time. As she walked, she became acclimated. She focused more on the present moment, the cars and the sounds and the people around her. She was one of them now, as much as the thought pained her. She was still an agent of her Father, and she knew that she was more than the humans around her. Her wings were still there, her holy light still deep within, but it was all contained within a fragile human shell. It was the difference between a beam of sunlight and the warmth that beam left behind.

She was Caitlin Priest, but the larger part of her was still Zerachiel. She took solace in the memories of her time among the other seraphim, closed her eyes and imagined the higher plain with the rest of her family, basking in the Father's light. Sometimes she hummed under her breath, swaying in her empty apartment to the sound of music coming from the church below. It was a balm to her soul, healing the many wounds and worries she accumulated over the course of the day.

But as another tremor of pain passed through her, she doubted even worship would help her. She bowed forward, resting her head on the back of the pew in front of her. "Help me, Father," she whispered. Tears fell from her eyes to the floor of the sanctuary, and she shuddered as she wrapped her arms around her torso.

It was hard enough for an angel to destroy a demon, let alone an angel that had descended to the mortal plain. She felt like she was going to be torn apart. She could feel the presence of the Duchess in her mind like the remnants of a terrible nightmare. Ephemeral, dark and silent, flashes of evil and hatred and pain from the corner of her eye. She knew it would fade in time, and all she had to do was bear with it until the last vestiges were nothing more than a memory.

But it was worth it. She succeeded, the Duchess was eradicated, and Gillian Hunt was, God willing, safe in the hospital. That was worth whatever happened next.

Priest knew that she may die because of what she had done. It was the tacit agreement made when she became a guardian angel. When her mortal body died - and it would die, there was never any doubt about that - she would return to Heaven to continue her existence until she was called upon again. She was eager to return, but she also knew she could wait for a very long time until that happened. She wasn't ready to leave Riley yet.

She finally felt able to sit up and face the front of the church. Rain washed down the stained glass windowpanes, and she closed her eyes to focus on the sound of the rainfall. It was only a few seconds after she sat up when she heard the footsteps coming down the aisle toward her pew. She instinctively knew it wasn't a priest, or anyone human, and she didn't have to turn to know who had been sent.

Michael sat across the aisle from her and pulled a hymnal from the slot on the back of the pew in front of him. He wore desert camouflage combat fatigues underneath a flak jacket. He was the quintessential soldier, combat boots placed far apart, holding the hymnal in one hand with the fingers splayed to keep the book from falling. He flipped through the pages until he found what he was looking for.

"Have you ever heard Maria, Mater Gratiae done out of doors? It can be... majestic." He hummed a bit of it and then closed the hymnal on his thumb.

"Hello, Michael."

"Zerachiel. You've looked better."

Priest smiled and nodded toward the altar. "Just give me a little quality time in the Father's house. I'll be fine."

Michael looked at her. "There was some commotion upstairs when the Duchess was destroyed. You took a mighty risk, Zerachiel. Gillian Hunt is not your responsibility."

"Riley Parra is. Saving Gillian kept Riley from going to pieces. Saving Gillian was, in effect, saving Riley."

"You've grown fond of your mortality, haven't you?"

Priest thought about it for a long time. She had never thought of it that way, but it was the truth. She finally said, "For ages we watched these people fight tooth and claw to stay alive. We never understood it. I've been a human for a handful of weeks now, and I can tell you why. To be alive is exhilarating. Emotions and pain and humor and grief. It's like nothing we've ever experienced."

"Our love for the Father..."

"...is similar," Priest admitted. "Stronger, perhaps, but it's nothing a human can comprehend or achieve. We always thought our way was better, and we pitied them. But it's just different. That's all. There's really no comparison."

Michael straightened his shoulders, staring at the crucifix at the front of the church. "There are those who would have you recalled. They believe you've grown too close to Riley. That you've been corrupted by your humanity."

"I have been," Priest said. "And I am close to Riley. It's what she needed, and I provided it. I will continue to provide it, with His blessing. Riley is special. She knows the chances, she can see the odds stacked against her, and she marches forward regardless." Priest smiled. "She goes where angels fear to tread, and she goes there willingly. Bravely. Without a moment's hesitation. Because it is what's necessary. Many angels could learn from her."

"Many angels could die by following her."

"But there is only me. There could be legions of angels here, standing by her side, helping her fight, but there aren't. The heavenly host is occupied elsewhere. I understand. But you would do well not to criticize the one person who is fighting the battle you are unwilling to join."

Michael chuckled quietly and said, "You seem to have gotten your strength back, Zerachiel."

Priest looked at the cross and realized he was right. She felt stronger. The pain was still there, but diminished. Just a bit. Enough to let her sit up straight and give strength to her voice. She was well enough to return home. She nodded and pushed herself up out of the pew. "So it would seem. Thank you for stopping by, Michael."

"She's dangerous," Michael said, not bothering to look up at her. "Riley. She's incredibly dangerous."

"I know." Priest smiled. "That's why Marchosias should be very afraid. Good-bye, Michael." She walked to the front of the sanctuary and dipped her fingers into the holy water. She watched it glisten on her fingers, the blessing of it tingling against her flesh. She closed her eyes and said a silent prayer before touching the water to her forehead, sternum and shoulders. "By this holy water, and by Your Precious Blood, wash away all my sins, O Lord. Protect Riley Parra. Protect Gillian Hunt."

She turned and looked back into the church, but Michael was already gone.

She rubbed her thumb against her fingertips until they weren't wet anymore. She smiled, took a final breath of the hallowed air, and stepped out of the church.

Angels Would Fall

12:32 am

The music is more of a blur than sound now, a dull thumping behind the eyes. It helps keep the fog in focus, makes her able to tell when she needs a new drink. She taps the bar with two fingers and she can tell that the bartender is thinking about refusing. She slurs something, maybe promising to make it her last drink of the evening, and the bartender finally moves to fill her glass. "Good man," she thinks she says as he takes her mug and holds it under the tap.

She presses the heel of her hand against her eye, trying to drown out all the voices all around her. Why are there so many people in her dive? God, is the place so depressingly bottom-of-the-barrel that it was hip? God save them all.

The beer is magically in front of her again, and she takes another drink. Some asshole laughs across the room and she wants to throw the mug at him. The only reason she doesn't is because she knows she'll miss and she doesn't want to be thrown out for destruction of property. She touches the tip of her tongue to her top lip, tastes the foam there, and runs a hand through her hair. It's been a while since she washed it, a longer while since she had an appropriate shower. She exhales through her nostrils and decides to see about crashing at someone's house. Maybe her partner has a shower she can use.

And then Ray Charles sticks his nose into her heartache by singing about Georgia.

Just because some jerk feels melancholy, she isn't about to sit through the whole song. She shouts for someone to turn that shit off, but no one complies. The song continues, and she can't help but think about Gillian and her retreat. Running away, across the whole damn country. They kept up with phone calls in the beginning, tried to keep connected. They quickly realized that it was too painful trying to act like nothing had happened, so the calls started to dwindle. It was five days since their last phone call, and she was starting to feel like they would never speak again.

Ray Charles won't leave her alone.

She spins around on her bar stool and says, "Would someone shut that damn thing off?" When the song continues to play, she pushes away from the bar and stumbles into the crowd. A few people bump into her, but she ignores them, focusing on the bright yellow and red toad squatting in the corner by the pool tables. She puts her beer down on a chair and grabs the jukebox, tries pulling it away from the wall, but it's too heavy.

"Hey, come on now," the bartender calls across the room.

"Just a second," she says. The jukebox stubbornly refuses to move, so she tries the next best thing. She picks up her beer glass and smashes it across the face of the machine.

As she bends to pick up a chair, someone grabs her arm and tries to pull her away. "That's enough. Closing time for you."

She swings out and her fist connects with a fleshy, doughy jaw. Someone shouts at her and her other arm is pulled back by another well-meaning jerk. She bends her knee, shifting her attacker's balance, and then throws herself back. She and the man holding her hit the jukebox, and the song finally, blessedly, stops. The light goes out, and the bar is silent except for the throbbing in her head and the angry voices in her head.

Someone grabs her by the scruff of her neck and pulls her forward. She stumbles along under the man's strength until they reach the front door. He pushes and she stumbles, then his foot meets the middle of her ass and she goes sprawling. She throws out both hands to keep from hitting the pavement and feels the grit digging into her palms. All the violence disturbs the contents of her stomach, and she throws up in the gutter.

"I don't care who you are," the bartender says. She looks back and sees him silhouetted by the doorway. "No one acts like that in my bar. Get the hell out of here."

He turns and shuts the door on her.

She pushes herself up and leans against the wall, making sure the wave of nausea is past before she tries standing. The sign next to the bar's door shows a bat hanging upside down between the words BAT'S and BELFRY. She stares at the woodcarving for a long time until she feels comfortable standing. She puts a hand against the brick wall to keep from falling and hisses as the brick touches raw, bloody skin.

Finally, still woozy, the world refusing to stay on a single axis, Riley begins the long walk to bed.

06:32 am
Riley had barely managed to fall into a fitful slumber when the door opened. It sounded like a submarine hatch, slamming and echoing through a room much bigger than the one she was actually in. She rolled onto her side and pulled the wafer-thin pillow over her head, burrowing into the warm blanket she had gotten from a nearby locker. "God, leave me alone," she said, her words muffled and distorted by the beddings.

"What's that?" Lieutenant Hathaway asked. She pulled the pillow away and tossed it onto the floor. "Did you apologize for your little tirade at the Bat's Belfry last night? Is that what you were saying?"

"Probably not," Riley admitted. She covered her eyes with her hand and said, "Could you turn out the lights when you leave?"

Hathaway stood next to the cot. "You're not on-call, Riley."

"Plenty of other beds for the other detectives," Riley said. "Or they can squeeze in next to me if they want. No funny stuff, though."

"Riley, get up." Riley grunted and forced herself into a sitting position. Hathaway shook her head. "God, have you looked at yourself lately? You look like shit. How many nights have you spent crawling from one bar to the next and then coming back here to try sleeping it off?" She sat on the cot next to Riley and said, "Burning yourself at both ends like this is just going to get you burnt out. I've had to replace too many people lately. I'm not going to replace you, too. I need my top detective back."

Riley sighed and leaned forward, her elbows on her knees and her hands covering her face. She wasn't even sure exactly how long it had been since Gillian left for Georgia. Three weeks? Four? Had she lost an entire month in her pity party? She sighed and pulled her fingers down her face, tugging her eyes and lips down in a parody of melting.

"You're right," she said. "Sorry, boss. I'll pull myself together."

Hathaway nodded and touched Riley's knee before standing up. Riley's hand shot out without thinking, slapping the hand away. Hathaway ignored the blow, and kept her hands to herself. "That's all I ask. We've all been through a bad break-up before. The trick is to just get back up and carry on."

"Yeah," Riley said. "Thanks."

"You feel up to taking an assignment?" Hathaway asked. "I've been kind of taking it easy on you and Priest, but people are starting to notice."

Riley nodded. "Sure."

"The information is on your desk. Splash some water on your face before you leave, and try to find some mouthwash. You look and smell like a drunk."

"Thanks," Riley muttered.

Hathaway went to the door and left Riley alone in the on-call room. The act of sitting on a bed with Hathaway made her tense. Hathaway seemed to have realized the line they crossed a few months back. Riley didn't know how she felt about their "encounter." She knew she should have reported Hathaway, probably gotten her fired. Or maybe Hathaway would have been safe and Riley would have quietly been reassigned. She didn't know why it didn't affect her any more than it did. She was sure Gillian had a lot to do with her getting through it unscathed.

She finally exhaled and pushed herself up off the cot. The adjacent locker room was dimly lit for the start of the day, several lockers standing open to announce they were available. Riley went to the locker she'd appropriated for herself and stripped out of her clothes. She took a rumpled maroon blouse from the locker, one of her last clean shirts, and put it on, tucking it into a pair of gray trousers.

At the sink, Riley turned on the hot water and finally dared to look at her reflection in the mirror. Hathaway's comment had been kind; what little sleep she managed to get was disrupted by dreams and nightmares, not to mention the fact that she passed out more than she fell asleep. Hardly restful. The on-call room was a terrible place to try and get any meaningful rest. People constantly came in and out, phones rang outside in the office all night long, and very few cops bothered to lower their voices when they came back from a late call.

She needed a real place to sleep, but her apartment was out of the question. She doubted the landlord would even allow her back in the building after a demon turned her bed into a chunk of charcoal. And Gillian's apartment... she just couldn't go back there and sleep alone. She had tried and she had failed. The on-call room was better than nothing, and she had no other options.

Although...

Riley splashed her face with water, finger-combed her hair, and left the locker room. It was a bad idea. A terrible idea. An idea that promised to cause nothing but strife and discord. But it would be better than nothing. In the bullpen, she grabbed the first cop she saw and said, "Is Hathaway in her office?"

"You just missed her. I think she's headed out." Riley thanked him and changed course for the stairs.

The main lobby of the four-ten precinct was the most impressive part of the entire building; mainly because it was the only place the majority of civilians would ever have to see. A long desk took up the east wall, manned by three or four sergeants depending on the time of day. The desk was backed by three huge arch windows, lit golden by the sunrise every morning. The floor was polished tile broken up by tall columns that were appropriated by bulletin boards and community information.

Riley reached the bottom of the stairs and saw Hathaway pushing through the large double doors onto the steps. "Lieutenant," she called, and hurried across the floor. She stepped out into the morning, the sunlight piercing her hangover like a knitting needle, and she squinted as Hathaway turned on the top step. Riley said, "Boss. Listen, I know it might be an awkward situation, but I was... wondering if I could... stay with you."

The kid in the cargo pants and red sweater was no more out of place than anyone else on the sidewalk, but Riley found her attention drawn to him in the middle of her question. A line appeared between her eyebrows as she watched him stride purposefully up the stairs toward the front doors. She was about to ask Hathaway if there was anything odd about him when he swung pulled the gun from the pocket of his pants.

Riley reached for her shoulder holster, pure instinct causing her to forget that it was still upstairs and she was unarmed. "Gun!" she shouted. She swung her left leg out and around Hathaway, twisting her body to cover as much of Hathaway's as she could. The stairs were mostly empty except for Riley, Hathaway and the shooter, a few pedestrians on the sidewalk and one detective pulling the door open to go inside. He turned at the sound of Riley's shout, just as the other man opened fire.

He shot six times, and the pedestrians began screaming with the first explosion. Amid the cacophony, she heard the glass front doors shatter. The sound reminded her of icicles dropping from the eaves outside of her apartment and crashing down to the dumpster in the alley, a deceptively gentle sound of destruction. As soon as the last bullet left the chamber, the kid spun on his heel and ran. Riley took half a heartbeat and turned to see if anyone was hurt.

Hathaway was already on her way down, three ugly roses blooming on the front of her white blouse. Blood spatter marred her throat and cheeks, her skin already pale as she dropped. Hathaway looked down at herself, hands shaking as she realized she had been hit. A uniformed cop suddenly appeared at Riley's side and she said, "Pressure, on the wounds," and focused on pursuit.

Riley launched herself toward the street, hitting hard enough to rattle her knees and throw her body forward. She hit the pavement with her hands, pain echoing the night before as her wounds were ripped open again. She didn't let her brain acknowledge the pain as she scraped her shoes against the pavement, heart pounding as she searched for traction. Then she was up and running.

The shooter had a good half block lead on her, but she wasn't about to let him out of her sight. She felt her hangover slip to one side to make room for adrenaline. She knew she would pay for it later, but that didn't matter at the moment. She pumped her arms and legs, willing her mind to work like a machine. All she had to do was run, and run faster than some punk kid. He looked over his shoulder and Riley tried her best to memorize his features, just in case.

A pain started in her back, a dull irregular pounding that made her worry for her heart. Her face was hot, her breath coming in angry pants between clenched teeth.

The shooter reached out and hooked his fingers around the lip of a trash can, sending it tumbling over in her path. Riley launched herself over it and hit the pavement again, losing another precious second as her shins protested the rough landing. Three more blocks and he'll be at the el station. He'll get away, a thought immediately followed by, The hell he will.

He knocked over another trash can, but this one was empty. Riley bent at the waist, grabbed the can by the handle, and hurled it. She shouted with exertion as the can left her hand, hitting the sidewalk with a metallic shudder and bouncing toward her prey. She put on another burst of speed as the can slammed into the shooter's back and knocked him off balance. He hit his knees and actually bounced on them, unable to get up immediately.

The few seconds were all Riley needed. She slammed into the shooter from behind, tackling him face-forward onto the pavement. She put a hand on the back of his head, forcing his face against the rough sidewalk as she settled her weight on top of him. "You're under arrest, you prick," she said, every work a painful gasp. Her face burned and she was sweating like mad. She tugged the gun from the biggest pocket on his calf and tucked it into the back of her belt. When she grabbed the back of her belt, she realized her handcuffs were with her gun. Way to be prepared, Riley.

Looking back the way she came, she saw a troop of uniformed cops closing in on her. "Handcuffs!" she called, holding out her hand. A pair of the silver bracelets appeared and she immediately wrenched the kid's hands back to attach them. "You have the right to remain silent. If you give up that right, the cops whose boss you just shot will delight in beating a confession out of you. Get your ass up."

She hauled him to his feet and turned him around. His cheek was torn where she'd pressed it against the pavement, beads of blood glistening on the unshaven skin. His lips curled in what was almost a sneer, almost a smile, and he said, "What makes you so sure I was aiming for her, sweetheart?" He winked and let the uniformed cop spin him around, nearly tripping on his feet as he was manhandled back toward the police station.

Riley walked behind them, trying to get her body back under control. She could barely breathe, her heart still thudding painfully against her chest. She was shocked to see the chase had barely lasted three blocks. It felt like they had crossed the entire city.

Riley said, "Around the back, guys. Take him through the back." The cops changed direction and Riley ran to the congregation of EMTs and cops. The front steps of the station were stained with blood, and cops were already taking care of blockading the scene. Riley had to show her badge to get in, thankfully the one thing she had managed to grab before leaving the lockers, and knelt next to Hathaway. A medic had already cut open Hathaway's blouse and was applying pressure to the three wounds. One was in her shoulder, the other two straddling her cleavage.

"Hey, boss," Riley said. "Looks like you got in the way."

"Looks like," Hathaway said.

Someone brushed through the crowd and knelt next to Hathaway's head. Riley looked up, surprised to see that it was Priest. "What happened?"

"Shooter," Riley said. "We got him." She looked down at Hathaway and said, "We got him. You'll get to toss him in jail for screwing up bathing suit season for you."

Hathaway smiled and tried to laugh, but it came out as a ragged cough. Blood smeared her lips, and she screwed her eyes shut in pain. "God..."

Priest reached out and brushed away the medic's hand. He didn't seem to realize he was being dismissed. Priest spread her fingers and covered the bloody pressure pads on Hathaway's chest. Riley watched, fascinated, as Hathaway's expression eased and she swallowed hard. "What are you doing?"

"Buying some time," Priest said. "Nina, I want you to look at me."

Hathaway's eyes opened, but it looked like doing so cost her quite a bit of energy.

"You're going to be okay."

"Caitlin?" Hathaway said.

"Yes, it's me, Nina."

"You're beautiful."

Riley said, "Priest, is there anything I can do?"

"Cover my hands with yours."

Riley did as she asked and Priest closed her eyes. "Nina, I want you to take care. I want you to focus on getting better. Let the professionals do their job and protect you. Everything will be all right."

"You have wings..." Hathaway said, her voice faraway as if in a dream.

Riley looked, but Priest's wings were out of sight.

Priest swallowed and said, "Sometimes, yes. Are you going to fight, Nina?"

"Yeah," Hathaway said.

Priest held tight for a moment, then withdrew her hands. The medic bent over Hathaway again, oblivious to the interruption in his care. Riley blinked and realized her hangover was no longer haunting the corners of her perception. She licked her lips and stepped back so the EMTs could load Hathaway onto a gurney. Priest said, "Riley, you're bleeding. Were you hit?"

Riley looked down at herself and saw the blood smeared over her fingers. She turned her hands over to reveal the scrapes from the night before. "It's nothing. I fell when I was chasing the shooter."

"Is that all?"

Riley ignored the question and said, "Come on. Let's go make sure the arresting officer hasn't broken any of the kid's bones."

07:08 am

Riley stood in the bathroom and watched the water spiral around the sink drain. The water was pink with her blood. She washed the wounds on her hands, wincing when she felt the tiny pebbles embedded in the torn flesh. She would have to get someone to pick them out for her. She looked into the mirror and saw that her throat and cheeks were speckled with a fine mist of blood. Lieutenant Hathaway's blood.

She wet a paper towel and carefully brushed away the stains. There were still some marks on her collar, but it would fade in and get lost with the maroon material. As soon as she was back in the building, the adrenaline wore off an all she could think about was watching Hathaway fall. The blood on her blouse, the shocked look in her eyes. And so much blood. Riley looked away from the mirror as if the memory was etched into the glass instead of behind her eyes.

She took her time cleaning up, but she finally knew she had to go back out among the living. She checked to make sure none of Hathaway's blood was in her hair before she tossed the paper towels and went back out into the main room. The bullpen was full of cops, the majority of them gathered around Hathaway's office door in a symbolic show of support. They were quiet, solemn, and Riley wished they would just go on with their day. Hathaway wouldn't want everything to screech to a stop just because she had been hurt.

She saw Priest and made her way over. "She's going to be pissed when she finds out we're losing an entire morning because of this shit."

"Maybe we just won't tell her."

Riley smirked and looked toward the stairs. "Where did they take the shooter?"

"I heard Embry saying he was still down in booking. They're going to print him, photograph him. Hopefully they'll find out if he has any priors."

"Let me know when he's safely locked away." She clapped her hands and the chatter died down. "Listen up, everybody. I was just with Lieutenant Hathaway downstairs. She was hit bad, but we've all seen people get up from things much worse. Don't start planning her funeral just yet. She's tough. We've just got to have faith that she'll pull through. Now let's all just get back to work. Hathaway will kick our asses if we fall behind because of this."

The crowd began to disperse, and Priest raised an eyebrow. "Nice job. That faith jab didn't even sound sarcastic."

Riley raised her voice, addressing the crowd but still looking at Priest. "And if anyone would like to pray, Detective Priest will be happy to lead the group."

Priest shrugged. "I actually would, you know."

"You're not fun," Riley said. "I'm going to get my hands looked at. Let me know when the shooter is through booking."

Priest nodded.

Riley looked at the wounds on her palms as she headed downstairs. The skin of her left palm was torn, the skin of the right merely abraded. If the wounds were any worse, she would have tried to annoy Priest with a stigmata comment. She barely remembered the initial injury, a testament to how drunk she had been, but the wounds were starting to sting. She rode the elevator down to the morgue without thinking, pushing the door open with her shoulder before she realized her mistake.

Dr. Millard Herron, Gillian's replacement, looked up from the latest corpse. He wore green scrubs, his wavy gray hair mostly tucked underneath a surgical cap. His eyes were wide and dark brown. He looked like an owl, the tufts of hair on either side of his head looking like mini-tornadoes. "Detective... Parra?" She nodded. "Good, nice to see you again. How may I help you?"

"I... uh, sorry. The other medical examiner used to... I won't bother you."

"Something wrong with your hands?"

"I hit them on the sidewalk. Scraped them up a bit."

"In pursuit of the ne'er-do-well that shot Lieutenant Hathaway. Ah, yes." He walked around the table and extended both hands to her. It was a moment before Riley shook the Frankenstein image and realized he wanted to see her injuries. She showed him her palms and he said, "Ah, nothing to fret about. I assume the other ME used to tend first aid to your wounds?"

"Yeah, something like that."

Herron shrugged. "Well, I'm not particularly accustomed to living patients, but I will do my best." He pointed to an empty table and said, "Disrobe and lie down."

Riley blinked at him.

He grinned. "A joke. Have a seat. I'll get the gauze."

Riley sat on the edge of the table and watched him walk away. The guy was a little odd, but she knew she would never accept anyone in Gillian's place. She'd never minded the morgue before. She was one of the few cops who didn't bother to smear Vaseline under her nose when she entered to view a body, and she didn't mind hanging out when Gillian was running a bit late. But now that Gillian was gone, the morgue seemed dark and foreboding. She just wanted to get out of there as quickly as possible.

Herron returned and placed the first aid kit next to Riley on the table. "This will be quick."

"I appreciate it."

"No problem, no problem." He washed out the wound, making sure all the little pebbles were gone, then sterilized the wound. Riley hissed and pressed her lips together. He wrapped her hand with gauze so that she looked like a bare-knuckle boxer. He repeated the move on the other hand and said, "A small wound for a great cause. I heard you caught the evil-doer who shot the lovely lieutenant."

"Word travels fast."

"Very good work." He gently patted her hands with his own. "You are good to go, Detective."

"Thanks." She slid off the table and started toward the door.

"Detective." Riley turned and Herron was walking toward her. He held out a CD and said, "This was left on the desk in the office. I assume if you're friends with the previous occupant, you could return it to her."

Riley took the CD and looked at the cover. Riley didn't know how she had missed it when she was packing; she was sure everything was in the box when she took it from the office. Maybe it fell out when she picked the box up. Or maybe she had been in such a damn hurry to finish the chore, she had gotten sloppy. Whatever the reason, she now had another excuse to make contact with Gillian. She smiled and said, "Thanks, Dr. Herron. I appreciate it."

"My pleasure."

Riley went back to the elevators and looked down at the disc.

There was shame in Gillian's eyes as she toyed with the leg of her scrubs bottoms. She wore a white T-shirt, her feet bare, and it was all Riley could do not to gather her up and hug her until she felt safe again. The apartment felt barren. Riley sat on the couch, Gillian sitting a few inches to her right. "I just need a few things from the office. Pictures, CDs, that stereo is mine. But I can't bring myself to go... back there."

"Ethan Winn is gone," Riley said. She touched Gillian's hand, warm and fine-boned. "He can't hurt you anymore."

"Maybe he can't," Gillian said. "But there will be others. That morgue is where I realized I was about to die. It's the place where I made my peace with it. Something... so much more powerful than me chose to let me live, but it could have gone the other way in a heartbeat. I know you understand what that's like, Riley. I know you do. So I hope you understand why you can't ask me to go back there. Not to pack my things, not to work."

"I understand. I'll pack your things tomorrow."

"Thank you." Gillian leaned in and kissed Riley's lips. Then she slipped off the couch and let her hand fall from Riley's grip. Riley let her hand fall, her fingers closing around the empty space where Gillian had just been.

Riley brought her hand up and pressed the gauze against her cheeks, letting it soak up her tears as she stepped onto the elevator.

07:20 am

The shooter was transferred from booking to a holding cell. Officer Sam Cooley crossed the bullpen and scanned the crowd. Riley walked up to him and put a hand on his shoulder. "Who are you looking for?"

"You, actually. The suspect demands to speak with you."

Riley kept walking. "We'll talk when his lawyer gets here."

"He doesn't want a lawyer. At least, he hasn't asked for one yet."

Riley stopped and looked toward the holding cells. "Did he ask for the cop who arrested him, or did he ask for me by name?"

"He said 'I want to talk with Detective Parra.'"

"Great," Riley muttered. She could make three guesses what a personal request meant. The shooting might not have been as straightforward as she thought. She sighed and said, "All right. Take him to the interrogation room. The one with the camera, not the two-way mirror."

"Yes, detective."

"Officer, be careful with him. Did you see *Silence of the Lambs*?"

"I read the book."

Riley said, "Impressive. Well, just think of Hannibal in Tennessee. Don't take your eyes off this prick for a second."

"Yes, ma'am."

Riley went to her desk and caught Priest's eye across the room. She motioned her partner over, and Priest weaved through the crowd. "What's up?"

"I think the shooter works for Marchosias. He asked to see me personally."

"That can't be good."

Riley shook her head. She braced her hands against the desk and closed her eyes. "Look, I would like you to have my back in there..."

"You've got it. Whatever you need."

"No. I meant that's what I want. But I think Lieutenant Hathaway needs you more. Get to the hospital. Stay with her."

Priest hesitated. "Riley, I'm your guardian angel. I don't know how much good I can do with—"

"Try, goddamn it," Riley snapped.

Priest looked like she wanted to argue some more, but she caught the look in Riley's eye and knew she would lose. "All right. I'll do what I can." She put her hand on Riley's shoulder and said, "Promise me you will stay safe. Just because we know he works for Marchosias, that doesn't mean we know what he's capable of."

"I'll be careful. Thanks, Caitlin."

"You're welcome. I'll keep you apprised of the situation."

Riley watched Priest leave the room, then left her desk to visit the interrogation rooms. She saw Cooley and another officer standing outside of Interrogation Room One, both standing at attention like Buckingham Palace guards. Cooley spotted her and gave a nod. She said, "Is he still cuffed and chained?"

"Yes, ma'am. Ankles chained together, wrists secured to the table."

"Good man." Riley knew she was risking the reputation of overkill, but she doubted any of the cops in the station would call her out over it. The punk shot a cop; whatever Riley wanted to do with him would probably be fair game. She said, "I'm going to let him sit for a while. Don't leave this door unattended even for a second. Get another officer to stand against this wall facing the door."

Cooley nodded and used his radio to call for another officer. Riley went down the hall and slipped into the observation room. The days of standing behind one-way glass weren't quite over, but they were on the way out. The observation room was an appropriated closet, filled with the best recording equipment the department could afford. A petite woman with owl-eye glasses sat in front of the monitors and looked up as Riley entered. She straightened when she recognized who had joined her. "Oh, Detective Parra."

"You're Barrett, right?"

The woman nodded. "Lauren Barrett." She was the technical expert for the station, usually found hunched over grainy security camera footage trying to turn a blob into a face. "They told me they were bringing someone into interrogation, so I thought I would get the cameras up and running."

"Good job," Riley said. The room was kept cool to protect the machines, and Riley always felt the chill as she crossed the threshold. She stuck her hands under her armpits and looked at the screen.

Both monitors showed the same image; Lieutenant Hathaway's shooter, sitting in the interrogation room. He was shackled and chained, as Cooley promised, and seemed content to sit there as long as necessary. His sneakers were gone, his white socks planted far apart on the floor. His brown hair hung over his forehead to his eyebrows. He looked like a preppie high school senior brought in for drugs.

"Are you... looking for something?" Barrett asked.

"Just wanted to get a feel for him before I went in."

Barrett nodded. "Well, he hasn't moved since the officers brought him in. He just sits there and taps the table with his fingers." She sucked her bottom lip into her mouth and then whispered, "I think he's really creepy."

Riley nodded. "You and me both, kid."

The floor of the interrogation room was carpeted after a suspect tried to beat his brains out on the concrete floor, but that was the only creature comfort. The walls were plain white drywall and offered nothing to draw a suspect's attention.

Riley rolled her shoulders and focused on the kid. She knew he was working with Marchosias, she just wasn't sure of his plan. Had he intended to shoot Hathaway and disappear into the crowd? Was Riley his real target? Or had the plan been to simply cause a commotion and get the cops to bring him inside? Maybe Hathaway was simply in the wrong place at the wrong time. Maybe they all were in the wrong place.

She sighed and looked at the video equipment. "If I tell you to stop recording, you stop. Got it?"

"That's not really..." Riley turned to look at her and Barrett pressed her lips together. "Got it."

Riley nodded and left the observation room. A third officer had appeared and stood in position as she requested. Cooley held out a manila folder and said, "Here's all the info we managed to dig up on the shooter."

"Good work, Officer Cooley."

He nodded, and Riley stepped into the interrogation room.

07:34 am

"Can I get something to eat?"

Riley shut the door, focusing on the front page of the rap sheet. "Leland Stark. Twenty-four years old." She whistled and sat down, leaving the folder open in front of her. "Wow, you've had a lot of attention in your short, miserable life. First arrest at the age of twelve for shoplifting. So you've been a criminal for half your existence. Not too shabby."

"I do what I can," Stark said. He leaned back in his chair and tried to look as casual as possible with his hands chained to the table in front of him. "Can we talk about you? Please? I would really like to talk about you."

"It doesn't work that way," Riley said. "Sorry to disappoint. You have a lot of really petty stuff on your sheet, Mr. Stark. So where did you suddenly get the balls to go out and shoot a cop?" She held up a finger before he could answer. "No, wait. That's not the question, is it? The question is why would someone tell you to shoot a cop? You're not that high on the totem pole. I would assume you're more of a... coffee boy. Is that it? You screwed up someone's order, so they decided to let you come here and get yourself killed. Get you out of their hair."

Stark suddenly lunged forward and pounded his fists on the table. He stared at her, breathing so hard that his nostrils flared. He narrowed his eyes at her, and then smiled. "Is that the right response, Detective? You question my manhood, and I spill my guts to show you just how wrong you are? 'Why, I'll show her. I'll tell her everything I know, and then she'll believe I'm one of the big boys.'" He leaned back and said, "Sorry, Detective. No go."

Riley flipped the file closed. "Well, if you're not going to talk, we're just wasting our time here. Right? Have fun in holding." She stood up and went to the door.

"Marchosias."

Riley stopped with her hand on the knob. She looked at the kid over her shoulder and he raised his eyebrows and spread his hands palm-out. "I'm perfectly willing to speak with you, Detective Parra. I just think it would be so much better to actually converse rather than interrogate. You'll get information, I'll get information. It will be so much better for both of us that way. Don't you agree?"

"You think I give a damn what works for you?" Riley said. She walked back to the table. "You are chained up, locked in a room, in a building full of people who would love five minutes alone with you. You shot someone who wore a badge. It doesn't matter if they knew her or not, it doesn't matter if we liked her or not. Because every cop knows it could just as easily been them on the ground. Do you think you're going to get the upper hand because you say a name and act like this is a cakewalk? You're just going to make me and every other cop in this building pissed off. So take your time. Debate. Think about what you want to tell me. Think about Lieutenant Hathaway, and you better pray she pulls through. I'll be back when you're ready to talk."

She left the room and said, "Nothing and nobody goes in. No water, no food, no anything. I don't care if he starts picking up the table and throwing himself against the walls. No one goes in until I say so. Clear?"

"Crystal."

Riley nodded and went into the bullpen. She searched the mess of her desk until she found her Rolodex, thumbing through until she found a number without a name written next to it. She used her cell phone to call, wandering toward the on-call room where she had spent the last dozen nights. After a handful of rings, the person on the other end of the phone picked up. "How much and where?" he said.

"Depends. How much information do you have to give me, Muse?"

"Oh, you know me. I've always got the goods. Whatever you need."

Riley leaned against the wall. "Leland Stark. Young guy. Ever heard of him?"

"You sure? That shit ain't heavy at all. You want something more powerful, I think. Something with more oomph. What you're talkin' about, it's nothing. Baby powder."

"Maybe he's on his way up in the world."

"Doubt it. But hey, miracles happen, I guess. You want me to see if I can find some of it for you?"

Riley said, "No. We've got him. He shot up the police station this morning. Hit a cop."

"Whoa, whoa, hold up." She heard him speak to someone else, and then she heard movement through the phone. A door closed, and Muse came back, his voice hushed. "You're telling me Leland Stark shot a cop?"

"I was standing right next to her when it happened."

Muse blew air through his lips. "Nuh-uh. Not the guy I know."

"Do you remember the crime boss you told me about? March? Does Stark work with him?"

"Hell, no. Stark is total small-time. I don't even work with Stark. Maybe he found some cojones since the last time I threw him into the street, but I doubt it. Kids like that stay kids, you know what I mean? They end up sacrificed for the greater good. Out here, it's survival of the fittest. And he ain't even close."

Riley considered the information and said, "Thanks, Muse. I'll be in touch."

"Let me know if I need to let people know about that little white boy. He could catch a lot of people off-guard if he suddenly got big and bad, you know? Nice to have a little warning that he's moving up in the world."

"Nice to provide you with info for a change, Muse. Stay safe."

"Back atcha."

Riley hung up and sagged against the wall. There was one explanation for how Leland Stark went from a joke to a menace; he was possessed. She had seen for herself just how completely a demon could overwrite someone's personality. When the Duchess hitched a ride on Gillian, Riley was hard pressed to see or hear anything that reminded her of the woman she loved. Maybe Marchosias put someone, or something, into the wannabe gang banger and helped him move up the ranks.

Or maybe the kid was just lying. Putting on a show to look bigger than he was.

Other cops were still wandering through the bullpen. She caught a couple sneaking glances toward Hathaway's office as if they expected her to come out and berate them for making a big deal out of her shooting. Riley sighed and checked her watch. She would let Stark stew for a while before she went back in to see him again.

08:24 am
Riley used the bathroom and had already started the faucet in the sink before she remembered the gauze on her hands. She settled for washing her fingers and flicked the water against the porcelain. She had spent the last half hour moping in the on-call room, berating herself for getting into a pissing contest with a demon. He was going to win. They always won. Even when she somehow managed to walk away from a confrontation with one, they were somehow the victor.

Marchosias watched her destroy an angel.

Alistair Call, Ethan Winn and the Duchess sent Gillian away.

She dreaded to think what this confrontation would cost her. She left the bathroom and crossed the bullpen to Hathaway's office. The other detectives watched her as she crossed the threshold as if she was breaking some kind of sacrament. She turned on the light and scanned the flat surfaces, trying to figure out what she was doing.

Hathaway's chair was pushed back, and Riley lowered herself carefully into it. The seat sagged briefly before it accepted her weight, but it kept her on her toes. She realized that every moment Hathaway sat behind the desk she was poised on her toes ready to run out the door. Definitely a good quality in a lieutenant. Riley glanced at the edge of the desk and had a flash of herself, on her knees, tugging Lieutenant Hathaway's trousers down over her hips.

Riley shook her head and exorcised the ghosts. Now was hardly the time to think about what had happened that day. Riley opened the desk drawer and searched for some kind of address book, anything to give her an idea of who she should call. She found a stack of memos from the desk sergeant on the edge of the desk and sorted through them.

Mother called - will call back.

The personal speed-dial spaces on the phone were mostly empty, but a few of them had cryptic codes. The paranoia of a cop; never let a snoop know how to contact your loved ones. She took the phone from the cradle and tucked it between her head and her shoulder. She pressed the top button and listened as the phone automatically dialed.

After a handful of rings, she got an answer. "Well, I didn't mean you had to get back to me so soon, Nina. I'm almost done with my laundry. You can talk while I sort."

Riley was thrown for a moment. "Uh, excuse me. Miss Hathaway?"

The woman on the other end of the phone seemed to freeze. Every noise on the other end of the call stopped. Finally, she said, "To whom am I speaking?"

"Ma'am, this is Detective Riley Parra. I work with your daughter. I'm afraid she's been taken to the hospital. There was a shooting this morning." Riley winced, knowing she was screwing it all up. She shouldn't have tried calling anyone.

"How is she?"

"I'm not sure. She was conscious and aware of her surroundings when they loaded her into the ambulance."

"Did you catch the motherfucker who shot her?"

Riley raised an eyebrow at the language. "Yes, ma'am."

"Good. Which hospital?"

"St. Anthony's is the closest," Riley said. She heard rustling on the other end of the phone and knew she was preparing to go. "She's most likely in the emergency room there."

"Thank you for letting me know, Detective Paris."

Riley didn't bother to correct her. "It was the least I could do, ma'am. I'll let you go so you can be with her. We're all pulling for Lieu—for Nina."

"I'm sure she knows, dear. Thank you again."

They hung up, and Riley leaned back in the chair. She checked her watch again and decided she had left Mr. Stark stew long enough. She got up and left the office, leaving the light on as a symbol of Hathaway's imminent return. The cops were still standing perfectly erect, still focused entirely on their work. Riley nodded to them as she passed, and stepped into the interrogation room once more.

08:29 am

Stark's head was down on the table, his fingers laced behind his head. When the door opened, he sat up and smiled at her. "Welcome back. Did you have a nice breakfast? I can almost smell bacon and sausage, I'm so damn hungry. Come on. Just a Pop Tart. I'll take a Pop Tart. But none of those whole grain bar things. They upset my stomach."

Riley pulled out her chair and sat down. "I don't think you realize the severity of your situation, Leland. You're not getting out of this building. I don't care who you work for. I don't care who pulls your strings. You have half a dozen witnesses who will swear up and down in court that you pulled the trigger. And every one of those witnesses wears a badge. You're fucked. Royally. I think you need to take that into consideration."

"What do you want from me?"

"I want you to tell me why."

Stark shrugged. "I does what I'm tolds."

Riley leaned forward and smirked. "I talked to a friend of mine. Apparently you're pretty small fry. Not even small fry. You're barely noticeable. See, we're starting to think that this was a suicide mission. Whoever sent you figured all us cops would just open fire on you. Cop goes down, you die a second later. Someone wanted to get rid of you in a very messy way."

"I'm on my way up. I know things now. I'm capable of things you can't even dream of." He looked up at the security camera and said, "May we speak frankly, Detective?"

Riley glanced up at the video camera and made a slashing motion with her hand. She gave Barrett a moment to stop taping before facing Stark again. "You want to talk, here's your chance."

Stark scooted to the edge of his seat and leaned over the table. "There's something in me. Something powerful. Even if you manage to keep Leland Stark in custody and put me to death, the thing inside of me is going to continue. It's going to get out. So you better think twice about messing with me, Detective. For I am ancient, and I have a very long memory. Your friend Muse was correct, as far as he knew. The Leland he knew was hardly worth the effort to spit on. But I've changed everything. And soon everyone will know my name."

"And what name is that?"

"Morax."

Riley laughed. "Borax? That's a hell of a name."

He sneered at her. "Careful, Detective Paris."

Riley held her hands out. "Fine. I just want you to realize that this is all just a formality. As soon as I decide we're done with you, that's it. You're going to disappear into the system. Your life will be in the hands of a bunch of cops. And let me tell you, there's not one cop in this city you'd be safe with. You can tell me all the lies you want about being able to hop into a different body. If you could do it, you'd have done it when I was chasing you. Your hollow threat to 'come after me in your new body' won't work." She winked. "So why don't you do all of us a favor and tell me who told you to shoot my boss? Marchosias?"

"I'm not one of his boys," Stark said. "I'm one of his boys' boys."

"Third tier. I'm shaking."

Stark lurched forward, his hands flat on the table. "You should be. Duchess, Call, Winn? They're all fifth tier. At most. You don't want to know what's waiting for you at the top of the slide. Oh, man. You'll put your own gun to your head and save us the trouble if you got a glimpse of that."

Riley shrugged and made a conscious effort not to lean back. "I've been in Marchosias' building, Borax. I survived."

"Barely. Do you really believe you'll be so lucky twice? Count your blessings and run to Georgia with your little whore."

Riley moved so fast even Stark wasn't prepared for it. Her hand made contact with the side of his face and knocked him to the side, her palm burning under the gauze. She pushed out of the chair, knocking it over in the process, and rounded the table. She grabbed Stark by the scruff of the neck and pressed his face into the table.

The door opened and Cooley took in the scene. "Everything okay in here, Detective?"

"Everything's fine."

Cooley backed out of the room and shut the door. Riley made a note of recommending him for a promotion. Riley tightened her grip and pressed Stark harder against the hard surface. "If you find it necessary to speak of Dr. Gillian Hunt, you will keep a civil tongue in your head."

"I'd rather keep a civil tongue in her—"

Riley swung her leg up, kneeing him in the side. The air erupted from him in a deep 'whuff!' and she said, "Am I clear, Mr. Stark?"

He coughed and nodded as best as he could.

Riley released him and backed up a step. "Sit up." Stark pushed himself up and brought both hands to his face. The cut on his cheek, from where she had tackled him, was open again. A trickle of blood curled down his chin like a ribbon. Riley went to the door and opened it a crack. "Get me a butterfly bandage, a towel, and some alcohol." She closed the door while the officer got the items she requested.

"So is that how it works?" Stark said. "You don't like what I say, you beat my ass?"

Riley sat down again. "If it gets what I want from you, why not. You saw the officer's reaction. No one is going to shed a tear if you get a little bump on your head."

Stark sighed and touched his cheek. He winced and said, "You're making it very difficult for me to like you, Detective. And I do so desperately want to like you."

The door opened and Cooley appeared with the first-aid kit. He glanced at Riley, and she nodded to let him know she would cover him. He put the kit down and opened it. He dabbed a cotton ball with alcohol and cleaned the blood from Stark's cheek. Stark remained still as his wound was tended, his eyes locked on Riley. Cooley applied the bandage with thick, blunt fingers and closed the kit again. "Need anything else, Detective?"

"No, thank you, Officer."

Cooley nodded and left the room.

"Why did you shoot Lieutenant Hathaway?"

"What was her first name? No one is willing to tell me." He touched the bandage on his cheek, opening and closing his mouth to see how it moved.

Riley shrugged. "Tit for tat. Maybe I'll tell you if I'm feeling charitable."

Stark rolled his eyes. "Kind of a small reward." He laced his fingers together and rested his hands on the table. "What if I give you something huge? Some revelation you haven't considered yet? What will you give me then? Are you prepared to give me my freedom?"

"That would have to be a pretty big something."

"Oh, it's huge," Stark said.

Riley shook her head. "Nothing you give me will buy you freedom. Maybe you'll get a nice cell with a view if you tell me who put the gun in your hand."

Stark pressed his lips together and shook his head.

"Come on, Stark. All you have to do is name a name. You said it yourself, we can't do anything to your bosses. What harm does it do for me to know?"

Stark laughed. "What harm? This from the woman who torched Alistair

Call from the inside out with holy water. We know that you're just a mortal. But you're bat-shit crazy. And that scares some of us right to death. We don't know what you'll pull next. So we're cautious."

"That makes me feel good. I thought you guys just considered me a nuisance."

"Oh, we do. You'll never make a dent in our numbers or our strength. But you'll take some of us out before you manage to commit suicide. Very few of us are willing to be the martyrs who go down in the course of events."

"Why were you willing?"

Stark made a fist and rested his chin on it. "Because I just had to meet the crazy cop bitch. I wanted to see if I could be the one to stop her for good. Worst case scenario, I get to spend time with a veritable celebrity."

Riley gathered up the file and said, "Call me when you're ready to give me something useful."

She was almost to the door before Stark spoke again.

"It's weird, isn't it? The timing."

Riley stopped and looked at the doorknob. She knew she should keep walking and ignore him. Instead, she said, "The timing of what?"

"Everything. This. Do you remember what happened right before Samael appeared in your apartment and this holy battle between good and evil dropped in your lap?"

"It's not so bad, right, Detective?" Hathaway said, her voice barely more than a whisper as she neared climax.

"Kara died."

"You blew her head off," Stark said. "But that's semantics. I meant right before you pulled the trigger and killed your partner. It was raining, you were fighting in the middle of the street. Something happened to you. Something violent. Think back."

Riley kept her back to the demon and closed her eyes. Riley sees an opening and lunges forward. Kara fires and the bullet slams into Riley's chest, her life saved by the Kevlar vest she thought to put on. Riley wraps her arms around Kara's waist and they grapple, Riley's hands wrapped around Kara's, holding the gun up and away. The rain soaks them both, rainwater running over her face like tears. Kara drops the gun and shifts her weight, throwing them back toward the car, and–

"My head hit the side mirror." Riley blinked and looked down at herself.

"Oh, my. How hard did you get hit?"

The mirror clattered on the ground. Riley barely paid any attention to it, too worried about stopping Kara, who had apparently gone insane.

God, how hard *did* she hit the mirror to knock it completely off?

Stark said, "A head injury, followed immediately by something as traumatic as Sweet Kara's death." He tsked. "And then... well, then you started seeing angels. You started fighting demons. Wouldn't it be terrible if everything you had seen and done since then was just a... hallucination?

"Imagine. Alistair Call, the Duchess, Ethan Winn. All three, dead. All human beings killed because of you. Because you thought they were demons. Your new partner is an angel, right? How lovely for you. How lucky."

Riley shook her head. "Other people... have seen what I've seen. Gillian..."

"Left you. Because she couldn't take the demons any more, and she couldn't cope with your war. Think about that. Gillian left because she was scared. Maybe she was scared of you. Maybe she was worried about how bad your injury was getting."

Riley said, "Shut up."

"Detective," Stark said, his voice totally different. "Detective, I don't know anything about demons. Please, I-I don't even go to Sunday school. I just want to-to talk to my lawyer. Okay? Please? Can I talk with someone else? Please?"

Riley forced herself to grab the doorknob, twisting it and slipping out of the interrogation room. She leaned against the closed door and closed her eyes, taking a moment to collect herself. She felt her heart beating - pounding - in her ears. Her mouth was dry. *What if he was telling the truth? What if everything in the past few months was just a hallucination? Oh, God, what if I've killed innocent people? Did Gillian leave because she was afraid of me?*

"Detective?"

She looked up and saw the three guards watching her. "Sorry," she said. She cleared her throat and pushed away from the door. She straightened her shoulders and avoided the eyes of everyone she passed as she went to the stairwell. She let the door swing shut behind her before she dropped down onto the top step. Her stomach rolled, her face hot as she tried to steady the ground under her feet.

"This can't be true. This can't be true. He's a demon. He lies. He lies..."

Her hand moved to the back of her head and sought out the spot where her head hit the mirror. Surely the impact from knocking off the side mirror of the car had left a bump. She didn't feel anything, and she didn't remember tending to the wound in the hours after the fight. Of course, she had a lot of other things on her mind at the moment.

If she made up the world of demons and angels, then she had to question everything else in her life. She shifted, and something in her pocket jabbed her side. She fished it out and discovered it was the CD Gillian left behind in her office. Oh, God, she didn't sleep with Gillian until after she hit her head. If she made up the angels...

Riley straightened and looked down at the CD. Everything swam into focus. Gillian touching my cheek, Gillian's expression when Riley told her the truth about what they were up against. Gillian's eyelids fluttering as she came, her fingers closing around Riley's wrist. Riley opened her eyes and tightened her fingers on the CD case. Angels were real. The thing sitting upstairs in the interrogation room was either a demon or possessed by one. Marchosias, Alistair Call, there was no doubt in her mind of their nature.

Because she loved Gillian. And Gillian loved her. That was something far more unbelievable than angels fighting demons in the streets of her city. She didn't doubt that love, not for a second. Not even when a demon tried to worm his way into her brain and weaken her defenses. She closed her eyes and pictured strands of hair, turned golden brown by the morning sun streaking through the window, feathered across a lightly freckled forehead. The taste of Gillian's forehead against her lips in the morning. Waking in her lover's bed.

She stood up, hand gripping the stair rail, and took a deep breath. The demon's words faded and doubt was erased. She pushed her hair out of her face and went back into the bullpen. Even though Gillian was currently lost to her, that didn't erase the meaning behind what they had. What they still had. Love that deep couldn't be manufactured or imagined. As long as she held on to the truth of that, the demon wouldn't get its claws in her.

09:05 am

Riley needed fresh air, so she went downstairs. The front steps of the station were still marked off with yellow tape that fluttered in the wind. Riley stopped just outside the doors, moving the shattered glass aside with her feet as she looked at the spot where Hathaway fell. She could still hear the gunshots, feel the blood burning in her face as her adrenaline kicked up to superhuman levels. She put her hands in her pockets and walked down to the sidewalk.

Television reporters stood across the street, speaking into large black or gray cameras. She thought to go back inside before someone saw her and recognized her as the one who made the arrest of the shooter. She had one foot on the steps when she heard her name called. She groaned and prepared her 'no comment' statement when she recognized the voice.

Priest sped up into a jog to catch up with Riley.

"I told you to stay at the hospital with Hathaway."

Priest stopped in front of the steps and looked up at Riley. "They did everything they could, Riley. It just... it wasn't enough. The damage was too severe."

Riley frowned. "What?"

"They had to let her go, Riley."

"They..." Riley's legs suddenly went weak and she dropped down onto the steps. Priest immediately moved to catch her, wrapping one arm around her waist and gently guiding her down onto the step.

Priest whispered, "It's okay. Just take your time, Riley. It's all right."

Riley pressed her hands against her face and her body shook with a series of violent tremors. Hathaway was gone. Everything that had happened between them suddenly solidified, suddenly became "done." She couldn't process the thought that they would never get closure. That she would never confront Hathaway about what she had done.

Priest held her, running her hand over Riley's back until the shaking stopped. "Her mother was there. She was able to say good-bye. Nina was unconscious, but... I let her know that she was heard. I was with Nina when she went. We spoke, and I helped her cross over. It was..."

"Don't say peaceful," Riley said. "That's a fucking lie. She was shot, and it took her an hour and a half to die. Do not dare to say it was peaceful."

Priest nodded.

"Are you going to be okay, Riley?"

"Yeah," Riley said. She pushed herself up and said, "Just as soon as we deal with the prick that murdered our boss."

09:22 am

Stark looked up as Riley entered the room with two of the officers who had been guarding the door. Riley said, "Stand up." Stark pushed off the edge of the table and stood up. One of the cops took Stark's chair and carried it from the room. The other officer unchained Stark from the table. He made sure that Stark saw the Taser on his belt. Riley said, "You're not going to give us any trouble, are you, Mr. Stark?"

"No, ma'am."

The two officers guided Stark out of the room, where the third guard was waiting with a baton. The bullpen was full of cops who looked ready to tear someone apart with their bare hands. Stark scanned the room and looked at Riley. "What's going on?"

Riley closed her hand around the back of Stark's neck and leaned in close. "Our boss just died. You're a cop killer. We have special rules for cop killers." She shoved him, making him stumble and trip over his chains. She hauled him back upright and shoved him forward. "Walk. Now, I'm going back to my theory. Someone wanted you out of the way, so they put a gun in your hand and told you to shoot at the police station. And you were dumb enough to do it. So here's what I'm thinking. If someone wanted you dead, then they wouldn't give you all the information you might need to survive."

Stark realized he was being taken toward Hathaway's office. The door was closed, but the lights were shining through the closed blinds. He smirked. "Oh, come on. Are you going to try to make me see her as a person? Are you going to make me feel oh, so bad that I'll give you whatever you want? I expected more from you, Riley."

Riley nodded at the guards, who backed off. Riley opened the office door and said, "No psychology. Just a room. Go on in, Stark. Take a look around."

Stark sighed and shuffled forward as best he could in the chains. As soon as he crossed the threshold, he froze. He furrowed his brow and closed his eyes. "Wait. What's... something..."

Riley put a hand in the middle of his back and shoved. Stark fell into the room, hitting one of the chairs in front of the desk. Riley followed him in and turned to the cops. "Don't open this door. Not for anything. Give us five minutes." She shut the door and twisted the lock.

Stark straightened and frantically searched the room. It didn't take him long to see Priest standing behind the door. She managed a smile, but to Riley it looked weak and sick. Priest crossed her arms over her shoulders and fixed an unwavering stare on the possessed kid. "Hello, Morax."

"You bitch!" Stark said. He tried to straighten, but it caused him too much pain. He wrapped his arms around his stomach and dropped to one knee. "What did you do?"

"She blessed this office. It's not hard to do. Not for an angel."

Stark lifted his head and squinted at Priest. "Which...?"

"Zerachiel," Priest said. "Pleased to meet you."

Stark trembled and pushed back against the desk. "It hurts. Stop it."

Riley crouched in front of Stark. "You see, my main problem is that I'm not sure what to do with you. You're a demon. Even the highest security prison wouldn't be much of a challenge for you to escape. So that left me with a predicament. But now that Nina Hathaway is dead, I'm less inclined to treat you humanely. So I'm going to give you to Priest. She's my partner. We give each other gifts sometimes."

"Yeah. I paid for her breakfast yesterday. She owes me."

Riley smiled. "You ever been alone in a room with an angel before, Leland?"

His red-rimmed eyes moved up to Priest and quickly looked away. He tried to touch the floor to push himself up, but his hands jerked back as if he'd been burnt. "You bitches..."

Riley punched him in the stomach and he folded. She put her hands on his shoulders and pushed him back up, shoving him against the desk. "Language, Leland. Didn't anyone teach you manners? You don't talk to women that way."

"Just get me out of here. Please, just get me out of here."

"Who gave you the gun?"

"No one!" Stark shouted. He laced his fingers behind his head, rocking back and forth. "No one. I just wanted to see. I wanted to see what you were like because everyone is talking about you. Everyone knows about you. Everyone is scared of you and I wanted to see why."

Riley leaned forward, her face inches away from him. "Do you know why now?"

"Yes," Stark said. "Get me out of here. Please."

"You're going to become our best friend, aren't you, Leland? You're going to give us everything you know on Marchosias and his operations. You're going to be a good little informant. And if I think for a second you're lying to me, or that you're starting to think you can trump me, I'll bring you back in here. I'll let Priest loose in whatever hellhole you call a home and I'll let her bless random objects. Your remote control. The food in your fridge. Your shower head. Imagine waking up to take your weekly shower, turning on the faucet, and getting sprayed with holy water."

Stark cringed and pulled his knees closer to his chest.

Priest lightly touched Riley's shoulder. Riley looked up at her, and Priest mouthed, "Enough," and nodded toward the door.

Riley stood and said, "Get up."

"It hurts..."

Riley grabbed Stark's arms and hauled him to his feet. The move left her slightly off-balance for a moment, and Stark took full advantage of it.

He rolled off the balls of his feet and tackled Riley, running her toward the wall. Riley hit hard enough to make the entire wall shake, and Stark grabbed a handful of her hair, twisting it as he hissed into her face. "You think you're in power, just because you used an angel against me? Angels aren't the only ones with power." He raised his free hand, the chains of his handcuffs dangling uselessly from his wrist, and grabbed Priest's arm as she was about to touch him. She gasped and dropped to her knees as his hand turned red, then black with power.

Stark's breath was hot in Riley's face. "Do you want the truth, Parra? I wanted to see how much fun you could be. And oh, I got my money's worth." He leaned in, his lips against the shell of Riley's ear, and said, "You're going to be so much more fun than Christine."

The explosions were deafening in the office, and Stark's eyes widened as he realized what they were. He looked down and saw Riley's gun pressed against his stomach, the shirt around the barrel still smoking. He stumbled, his grip weakening. Riley pushed him away, and he let go of Priest's hand. Priest, suddenly free, cradled her burnt hand to her stomach and rolled away from him. She came to a stop a few feet away, perched on her haunches like a cat ready to pounce.

The door burst open and two cops appeared, guns drawn. Riley said, "Don't!"

They opened fire on Stark. He fell back against the desk, jerking with the force of their bullets. He turned his face toward Riley and smiled, then looked up toward the ceiling. Riley dropped down and grabbed Priest, helping her to her feet. "Get out! Now!" She could feel the heat building in the room. The fluorescent lights of the bullpen flickered, energy being drawn from them as Stark tried to overwhelm the barriers of Priest's blessing.

Riley slammed the door and shouted, "Take cover!"

The office erupted in a wave of heat and unnaturally smokeless flame. Riley took cover behind a desk, helping Priest move as well. The entire office seemed to shake for a moment before the power died down. Riley turned to Priest and grabbed her arm, examining the wrist Morax had grabbed. The sleeve was charred and brown, the skin underneath blistered. "Are you okay?"

"Weak, but I'll be fine. I can heal." Priest looked around the corner of the desk and said, "He overcame the blessing."

Riley looked over the edge of the desk at the flickering lights in Hathaway's office. "I think it took absolutely everything he had. He's burning out."

"He's going to take this building with him. I have to stop him."

"Yeah, but at what cost?"

Priest hesitated. "There are other angels."

Riley shook her head. "Nope." She got to her feet, ignoring Priest's attempts to stop her. She pushed Priest's hands away and said, "You've done enough already today. My turn." She returned to the office door and took a steadying breath. She threw open the door and stepped into the maelstrom.

09:37 am

Morax stood in front of Hathaway's desk, most of his clothes burnt away. The skin of the being who had once been Leland Stark was gone, replaced by a sleek red expanse of muscle. The bullet wounds in his chest were filled with thick black smoke that rose to curl around Morax's head. When he focused his eyes on her, she saw only the inhuman yellow glow of a demon. Riley felt sick, picturing Gillian with one of these... things inside of her. She pulled out her gun and Stark laughed.

"Are you going to shoot me, Detective?" He gestured at the wounds. "I doubt it will do much. But keep your talisman if it makes you feel safe."

"What did you mean?" she asked. Her eyes burned with the heat, but she refused to close them. Not when he had nothing to lose by taking her out. "About Christine? Christine Lee?"

Morax grinned and said, "You remember her well, I assume."

Riley definitely remembered Christine Lee well. Christine was the one who inspired Riley to be a cop, the one who gave her the tattoo on her shoulder. "What do you know about her? Was she like me?"

He shifted against the desk, but made no move toward her. "No. She was far dumber than you, Detective Parra. She became infatuated with a yearling. She had protection, but she sacrificed it for an idea of love. She transferred her protection to you, Riley. And she died for her ignorance. This city has had so many protectors. And they all fall. Every last one of them. The demons always survive. Perhaps it is time you got a lesson in just how deep of a hole you have dug for yourself."

"Christine Lee gave me the tattoo. Did she... mark me? Is that the reason I'm in this mess?"

"One of many."

"Thanks for the info," Riley said. "The blessing is still intact, isn't it? It's tearing you apart to be in this room, but you're still in here. Why? I think you don't have enough power to leave. I think you're planning to use every ounce of strength you have to take this building to hell when you go."

He smiled. "And there's nothing you can do to stop it. So why try? I would be running for the door at this time, Detective."

"Maybe," Riley said. "But this room isn't the only thing Priest blessed." She lifted her gun and fired at the sprinklers. The heads were fused from the heat Morax put off, but the pipes were fair game. The water erupted from the hole punched by her bullet, and the room was suddenly doused with water.

Water from a reservoir that Priest had blessed on their way upstairs.

Morax screamed as the water hit him, and the heat and smoke suddenly seemed to wrap itself around him like a cloak. He dropped to his knees, hands over his head in a vain attempt to stop the water. The only thing he managed to do was burn his hands.

Riley leaned against the door and watched the demon convulse, then his body began to smoke. It rose from him in waves, wafting toward the ceiling in narrow wisps. Finally, he was gone, and the sprinklers were cascading down on nothing at all. Riley slumped against the wall and slid down until she was sitting. She put her elbows on her knees and put her hands on her forehead.

The door opened and Priest examined the room. "Riley."

"He's gone."

Priest knelt next to Riley. "Are you okay?"

Riley closed her eyes, inhaled through her nostrils, and finally nodded. "Yeah. I think so. I just need a minute."

Priest sat down next to Riley and looked at the spot where Morax had disappeared. "Everyone is busy trying to salvage their paperwork from the sprinklers." After a moment, Priest added, "It was a good plan, Riley."

"Yeah, but what's it taking out of you to save my ass all the time?"

"Nothing I can't get back."

Riley made a fist and held it out in front of her. Priest stared it at. Riley sighed and picked up Priest's hand. She curled the fingers into a fist, and then bumped Priest's fist with her own. She leaned back against the wall and said, "It's a thing. Don't worry about it."

Priest looked at her fist for a moment and shrugged.

"This Morax guy. He was nothing, right?"

"Pretty minor."

Riley closed her eyes. "I'm in trouble."

"Yes, you are. So what else is new?"

Riley smirked. "We're going to have to come up with something to explain this away."

"Leland Stark, a career criminal, opened fire on the police station in an attempt to improve his standing in his gang. He was apprehended by Detective Riley Parra, who interrogated him and learned his motives. When Lieutenant Hathaway died, Detective Parra decided to show Mr. Stark the life he had ended. In Hathaway's office, Stark took Detective Parra's gun and ended his own life."

"And the fireworks?"

Priest shook her head. "People won't remember. They can't be explained away, so they'll just be put aside. It happens far more often than you might think."

Riley relaxed against the wall. The adrenaline of the morning was starting to wear off, and the hangover was making itself known. She pressed her thumb into the hollow between her eye and nose and grunted. "I think I'm going to call it a day. What time is it, anyway?"

Priest looked at the clock in the corner. "A quarter to ten."

Riley frowned. "Already?"

"Ten in the morning."

"Oh, that can't be right," Riley muttered.

Priest smiled and looked at the ceiling as the sprinklers finally stopped. Finally, Riley said, "All right then. There's someone I need to see."

10:45 am

The nurse barely needed to look at the badge before she agreed. Riley wore the events of the morning like a yoke around her shoulders, leaning against the nurse's station like it was a crutch. They walked down the narrow corridor together, Riley struggling to find the strength to remain upright. The nurse stopped at a pair of double doors and said, "Right inside there. Don't take too long. They'll have my ass if they find out I let you in, badge or no badge."

"Thank you. I appreciate it."

Riley waited until the nurse was gone before she went into the morgue.

Nina Hathaway's body was on the farthest slab, covered by a white sheet. Riley approached slowly, still gathering her courage. When she reached the bed, she pulled back the sheet and forced herself to look. Hathaway's black hair was slicked back against her skull, her lips slightly parted. She was blue, which Riley hadn't expected. Someone had taken the care to wash the blood spatter from her throat and face. Riley had left the sheet at Hathaway's shoulders, but she could still see one puckered bullet wound above her collarbone.

"Hey, boss."

She sighed and pressed her lips together. She rolled her shoulders and rested her hand on Hathaway's forehead.

"You were a good boss. I'm sorry I didn't... care for you the way you wanted. You had no right to do what you did to me. I'm sorry that this happened to you. I wish..." She closed her eyes and shook her head. "I don't know what I wish. You deserved better than that. I guess I wish you peace." It wasn't closure. It wasn't the angry shouting match she wanted, but it would have to do. She had enough emotional baggage without carrying Hathaway's sin with her. She would find a way to live with what had happened. She took her hand from Hathaway's forehead and resisted the urge to wipe her palm on her jeans. "Good-bye, Nina."

She covered Hathaway's face and left the morgue. Priest was waiting in the hallway, leaning against the wall with her hands in her pockets. "The press is having a field day with Stark's death. They want a full investigation of police brutality."

Riley rolled her eyes. "Of course they do. I don't suppose you can do anything about that. Maybe wave your hands and make it go away. 'These are not the droids you're looking for.'"

Priest frowned.

"God," Riley muttered. "We have to get you a DVD player."

Priest shrugged and pushed away from the wall. "The investigation won't turn up anything untoward. Everything was by the book. The videotape will show that you didn't harm Stark during the interrogation."

"Yeah, like that's going to be admitted any time soon."

"There was no audio," Priest said. "No one could hear what he was saying to you. It's obvious he spent the entire interview period attempting to make you attack him and you resisted. That will go a long way into shutting up the reporters. It'll just take a little time."

Riley nodded.

"Where are you going next?"

"I don't know. Before all of this started, Hathaway told me I had a new case on my desk. I guess I should get started on that."

Priest nodded. "Right back on the horse?"

"Yeah," Riley said. "Otherwise I might never get back on."

Priest put her hand on Riley's shoulder as they stepped onto the elevator. Riley leaned against the back wall, eyes closed, and let the motion of the car soothe her headache. She needed to stop drinking. She needed to move on with her life. The demons had already cost her too much. Sweet Kara was gone, Lieutenant Hathaway was gone... Gillian was gone, but she would be back. Riley had no doubt about that whatsoever. She might not be able to win the war, but she damn sure wasn't going to let the war take everything away from her without a fight.

Open and Shut, No. 3:
Beautiful Night

The windshield was speckled with raindrops as soon as she left the garage. Ingrid Elliot drummed her fingers on the steering wheel and decided to go west, without any real reason. As she pulled out of the driveway, she thumbed the remote to close the garage door behind her. Someone on the street raised his hand, and she almost pulled over before she noticed the cell phone in his hand. People were always taking pictures of her when she was working, amazed to see an actual checker cab out on the street. She continued on after he snapped the picture, on the lookout for real customers.

She wore her black hair underneath a Kangol cap; not exactly uniform, but she didn't have to answer to anyone but herself. She did attempt a uniform of sorts. Every night, she wore a crisp white dress shirt with the sleeves rolled up to the elbows, gray slacks, and a black vest. Though the majority of people only saw her right shoulder, being in uniform made her feel more like a professional.

Ingrid reached the first stoplight before someone waved her down. She pulled to the curb and the man opened the door to lean in. "Grant and Eighth?"

"Sure thing."

The man climbed into the car and shook the lapels of his coat, running his hand through his hair. "Didn't think it was supposed to rain today."

"I'm not surprised, as humid as it's been."

Ingrid was grateful when the man's cell phone rang and spared her any further commentary about the weather. Sometimes she wondered who decided that the weather became the default topic of conversation between strangers. The rain, really just a drizzle, was already starting to die off anyway.

"...raining there, too? I'm still in New York."

Ingrid glanced in the rearview mirror at the man in the backseat. It wasn't her place to catch him in a lie, but she found the lies her fares told to be entertaining. She only got to be a part of these people's lives for a couple of minutes at a time, but the conversations were always worth listening to.

"Hopefully the storm won't delay the flight. No, eight. Yeah. No, I'll just take the shuttle or something. Yeah. Miss you, too. Love you. See you tomorrow." He hung up and slipped the phone back into his pocket, his urge for conversation obviously expiring. He looked out the window and Ingrid was grateful for the silence. When she reached Eighth Street, she said, "Where on Grant?"

"The third brownstone," he said. "The one with the archway in front."

She pulled up to the curb, and the front door of the building opened. A blonde woman in a clingy robe stepped out onto the porch. She hugged herself and craned her neck out, getting her hair wet as she looked at the clouds.

"Six seventy-five," Ingrid said.

The man handed her a ten and said, "Keep the change."

She thanked him as he climbed out of the cab and hurried up the stairs. He put his hands on the robed blonde's hips, bent to kiss her, and shuffled her back into the apartment building. Ingrid checked over her shoulder and merged back onto the main street. She turned on the radio and hummed along with the music as she drove down Grant.

Technically, what she was doing was illegal. She wasn't licensed as a cab driver, but cabbies started to dry out as the city began to decline, and the few who were left were unwilling to cross the invisible barrier to No Man's Land. The cops knew about her and they left her alone, for the most part. She routinely went in to let the cops know she was working, that her driver's license was up to date, and that she wasn't a danger to herself or others. As long as she kept everything kosher, they were happy to leave her alone.

She drove at night because that was the time she liked the best. Most of the city was shut down, and the few places that were open stood out like beacons in the darkness. Plus, at night, it was harder to notice the downslide the city was taking. The night covered buildings like a veil, so it was easy to ignore that windows were busted out or that sidewalks were cracked with weeds growing through them.

Her cell phone rang and she placed it on the seat next to her. She flipped it open and answered without looking, turning it to speakerphone. "City Cab. Where can I take you?"

"I need to get to the waterfront. You got anyone going down there?"

"Yes, sir. I just need the pick-up address."

He gave her an address three blocks away. "All right, sir. I'll have a car there in about five minutes." She hung up and left the phone next to her on the seat. People usually assumed the person they called was a dispatcher. No harm, no foul. It would just make people suspicious if they knew she was operating on her own.

Two minutes later, she saw the man standing outside of his apartment, hands in his pockets, hunched against the rain. He stepped to the curb when he saw her approach and slid into the backseat. "Anywhere specific you need to go?" she asked.

"Just down to the waterfront," the guy said. "Anywhere is fine."

Ingrid nodded and drove. The guy settled back in his seat and sighed heavily, rubbing his chin and then running a hand through his hair. "Is it supposed to keep raining all night?"

"Not sure." Ingrid prayed she wouldn't get roped into another conversation about the weather. Anything but that.

"Someone told me about your cab. Not many willing to go down so close to No Man's Land, especially this time of night."

"Just cuts down on my competition."

The man chuckled and checked his watch. Ingrid kept an eye on him in the rearview mirror. One of the dangers of working only at night and crossing the line to No Man's Land meant that she had been almost robbed a half dozen times. The cops who okayed her business didn't know about the gun in her glove compartment, but she doubted they would have much of a problem with it. She had to protect herself, after all.

But the guy in the backseat kept his hands in sight, and seemed more interested in the world going by the window than he was in her.

Ingrid drove the man to the waterfront in silence, listening to the radio playing quietly. She was grateful for the people who didn't feel the need to make conversation. The rain had stopped and the few working streetlights reflected off puddles of collected rainwater on the sidewalks. A handful of people were out on the streets, despite the late hour. She figured half of them were homeless, the other half criminals.

She stopped at the T shaped intersection with the waterfront directly ahead of her. "Here we are, sir. That'll be twelve ten."

The man fumbled with his wallet and withdrew a ten and a five. He handed it through the slot in the safety glass between the seats. "There you go. Keep it."

"Thank you, sir. Have a good night."

He got out of the cab and Ingrid waited until he was a few feet down the streets before she drove away. She drove along the waterfront and thought about why it always seemed to be brighter near the water. She spotted a few women standing on a nearby corner and realized she had forgotten a demographic of the nightlife: prostitutes. One of the women waved, and Ingrid lifted her fingers from the wheel in the barest minimum of politeness as she drove by. They weren't flagging her down, they were just acknowledging the passage of another night owl.

Ingrid meandered through the streets of downtown, skirting the edge of No Man's Land as she looked for fares. There were a few bars she knew she could stake out, waiting for someone to stumble out and discover their keys have mysteriously vanished. She parked down the block from the Bat's Belfry and waited for the first drunk of the night to show up.

She didn't have to wait long. She kept a book under the front seat for times like this, but she barely read one whole page before someone knocked on the window. She lowered her head to peek at the person, who was bent at the waist and looking into the front seat. The woman gestured at the back seat. "Are you available?"

Ingrid nodded and replaced her bookmark as the woman and her friend got into the backseat. The woman was in her forties, upswept black hair, and a business suit that passed its eight-hour lifespan at least four hours earlier. The man was tall, bald, his shirt unbuttoned at the collar and his fingers were working the buttons of his shirt cuffs. The woman sighed and settled against the seat, digging in her purse for something. Ingrid waited and then twisted in her seat. "Where to, ma'am?"

"Oh, uh, just home."

The man said, "She needs the address."

The woman sighed and touched two fingers to her forehead. "Oh, oh, oh. Uh, six. Six Monroe Street."

Ingrid started the engine and the woman sagged back in her seat. The man finished unbuttoning his cuffs and rolled his sleeves up to the middle of his forearm. Ingrid eyed him carefully as the woman groaned and rubbed her forehead. "Everything all right?"

"It will be once I finally discover what my limit is. I'm getting closer. I've only been trying to find it since I was nineteen. One of these days..."

Ingrid smiled. "Don't worry, I've only had seven so far tonight."

The woman just grunted. The man ignored them both.

Ingrid shrugged and mentally figured out the quickest route to Monroe Street. She turned next to the bar her current passenger had exited, and the woman said, "Bunch of thieves and liars in that place. Talk about bullshit."

"Why don't you just let it go?" the man said, trying to keep his voice low.

"Why don't you shut up, Leonard?" she snapped. She rearranged herself in her seat, body language drawing a line between her and Leonard. He shook his head and looked out his own window. In the rearview mirror, Ingrid saw tears glistening in the woman's eyes. She'd had her share of emotional drunks weeping all over the backseat. But when you were ferrying drunks home from the bar, tears were preferable to any other bodily fluid.

The woman said, "When did people become such assholes?"

"Are you talking to me, ma'am?"

The woman didn't seem to be expecting an answer, and ignored Ingrid's question. The el train rumbled by overhead and Leonard said, "See, I told you we wouldn't have gotten to the stop in time."

"Oh, shut up," the woman muttered, her lips stumbling over the words.

Monroe Street had once been a pretty nice neighborhood, but apathy and gang activity ruined it. The crime rate went up and people started moving out. No one moved into the empty apartments, so they either sat empty or became squats for the increasing number of homeless people. A fire had laid waste to the first building on the corner, turning it into a husk of a landmark. The upper three stories were exposed to the air like a cutaway dollhouse.

Ingrid slowed and began looking for the address. The man said, "Just up here on the left. The one with the mailbox in front of it."

Ingrid stopped in the middle of the street, since there were no spaces available, and checked the meter. "Eight fifty-five."

Leonard paid her as the woman climbed out of the cab. Ingrid watched as Leonard put a hand in the small of her back, guiding her between two cars and onto the sidewalk. The woman put her arm around his waist and sagged against him, forcing him to all but carry her into the lobby of their apartment building. Their disagreement in the cab was apparently forgotten as he ushered her inside.

Ingrid had seen all versions in her backseat; yelling arguments, attempted physical fights, sobbing accusations, and more than her share of attempted sexual reunions. She tried to ignore them as much as possible, but once or twice she had been forced to call the cops and let them deal with the violent or amorous passengers.

She stopped at the next corner and rested her hands on top of the steering wheel. Her three fares of the night had taken her progressively deeper into No Man's Land. People running toward her car now were equally likely to be trying to mug her or steal her wheels as to be potential fares. The el train she passed on the way to Monroe Street rattled overhead again, and she leaned forward to watch it pass. The windows glowed, an oasis of light in the darkness, and she glimpsed a handful of people inside and wondered where they were going.

Ingrid was about to pull away from the stop sign when something hit the back bumper of the cab. She reached instinctively for the glove compartment and pulled out her gun before she looked out the back window to see what happened. A woman with layered blonde hair had apparently run into the back of the cab and was trying to pull up the handle on the driver's side door. Ingrid always kept that door locked so people would have to get in on the passenger side and she could keep her eyes on them.

The woman shouted, her voice muffled by the glass, and pounded on the window once before she pushed away from the cab. Behind her, Ingrid saw three men in hoodies running down the middle of the street. The one in front was carrying what appeared to be a belt. Ingrid cursed and pushed open her door and stepped out into the street. "Hey! Lady!" The woman was at the intersection, apparently torn about which was to go. The deer in the headlights effect, frozen by a multitude of options.

"Lady, get in the cab," Ingrid said. From the corner of her eye, she saw the woman look at the cab and then run back toward her. Ingrid raised the gun and fired over the heads of the men. They were nearly to the cab, and the gunshot echoed off the buildings around them. All three men skidded to a stop as Ingrid lowered the gun to center mass. "Stop right there. Turn around. Go home."

"Bitch, you—"

Ingrid fired, twitching her wrist just barely so the bullet hit the ground in front of them. "You might want to rethink that. Back away."

The trio seemed to consider their options. The farthest two began to back away, and the leader tightened his grip on the belt. "You're in for a world of hurt, sweetheart."

"That's a real nice cab you got. Real nice. Distinctive."

Ingrid said, "I have four bullets left. I won't waste them."

The man pointed at her before he turned and ran off with his two friends. Ingrid waited to make sure they were far enough away that they couldn't ambush her, then got back into the cab. The woman was sitting on the passenger seat, knees pulled against her chest, hunkered down so that as much of her as possible was hidden by the back of the seat. Ingrid said, "Get in the back."

"The... door's locked."

"Not the passenger side. Go on."

The woman got out of the front seat and climbed into the back. Ingrid got behind the wheel and locked all the doors, checking the rearview to make sure their little friends were truly gone. She caught the woman's frightened expression and said, "Those guys are pussies. As soon as someone steps up, they back off."

The woman twisted around and looked through the back window.

"Where do you need to go?"

"I-I don't have any money."

"Yeah, well, I think it's a pretty good idea to get both of us away from here as soon as possible. So I might as well take you somewhere."

She bit her bottom lip and said, "Out of No Man's Land. Just... somewhere nicer."

"I can do that. I'm Ingrid."

"Michelle."

Ingrid finally pulled away from the stop sign, keeping an eye on the sidewalks in case their friends decided to circle around and get their revenge. "So, Michelle. Those guys back there friends of yours?"

"They..." She swallowed hard. "One of them kept trying to buy me a drink at the club. I told him I wasn't interested, like, three times but he wouldn't take the hint. When I left, he was waiting outside. He tried to grab me, him and his friends. He said if I wouldn't take his drink, then he would make me..." She swallowed hard and looked out the window. "I stomped on his foot and ran. I thought I was..."

"Well, they'll probably give up. Guys like that go for the easy target." She looked in the rearview. "Did they hurt you?"

Michelle shook her head and then looked down at her arms. "The big guy bruised me a little bit, I think, but I'm fine. I-I'm fine."

"You sure I can't take you anywhere specific? The police department, maybe?"

"No. But... can you take me home? I just need..."

"No problem. Where do you live?"

Michelle hesitated. "The Cobblestones."

Ingrid suddenly put all the pieces of the night together. Michelle, and maybe some friends, decided to be "dangerous" for a night. They dressed up and went to a bar in No Man's Land, tempting fate, proving their invulnerability. Death, pain, danger, it can't touch them, because they're young and stupid. Ingrid resisted the urge to give a speech; she was just a hack driver. She changed lanes and took the quickest route out of No Man's Land.

Cobblestone Square was one of the few neighborhoods in the city that could still be considered nice. The homes were originally owned by the city founders, impressive two-story houses flanked on the corners by two mansions that were converted into apartments sometime in the fifties. The people who lived there still cared about their homes, and had the means to hire people to take care of their lawns. Ingrid hated it more than No Man's Land; it seemed less real. At least the people in No Man's Land were honest about who they were. She would trust anyone from No Man's Land before anyone from this super swanky part of town.

Michelle regained her composure and pointed toward one of the apartment buildings on the corner. Ingrid parked at the curb and turned to look into the backseat. Michelle was hugging herself, staring up at her house, and Ingrid couldn't resist a bit of preaching. "Look, I know it's a thrill to go down to No Man's Land. But let tonight be a lesson, okay? You could have been jumping from the frying pan into the fire when you got into my cab. Maybe you need to get your thrills from TV and the movies from now on, huh?"

"Yeah," Michelle said. She opened the door and said, "Look, I feel stupid. I feel like a child. But would you mind... would you walk me to the door."

Ingrid almost refused on the basis she couldn't leave her cab. But there really was nothing to fear in The Cobblestones. She sighed and shut off the engine. "Sure." She got out of the cab and walked around to the other side. She led the way up the path and through the front door. The foyer still felt like a house, with a communal kitchen to the left and a flight of stairs on the right. Ingrid was always uncomfortable going into a stranger's home, especially at night. There was something awkwardly intimate about it.

Michelle undid her jacket and shrugged it off her shoulders. "I'm on the top floor."

"I think you can make it on your own. Sleep well, Michelle."

"Thanks. A-and thanks for the ride. And everything."

Ingrid nodded. "No problem. Glad you got home all right."

Michelle turned and started to ascend the stairs, and Ingrid stepped back out into the night. Her phone was ringing when she got back to the car, and she answered as she fastened her seatbelt. "City Cab. Where can I take you?"

"Yeah, bartender took my keys, so I guess I need a ride. You come to No Man's Land?"

"Just give me a cross street, and I'll be there," she said.

She heard quick muttering and then the caller said, "You know Van Buren Avenue is?"

Ingrid kept her voice even. "Yeah, I can manage that. It'll be about ten minutes."

"Okay, you can pick me up there."

The caller hung up, and Ingrid closed her phone and tapped it against the steering wheel. Some streets in town had been renamed after Presidents of the United States as part of an Independence Day celebration during the bicentennial. The majority of the streets were named in order - Washington ran along the waterfront, Adams and Jefferson branching off of it. But after a while, things got a little sloppy. But Ingrid was positive that Van Buren Avenue was only two blocks away from Monroe Street, where she had picked up Michelle and sent her pursuers running.

Did any of those Neanderthals get a look at the phone number on the side of her cab? Could she risk it? She took the gun from the glove compartment and checked the load. Four bullets, just like she told the guy. She had ten minutes to get back to Van Buren Ave. That didn't leave her much time to plan for an ambush.

She got out of the cab and went around to the trunk. She peered inside and looked at the tools she'd acquired. At the time, she thought she was just being paranoid. But that didn't stop her from stocking up. When you spend your nights in a place like No Man's Land, it's best to come prepared.

The cab rolled slowly down Van Buren Ave. Ingrid had the headlights off, but the "off-duty" sign on the roof glowing. She floated down the streets like jetsam on a wave, keeping her eyes peeled for movement. She stopped under a streetlight, engine idling and smoke trailing from her tailpipe to mix with the clouds to obscure the stars. She slumped down in the seat, turned off the interior lights, and waited. The streetlight turned her windows into mirrors, making her invisible to the outside. She used the side and rearview mirrors to watch for her alleged fare.

After about three minutes, they arrived. Belt was in the lead, rolling his shoulders as he strode across the street. She waited until they were just out of arm's reach, the leader's hand extended to grab the door, and she pressed her foot down on the gas. The cab lurched forward about five feet and came to a stop again. She was out of the streetlamp's protection, but she hoped the shadows would protect her.

The leader stepped forward again, and Ingrid lurched again.

"Bitch!" the guy growled, and any doubt was erased; they were the guys who had been chasing Michelle. She let the leader grab the handle and yank it up, but the door was locked and wouldn't give. She shifted into reverse, stood on the gas, and the tires squealed as she backed up. Belt Man was thrown off balance. His knees hit the ground and his hand was wrenched away from the car door. She reversed until she was behind the three men, and then she switched the headlights on bright.

The guys blinked in the sudden brightness and Ingrid opened her car door. One of the men was carrying a baseball bat, and he swung it at the shape her body made in the beam of the headlights. The bat slammed against something hard and came up short, Ingrid twisted her arm, the aluminum bat in her hand easily pushing away the Louisville slugger. She pivoted on one foot and buried the blunt head in Baseball Man's gut. He doubled over and Ingrid swung the bat as he fell to his knees. She hit the third, apparently unarmed, man in the thigh and he howled in pain as his muscles contracted.

Belt Man came at her from behind and wrapped his belt around her throat. Ingrid was expecting him, though, and contracted her body. He was forced to compensate, rising onto the balls of his feet. When Ingrid threw herself backward, he lost his balance and they both went down hard. Belt Man took the brunt of the fall, and Ingrid freed herself from his makeshift garrote. She put her hand on his hip, as if to help herself stand, and positioned herself over him as she slipped the wallet from his pocket. She placed the tip of the bat against his cheek as he glared up at her.

"What were you planning to do to that woman tonight? Huh? Whatever it was, I think a bat to the face is meager in comparison. What do you say?" She flipped open his wallet and looked at the driver's license. "I asked you a question, Eddie Congers."

"You bitch..."

Ingrid tapped his shoulder with the bat, pinching a nerve, and Eddie convulsed. She turned and saw that his friends were on the opposite sidewalk, shuffling away. She looked down at Eddie. "Just me and you, Eddie.

You think you're a badass? Think you have to take down a woman because she showed you up? This ends right now, Eddie. You better make me believe that you'll walk away, or I'll make sure you don't ever get up." She cocked her gun and Eddie winced. "What's it going to be?"

"It ends now."

"You stay out of bars. You don't speak to women unless they speak to you first. You will keep to yourself and you will convince your friends to take vows of chastity. Because I'm out here every night, Eddie. And I know your face. I know your name, and where you live." She dropped his wallet on his chest, minus the driver's license. "You think I have to be scared of you and your boys? You should be scared of me." She put her foot on his left hand and stepped down, pinning it against the asphalt.

"Do we have an understanding, Mr. Congers?"

"Yes."

"If you and your buddies ever need to get somewhere... walk. Trust me. It will be much healthier for you."

Ingrid took her weight off his hand and walked back to the cab. She got behind the wheel and waited until Eddie Congers got to his feet before she gunned the engine. She barely missed him with the curved front bumper, forcing him to jump back to avoid being hit. She ignored the stop sign at the end of the block and turned right, leaving Eddie and his goons behind her. She exhaled, rolled her shoulders, and tried to steady her jangled nerves as she drove along the quiet waterfront.

The phone rang next to her on the seat. She picked it up and answered without looking. "City Cab. Where can I take you?"

Ingrid accepted the twenty from the young couple, neither of whom looked like they would make it all the way to their apartment before they ravaged each other. She thought about telling them they were giving her an eleven dollar tip, but they had bigger things on their mind. She watched the man's hand slip down to the woman's butt as they climbed from the car, and she giggled and squirmed but didn't really try to get away. Ingrid had to force herself to look away. It had been a long time since she heard a woman make a noise like that.

She sighed and checked the clock. The sun was rising and the darkness had acquired a velvet blue tint. All-night parties were letting out, people were stumbling away from one night stands, and parents were waking children to meet their bus. It was the moment of the day when Ingrid's world overlapped with that of everyone else. She flipped the rooftop sign off as she drove through the neighborhood. There was a new gap between two buildings where an office had once stood, now occupied by piles of rubble and a cracked foundation. She wondered if it was a victim of arson, accident or the forward march of progress. Doubtful, on that last mark. Very little marching was going on these days.

Ingrid drove to the waterfront and pulled off the road. She parked with the front of the cab pointing toward the water and opened the glove compartment. Tucked next to her gun was a plastic bag that held a cheese sandwich, an apple and a juice box. She took them both, tucked the keys into her pocket, and walked to the front of the car. She stepped up on the bumper and sat on the sloped hood. She leaned back, propping herself up on her elbow, and unwrapped the sandwich.

Slowly, the city came to life behind her. She ignored it. She was only interested in the night; the day belonged to others. She ate slowly, watching as the light bled across the cloudy sky, spilling diamonds into the waterfront. At dawn, it was easier to believe the city wasn't too far gone to save.

All she wanted to do was go home, shower, climb into bed, and sleep through the day. She craned her neck, working the muscles, and decided maybe a bath would be better. It wasn't every night someone tried to choke her to death with a belt. She sighed and took a bite of her sandwich.

"Excuse me. Are you available?"

Ingrid shifted and looked over her shoulder. "Sorry, I—"

The woman was standing on the side of the road, a pair of high heels dangling from her fingertips. She wore a black dress, the kind that looked great on the dance floor but always looked a little sad in the early morning light. Her hair was mussed, and she looked like she had been crying. She was composed now, however, and looked ready to keep walking if Ingrid turned her down.

The woman nodded down the road. "My car broke down." Her voice was tinged with a British accent. "I spent the entire night trying to convince this bastard to hire me, and then... well, I guess he liked my bar tab better than my résumé." She grinned and pushed her hair out of her face. "Sorry. I'll, uh, let you get back to your lunch."

"No," Ingrid said. She gathered her lunch and slid off the hood. "I think I've got time for one more ride."

She gestured at the passenger side back door and then got behind the wheel. She watched as the woman slid into the backseat. "Thank you. I mean... really. You're saving my life here."

"No problem," Ingrid said. She turned, arm on the back of the seat, and said, "Where can I take you?"

The Martyr

Chapter One

Kenzie woke at twenty-nine minutes past five in the morning, same as always. The only difference was that, this night, she had hardly slept since putting her head to the pillow. Three of the four hours she spent in bed were spent staring at the water stain on the ceiling that was shaped like France. When her watch alarm finally chirped to signal the start of morning, she pulled it off the nightstand and silenced it immediately.

As she slipped the watch onto her left wrist, her fingers brushed the slip of curved metal that was already there. She ran the tip of her index finger over the engraved words, closing her eyes as she pictured a face for each name. "Miss you guys," she said, pushing herself up and putting her feet on the floor. Her dog tags swung back into their proper place as she sat up, dangling between her breasts.

After a long moment, she got up and found her tangled tank top. She pulled it on and tugged the dog tags out so they rested against the fabric. She moved to the window, braced her hands against the frame, and looked out at the alley. A few laundry lines stretched between her building and the next, clothes waving in the pre-dawn breeze like flags of surrender. She could smell the stink of garbage on the waterfront, sewage making its way to a larger body of water. Below her, something caromed off a garbage can with a metallic echo and stumbled on. Either a drunk or a large stray dog. Whichever, she didn't care to find out.

Kenzie was eager to leave, to start the day, but routine demanded to be followed. Besides, the odds of doing what needed to be done were slim at such an early hour. So she dropped to the floor and did a set of fifty push-ups. She rolled onto her back and did one hundred sit-ups. When she finished, she did the reverse; one hundred push-ups and fifty sit-ups. Muscles burning, body fully awake, she went into the bathroom and took a quick shower. She didn't mind the crappy old building's pipes taking ten minutes to heat the water. She liked the cold.

She cupped her hands under the spray and dumped it over her head. Her hair was short, the color of oak, and a wing of it fell loose over her right eye. She pushed it out of the way, flattening it to her skull, and finished bathing a few minutes after the water finally got hot.

She dressed in a pair of jeans and a loose silk blouse over the tank top, leaving the blouse unbuttoned. She tucked a gun in the back of her belt, making sure the tail of her blouse covered it. Her black boots were by the door, and she put them on as she left the apartment. She hid her eyes behind a pair of aviator sunglasses, a memento of her time overseas.

Her hair fell over the right side of her face again as she left the apartment and headed downstairs. A few people were in the lobby, the indigent population preparing to give control of the day over to those more fortunate, packing away their meager possessions and disappearing into the shadows of the early morning.

The day was already humid when she left the building, promising more rain in the future. The general store on the corner was just opening for business, and a street sweeper lumbered slowly down the street toward her. Washing away the night to make a new day. She bought an apple from the general store and watched as the sweeper moved past her. She tossed the apple core into the trash and started off down the street. The elevated tracks above her rattled and hummed with the passage of a sleek silver train, but she preferred walking to riding. She put her hands in her pockets and watched the people moving around her.

People in wrinkled suits leaving buildings, checking their watches as they headed for cars or bus stops.

Other people wearing everything they owned as they shuffled between buildings and found a place to keep out of sight while the sun was out. Real-life vampires, shunning daylight and human contact for own survival. If they allowed themselves to be seen, they would be run off. Better to just hide.

Kenzie was surprised how much larger No Man's Land had grown since her last visit. Storefronts she remembered as laundromats and barber shops were empty husks, hiding behind dirty windows and lowered blinds. More than a few buildings looked like they had been burned and then left to fall, waiting for a strong wind gust to finish the job the flames started. Stacks of black garbage bags stood on the sidewalk, forming stinking mountains, and she stepped into the street to avoid them.

She reached her destination before she knew it and stopped to get the lay of the land. She leaned against the wall of a building cater-cornered to the police station, watching as cops streamed in and out of the front doors. Plywood had been put up in place of the glass, and she idly wondered if the police station had become part of No Man's Land, or if there had been some kind of incident.

The street was lined on both sides by shining police cars, marked and unmarked. As she watched, about half of them were taken out by uniformed officers. At a quarter past seven, a faded yellow Chevy Nova drove past her and pulled into an available spot in front of the station. She recognized the profile of the driver and pushed away from the brick wall. She rolled her shoulders and took off her sunglasses, hooking one earpiece in the scoop neck of her tank top. She waited for an ancient yellow Checker taxi to pass before she started across the street.

Riley Parra got out of the Nova, and a woman with short blonde hair got out of the passenger side. Riley slammed the car door, checked the handle to make sure it was locked, and tucked the keys into her pocket as she stepped onto the sidewalk. "It could use some work."

"Yes," the blonde woman said.

Kenzie was coming up from behind them, moving quickly, but not fast enough to attract attention of the cops swarming all around them. She waited until she was right behind them before she pulled the gun from the small of her back, and pressed the barrel into the small of Riley's back. "Your money or—"

She was cut off by a strong arm wrapping around hers and twisting. Kenzie didn't even have time to cry out in shock as someone used an amazing amount of strength to lift her feet off the sidewalk. Kenzie was airborne for a half-second, and then slammed into the sidewalk with the force of being hit by a Humvee. All the air rushed out of her lungs, every bone in her body vibrated, and her eyes bugged out as she tried to make sense of what had happened.

Her gun was yanked from her hand and she felt the cold barrel press against the bare skin above her tank top.

Riley's face appeared in her field of vision, the corners of her lips forced down to keep a smile from intruding. She held out her hand and said, "Bad joke, Kenzie. Let her up, Priest."

The weight of the gun vanished, and Kenzie let out the breath she was holding. She clasped her hand to Riley's forearm and pulled herself back to her feet. She brushed off the seat of her pants and eyed Priest. The woman was deceptively lithe, slender and boyish. She wore a white blouse, unbuttoned at the collar, and a gray vest. She was still eyeing Kenzie warily. Kenzie nodded to her and said, "Well, Rye, I guess I don't have to worry about your new partner being a lightweight."

"*New* partner...?" Priest said.

Riley said, "Caitlin Priest, I would like you to meet Mackenzie Crowe."

"Major Mackenzie Crowe, actually," Kenzie said. She extended her hand. After a moment, Priest took it and squeezed. "You have some nice moves, Katie."

"It's Priest."

"I'm going to call you Katie."

Priest pressed her lips together.

Riley said, "You picked a really bad time to pull that joke, Kenzie."

Kenzie looked at the front doors of the station and realized what might have broken the glass. "Ah, shit, Rye. I didn't..."

Riley shook off the apology. "When did you get back?"

"Yesterday. I'm not sure I'm back for good yet." She sighed. "Truth is, I'm here because I need your help, Riley."

Riley nodded, looked at Priest, and checked her watch. "We got some time. Let's grab some breakfast."

The closest diner was a dive called Coach's. Priest returned Kenzie's gun as they walked there, mumbling an apology for her reaction. "Don't worry about it," Kenzie said as she tucked the weapon back into her belt. "Given the circumstances, I would have been upset if you let me get any further than I did."

"As long as you know how to use that thing," Priest said.

"Six years as a cop, twelve years in the army. I think I got a handle on it."

She smirked and led the way into the diner. The counter stood against the back wall, with booths built into the front of it so the short-order cook could deliver the food directly to the customers. Riley guided them toward a table at the far end of the room, well away from the cloud of smoke and spatter of grease coming from the so-called kitchen. She pulled out a chair and sat facing the door.

Kenzie sat with her back to the window. "It's good to see you again, Rye. It's been way too long."

Riley smiled. "What brought you back?"

Kenzie's smile faded and she looked down at the tabletop. "Bad news, I'm afraid." She glanced at Priest and said, "Maybe she shouldn't hear this."

"Anything you say to me, you can say to her," Riley said.

"It's not that I don't trust you, Katie. It's just that I don't want to get you in trouble."

Priest looked ready to leave, but Riley shook her head and put a hand up to keep Priest in the booth. "She stays."

Kenzie shrugged. "Your call." She sighed and leaned back in her chair. "First, a little background. Let's do a hypothetical. Let's say that you walk into a room, and you see me standing over a dead body with a smoking gun. What would you do?"

"This is totally hypothetical, right?"

"Yes."

Riley said, "I would arrest you and investigate until I was satisfied about what happened. One way or another."

Kenzie nodded. "Good enough for me." She leaned forward and rested her elbows on the table. "I got a call from a soldier from my platoon, guy called Coltrane. He said he was in trouble, afraid for his life, panicked. He wanted to meet me, but he didn't know where would be safe. So I told him to come to the city and I would meet him here. I showed up early last night, found his hotel room. He was dead. Shot twice in the chest."

"Did you report it?"

"I'm doing it now."

Riley rolled her eyes. "Okay. Was someone standing over his body with a gun?"

"No," Kenzie said. She tapped her fingernail against the table's surface and exhaled sharply. "Coltrane is the third guy from my platoon to die in the past six months. I didn't think about it when I asked him to meet me here, because two doesn't make a pattern. But three..." She shook her head. "I mean, the first one, we were sure it was suicide. The other was just an accident. Or so we thought. Now that Coltrane is dead, I'm not sure what to think."

"You think someone is out to get your people?" Priest said.

"Maybe, Katie. But what I do know is that three of my guys have died since coming back. And all three times, the same soldier was nearby. He was in New York for Charlie, he was the last one to see Marks before he committed suicide... and he lives here now."

Riley nodded. "Okay. We'll round him up and ask him some questions.

But first you need to make an official report."

"No."

"Kenzie..."

"No, Rye. I don't want this on the books until I'm absolutely sure."

Riley said, "The guy who was in all three places. He's special to you, isn't he?"

"Damned special," Kenzie said. "He saved my life."

Chapter Two

"We were patrolling the border between Afghanistan and Pakistan, the ten-thousandth time we had been over the same rocks and sand. Mountains and caves, all of it exactly the same but different. Because we knew there were Taliban in the hills, we knew insurgents were tracking us in their crosshairs. A lot of times, we only survived because they didn't feel like wasting the ammo. But one day, I don't know. Maybe they were pissed off, maybe they were trying to get revenge for some slight or another. We gave candy to the children of the neighboring village and not to theirs. Whatever.

"The Humvee in front of us went up like a firecracker, and then they opened fire. We weren't even sure where it was coming from at first. We got out and took cover, and Coltrane spotted the Taliban fighters on a ridge about a hundred yards up. I laid down cover fire for my guys while they outflanked the insurgents. One of my guys, Radio, checked on the other Humvee, but there weren't any survivors. He's a black guy, but he was pale as a ghost when he came back to report. When I finally got a look at what he'd seen, I don't..." She pressed her lips together, swallowed hard, and shook her head.

"I wanted to get better cover, and I went around to the back of the truck. I just wanted a better position. Next thing I knew, Radio had slammed into me and knocked me down. I thought he snapped. Seeing what he did, I just thought... but he pointed to the spot I had been five seconds from kneeling down on. There was an IED buried in the sand. I don't have a clue how we missed it with the truck tire, but I was about to trigger the thing with my knee."

Riley stared at the empty table in front of her, wishing she had ordered a coffee or water or something to occupy her hands. She signaled to the cook, mimed drinking and held up three fingers. He nodded and went to the cooler.

"Radio is the guy who lives here now, right?" Riley said.

"Yeah. He didn't have any family, nowhere to go. When they let us come home, he asked me for suggestions of a good place to settle down. I told him this was the only place I called home. I got a postcard from him a while back. He thanked me for making the recommendation and said it was great here. He really liked it."

"Where were you?"

"Virginia."

Riley leaned back and said, "They let you, Radio, Coltrane... all of you came back at the same time, and you went to Virginia?"

Kenzie nodded. The cook brought over their water and Kenzie took a long drink.

When they were alone again, Riley said, "Walter Reed." Kenzie touched her top lip with her tongue and, after a moment, nodded again. Riley looked over Kenzie's body and didn't see anything amiss. "Where?"

"Coltrane got shrapnel in the thigh. They took most of it out, but it was still going to be hell at airport security. Most of the other guys got shrapnel in the back, sides. Charlie lost his leg."

"Where?" Riley asked again.

Kenzie reached up and pushed her hair away to reveal the right side of her face. A line of scar tissue ran from her hairline down to the curve of her jaw, her ear a mangled mess. She let the hair fall, covering the damage. She swallowed hard and said, "I was in the burn ward when I told Radio about living here."

"How bad was it?"

"Not too bad. Just my face and a little bit of my shoulder. Radio blocked a lot of it." She drank the last of her water, working her top lip with her bottom teeth. She put the bottle back on the table and said, "His entire back. Shoulder to hip, some of his legs and ass."

"The IED you were about to kneel on."

"It went off a few seconds after Radio saved me. Because of where we ended up when he tackled me, he got the majority of the blast." She tapped her fingernail on the table again and said, "Three of my people died after they came home, and Radio was there every single time. Dropping by for a visit, or responding to a call for help. He took a bomb meant for me, Riley. I'm not giving him the benefit of the doubt, I'm giving him all the doubt I can spare. If he did it, I don't want him to get off. I just want to be absolutely certain that he won't get railroaded."

Riley glanced at Priest. "I'm not sure what you expect from me."

"I'll report Coltrane's murder, and I need you to request the case. Once you're on the case, I can relax. Whatever you decide. I trust your judgment."

Riley took a moment to think about it. She pictured herself in Kenzie's position, desperate to give the man who saved her life a fair trial. Kenzie wasn't really asking her to do anything she wouldn't have done anyway. She nodded and said, "Okay. I'll see what I can do."

Kenzie walked them back to the police station and sighed as they entered the frigid air of the lobby. "You don't appreciate air conditioning like this until you're in Afghanistan in July in full gear." She grinned and looked toward the sergeant's desk. "Guess this is where civilians do their civic duty."

"If you can get in," Riley said. Groups of people filled the blue plastic chairs, waiting for someone to take their statement. More likely, the cops were waiting for the people to give up and go home. Less paperwork that way.

Kenzie said, "I'll keep in touch while I'm in town." She wrote down her cell phone number and the address of her hotel. "Same goes for you."

Riley looked at the address and raised an eyebrow. "No Man's Land? Brave."

"Broke," Kenzie said. "It's the only place I could afford for any length of time. It's not so bad. I like it there."

Riley nodded and, after considering it for a moment, stepped forward to embrace Kenzie. "I'm glad you're okay. Take care of yourself. I'll come by after I get off tonight and fill you in."

"Thanks, Rye." She turned to Priest and held out her hand. "Nice to meet you, Katie."

Priest looked at Kenzie's offered hand and finally took it. "It's Priest."

"No, it's not." She winked and backed away from them. "I appreciate this, Rye. I owe you."

"Big time," Riley said.

Riley watched Kenzie go into the sea of chairs, speak to the desk sergeant, and then take her seat amid the "civilians." She tapped Priest's arm and gestured to the stairs. "C'mon. We're going to be late."

"How do you know that woman?"

"You heard her. Six years as a police officer. She was my partner back when I was in uniform."

Priest fumed. "I don't like being called Katie."

"You think I like being called 'Rye'? It's one of Kenzie's things. Don't let it get to you. She picks a nickname for you, and that becomes her... call sign for you. If I see something addressed to Rye, I know who sent it. If you hear someone calling for Katie, you know who wants you." She glanced back to see Priest was still irritated. "I didn't say it wasn't annoying. You get used to it."

When they reached the office, Riley barely made it halfway to her desk before someone called their names from across the room. "Detectives Parra and Priest, I presume?" Riley looked up and saw an Asian woman standing near the open door of Interrogation Room One. She had bad memories of that room. She nodded, and the woman waved them over. "I've been waiting for you."

Riley used the time it took to cross the room to examine the woman. She was tall and slender, with long black hair. She wore a green turtleneck and a gray skirt, her badge hooked on the belt. She stepped to one side and allowed Priest and Riley to enter the interrogation room ahead of her. The table in the middle of the room had been moved to the back wall and was covered with various files and stacks of paperwork. A phone and a laptop stood on the far end of the desk, wires from both running out of the room to some distant jack.

Riley walked in and turned to face the woman as she shut the door. "What is this? IA?"

"Why? Does Internal Affairs have some beef with you I should know about?"

"Depends on who the hell you are."

"Lieutenant Zoe Briggs. I'm your new boss. Interim new boss, actually." She smiled as she leaned against the table. "You missed orientation, so I'll give you the bullet points. I've been a cop for a long time, and I've been in charge of cops for about half of that time. I'm very good at what I do. Your precinct has been doing well in terms of crime rate, and I don't see any reason to change things just because I'm in charge now. If it's not broken, why fix it. Like I said earlier, I'm just your interim lieutenant, but I hope to make it permanent. I like it here. I'll like it even better when my office is habitable again."

She looked at Riley, hinting that she knew whose fault it was that Lieutenant Hathaway's office had been destroyed.

"I look forward to working with both of you. You can go." Priest opened the door and was halfway out before Briggs said, "Parra. Stay a moment."

Priest looked at Riley, who nodded that it was okay. Priest left the room, and Riley closed the door behind her.

"I've been reading some of Lieutenant Hathaway's notes about you, Detective. Seems you and she had a... special relationship."

Riley didn't want to comment on that, so she remained stoic.

"She let you get away with a lot of things. Off-the-books investigations, going off the reservation without letting anybody know where you were going... You spent a lot of time outside of the station doing God knows what with God knows who, and Lieutenant Hathaway let it slide because you got results. But where I come from, that raises all kinds of red flags. I see a secretive cop who disappears for entire shifts, and I think corruption. Do you understand where I'm coming from, Detective?"

"I do, ma'am."

"I don't want to imply you're corrupt. Your record speaks for itself. I just want to know I don't have anything to worry about when it comes to your police work."

"You don't have anything to worry about."

Briggs smiled. "Great to hear it. Thank you for putting my mind to ease, Detective Parra. You may go now."

Riley nodded and left the temporary office, shutting the door behind her. She sagged against the wall and cursed silently. New boss, new rules. No more running after Marchosias and his cronies during work hours. Fine. She could make that work. But the real panic came from Briggs hinting Riley might be crooked.

With everything that had happened since, Riley had forgotten what led to the "interlude" in Hathaway's office after Sweet Kara's death. Somewhere in Lieutenant Hathaway's office was a letter, fictional but believable, detailing Riley's criminal activities. Riley sexually serviced her boss to keep that letter out of the public eye, but she didn't know what happened to it after that. Had she destroyed it? Or was it sitting in the ruins of Hathaway's office waiting to be found? She bumped the back of her head against the wall a couple of times before she pushed forward and crossed the bullpen to her desk.

"Everything all right?" Priest asked.

Riley said, "New world order. No off the books investigations, no special favors, no wiggle room."

"What does that mean?"

Riley nodded for Priest to follow her. "It means we have to stop Kenzie from reporting what she saw last night. We're going to do this quietly, on our own."

"Briggs won't be happy about that."

Riley looked toward Hathaway's office. The door was crossed with yellow crime scene tape, locked off until someone could get in to clear out the water- and fire-damaged furniture. Somewhere in that office was a piece of paper that could end her. "I'm going to do what I can, while I can. There's a chance I won't be a cop too much longer anyway."

Chapter Three

They made it downstairs before the desk sergeant decided to pay attention to Kenzie. Riley pulled her from the waiting area and escorted her outside. Kenzie put on her sunglasses and said, "What's up? They decide murder wasn't a crime anymore?"

"No," Riley said. "There's a new sheriff in town. I couldn't guarantee we would be the ones investigating it. Your friend deserves better than that."

"Thank you, Rye. I appreciate that."

Riley shook her head. "Don't worry about it." They headed to Riley's Nova, a piece of crap she had picked up at the police auction. It had the benefit of being too decrepit to worry about anyone trying to steal it, but it was a bit of an eyesore. She unlocked the driver's side and said, "Priest, I need you to run interference for me. I don't care what case you follow up on, just make sure it's official. I need plausible deniability."

"I'll do what I can," Priest said, eyeing Kenzie. "But are you sure you don't want me to come with you?"

"We'll be fine," Riley said. "Keep in touch."

Priest nodded. "Okay. Be safe, Riley."

Riley got into the car and leaned across the seat to unlock Kenzie's door. Kenzie slid into the seat and settled against the fabric, twisting to look in the backseat. "Nice car."

"Thanks."

"I like your partner, too. She's a doll."

"Yeah," Riley said. "A real angel." She smirked and then laughed when she caught Kenzie's confused expression. "Sorry. Inside joke. What do you know about Radio? Any idea where he lives?"

"I have an idea, yeah," Kenzie said. "But I think we'll need to do a bit of planning before we go to find him."

"I don't like the sound of that," Riley said. "All right. We'll head to your hotel to come up with a plan." She started the car, turning the engine over on the second try, and pulled away from the curb.

Kenzie looked around the car and shook her head. "Seriously, Rye..."

"It's temporary. My other car was... there was an incident."

"Towed?"

"Hit by a fire truck."

Kenzie raised her eyebrows.

"It's okay. I was driving the fire truck at the time."

Kenzie laughed. "Okay. I definitely made the wrong choice joining the army."

"I tried telling you that twelve years ago."

"Just drive, Rye." Kenzie chuckled and made a show of fastening her seatbelt as Riley took a corner. Riley smirked and remembered their first night as partners, patrolling the streets of No Man's Land like sentries. Kenzie was Riley's second partner, following the death of Donald Rafferty. Kenzie understood the pain of losing a partner and gave Riley time to warm up to the fact of riding with someone new.

After a week or so of moping, Kenzie slapped Riley on the side of the head and said, "I know he meant a lot to you, and I know you miss him. But there's nothing you could have done. You weren't there, you couldn't have been there. Right now, there's someone else relying on you to have their back. Namely, me. I want to know I can trust you when we're on a call."

Riley promised she would get her head in the game and, after that, she had. Before long, she and Kenzie were simpatico. They developed their own form of shorthand, learned each other's way of thinking so they could anticipate. They were the best pair of uniformed cops on the streets.

Until Kenzie's father was died. A career soldier, he was slowly killed by cancer eating away at him until he withered to nothing. Kenzie made him a promise before he died, and Riley assured her that she supported her decision. Kenzie turned in her badge the next day and joined the army. Riley, in turn, began preparing to take the detective's exam. If she couldn't ride with Kenzie, she didn't want to patrol at all.

More than a decade later, Detective First-Grade Riley Parra and Major Mackenzie Crowe parked in front of the Gold Hotel.

Riley got out of the car and looked up at the building. It seemed to lean slightly to the right, like a drunk trying to lean on the guy next to him to keep from falling on the floor. Riley pocketed her keys and said, "Nice place. Maybe when a rat family moves out, I'll see if I can get a room."

"The rats don't mind sharing."

Kenzie led the way upstairs, turning at the waist as they reached the first floor landing. "Don't lean on the railing. Or touch it. Or look at it weird." Riley moved closer to the wall and followed Kenzie up to the third floor. Someone was shouting in one of the rooms, and Riley heard daytime TV blasting in another room to drown out the sounds of the argument. Kenzie unlocked her hotel room door and said, "Home sweet home." She went inside and Riley followed, closing the door behind her.

Kenzie put her hands on Riley's waist, spun her, and pinned her against the wall. Riley barely managed to say Kenzie's name before her lips were caught in a kiss, her shirt quickly being tugged from her pants. She twisted her head to break the kiss and said, "Kenzie..."

"Riley... God, I've missed you," Kenzie said, forcing Riley's head back so she could kiss her again. Riley squirmed against the wall, willing her body to shut down before it got the wrong idea. It had been a while, and she was in danger of making a very stupid mistake. Kenzie broke the kiss and said, "Get your pants off."

"Kenzie, stop. Wait. I'm with someone."

Kenzie froze, her hands on the buttons of Riley's shirt. Her hair hung down in her eyes, and she tried to catch her breath and process what Riley said at the same time. "What?"

"I'm dating somebody."

Kenzie backed away, but kept her hands on Riley's shirt. "Shit. I didn't... when you said we could come back to my hotel room, I thought you were..." She finally dropped her hands. "God, I'm sorry, Riley."

"It's all right," Riley said. "I'm not saying I didn't enjoy it."

Kenzie chuckled and cleared her throat. "Uh. This is a little awkward now."

Riley shook her head. "No. It's not. Come on, Kenzie, it's us."

"Yeah? No harm, no foul?"

"Right."

Kenzie nodded and gestured for Riley to go on into the room. The space was divided into a bedroom and a kitchen, the chairs flanking a card table under the window standing in as a living room. Riley went to one of the chairs and sat down while Kenzie put her gun back on the nightstand. She sat on the edge of the bed, elbows on her knees with her hands clasped together between them. "Okay, back to business. The murder."

"Yeah," Riley said.

Kenzie pressed her lips together, then raised her eyebrows. "It's not

Katie, is it? I mean, she's nice and all, but if you're dating that stick in the mud..."

Riley laughed out loud. "God, no. No. I am not dating Priest. It's... her name is Gillian."

Kenzie smiled. "Pretty name."

"Yeah."

"Is it serious?"

"It's... complicated."

"Is she into threesomes? I have a cell phone. We could call her..."

Riley chuckled. "Kenzie. Please. Focus."

Kenzie stood up and stuck her hands in the back pockets of her jeans. "I've been going over and over it in my head. I'm trying to picture Radio doing it. The picture just doesn't come together in the end. I mean, it's like trying to picture the Pope wrestling an ostrich."

Riley blinked. "It's that unlikely? The man was a soldier, Kenzie."

"Not all soldiers are killing machines, Riley."

"I didn't mean that. I just meant that things he saw over there... he may not be the guy you remember. He might not be completely there." She tapped the side of her head.

Kenzie paused in her pacing. Not much, but just enough for Riley to notice.

"What?"

"Radio... was odd." Riley stayed quiet, waiting for Kenzie to elaborate. She finally sighed and sat in the chair opposite Riley. "We called him Radio because he chose to communicate through song titles. He could speak normally. We heard him all the time, on the sat phone and talking to commanding officers, he was erudite and clear. It was just a game to him."

"What do you mean he communicated through song titles?"

"Ask me some questions."

Riley frowned and said, "Okay. What did you have for breakfast?"

"Brown Sugar."

Riley smirked. "Did you have eggs with that?"

"A Taste of Honey."

"How was that?"

Kenzie shrugged. "Getting Better."

Riley said, "He would have entire conversations like that?"

"Always."

"Stop it."

Kenzie held out her hands. "I'm Sorry."

Riley reached down and put her hand on the butt of her gun.

Kenzie said, "All right, I think I've made my point. And he was a lot better than me. He could have entire conversations with someone. Country, blues, classic rock, modern music, it didn't matter. We had people writing down a lot of what he said, so we could check they were actual songs. He never slipped up once. After the attack, he did it non-stop. I don't know if it was because of what he saw, or the injuries... whatever it was, he wouldn't speak normally. If he couldn't come up with a title, he just kept quiet until whoever he was talking to rephrased the question."

"Guy like that shouldn't be hard to find."

"Well. I know where we can find him, but I don't know exactly where he is."

"That doesn't make much sense, Kenzie. Either you know where he is, or you don't."

Kenzie looked at the window and tapped the heel of her shoe against the floor. In the silence, Riley heard sobbing from next door; the fight's inevitable conclusion. Finally, Kenzie said, "I didn't want to tell you this until it was too late for you to back out."

"We're there," Riley said. "I'm out on a limb here. We need to find Radio as soon as possible so we can question him about this whole mess. Spill it."

Kenzie exhaled and said, "He's Underground."

Riley closed her eyes and covered her face with both hands. "Of course he is."

"That's another reason I came to you. I knew I was going to have to go down there eventually. I don't want to go alone, and I don't want to go with someone I don't trust completely."

"The Underground," Riley muttered. She shook her head. "I knew from the moment you showed up that this wasn't going to be easy. I wish I'd realized it would be suicidal."

"There's nothing inherently dangerous about the Underground."

Riley barked a laugh. "You've been gone for over ten years, Kenzie. Things have changed. And not for the better. I haven't even thought of the Underground since I walked the patrol. For all I know, there are..." She nearly said demons, but caught herself at the last moment, "...there are entire gangs of criminals down there. It could be Mad Max down there and we wouldn't have any idea."

"Rye... please. I owe this guy. I would prefer to go down there with you, but I'll go alone if I have to."

Riley pushed herself out of the seat and muttered under her breath. If Marchosias and his demonic legions had control of No Man's Land, she could only imagine what kind of power they had down below. It would be like walking into the mouth of Hell and announcing her arrival with a bazooka. But as much as the thought terrified her, she couldn't imagine letting Kenzie take the risk on her own.

She turned and said, "All right. I'll go with you."

Chapter Four

The Underground was not officially a part of the city. Nearly a hundred years earlier, a fire decimated several city blocks, creating entire neighborhoods of uninhabitable buildings. The city leaders decided to regrade the streets two stories higher and start rebuilding from the ground up. The project was massive, and took several years to complete. When it was finally finished, it created a large underground labyrinth of abandoned buildings. The Underground was originally meant to be sealed and forgotten about, but it quickly became a refuge for the homeless and criminal element.

On countless patrols, Riley and Kenzie had chased a suspect through alleys and down hidey-holes only to have them duck into an "Underground Entrance." They would call dispatch, who would tell them to throw in the towel. The higher-ups figured the Underground was too risky, and the criminal would probably never be seen again after venturing into the maze unprepared. A few reckless souls had tried to map the Underground, using antique land surveys and a minimal amount of spelunking, but the resultant guides were unreliable at worst and completely confusing at best.

And I just promised to go down there, Riley thought. She looked at Kenzie and said, "How certain are you that he's even down there?"

Kenzie went to the nightstand and took a postcard from the drawer. She handed it to Riley without saying anything, letting her make up her own mind. The words on the postcard were close and small, written with a very steady hand. "Major Tom. Diggin' up bones, here there and everywhere. Got to get you into my life. Let's spend the night together (you can't always get what you want). I'm under the boardwalk. Time is on my side. I can see clearly now, here in the real world. I'll be seeing you. Radio."

Riley looked up. "You can actually understand this?"

Kenzie nodded. "He'll change names to refer to specific people. It's his main cheat. And it took some education, but I can translate. He says he's going through the past, moving around, which tells me that he was visiting his fellow soldiers in New York and Chicago. He admits to being there. Then he says he wants to see me." She smiled. "He implies we should sleep together, but he knows that'll never happen. As for 'under the boardwalk,' where in this city would that describe?"

Riley gave her the point.

"Time is on my side means that he's not in any rush. That last part means he understands something. I think he's innocent of the murders, but he knows who is doing it."

"What about the first line? That's not a song title; it's from Space Oddity. Does he do that often?"

Kenzie nodded. "Now and again when he wants to refer to someone specific. I was Ride, Captain, Ride until I got my promotion. Usually he would just start letters with Hello, It's Me."

Riley tapped the postcard against her thigh and looked out the window. "It's going to be hell trying to question this guy. Even if we are able to find him down in the Underground."

"We'll find him. Most people in the Underground are hiding. They'll run from us. But Radio wants to be found. We go down there, we make the effort, and he'll find us. Trust me. You do still trust me, right, Riley?"

"Yeah," Riley said. "I just need a little time to psych myself up to going down there."

Kenzie nodded. "Take all the time you want. I was planning to head down closer to night. Seemed like a pretty nocturnal place last time I was here." She stood up and said, "You're welcome to hang out for a bit if you want. I'm just going to hop in the shower."

"I think I'll track down Priest. Try to keep from being fired."

"All right." Riley stood, and Kenzie moved to intercept her. "Listen, Riley. The whole... groping, kissing incident aside, it's really great to see you again. I've really missed you." She took Riley's hand and squeezed it. "Even if our reunion can't be quite as... horizontal as I was hoping, I'm really glad to just be with you again."

Riley leaned in and kissed Kenzie's cheek. "I don't have a lot of friends. I think you're it, in fact. And you were the first woman I slept with that I didn't want to kill after we broke up. Maybe we're just meant to be friends."

"Maybe," Kenzie said. She grunted and shook her head. "Such a frustrating thought."

"I'll see you tonight, Kenzie."

Kenzie released Riley's hands and headed for the bathroom. She paused in the doorway and said, "Hey, your partner, Katie..."

"I'll be here around five."

"Is she single? Is she gay?"

"Okay, five it is."

"Come on, bitch, don't hold out on me."

"Nice seeing you, too, Kenzie." Riley shut the hotel room door behind her and shook her head. The last image she needed in her head was Priest and Kenzie rolling around naked on a bed. She wondered if Priest would unfurl her wings when she came. Against her will, the image popped into her head fully formed. Riley's laughter echoed up the stairs as she headed back to her car.

Their first time had been after a particularly nasty shift. An anonymous 911 caller reported a group of people going in and out of a supposedly abandoned warehouse at all hours. They got the call, and rolled up at a few minutes past three in the morning. Kenzie took the back door while Riley checked out the front. The building was supposed to have a security guard, but he was nowhere to be seen.

The first shots came from the back of the building, where Kenzie was. Riley pulled her gun and made a break for the front door. She burst through and found eight men, all armed, facing the opposite direction. Riley shouted her identification, and three of the men turned toward her with their weapons leveled. Riley opened fire, and the three went down. All three were hit in the leg, and the others scattered like cockroaches.

Riley used the radio to coordinate the back-up units, drawing a tight net around the warehouse before the guys could get away. Riley made sure the wounded shooters wouldn't bleed to death, then handcuffed two of them together. It was the best she could do with one set of handcuffs. She thumbed her radio. "Kenzie, I need your cuffs. I got three of the bastards down." No answer, and Riley's blood ran cold.

"Kenzie." Riley didn't bother telling the shooters to stay put; they were too busy focusing on the new holes in their legs. She went to the back door, which was standing open and revealed a wide concrete loading dock. A security light bathed the entire area in crisp, white light, like a spotlight on a stage.

Kenzie was lying in the center of the light, a black body shape that looked like spilled oil. Her arms were spread out to either side, her right leg bent at the knee.

"Mackenzie," Riley gasped, her shoes making skittering noises on the concrete as she ran. She dropped to her knees and cradled Kenzie's head in her lap, brushing the hair out of her face and looking for the wound. Kenzie's eyes fluttered open, and she coughed weakly, scanning Riley's face for answers. "What..."

Riley laughed and touched the front of Kenzie's bulletproof vest. POLICE was written across the chest in white block letters, and the fourth letter had the circular butt of a bullet embedded in the center of it. Riley laughed again, shook her head, and said, "They shot you in the 'I'."

Kenzie looked down at herself, laughed, and groaned as the action caused her bruised chest to move. Riley, the thoughts of a flag-draped coffin erased from her mind, her partner alive and groaning in her arms, was too caught up to think of the potential damage. She bent her head and kissed Kenzie, long and hard, her heart soaring when Kenzie returned the kiss.

"Couldn't help it," Riley said when they finally parted.

"Wouldn't want you to," Kenzie said, her face flushed.

Riley kept the kiss in her mind as she replayed the entire confrontation with her superiors. They took her gun, standard procedure, and made her put her statement in writing. At seven in the morning, they were finally allowed to leave. Kenzie waited for Riley outside the station, dressed in jeans and a white T-shirt, and said, "I'm not going to pussyfoot around, Riley. Come home with me. I'd really like to make love to you."

Riley was grateful that she wouldn't have to be the one to ask.

They decided to take it all the way, not content to leave it as an "adrenaline thing." Riley confessed she had wanted Kenzie for years, while Kenzie was willing to explore the idea of Riley being more than her work-partner. "The women I date," she explained, their bare legs twisted together under the blankets, "always use my job against me. The danger. The butch factor. Might be nice to throw that all out and just... be with each other."

Riley moved her hand down between Kenzie's legs and said, "Sounds good to me."

After that, they took every opportunity. The backseat of their squad car, sometimes a simple hand job in the front seat, sometimes a quickie in the on-call room. Kenzie admitted that one of the draws to becoming a cop was the uniform, so Riley wore it during sex whenever possible. It got to the point where simply putting on the uniform to go to work would turn her on.

When Kenzie handed in her badge, she went to Riley's apartment to tell her she wasn't quitting the relationship. But Riley was torn between loyalty to the force and loyalty to a woman she thought she loved. "That thing you said about women using your job against you. The women who used the danger as a reason not to be with you. I don't want to be one of those women. But I think I am. I don't think I could handle knowing you were over there. In danger. I'm sorry, Kenzie."

Kenzie took the news well. She smiled, nodded, and called it a clean break. They would end their relationship the morning Kenzie shipped out to basic training. They spent the time between making love, giving each other good memories to last until they met again. When Riley woke the next morning, she expected Kenzie to be gone. But she was sitting on the edge of the bed, watching the sun rise through the window. Riley kissed her shoulder, pulled her close, and offered to drive her to the airport.

Riley sat in her Nova, the engine chugging even though she was parked at the curb. Groping with Kenzie in the hotel room brought back the memories of their time as a couple. It seemed like ages at the time, the longest relationship she had ever been in, but looking back it was barely more than a footnote. But it was one of the most influential relationships in her life, and she had just let it end. She let it slip through her fingers because it was kind of hard.

They had parted with a hug and a promise to keep in touch, and Riley watched Kenzie disappear through security. A few letters both ways, one or two risqué pictures that made it past the military's mail security, but they eventually fell out of touch. She tried to remember the last exchange, tried to remember the last thing they wrote to one another, but she drew a blank.

Riley refused to see parallels between her relationship with Kenzie and what she was currently going through with Gillian.

So why are you sitting here staring at your cell phone trying to keep yourself from dialing her number?

Riley opened the phone and dialed a number, listening to the metallic tone on the other end. After three rings, the call was answered.

"Hey, Priest," she said, hating herself for surrendering. "Where are you?"

Chapter Five

Riley pulled up at the address Priest gave her, and immediately spotted her partner sitting on a brick retaining wall that surrounded an outdoor diner. She parked along the curb and approached from behind, walking in Priest's blind spot. Regardless, as she approached, Priest held up a plastic bag with a sub sandwich and a bag of chips. Riley took it from her and took a seat on the wall next to her. "That's creepy."

Priest shrugged. "I'm your guardian angel, so I can sense you when you're nearby. I can feel your presence."

"I know. That is creepy."

Priest smiled.

"So what did we do today, in case the boss asks?" She opened the sandwich and saw it was her favorite. Some days it was good having her guardian angel as her partner.

"Canvassing. The Benedict murder."

Riley nodded. "Good choice."

Anthony Benedict was murdered in the city's one nice hotel, dropped from one of the higher floors to land in a bloody pile in the middle of the lobby. The lobby was an open-air pavilion, and people on every floor had a clear view of the man dropping like a stone. Canvassing would involve tracking down every single person who could have conceivably seen the drop and asking if they saw anything else that might be of use.

Riley took a bite of her sandwich and said, "Listen, Priest. Thanks for filling in for me."

"No problem. Protecting you means more than just following you on suicide missions." She took a chip from her bag and chewed it slowly. "What's your take on the new boss?"

"I don't know. She's probably a good boss if you're willing to follow the rules."

"Some people just have unreasonable expectations."

"Tell me about it," Riley said. She watched as Priest ate another chip, and pointed at the half-eaten sub sandwich with her pinkie. "Do you need to eat?"

"This is basically a human body," Priest said. "Just with a bit different in the way it was put together. I need to eat just like anyone else."

"Huh. Good to know."

Priest chewed and stared across the courtyard. Riley remembered the place in its heyday, which only made seeing its present state of decline sadder. Weeds stuck up through the broken tile of the dining area, and a few of the umbrellas covering the tables were tattered and torn. A handful of people were eating their lunches there, businessmen and women from the surrounding buildings.

"So what is Kenzie asking of you?"

"She thinks Radio is in the Underground. She needs me to watch her back."

Priest tensed. "The Underground."

"I know," Riley said. "I'm not happy about it, either. It's dangerous as hell, we have no idea what's down there..."

"You're wrong," Priest said. "It is just as dangerous as Hell - actual Hell - and you don't know who is down there. Riley, it's a forgotten realm. Demons have full reign down there. I know you understand what that means. I know you know what going down there will mean. The second you step foot on their territory, they will know. Marchosias and everyone under him. They'll know, and they'll come after you."

Riley said, "Then we'll have to move fast."

"That tattoo on your back. The one that protects you up here. It will still work in the Underground."

"Good to know."

"It will be all that's left. A charred remnant, a flapjack-sized piece of charred flesh. They will show you no mercy, Riley."

Riley said, "I'm not going to change my mind. Kenzie needs my help. I'm going. That's the final word."

Priest pressed her lips together. "Sometimes a guardian angel has to take drastic measures to protect their wards. Sometimes they have to go to extremes."

Riley straightened and rubbed her hands together. She kept her eyes locked on the opposite side of the courtyard, aware that Priest was looking at her. "I would think long and hard about doing that, Caitlin. Because I would be done with you."

"You don't decide that."

"Want to test that theory?"

Priest was quiet for a long time, and then began gathering her trash. She stood up, carried it to the trash can, and turned to face Riley. "I'm not going to hurt you, Riley. You have enough bad things to watch out for without that. Besides, I think you would drag yourself to the Underground with two broken legs. But I'm not going to watch you kill yourself. If you go to the Underground, you're going alone."

Riley finally met Priest's gaze. "I'm used to it. Got along just fine before you came along."

"Things have changed, Riley."

"Yeah. They have." Riley stood up and said, "I'm going to back up my friend. My partner. It doesn't matter that she turned in her badge, she's still my partner. I know you understand that, Priest. I can't back away, and I can't turn my back on her when she needs my help. That's who I am."

They stared each other down for a long time, neither one willing to break the silence. Finally, Riley said, "So I guess the question is who do you want to be. Are you my partner, or are you just my guardian angel?"

"I'll cover you with Lieutenant Briggs."

Riley relaxed and said, "Thank you."

"But I can't be in two places at once. If I'm covering your ass, I won't be able to protect you in the Underground. You'll be on your own."

"That's fine," Riley said. She tossed her trash into the can, and said, "The important thing is that Kenzie won't be alone." She checked her watch and said, "I'm going to head back home and grab a nap. We're going into the Underground tonight at twilight."

"Look, Riley... I apologize in advance. I know you don't like me to say this, and I know you don't believe in it... but I'll pray for you."

"No need to apologize," Riley said. "I'm going to need all the help I can get."

The hardest part of returning to Gillian's apartment was facing the memories every time she opened the door. Simply stepped into the living room was enough to cause vivid flashbacks to the first time she visited, bleeding to death and weak from her first true face-off with the demons that inhabited No Man's Land. The kitchen reminded her of domestic mornings together, eating freshly scrambled eggs and sitting across from someone who had just hopped out of the shower. The bedroom caused the most splendid and most dangerous memories of all.

In the weeks following Gillian's departure, Riley hadn't even been able to walk through the front door without breaking down. But recent events at the police station had made it just as bad, in terms of nightmares and lack of calm. Rather than seek out a whole new port in the storm, she decided to face up to her fears and returned to Gillian's apartment. The memories were still strong, and painful, but she was overcoming them.

She emptied her pockets and took off her shoulder holster, kicking off her shoes as she sat on the edge of the bed. She rolled the kinks out of her neck and stretched, settling down on the cool blankets. With her eyes closed, Gillian's scent all around her, she could imagine that Gillian was really there and not thousands of miles away. But if Gillian was there, she wouldn't have to take off her own blouse.

Her mind wandered to the few times she had come home after a shift, the handful of nights Gillian was waiting to greet her. Soft kisses, shoulder massages, and a slow, loving undressing. Riley had never felt so pampered or more loved than those nights. She ran her hand over her chest, fooling herself that it was Gillian's hand. Slowly, she undid the buttons of her blouse and ran her fingers over her chest.

Kenzie is back. She wanted you. You were in a hotel room, with Kenzie Crowe kissing you, and you did... nothing.

It was the true test, as far as she was concerned. She hadn't realized how deep her feelings for Gillian went until the moment she was pushing Kenzie away.

She moved her hand down to her belt, resting the palm against the crotch of her jeans. She licked her lips, swallowed, and lifted one leg as she began to rub through her pants. Gentle kisses, Gillian breathing against her hair, breath washing against her neck. Long days and aching muscles were a small price to pay knowing that Gillian would make it all better in the end. Now, the days were just tedious and the muscles went without a massage.

Riley opened her eyes and looked at her cell phone on the nightstand. *Call her. Just pick up the phone. Take the first step, damn it.*

She couldn't bring herself to do it. Gillian was the one who left. Gillian was the one who made the calls. She needed the space to figure out what she wanted to do. She would come back when she was ready. If she was ready. She didn't need Riley pressuring her to make the decision faster.

But she needs to know you care. That you're waiting. She needs to know you love her.

Riley made a fist with her free hand and bumped it against her forehead. She moved her hand faster between her legs and arched her back as she came.

Nothing was going to happen with Kenzie. She was still in a relationship with Gillian, and it would stay that way until Gillian told her otherwise. Riley sat up, still breathing hard, and picked up her cell phone. She was grateful for the speed-dial, taking away her option of stopping mid-dial and immediately connecting her to Gillian's phone. Three rings, Riley's breath caught as the call was answered.

"Hi..."

"It's me. I miss..."

"...reached Dr. Gillian Hunt's phone. Please leave a message and I'll get back to you when I can."

Riley crumbled and felt like crying. She listened to the white noise on the other end of the phone for a long time, hand balled into a fist around the comforter. She swallowed, tears burning her eyes, and said, "I miss you. I love you." She closed the phone and dropped it on the bed next to her. The tears finally came, and she curled up on Gillian's side of the bed to let them flow.

Riley got back to the Gold Hotel at ten minutes to five. She headed up to Kenzie's room, making sure she didn't look like she had been crying. She knocked on Kenzie's bedroom door and, when there was no answer, tried the knob. A knot of tension grew between Riley's shoulders as she stepped into the quiet room, well aware that Kenzie wouldn't purposely leave her room unlocked. Not when several of her soldiers had just been killed.

From the doorway, she could see into the bedroom. Kenzie was curled on the bed with her back to the door, her right leg stuck out and the left pulled tight against her chest. She had one fist curled next to her head, trembling violently and rocking her head against the pillow. Riley lowered her gun and said, "Kenzie?"

"No," Kenzie groaned.

Riley crossed the room and sat on the edge of the bed. Kenzie's eyes were open, but unfocused. Riley put her hand on Kenzie's shoulder, and her wrist was immediately locked in a vice grip. Kenzie's eyes swam into focus, her hair falling back to reveal the scars on the side of her face. Riley managed not to recoil, but it was difficult. She swallowed hard and said, "Kenzie. It's me. You're safe. You're home."

Kenzie looked past Riley at the hotel room and relaxed slightly. Her fingers relaxed and she pushed herself up. "Rye. God."

"You okay?"

Kenzie nodded. "Yeah." She exhaled sharply and looked at her watch. "You ready to make the descent into purgatory?"

"Yeah." Riley took Kenzie's hand and pulled her off the bed. "I've still got your back."

Kenzie grinned. "Good to know."

Chapter Six

The bus station was a long abandoned mess, the parking lot ringed with a chain-link fence that seemed to work better as a trash-catcher than a deterrent to trespassers. A sign for "Ann/Dras Developments" hung lopsided from the links. Riley parked outside the fence and Kenzie got the padlock off the fence with a modicum of effort. She pushed the gate open just enough for Riley to slip through, then closed it behind her. The Depot, as it was known among the criminals she and Kenzie chased through the lot, was infamous as an entry point to the Underground. Few people were insane enough to venture inside.

Riley led the way across the loading area. The front door was long gone, the entrance a gaping hole in the side of the building. They were halfway there when something inside shifted, and a person stepped out of the shadows. Both Riley and Kenzie had their guns drawn before they recognized who it was.

"Damn it, Priest," Riley said as she returned her gun to the shoulder holster under her jacket. "What are you doing here?"

"Watching your back," Priest said. She wore a lightweight jacket, the pockets weighted down with supplies. "You and I are staking out a suspect in the Benedict murder. Should take all night."

Riley nodded. "Thank you."

Priest gave a slight incline of her head, still obviously annoyed that Riley wouldn't listen to reason. "I'm your back-up. I can't let you go down there alone."

"She wouldn't have been alone," Kenzie said. "How did you find this place, anyway?"

Priest glanced at Riley and said, "I had a hunch." She looked at the sky. "It's going to be dark soon. We should get in and out as quickly as possible."

"Sounds like a good plan," Kenzie said. "Lead the way, Katie."

Priest glared at Kenzie before she turned around and went back into the Depot. The red light of the setting sun made the interior look like it was aflame, rotting benches and piles of trash casting long shadows across the tile floor. The ticket agent's booth was in the process of falling down, slowly but surely, and it was here that Priest led them. She took a flashlight from her pocket and aimed it into the square skeleton of the booth. The floor was gone, replaced by a jagged hole. A wooden ladder led down into the darkness. "This just goes to the basement," Priest said. "There's a staircase on the other side of the building, but the ladder actually looks safer." She aimed the flashlight at Riley and Kenzie. "Who is going first?"

Kenzie said, "It's my stupid mission. Might as well be the canary in the coal mine." She brushed past Riley and stepped into the booth. She tested her weight on the top rung of the ladder and slowly began to climb down. "The, uh... fourth rung from the top is a little weak. Katie, you may want to be careful of it since I think you weigh the most of us."

Riley stepped closer to Priest and whispered, "Don't smite her."

"I don't smite."

"Well, whatever you do. She's just testing the boundaries, seeing how far she can push you. Don't let her get to you. It's her way of bonding."

Priest sighed and leaned over the hole. "Thank you for the information, Mac."

Kenzie looked up, squinting into the light of Priest's flashlight. "Hey, what do you know, she bites back. Good to know." A second later, she said, "All right, I'm down."

Riley motioned for Priest to go, and followed a few seconds behind her. Priest dropped her flashlight at Kenzie's request, and Kenzie examined the confines of the basement. "Over here," she called. Riley and Priest made their way over to a concrete set of stairs that seemed to lead into the ground. Kenzie crouched and felt around, finally finding a hatch. "Here we go. You're both sure you want to go down here?"

Riley said, "I promised, didn't I?"

"How about you, Priest?"

Priest glanced at Riley to make sure she'd heard right. Riley raised her eyebrows and shrugged. Priest said, "Riley is your partner, and I'm hers. I'm going."

Kenzie opened the hatch and said, "Well, then here we go."

The hatch covered a stone staircase, tight walls on either side giving the impression of a tomb. Kenzie aimed the flashlight up at the curved ceiling, her free hand pressed against the stone walls on either side to keep her head from swimming. The stairs seemed to go straight down, their bodies pulled forward by gravity. Riley and Kenzie both had to fight the feeling they were falling, but Priest managed to descend without much trouble.

The bottom of the passage was capped by an ill-fitting door, light pouring through on all four sides. Kenzie pushed the door open and they emerged into a wide, low space that looked like the lobby of an apartment building. Directly across from the entrance was a latticework of lumber wrapped in wires and extension cords. An iron grid formed a ceiling over their heads, bare bulbs hanging from bare wires. The light was dim, but bright enough for Kenzie to turn off the flashlight.

"Where do they get power?"

Riley went to the wall, where several holes had been punched in the Sheetrock. She peered into the hole and knocked on the wall with a knuckle. "They hook into the power of buildings above them. Leech it out. They only take a little so it won't be noticed. Same with water." She looked at Kenzie and saw she was smiling. "What?"

"Come on, Rye. How many times did you wish we could come down here after some crook? Now here we are."

Riley smirked. "Keep your mind on the mission, Kenzie."

The east and west sides of the "lobby" were fronted with brick archways. Riley randomly went to the east entrance and peered through to the darkness. Another thin passageway led to her right and left, lights hanging at five- or six-foot intervals along the wall. "Okay. East or west, right or left? We could split up, but I don't like the idea of any of us going off on her own."

"Good point." Kenzie joined Riley at the entrance and shrugged. "This way is as good as any. The hard part is going to be remembering the way out."

"I've got it," Priest said.

"Glad you came, then, Katie." Kenzie checked her watch and said, "Okay. We'll give this way fifteen minutes. If we don't find anything, we'll come back and try the other direction. Sound good?"

"Works for me," Riley said. She stepped through the archway and found herself completely in the Underground. Nightmares, urban legends, lies told by parents to make their children behave, all came flooding back to her memory. She exhaled and looked at the expanse of dark brick in front of her. The ceiling arched over her head, thick strips of wood stretching from one wall to the other and supporting the stone ceiling. Riley pushed aside irrational fears to make room for the rational fears and began walking. She resisted the urge to pull her gun; the people down here were jumpy enough without her adding a weapon to the mix.

Most of the buildings had been demolished when the city was raised, replaced by thick stone supports. But here and there, they found buildings hiding in the shadows. Doors, windows and signs were all gone, but there were obvious signs of occupation. A flat pillow here, tangled blankets there, a barricade built out of shoeboxes and plastic bags, little hints of an attempt at civilization.

The streets, such as they were, varied wildly in width. Sometimes Riley and Kenzie were able to walk side-by-side, while other times they were forced to turn sideways and scoot, clothes brushing against the stone walls as they walked. They heard voices raised in the distance, music playing somewhere, but they never crossed paths with anyone. Occasional shadows fled across the walls in front of them, and Riley knew that their presence was known. The citizens of the Underground were evading them.

"I guess that's good," Riley said as she heard scuttling footsteps coming from up ahead. "Like rats. They're more afraid of us than we are of them."

She turned a corner and shined the flashlight into the grinning face of a pale man. She recoiled, shocked at finally seeing another person. He was standing in a gap in the wall, his shoulders hunched to make room, his eyes blinking rapidly at the light. His grin widened and he sniffed the air. "Riley Parra. Oh, good, good. Riley Parra."

Riley tensed and moved her hand to her gun. "That's right, pal. Who's asking?"

The man erupted in laughter and turned, scooting down the gap with the speed of a spider. Seconds later, he was out of the flashlight's range.

"How the hell did he know your name?" Kenzie whispered. Her voice was more surprised than angry.

"Don't know. Maybe they get the papers down here. I'm kind of a big deal."

"Right," Kenzie chuckled.

They continued on until they found a long shack with an open front. Tables stacked with baskets and bowls filled the empty space under the wooden roof. Underground residents shrunk away from the newcomers, but they didn't flee. Kenzie moved past Riley and led the way into the apparent marketplace. "Excuse me. We're looking for a friend of mine. We were wondering if you could help."

The person closest to Kenzie, someone so enshrined in rags that Riley couldn't tell if it was a man or a woman, shook their head rapidly and backed away.

"He's a tall man, uh... light-skinned black guy. He was a soldier, like me." She pulled her dog tags out, and a few of the people stopped shrinking away. "I just want to talk to him. He's a good friend of mine. He's called Radio because—"

"He talks like a radio."

Riley and Kenzie both turned and saw a man wearing a fedora watching them. He eyed Priest and moved closer, his right foot dragging behind him. He looked at Kenzie's dog tags and said, "You really his friend?"

"I was his commanding officer in Afghanistan. I just want to make sure he's okay."

"People who end up down here, sometimes they don't even want to see their friends."

"I'd like to let him make that choice, sir."

The man pursed his lips and made little 'bup-bup-bup' sounds with his lips. Finally, he dipped his chin and said, "Okay. Name's Jeremiah." He eyed Riley and Priest and said, "You two are cops?" They nodded. "Ain't got no jurisdiction down here. You best understand that 'fore we go anywhere."

"We understand. We're not here to arrest anybody. We just want to talk."

Jeremiah held up his large, gnarled hands. The joints were swollen and reminded Riley of old tree branches. They weren't pretty, but they were strong. He dipped his chin and said, "Good enough for me. But if he wants you to leave, you leave. On your own, or we'll make you. Clear?"

"Perfectly clear."

Jeremiah looked at Priest again, and said, "All right. Follow me." He motioned them toward one of the tributaries that branched off from the clearing. Kenzie walked behind him, with Priest and Riley bringing up the rear.

"*Riley Parra!*"

Riley and Priest both turned, even though the shout came from some distance away. It was impossible to tell exactly how far in the tunnels. Riley glanced at Priest and said, "In and out as quick as possible. Works for me."

"Me too."

They turned and followed Jeremiah and Kenzie deeper into the Underground.

Chapter Seven

Jeremiah asked them to stop at the next crossroads, raising one old hand as he continued deeper into the maze. They heard his voice, and then someone answered him. Kenzie straightened and said, "That's Radio." She started to move, but Riley put a hand on her arm.

"Let's do this the way Jeremiah wants. Let's show the old guy a little bit of courtesy and see how far it gets us."

Kenzie nodded and relaxed again, but craned her neck to look down the corridor. A moment later, Jeremiah returned. "He said he'll see you. Said he's been waiting."

"He said that?" Riley said.

Jeremiah's lips curled into a smile. "Actually he said I've Been Waiting for You. Neil Young, 1968."

Kenzie smiled. "Thank you, Jeremiah. You've been a big help."

He nodded his head and stepped aside. "Go on in."

Kenzie led the way around the corner. Radio was pushing himself to his feet, brushing his hands over his dirty jeans. He wore a red hoodie under a black jacket, the hoodie pulled up over his head. He was tall, but not lanky, so it was difficult to tell how big he was until Kenzie stepped up next to him. He wore a beard that had once been neatly trimmed but was starting to grow up in rough patches on his cheeks. His skin was ruddy, dark but suffering from a lack of sunshine. He grinned when he spotted Kenzie and wrapped his arms around her.

Kenzie chuckled as he squeezed her. "I've been waiting for you."

"Jeremiah told me you already used that one," Kenzie said when he let her go.

Radio chuckled and put his hands on her shoulders. "Hello." He looked at Riley and Priest, his smile fading. "Goodbye, stranger."

"No, it's fine, Radio. They're good. I trust them." She pointed at Riley. "She was my partner on the force. She's just here to watch my back, make sure I stay out of trouble."

Radio seemed to debate himself about their presence, and Riley said, "Why can't we be friends?"

Radio's grin returned and he relaxed. "Good enough." He gestured at a low divan sitting against the far wall, threadbare cushions on a rickety wooden frame. Kenzie and Riley sat down, but Priest remained standing. Radio looked at her as he sat down, then turned his grin back on Kenzie. "Welcome back," he said.

"It's nice to be back," Kenzie said. "It's nice to see you, Radio. Are you well?"

Radio held his hands out. "I will survive."

Kenzie smiled. "Good. I'm glad." She glanced at Riley and said, "We should talk about why we're here. I got your postcard. I know that you were looking into something, and it's causing a lot of problems. Do you know about Charlie and Coltrane...?"

Radio looked down at his hand and shifted on his seat. He nodded. "A Day in the Life."

"Heard the news today," Riley said. Radio nodded. Kenzie raised an eyebrow, and Riley shrugged. "I'm learning."

"Hard to say I'm sorry," Radio said.

Kenzie reached out and touched Radio's hands. "It wasn't your fault."

"What a fool believes."

"Hey," Kenzie said. "I'm trying to help you here, you son of a bitch."

Radio pressed his lips together and closed his eyes. Finally, he nodded and covered her hand with his. "I'm sorry."

"It's all right. Okay, we know that you went to see Charlie and Marks before they died. Can you tell us why?"

Radio's tongue poked between his lips and he rocked back and forth on his seat. He rubbed his hands together, searching for the right thing to say. Finally, he said, "Livin' on the edge. Suspicious minds. Daytime friends."

Riley leaned forward. "Look, Radio. I understand this defense mechanism. Trust me. But we need you to just tell us what you saw."

"If you don't know me by now."

"No, I understand. You want to use this thing to protect yourself. But there have been three murders that all seem to point to you. I need to know what you had to do with them."

"Cut him some slack, Riley."

Riley closed her eyes. "This isn't a game, Radio." She turned to Kenzie.

"What's his real name?"

"Russell Miller."

"Russell, please. Just stop this game and tell us what we need to know."

Radio stood up and waved them away. He glared at Kenzie. "I should have known better."

Kenzie and Riley both stood. "Radio, stop. Please, let's just..."

"We'll take you to jail. Maybe you'd feel more comfortable talking there." Kenzie glared at Riley, but she wouldn't be stopped. "You break the rules when it suits you. Switching to lyrics if the title doesn't suit you, like calling Kenzie Major Tom. You'll break the rules for a letter, but not to catch a murderer?"

"I can't help myself," Radio said, his voice trembling.

"I think that's bullshit."

Kenzie said, "Wait, Radio..."

He shook her off. "It's too late."

Kenzie moved between Riley and Radio and held her hands out to them. "Just hold on. Radio, please. You came to me for help. Riley is... she doesn't understand, okay?"

Radio glared at Riley and his shoulders sagged. He nodded to Kenzie. "For you." He returned to his seat, glaring at Riley. "Sorry seems to be the hardest word."

"I'm not apologizing to you. This is nonsense."

Radio glanced at Kenzie, shrugged, and held his hands out. "We can work it out. If you could read my mind."

"Sorry, left that superpower upstairs," Riley muttered.

Kenzie sighed and turned to Riley, "Look, you're probably not going to be much help. So why don't you and Priest just... step outside? Radio and I will get through this. I have practice, I know how to parse what he's saying. Just give us five minutes. Please, Riley."

Riley stood up and said, "I still think you could tell us without this song and dance. For what it's worth."

"Would I lie to you?"

Riley scoffed and motioned for Priest to lead the way out. They stepped out of the room and Riley heard Radio begin speaking immediately.

She crossed her arms over her chest and looked down the "street." Radio's apparent home was separated from the public thoroughfare by a simple wooden wall with a door cut into the side. To the right was a brick wall, weeds growing through the foundation and snaking up through the mortar.

The entire area was cast in shadows, just enough light coming from the weak bulbs for her to realize how close the walls and ceiling were. She felt like she was in a crawlspace under a house. She glanced at Priest and saw she was valiantly trying to hide her own discomfort.

"How are you holding up?"

"As well as can be expected."

"I'm glad you came."

Priest looked Riley in the eye. "I didn't have a choice. You were coming down here no matter what. If you died..." She shook her head. "You're stubborn, Riley. I knew that when I accepted the chance to watch over you. But I thought you would stop short of suicide."

"Sometimes you have to put yourself at risk to protect someone you care about."

"Apparently."

Riley looked back in the direction they came. "Do you still remember the way out?"

"I do."

"Just making sure. This place is..." She swallowed and stuck her hands into her pockets. "I don't know what it is."

"We're underground," Priest said. "It's instinctual. You equate being underground with being buried. Death."

Riley nodded. "That, and the fact you told me this place was worse than Hell."

Priest allowed herself a small grin. "Well, there's that, too."

"Seriously, Priest. I want to thank you. If you hadn't..."

She was interrupted by Kenzie raising her voice inside Radio's hovel. "Think," Radio shouted. "Please! Think."

Kenzie stormed out of the home as Riley and Priest reached the front door. Her face was red, her eyes wide and wet with tears. "Get out of my way, Riley. We're out of here."

"What did he say?"

"He's a damn liar," Kenzie said.

She put her hand on Riley's shoulder and tried to shove her out of the way, but Riley anticipated the move. She grabbed Kenzie's arm, pulled it down, and twisted. She put her arm around Kenzie and pulled her close to her chest, her chin on Kenzie's shoulder. Kenzie fought, but Riley had the upper hand.

"What did he say?"

Radio came out of his home and said, "The cold hard truth."

Kenzie brought her hand up, aiming her finger at Radio. "You shut your damned mouth!"

Priest said, "Riley..."

Riley looked over her shoulder. Jeremiah had arrived, drawn by the commotion. A group of fellow Undergrounders stood behind him, craning their necks to get a better look at the commotion. Jeremiah kept his hands clasped behind his back, looking at the scene before he calmly asked, "Is there some sort of problem?"

"No problem," Riley said. "Right, Radio?"

Radio nodded and gave Jeremiah a thumbs-up.

Kenzie fought to escape Riley's grip and said, "We're done here. You can fry, for all I care. Screw you, Russell."

Riley frowned and said, "Let's just all calm down and talk this out."

Radio's eyes widened and his lips moved for a moment before he finally shouted, "Help!"

"What—"

Something came down hard across Riley's shoulders and she went down hard. Kenzie fell with her, and they landed in a heap on the ground. Riley rolled onto her side and saw one of the Underground dwellers pinning Priest to the wall with a baseball bat across the chest. He had one hand clamped over her mouth, pressing her hard against the stone of the wall. Jeremiah lifted his lead pipe, wielding it like an axe, and said, "Sorry, Detective Parra. You understand how it is. Loyalty and all."

Jeremiah swung the pipe down toward Riley's head. The wide arc of the blow was deflected by Radio's arm, which appeared out of nowhere at the last second. The pipe hit hard enough to make Riley wince, Radio's lips pulled back over his teeth as he spun on Jeremiah. "Respect!" He shouted as he shoved Jeremiah away from Riley. Jeremiah stumbled and his feet came out from underneath him. He landed on his ass, sprawled in the middle of the street.

Radio had already turned on the man holding Priest. They grappled briefly, the man releasing Priest to focus on the true threat, and Radio managed to drop him as well. Kenzie stood and helped Riley to her feet, their disagreement forgotten for the moment. Priest looked toward the ceiling, eyes closed, and said, "There are more on the way."

"How do you know that?" Kenzie asked.

"She knows," Riley said. She grabbed Radio's arm, forcing him to look at her. "Is there another way out of here? Another way back to the surface?"

Radio thought, and then nodded quickly. He motioned for them to follow him. They ran past his home, down a side alley. Riley was reminded of the old TV show Fraggle Rock and had the insane urge to start singing. The urge passed when an inhuman voice howled in the caverns behind them. It was echoed by a series of hoots and catcalls, and then another shout of "Riley Parra!"

Kenzie looked at Riley as they ran. "Guess you really are famous."

"Fame is overrated," Riley said. "Go. Run." She looked over her shoulder and discovered Priest had vanished. "Damn it, Caitlin," she muttered. She didn't have time to go back; she just hoped that Priest would be able to find them wherever Radio was leading.

Chapter Eight

Trying to make sense of the twists and turns in the path would have driven Riley crazy, so she just focused on the back of Kenzie's blouse and prayed Radio knew where he was going. Occasional howls echoed after them, the thrill of the hunt. Kenzie glanced back a few times to make sure Riley was still behind her. At one point, she said, "Priest?"

"Watching our backs. Go!"

Kenzie shook her head as she ran. "Those howls. They don't... sound human."

"Bad moon rising," Radio muttered up ahead.

Riley said, "That is really not helpful, Russell."

He stopped at a dog-leg turn and pointed to a wooden shack. "Up around the bend. Get together." He waited and then grabbed Riley's arm. "One?"

"She's watching our back. It's okay. She'll find us."

Riley and Kenzie went into the building with Radio watching back the way they had come. When they were safely inside, he closed the door and set his shoulder against a section of counter that had broken away from the wall. Kenzie flipped on her flashlight and joined Riley and Radio in the effort to get the door blocked. Kenzie said, "How is Priest going to know where we are? We can't just abandon her out there."

"It's okay," Riley said. "Trust me. Priest is... resourceful. She'd be angrier if we put ourselves at risk for her."

Radio said, "She works hard for the money."

Kenzie, suddenly reminded of their argument earlier, shot him a look of pure venom. "You don't speak to me. Ever."

"Don't bring me down."

"Shut up," Kenzie growled. She got in his face and said, "Just shut the hell up, okay, Radio? For once in your goddamn life. Sounds of silence, right?"

Riley stepped between the two of them and whispered, "We have everybody in the Underground chasing our asses. Isn't that enough without fighting amongst ourselves?" Kenzie backed away, tossing the flashlight onto the counter as she passed. Radio nodded, his face twisted into a distraught expression as he backed away as well.

"Great. Good." She sighed and examined their hideout. It was the front room of a restaurant, tables and chairs and accoutrements all long-since scavenged. The walls were ripped apart, the innards removed for some sundry construction project or another. Most of the ceiling tiles were gone, the remnants sagging in their frame like rotten teeth in a diseased mouth. Kenzie's flashlight was the only thing between them and total darkness, so Riley fervently hoped that Priest put in new batteries before she left. Or that she used holy batteries.

Riley started to follow Kenzie into the kitchen, but she was reluctant to leave Radio on his own without the flashlight. "Will you be okay out here?"

He smiled. "Solitary man."

"Right. Yell if someone besides Priest tries to get in here."

"You got it."

Riley went into the kitchen and found Kenzie standing over a sink. She was violently twisting the faucet with one hand, working one spigot with the other. She heard Riley approach and slapped the side of the sink with her hand. "Stupid piece of shit."

"Well, it has been out of service for over a century."

"People down here have lights, they have damn neighborhoods. They can't hook up the water? For fuck's sake." She rubbed the hand she'd used to hit the sink and glared at Riley. "You look like shit."

The sweat on Kenzie's face had drawn all the dirt particles out of the air, giving her already dark complexion an added layer of grime. Her hair was rearranged from repeatedly raking her fingers through it, the ends limp and dripping sweat onto her collar. "Good, because you're a beauty queen, and otherwise people wouldn't be able to tell us apart."

Kenzie scoffed and unbuttoned her blouse.

"That wasn't a come-on."

"Oh, get over yourself." She shrugged out of her blouse, leaving her in a white t-shirt. She balled up the shirt and used it to wipe some of the dirt off her face. The result was a smeared, smudged mess. Riley halfway wished Kenzie was wearing a tank top just so she could see how bad the burns on her shoulder were, and she felt like a pervert for thinking it. When Kenzie finished wiping her face, she wrapped the sleeves of her shirt around her waist and began to pace.

"What the hell happened with you and Radio? What did he say?"

"I'm not going to talk about that."

"Come on, Kenzie. It's the whole reason we're down here. Priest is God-knows-where because we're helping you out. And now we're just going to forget it because you didn't like what you heard? You didn't believe Radio was a murderer. Has that changed?"

"No."

"Do you think he's the kind of person who would lie to you?"

Kenzie clenched her jaw and crossed her arms over her chest. Finally, she said, "No. He wouldn't."

"So what did he say?"

Kenzie found a milk crate at the back of the room and turned it upside down, testing the weight with her foot before she sat down. "There was a member of our platoon we called Player. Travis Unger. He was always regaling us with stories of his many conquests back home. If someone said they dated a model, Travis dated a supermodel. If someone said they slept with an actress, Travis had an orgy backstage at the Academy Awards. We all thought he was full of shit, but we humored him." She smiled. "Then one day he got a package. It was full of pictures. Boy, he acquired a crowd as he started to put them up over his bed. It was like an issue of the National Enquirer. Famous names, famous faces, and all of them draped all over Player like he was the second coming of Don Juan.

"Player wasn't in the ambush where we all got hurt. When we came back, he stayed over there. But he got back recently. Radio said Player came to see him when he came home and wanted to catch up. I didn't even know he was home. I don't know. He didn't contact me." She toyed with her fingernail and shook her head. "Player told Radio that he was just touching base, but something got Radio spooked. He ended the visit as quickly as he could and sent Player away."

"Player met with Radio down here?"

"I guess so."

"Brave guy."

"Soldier."

Riley nodded.

"Something got Radio so spooked that he decided to go check on the others. He says I had the timeline wrong. He got to New York just after Charlie died. He was in Chicago in time to find Marks after he killed himself. Everyone died right before Radio got there."

Riley frowned. "Someone is picking off members of your old platoon? Why didn't he get Radio?"

"Would you try to kill someone down here? These guys look out for each other, for better or for worse. Do you really think we would have found Radio so easily if they thought we weren't friends? Radio had protection. Charlie, Marks and Coltrane weren't so lucky."

"Why didn't Radio get in contact with you?"

Kenzie looked past Riley to the door. "He didn't think I would believe him. He's telling me that Player is the one killing our people. And I just cannot accept that. I cannot believe someone under my command is capable of such... evil. And what does he have to gain from it?" She shifted her feet on the floor. "I think you're right, Riley. Maybe Radio is cracking up for good. Maybe he's making all of this up."

"Sisters of mercy," Radio said from behind her.

Riley turned and saw his silhouette framed by the door. He hung his head and stepped into the room like a child knowing he's about to be scolded. "Wicked game. On the road again. Held up without a gun, looking for the next best thing. Love is a many splendored thing. Blue eyes crying in the rain. Blinded by the light. Love on the rocks. Ain't no cure for love."

Riley looked at Kenzie. "Did you understand any of that?"

Kenzie was frowning up at Radio. "Who?"

"Woman." Radio shrugged.

"What woman? An Afghani woman?"

"You got me, babe. Rumors. Other side. Play with fire."

Kenzie stood up. "You better be damn sure. Rumors are one thing..."

"I saw her standing there."

Riley said, "Will someone please translate for me?"

Kenzie sighed, keeping her eyes on Radio as she spoke. "Radio claims that Player had a thing with some woman over in Afghanistan. If you've ever seen some of the women over there, you would understand. Gorgeous. Bluest eyes you've ever seen. Player met her when he was... on patrol?" Radio nodded. "They had sex, and Player apparently fell for her. Kept the relationship secret. He thinks... Player inadvertently set up the ambush that got us all hurt."

"What?" Riley said.

"When will I see you again?" Radio said.

"She wanted to meet him. Player told her that we would be out on patrol that day. Oh, God. She used him to get information about our movements."

Riley said, "So why is Player killing you guys now?"

"Do you hear what I hear?" Radio said. "I can see clearly now."

"Player is worried we saw or heard something that made us realize what he'd done. He's trying to cover his ass because he got used. He's trying to finish the job his whore started."

Radio nodded sadly. "The boys are back in town."

"Shit. He killed Coltrane last night. Odds are he's going to come after Radio again."

"Don't worry," Riley said. "No one's going to get past that barricade."

Priest stepped into the room, eyed everyone, and said, "Hey."

Kenzie was on her feet, gun in hand, before she realized who the new arrival was. Her jaw dropped and she gave Riley a confused look.

Priest, oblivious, walked across the room. Her clothes were dirty and torn, a mixture of blood, sweat and grime coloring one side of her face. She pointed at the sink and said, "Does that work?"

Kenzie lowered her gun. "What the hell?"

"Relax. I meant that no one except Priest can get in." Radio went back into the main room to make sure the door was still blocked. Riley walked up to Priest to make sure she was all right. The few wounds she could see were superficial, and the majority of the blood seemed to belong to someone else. "What happened out there? Are you all right?"

"Fine. The sink?"

"Broken," Kenzie said.

Priest sighed and pressed her hand against her temple. "Wonderful." She fished in her jacket with one hand and withdrew a bottle of water and a handkerchief. She handed them to Riley, who twisted the bottle open and wet the hanky. She cleaned up some of the blood from Priest's cheek and pressed the wet cloth to a wound near Priest's hairline. "Local boys?"

"Yeah. From downtown," Priest said.

"Great," Riley muttered.

Kenzie said, "What the hell is going on with the two of you?"

"Nothing," Riley said. "Why?"

Radio came in and shrugged at Kenzie.

"How did she get in here?"

"I told you," Riley said. "She's a good partner." She took Priest's hand

and placed it on top of the compress. "Are you going to need... confession?"

"No. Church can wait until morning."

Riley took that to mean she hadn't overused her powers as an angel. She figured it was the closest approximation to good news that they would get, so she took it without complaint.

"And you say Radio is hard to understand," Kenzie said. "What's going on out there?"

Priest sagged against the wall. "A bunch of locals got all riled up by outsiders. They discovered Riley and I were down here, and they figured we were fair game. Because we're cops, and we don't have any jurisdiction."

Riley nodded. "Yeah. We've made our fair share of enemies."

Kenzie decided to drop the subject. "Radio, is there any route to the surface near here?"

Radio rubbed his face with both hands and paced for a moment. He snapped his fingers and said, "Proud Mary."

Kenzie frowned.

"Maybe he means a lyric," Riley said. "Good job in the city... working for the man?" Radio said nothing. "A minute of sleep, rolling on the river?"

Radio snapped his fingers and pointed at her.

"River... the waterfront. The waterfront?" Another nod, this time a wide smile.

Kenzie said, "You're getting good at this."

"Don't get too excited," Priest said. She went to the wall and said, "Riley, shine the flashlight over here." Riley lit up the wall, giving Priest a wide shadow as she used a charcoal pencil to draw a rough box-shape on the wall. She quickly sketched a row of lines, and then added a few landmarks. Kenzie watched as the map appeared on the wall. "We're here," Priest said. "Give or take, we're underneath Cleveland Road." She made a quick series of lines leading down and to the left. "This is the path we took to get down here."

"If you say so," Kenzie said.

"The waterfront is here. It's about ten blocks away from where we are right now. And right now, the people who want us dead are here, here, here and here." She made marks that showed they were pretty much completely surrounded. The waterfront was cut off from them.

Kenzie groaned and looked at Radio. "Any other nearby exits?"

Radio winced and nodded.

"Is it cut off?"

Radio looked at the map Priest had drawn and reluctantly shook his head.

"Great. Show us the way."

Another negative shake.

Priest said, "Why not? Is it a bad place?" He nodded emphatically. "In No Man's Land?"

Radio nodded.

"So it's in No Man's Land. We'll fit right in with the homeless."

Radio looked hopefully at Priest. "It comes up... in a bad building. The basement of a bad building."

"Bad, bad Leroy Brown."

"'Baddest man in the whole damn town. He means it comes out in the worst building in town," Priest corrected. Realization dawned and she said, "Oh."

"What?" Riley said.

Priest leaned against the wall and checked her handkerchief. It was smeared with blood and dirt, but the wound had closed. She looked at Kenzie. "The reason the nearest available entrance is because a lot of the bad guys chasing us used it to get down here. It's the basement of the biggest crime boss in No Man's Land." She looked at Riley. "Guy goes by the name March... or Marchosias."

Riley said, "And that's the only way back to the surface?"

"At the moment," Priest said. "Yeah."

Riley leaned against the wall and slid down to the floor. "Of course it is."

Chapter Nine

"Who is March Otis?" Kenzie asked.

"No one you need to concern yourself with," Priest said.

"If I have to fight my way out of his building, I would like to have some background. Who is he? Some guy you and Rye took down?"

Priest said, "Imagine a criminal mastermind. Some business-minded villain who decided to start up his own crime empire. He's the puppet master. He hires people to do his dirty work on the street and then just sits back to reap the rewards of his ill-gotten gains. Because he has someone else doing all his dirty work, the cops can't touch him. He's bulletproof. Al Capone times a million."

Kenzie said, "And that's March?"

"No. March is that guy's boss."

Kenzie raised an eyebrow. "Okay. I take it you two have some history."

"He nearly killed me," Riley said. "Well, his boys. I barely managed to get out with my life the first time. The second time I only made it out because I had an ace in the hole." To Priest, she said, "There's no way."

"There's no other way," Kenzie said. "Look, we'll probably be in and out before Otis even knows we're there."

Radio said, "Santa Claus is watching you." Everyone turned and stared at him, and he waved his hands. "Private eyes."

"He's right," Riley said. "March knew we were down here seconds after we showed up. He's going to know we're in his building. His turf, his rules."

"Well, we can't stay down here forever," Kenzie said. "In case you didn't notice, these people don't seem to like you much, either."

Priest said, "We'll go in the morning. March is nocturnal. He'll be at his weakest at sunrise. With luck, we'll reach him at just the right time and we'll be able to get out before he can gather his strength. The downside is that we'll have to spend the night here."

Kenzie shrugged. "Spent the night in worse places, with worse company.

How will we know when it's safe to go?"

"I'll tell you."

Radio said, "Countin' on a miracle?"

"You'd be surprised," Riley said. She looked at her watch, but it was too dark to read. Probably for the best. "Okay. Kenzie, Radio, you guys set up camp here. Maybe Priest has a tent and some sleeping bags in that jacket of hers. I'm going to see if I can find anything of use. Maybe someone was using this place as a squat and forgot their freezer full of TV dinners."

"Look for a microwave, too."

"I'll get right on that. Priest, want to give me a hand?"

They left Kenzie and Radio in the back room with the flashlight and went into the darkness. Priest took a second light from her pocket and clicked it on.

"Okay, seriously. What do you have in those pockets?"

"I have what I need," Priest said. She kept her voice low so that it wouldn't carry back to the others as they moved through the shell of the building. "We're not just facing demons. A lot of the people down here have been recruited by Marchosias' minions. They're paying, and they're paying well. By morning, every single person and demon down here is going to be looking for you. Dead or alive."

"Eh, why should life be easy?" Riley moved a stack of garbage and smelled brimstone. Either there was a fire at some point in the building's history, or a demon had been squatting in the corner. Maybe both. She turned and caught a glimpse of Priest in the backwash of the flashlight. "What about you? Looks like you took quite a beating."

Priest gingerly touched her forehead. "Yeah. I kind of got into a brawl with a whole group of people. Close quarters like that, I couldn't tell the humans from the demons. I didn't want to risk torching some mortal, so I had to rely on brute strength. I'm not used to that."

"Looks like you did a good enough job."

"I just scared them a little. They'll be back."

Riley found a door and managed to shoulder it open, the wood so warped that it cracked as she pushed it open. She took the flashlight from Priest and used it to destroy some gossamer spider webs before she stepped into the room. Shelves hung from brackets on the wall, ready to collapse if another ounce of weight was placed on them, and a ladder leaned against the back wall. Riley scanned the floor with the flashlight and bent down to pick up a discarded tablecloth. She folded it as best she could and picked up a second one that was bundled against the wall.

She came out of the storage room and looked toward the kitchen. The flashlight was still on, and Riley could see Kenzie's shadow moving across the far wall. "All right, here's the plan. We camp out here until you tell us it's clear. Then we walk the ten blocks to the exit, slip out through March's basement, head home and forget this ever happened. What about March? Do you think he's going to be that big of a problem?"

Priest raised an eyebrow.

"Fine, bad choice of words. Do you think we can handle him?"

"I don't know. He may be reluctant to show his true colors with humans around. But don't count on it. This isn't going to be a cakewalk."

"It never is." She gave up on the storage room and went back to the former kitchen of the restaurant. Kenzie had laid out her blouse on the floor, padded with Radio's hoodie. Radio himself had shed at least three layers and was making a bed for himself. He saw Riley and Priest return and pointed to another pile of clothes in the far corner. "Wow. Guess there's a benefit to dressing in layers."

Kenzie was sitting on her pile, arms folded across her knees and her face pressed into her elbow. Riley nodded to the clothes and said, "Thank you, Radio."

He nodded and smiled.

Riley tossed the tablecloths onto the floor in the middle of the room and said, "In case anyone wants a blanket. You might want to kick it a few times to make sure there aren't any spider nests."

"Thanks for putting that image in my head, Rye."

Riley took off her shoes and shoulder holster, laying them on the floor near the bed before she rearranged Radio's borrowed clothes. She sat with her back against the wall, her socks looking like neon lights in the darkness.

"Goodnight, my someone," Radio said.

"Night, Radio," Riley said.

"Night, Riley."

"Goodnight, Kenzie."

"Goodnight, Priest."

"Goodnight, Kenzie."

"Goodnight, John Boy," Riley and Kenzie said together. Riley chuckled and rested her head against the wall. "I'm going to stay up for a while. I'll wake you in a couple hours, Kenzie."

"Sounds good."

Riley shut off the flashlight and the room was thrown into total darkness. Riley closed her eyes, trying to ignore the shifting and settling in of her fellow prisoners, focusing on sounds outside. She kept hearing voices, skittering noises in the walls, and hushed orders. It sounded like rats, but it was hard to be sure. Demons had possessed a group of pigs in the Bible, right? So why not rats? It would be hard to find better scouts.

Something shifted in the darkness nearby and Riley tensed, but Kenzie whispered, "It's me, Rye. You're here somewhere, right?" Riley stuck her right leg out until it met Kenzie's shin. Kenzie grabbed Riley's leg and let her hand slide down it as she moved toward the wall, her palm skimming over Riley's knee, her thigh...

"Hey, hands."

"Sorry." Kenzie sat down next to Riley in the darkness and whispered, "Couldn't sleep. Thought I would keep you company."

"Just talking, right?"

"I'm no home wrecker. Try though I may."

Riley smiled into the darkness.

"Tell me about Gillian."

"She's... she was the medical examiner. It took me a long time to realize I had feelings for her. Some really bad stuff was going on, and she got caught in the middle of it because of me. She was in the hospital for a while. When she got out, she told me she needed some space. I just wanted to make her happy. But now..."

"You miss her."

"I miss her like hell. But... I can't ask her to come back."

Kenzie scoffed. "Why not?"

"She left. She needed space. It has to be her choice to come back."

"True. But she has to know you want her back, Riley. You know that saying, if you love something, set it free? Of course you know it. You're living it. That saying is stupid. Sure, fine, if you love something, give it space. But don't just give up. Fight. Gillian's been gone how long? And you're still saying you're with her. You're not with her, Riley. She's gone, and you're both alone. It doesn't have to be that way. You don't need to martyr your relationship just because you think it's her responsibility to make the first move."

"What if she thinks I'm being... overbearing?"

"She won't. I know what she's going through, Rye. She had to leave you, and it killed her. She doesn't want to be the one to always make the first move. She wants to know she's missed. If she retreats, you move forward.

If she turns her back on you, walk around her. Don't give up until she tells you she's absolutely done."

Riley said, "Kenzie, when you left for Afghanistan..."

"This isn't about me, or what might have been. You don't need to defend yourself to me. We had something good, and we both decided to let it go. You have a second chance at that. Don't let it go again."

Riley was surprised by a sudden kiss on her cheek.

"That was your cheek, right?"

"Yeah."

"I realized after I leaned in, I wasn't sure how you were... anyway. You deserve her, Rye. And she would be a fool to let you go easy."

"I'll keep that in mind."

She heard clothes rustling in the darkness, and then the presence next to her was gone. A few seconds later she heard Kenzie stretch out on top of her bedding.

Riley rested her head against the wall and closed her eyes. Since discovering the true nature of No Man's Land, learning the truth about Marchosias and angels and demons and eternal warfare, it seemed like everything had been taken from her. Kara, Gillian, her apartment, her car, even Lieutenant Hathaway. But Gillian could be brought back. She didn't have to let them take her away. She could fight. She lifted her hip and pulled out her cell phone, flipping it open to check for a signal.

"You're Going to Die" was written across the screen in blood red letters.

Riley nearly dropped the phone, but the message vanished before the message from her brain got through to her fingers. She was shaken, but she pushed past it and looked for the reception bars. Absolutely nothing. She closed the phone and slipped it back into her pocket. She bent her knees and rested her arms on them, her hands dangling. It was going to be a damn long night.

Chapter Ten

Riley woke early the next morning to the sound of whispered conversation. She rolled onto her back and saw both flashlights were aimed toward the ceiling, forming a giant X that illuminated dust motes swirling in their beams. Priest and Kenzie were crouched next to them consulting a map Priest had drawn with her charcoal. Radio sat at the far end of the room, obviously still in Kenzie's doghouse.

Riley pushed herself up and grunted, shaking the sleep from her brain. Priest and Kenzie both looked over at her and returned to their map without a word. Radio smiled and said, "Good morning, star shine."

"Morning, Radio," Riley said. She stood up, stretched, and said, "Is there a bathroom in this place?"

"There's a bucket in the farthest room from this one," Kenzie said. She picked up one of the flashlights and handed it to her. "Ignore the smell."

Riley grunted and disappeared with her flashlight. She found the farthest room and quickly began listing the species that might have died within its confines. She took off her undershirt and wrapped it around the lower half of her face before she dared enter. By the time she stumbled back out, her list of possible deaths included seven species of animal, including humans, and she wondered if they had all been diseased when they crawled there to die.

She tossed the flashlight back to Kenzie when she got back. "You sure know how to pick them."

"You should have smelled the actual bathroom."

Riley put her blouse back on and checked her watch in the flashlight. It was fifteen minutes past five in the morning. "What do you think, Priest?"

"Close enough. I don't want to be down here any longer than necessary."

Kenzie said, "Your girl is pretty good, Rye. You definitely traded up, partner-wise."

"Says you," Riley said, crouching by the map. "This one doesn't rub my feet."

"Does she do that thing I showed you...?" She held up two fingers and wiggled them.

Riley smiled. "Not with me, she doesn't. Gillian, though..."

Priest thumped the ground with her knuckle. "Can we focus on the escape route, ladies?" Riley chuckled and nodded for Priest to take the floor. "I got the gist of the layout from Radio. There are a couple of blind turns, some dead ends, all of which are probably going to be full of people waiting to take us out. We have to move fast."

"Nobody gets left behind this time," Kenzie said, looking at Priest.

"Trust me, I learned my lesson."

Kenzie stood up and put her blouse back on. Grime and blood stains covered the back like an abstract art project. She spoke to Radio without looking at him. "Are you ready?"

"Born to run."

"Priest, you want to make sure the coast is clear?"

Priest nodded and got to her feet, taking one of the flashlights into the main room.

Riley straightened and looked at a spot above Kenzie's head. "Orders, Major Crowe?"

Kenzie playfully clipped Riley on the chin. "Just hang back and look pretty, Private." She made sure they had all their things and picked up the second flashlight. As they went into the main room, Priest was returning from outside. "No one is coming."

"How did you move that counter by yourself? It took all three of us last night."

"Pilates," Priest said. "Let's go." She waited by the door while everyone else filed out. Riley stopped and looked back, watching Priest bow her head and move her lips as she silently mouthed a prayer. Riley watched Kenzie and Radio carefully moving into the corridor and went back, sliding her hand into Priest's. Priest squeezed and finished the prayer, then pulled the door shut. "Thanks."

"Couldn't hurt," she said.

She turned and followed Kenzie down the corridor. The lights hanging from the wall were dim, but they were still brighter than the pair of flashlights. The corridor was practically lit by the sun compared to their pitch black night. Radio stopped at a crossroad and leaned out to make sure no one was coming. Riley figured they were safe; the denizens of the Underground might be willing to spend a few hours looking for someone, but practical needs outweighed anything else. They needed to get out and scrounge before the sun came up and the respectable people reclaimed the world aboveground.

The ground beneath their feet, uneven and covered with a loose layer of gravel and stones, kept slipping them up and forced them to move slowly. Priest stopped and peered into the relic of an old apartment building and then hurried to catch up with the others. Kenzie tore the sleeve of her blouse on a particularly tight corner and cursed quietly. Priest brought up the rear and occasionally reported sounds she heard coming from behind them. "Muttering. It's close," she whispered, and Riley nodded. Not much they could do about it in such tight confines.

Riley figured they had gone about six blocks when all hell broke loose. Radio had gone around a corner, Kenzie right behind him, when Priest suddenly shouted, "Everybody down!" The first bullets ricocheted off the walls, raining chips of stone down on them. Riley and Kenzie both pulled their weapons and spun around to return fire. The explosions were deafening in the confines of the caverns, and Riley's nostrils burned with the scent of gunpowder.

She tried to retreat, but Radio slammed into them and said, "Get back!"

Kenzie barely avoided a swinging baseball bat to the skull, ducking at the last moment before it would have taken off her head. She twisted at the waist and fired behind her, catching the wannabe Babe Ruth in the chest. He fell back into the people shoving down the path behind him and tripped them up.

"Not this way!" Kenzie called.

Riley said, "We're blocked here, too." She glanced at Priest. "So much for the power of prayer, huh?"

Priest ignored her. "Remember the apartment building we passed two blocks back?"

"Yeah."

"Can you get back there?"

"No one gets left behind. Especially not you. You've risked your life enough for me."

Priest said, "Okay. Kenzie, Radio, cover your eyes!" Riley didn't realize the warning was meant for her as well; she thought Priest merely wanted privacy to spread her wings. She was caught off-guard when Priest held her hands out and an explosion of light burst forth from the palms of her hands. Flames licked the walls of the corridor and the people swarming them fell back so they wouldn't get burned. A crowd of screaming faces retreating in fear was the last thing Riley saw before her vision went black.

"Okay, we... Riley?"

Riley grabbed Priest's arm to keep from falling, blinking rapidly to clear the spots and fuzz from her vision. "I'll be fine. Just go. Go!" She pushed Priest forward, holding on to her for dear life. She felt Kenzie's hands on her back, keeping her on the path as she ran. Their feet scraped the stone, echoing through the winding corridors of the Underground, and Riley suddenly smelled everything all around them; garbage and decay, vermin and unwashed flesh. Some of the latter may have been coming from her own body, but that didn't make it any less disgusting.

Riley was guided into the lobby of the apartment building, and she heard something heavy skidding across the floor. She widened her eyes, trying to focus and failing. She could see blobs of shapes dyed red, swirling bugs of yellow and white swarming in her eyes. Someone touched her arm and Riley said, "It's all right. I'll be fine. It's just..."

"What the hell did you use, a fucking flamethrower?" Kenzie asked.

"Never mind," Priest said. "We need—"

"Everyone shut up," Riley said. She held her hands out in front of her and listened. "Something is upstairs. Coming down quick."

Priest and Kenzie ran across the room, and Riley felt Radio's hand on her shoulder. It was large, but surprisingly gentle as he guided her across the room. "Everybody hurts."

"You can say that again, buddy."

She recoiled as gunshots filled the air. In the silence that followed, Riley's ears rang and she feared she had lost another sense. "Priest? Kenzie?" Thank God, she could hear her own voice. "What happened?"

"Ugly motherfucker," Kenzie said. "Anyone else?"

Riley listened hard and then shook her head. "All quiet on the western front."

"Good. Come on." Someone, she wasn't sure who, grabbed her hand and she was pulled up the stairs. After a few shaky newborn colt steps, she managed the staircase with minimal help. By the time they reached the top floor, the red had faded a bit and she could see a hazy cloud she thought was Kenzie moving in front of her. "We're going to have to go through the ceiling."

"You're kidding, right?"

"You want to try running the gauntlet again?"

Kenzie sighed. "You're insane, Katie. Luckily, I like that in a woman."

Riley heard banging and cursing as they used the old furniture that was left behind the punch a hole in the ceiling. She blindly moved to her right and wrapped her hand around the stout leg of a table. She stumbled forward, bumped into Priest from behind, and joined the fray. Sheetrock washed down over them, peppering Riley's face and shoulders. It was all she could do to keep her eyes and mouth shut; she didn't know if asbestos had been invented when the building was put up, but it was the least dangerous thing endangering her at the moment.

"I think I'm feeling some resistance..." Kenzie said.

Riley heard a hollow echoing sound every time Kenzie thrust upward. "I think you're getting somewhere, Kenzie."

Kenzie grunted. "Just a little..."

Something broke, and a tidal wave slammed Riley and Kenzie off their feet. They sputtered and coughed, their fall broken by a rickety banister that kept them from riding the wave all the way back to the ground floor. When Riley opened her eyes, the blobs had transformed themselves into actual blurry human shapes. Priest stood over her, offering a hand. Riley clasped her hand around Priest's forearm and let herself be pulled to her feet.

She turned to face Kenzie and smiled. "Well, well."

Kenzie's hair was plastered to her head, her T-shirt clinging to every curve. She spit up a mouthful of water and said, "What?"

Riley smiled. "Definitely worth getting my eyesight back."

"Flirt."

They went back to the hole, which was still raining down like an insane water feature. Priest said, "We still have to get through there. It's just water."

"Right," Riley said. "Better than going through March's building."

"Much better," Priest said. She looked at Riley and said, "What was that you were saying about the power of prayer?"

"Big guy lend a hand?"

Priest smiled.

"Yeah, yeah, mysterious ways. Maybe God just wanted to watch a wet T-shirt contest." She looked around the landing and found a chair that looked sturdy. She brought it over to the waterfall and gestured at the seat. "I would say ladies first..."

"But there are no ladies present," Kenzie said. "Up you go, Rye."

Riley grabbed the edge of the hole they had punched out and, with an assist from Radio and Kenzie, pulled herself up through the deluge. She sputtered, completely underwater for a few seconds before she emerged in the center of a whirlpool. She gasped and spit up mouthfuls of water, swimming for the edge of whatever body of water she happened to be in. She grasped a smooth stone lip and pulled herself up, her clothes hanging from her like sandbags. She sat on the edge and watched as Priest appeared, followed by Kenzie. Riley helped them up and out of the water, before she turned to see where they had come up.

They were in a lobby that stretched twelve stories straight up. People stood next to the waist-high barriers on every floor, looking down at the spectacle taking place below them. Riley looked behind her and saw people in identical navy blue suits rushing toward them. She recognized the building and laughed, taking the badge from her belt and holding it over her head. "Police. Police business. We're investigating the death of Anthony Benedict."

Security officers, dedicated to keeping their hotel as the one four-star stay in the city, stopped short, but didn't relax. Kenzie helped Radio out of the whirlpool, which was now just a swirl of water circling the make-shift drain. The fountain was almost empty now.

Riley climbed out of the fountain and helped Priest, Kenzie and Radio out as well. She wiped the water from her face and walked up to the closest security guard. "You might want to tell your boss that the foundation under that fountain is weak. Probably would have been an issue before too long even without us tunneling up through it." She smiled and walked on past him, her shoes squelching on the tile as she headed for the doors. From the sounds of their shoes, she knew that the others were right behind her.

She stepped out into the sun which, after a night in the Underground, seemed unbelievably bright. She shaded her eyes with one hand and turned to see Radio had both hands covering his eyes completely. "Ain't no sunshine," Radio said. "Where I come from."

"Where to now?" Kenzie said.

Riley said, "First, we get some dry clothes. Then we find Player and make him pay for what he did."

Chapter Eleven

Riley got a dry outfit from her locker at the station, while Kenzie took Priest and Radio back to her hotel room to get them changed. Riley left the locker room with her blouse unbuttoned over a white tank top, hurrying to catch the cab that was going to take her back to the Depot to retrieve her car. It was hard finding a cabbie willing to go into No Man's Land, rarer to find one willing to wait while she changed clothes. She prayed he would still be there, and that the Nova would still be outside the Depot.

Halfway across the bullpen, someone called her name. "Detective Parra."

Riley considered just barreling on, but she knew it would cause more problems than it solved. She turned and faced Lieutenant Briggs, very aware of the clock ticking downstairs. "Yes, ma'am."

"I haven't seen you since our little powwow yesterday. I assume you and Priest have been keeping busy?"

"Yes. Very busy. In fact I'm..."

"In the middle of a case?" She crossed her arms. "I would love to hear about it."

Riley didn't know the name of the person she and Priest were supposedly staking out all night. And she had no idea how to dovetail that cover story into the true fact that she and Priest were seen climbing out of a hotel fountain at a quarter to six in the morning. She said, "Detective Priest and I have been investigating a murder, off the books. We needed to find a witness. In order to do that, we needed to go into the Underground. Found the witness, got a suspect, we're on our way to bring him in now."

She stopped talking and waited for Briggs to request her badge.

"You'll need back-up. Take a tactical team."

Riley blinked. "Yes, ma'am."

"You should have had one in the Underground with you last night."

"All due respect, ma'am, that would have just scared everybody off. We never would have gotten anything."

Briggs stared at her, then nodded. "You have a point, Detective." She turned and said, "Charleston. Get SWAT together. Detective Parra will tell you where to go."

"Thank you, Lieutenant."

"It's not always better to beg forgiveness than to ask permission." She held up a finger. "Last warning, Detective."

"Understood."

Briggs said, "Come with me to my office." Riley followed Briggs to the interrogation room and waited patiently while the new lieutenant coordinated a SWAT team to accompany them on the raid of Player's apartment. She chuckled, shook her head, and said, "Honesty. Who'd have thought?" She looked at her watch, halfway hoping the cabbie was still waiting and also hoping she wouldn't put the guy's kid through college with her fare.

Riley led the team up the stairs, the bulletproof vest digging into her shoulders. She stopped at the top of the stairs and looked back to see Priest pressed against the opposite wall. She nodded, and Riley moved toward the door. Room 4-F, assigned to a Sergeant Travis Unger. He used his real name so he could take advantage of the military discount. Kenzie knew he would go for the cheapest option while still staying above the poverty line. He had been easy enough to track down after that.

Riley pounded on the door. "Mr. Unger? Police, we'd like to ask you a few questions."

A SWAT team member in her earpiece said, "Suspect's window just opened; he is attempting to flee."

Riley turned and planted her foot just under the doorknob. She was inside the apartment before it hit the wall, crossing to the window on the opposite side of the room. Unger was still leaning out, trying to figure out why there was no fire escape, when she grabbed the back of his shirt and hauled him back into the apartment. She used the momentum of her pull to toss him onto the floor, where he sprawled face-down with his arms splayed to either side.

"Travis Unger," Riley said as she took the gun from the back of his belt, "you are under arrest for the murders of Charles Deluca, Timothy Marks, and Colin Tran. You have the right to remain silent. If you give up that right..." She looked up as she continued to recite the Miranda rights, and saw Kenzie enter the room. She was decked out in the same protective gear as the rest of the team, but she was unarmed.

Riley hauled Unger to his feet and said, "Former Officer Crowe, would you take the prisoner downstairs?"

"Gladly," Kenzie said. She roughly grabbed Unger's arm and forced him to lead the way out of the apartment. She stopped at the doorway and turned back. "Hey, Rye."

"Yeah," Riley said, adrenaline still pumping.

"Take a picture of yourself in that get-up. Vest, sweat glistening on your forehead. Put it in an envelope, send it to Gillian. Her reaction will be worth the postage."

Riley chuckled and said, "Take the prisoner downstairs, you has-been."

When Kenzie left, Priest came inside. "Nice bust."

"Thanks. You look kind of odd in that gear."

Priest looked down at herself and thumped the middle of the vest. "I've always got the full armor of God. Sometimes you need the armor of Man, as well."

"Amen," Riley said. She motioned for Priest to follow her out of the apartment, pulling the ruined door shut behind her.

The hotel was blaming Riley for the broken door. The department was willing to cover the cost, but it required extra paperwork. Riley, as a show of cooperation to the new lieutenant, decided to get it out of the way as soon as possible instead of putting it aside for a slow day.

The bullpen was dark, since Riley's procrastination kept her at her desk long after everyone else went home. She was seeing double by the time Radio and Kenzie appeared in front of her desk. She leaned back, dropped her pen on the file, and said, "Well. Look who is back among the living."

Radio smiled, and Kenzie said, "Radio's done giving his statement. Written, of course. They want him to stay close in case he has to testify, but Player has pretty much given up trying to hide what he did. Everything Radio said was true. Unger met the woman on patrol, and she seduced him. She used what he learned to set up the ambushes. His father was a career soldier, like mine, and he couldn't bear the thought of what happened getting out. Death before dishonor."

"So he murdered three people. And he was going for four."

"Under pressure," Radio said. "Evil ways. No way out. Dust in the wind."

Riley smirked and shook her head. "Radio, you're one weird dude. But I'm glad I got to know you." She held out her hand, and Radio shook it.

"Someone saved my life tonight."

Riley said. "You did some saving of your own. Take it easy."

Radio grinned. "I'll be around."

"Where are you going?" She looked at Kenzie and said, "Dave Matthews Band, back in oh-two."

"California Dreamin'."

Riley nodded. "It never rains in southern California."

"Last train to Clarksville."

Riley said, "North to Alaska."

"Oklahoma."

"Positively Fourth Street."

Kenzie held up her hands. "All right, you guys, stop it. Radio, head on down to the car. I'll drive you to the station."

"Never been to Spain," Radio said as he retreated.

"Go your own way," Kenzie called after him. She sat on the edge of Riley's desk and said, "So. It was nice working with you again, Parra. You've got some chops. A couple of moves I haven't seen. Shame I couldn't see what you were capable of in bed."

"Yeah, well. You can't always get what you want."

"But if you try sometimes, you get what you need." She bent down and kissed Riley's lips. It was a gentle kiss, chaste, a memento of what they once had. She smiled and slid off the desk. "I'll see you around, Rye."

"Really?"

"Oh, yeah," Kenzie said. "Something's going on in this town. Could be fun to stick around and get in my share of trouble."

Riley sighed. "I'll start your file now."

Kenzie saluted and looked past Riley's chair. She smiled. "Hey, Katie. It was nice working with you."

"Take care, Mackenzie."

Riley watched Kenzie go downstairs before she turned to Priest. "Where have you been?"

"Hathaway's office." Priest dropped a singed manila envelope on Riley's desk. "You can do whatever you want with that."

Riley straightened in her seat. "Is that...?"

"The fake note Kara was forced to write. Yeah." Priest took her jacket off the back of her seat and shrugged into it. "I'll see you tomorrow, Riley."

"Caitlin." Priest stopped at the top of the stairs and said, "Thank you. You're a good partner. I need to stop taking advantage of that."

"You're a good partner, too, Riley. I'll let you know when you're taking advantage." She smiled and waved over her shoulder. "Good night."

"Night." Riley slumped in her seat and stared at the burnt file on her desk. She chuckled, squeezed the back of her neck, and went back to her paperwork.

Epilogue

Riley ached. She was bone tired, stiff from spending the night before on a concrete floor. Everything hurt. She went to Gillian's apartment, too tired to even entertain the ghosts and memories she usually had to tap dance around. She stripped down to her underwear and dropped on top of the blankets, sighing as the blankets seemed to mold to her body. It was exquisite. She felt herself beginning the backward slide to sleep, her body slowly drifting away from consciousness, her mind fading.

Her cell phone chirped.

Riley groaned and pulled the pillow on top of her face. No more distractions. No one got murdered, no one got hurt. No one else she loved was in danger. She was unnecessary for the next eight to twelve hours. It was a nice fantasy. But not one she could entertain for long. She rolled to the edge of the bed, found her jeans, and freed her phone from the pocket. She flipped it open without bothering to look at the Caller ID. "Parra."

"I love you, too."

Riley's heart seized. She felt as if someone had punched her in the chest, sucked the air from the room, and her mouth tried to form words. When the dam finally broke, the tears began to flow as well. She sobbed into the mouthpiece and finally managed to say, "Gillian?"

"I got your message. Are you okay?"

Riley rolled onto her back and sucked in a deep breath of air. She closed her eyes, thousands of miles closed in the space of four words. She smiled and said, "Yeah, Jill. I'm... doing well. Now."

"Are you busy? Can you talk?"

"Yeah," Riley said. She pushed herself up, leaning against the headboard. Exhaustion vanished as she rearranged herself on the bed. "Yeah, I have a couple of minutes." She wiped her cheeks and said, "How have you been?"

Open and Shut, No. 4:
Heaven is Overrated

When Gillian Hunt ran away, she went to the one place she still felt safe; the one place she had ever truly thought of as home.

The bedroom at the top of the stairs was the same as she remembered; originally part of the attic, part of the room was cut off by the slope of the roof. Her bed was tucked under the angle, and a curtain hung from the ceiling and draped over the bed. She remembered waking every morning before school and watching the material catch the new sun's rays. Now, though, rolling over and seeing that curtain made her feel like a coward. She was hiding.

Every morning also brought new horrors. She never remembered full dreams, but what she did recall was bad enough. She dreaded falling asleep because she knew what waited. Screeching, like nails on a blackboard, and horrific laughter. She never knew laughter could be evil, but there was no other word for this soulless cackling that filled her head.

Gillian spent her first three days in Georgia in church. Praying, lighting candles, listening to the music, anything to get the images out of her head. She was still traumatized by the demon assaulting her in the morgue, but that paled in comparison to what came next. The darkness, the touch of a cold hand on her forehead and then... it was inside of her. She couldn't begin to describe the feeling accurately. It was being blind, deaf and dumb to the outside world while something else controlled your body.

And when the veil finally broke... oh, the pain. Caitlin Priest, Riley's partner and guardian angel, was holding her in a bear hug. Her body burned where the angel touched her, the light searing her flesh. It was like the worst sunburn she'd ever had, like acid burning through her skin. Priest whispered in her ear the entire time, words and verses meant to be soothing. But the pain they caused the demon was transferred to Gillian.

She eventually passed out from the pain. When she woke an indefinite amount of time later, Riley was by her side. The pain had fled, as if she was a terminal patient whose doctor found a miracle cure. But she couldn't rejoice. The Duchess had fled, she could tell she was truly gone, but the scars would take time to heal.

Gillian wasn't like Riley. She couldn't handle the thought of demons coming after her, trying to kill her. She sat on the edge of the bed, fists against her eyes, and chided herself for the comfortable lie. Riley wasn't better at handling the demons in her life. She was just as terrified as anyone else would be. But she didn't run. She faced it down.

Their first night together, Gillian stayed up with a battered Riley in her bed. The gash on Riley's side terrified her, and the way Riley kept tensing and murmuring in her sleep... Gillian couldn't imagine the hell she had gone through. The hell she had survived. And she was still there, still facing the demons, but she was alone.

She picked up her cell phone off the nightstand and flipped it open. The message from Riley was still there, and she replayed it for the millionth time since it arrived the day before. "I miss you. I love you."

She closed her eyes and dialed. She chewed her bottom lip as she waited for an answer, praying Riley was somewhere—

"Parra."

"I love you, too."

She heard a sharp intake of breath and then a sigh. She closed her eyes. She wanted suddenly to have Riley with her, in her arms, to hold and kiss her. Why, God, was she so far away? Because of you. Because this is where you ran.

"Gillian?" Riley whispered.

"I got your message." A tear rolled down her cheek. "Are you okay?"

She could hear the relief in Riley's voice. "Yeah, Jill. I'm... doing well. Now."

Gillian used a fingernail to toy with the skin around her thumbnail. "Are you busy? Can you talk?"

"Yeah," Riley said. "Yeah, I have a couple of minutes. How have you been?"

Gillian smiled. "I don't know where to start."

"Tell me it's an easy one," Riley said. "Start at the beginning, Doc."

Gillian laughed. She was immediately transported back to the dingy apartment of a dead junkie. His blood was splattered all over the window, and he lay on a pile of old newspapers with his arms splayed out to either side. Detective Riley Parra walked into the room and Gillian introduced herself. Riley shook Gillian's hand, made the briefest eye contact, and then looked at the body. And then she said, "Tell me it's an easy one. Start at the beginning, Doc."

Following that moment, Gillian stole glances at Riley whenever they were at the same crime scene. When Riley and Sweet Kara would come into the morgue to see what she had found, Riley never acted like the place sickened her. Gillian didn't blame people for their reactions to the dead bodies; it was just human nature. But the fact that Riley was willing to visit her without gel under her nose, that she could hold a conversation over a dead body without wincing or gagging, just secured her place in Gillian's heart.

The magical moment they kissed, and then their first night together, was still like a dream. She couldn't believe Riley actually had feelings for her. And then, like a flash, it was over and they were apart again. All because of her.

"Nothing's easy anymore," Gillian said.

"No."

"I feel like... I need you here. But I know you can't leave. And if I go back to that place, I feel like I'll never find the courage to get out of bed in the morning." She realized she was still sitting in her own bed, after her early evening nap, and stood up. She went to the window and looked out at the backyard of her youth. "Riley, I'm sorry I ran."

"Don't," Riley said softly. "Please, I understand. I know why you left."

Gillian rested her head against the window and closed her eyes. "I still have nightmares. And if I woke up from one of them, and I was still in that city..."

"What if you were in my arms?"

A tear slid down Gillian's cheek. "I think that would really help."

"I'm lying in bed right now. Your bed. I want you to imagine waking up with me holding you, Jill."

Gillian wrapped her free arm around herself and said, "Feels good. Feels safe. I never feel anything less than safe with you, Riley. I just feel like I spent so long looking for you, and then I had to give you up as soon as I found you. I'm so sorry I put you through that."

"Even if you never come back... even if you feel like you can't ever show your face in this town again, I'll treasure what we had."

Gillian could hear the tears in Riley's voice, and she knew how much the words had cost her. She walked back to the bed and said, "I'm trying, Riley. I want you to know that I'm trying."

"I know."

"I miss you."

"I miss you, too."

"How... how are things going?"

Riley chuckled. "Not well. I don't want to get into it. But... yeah. Things kind of got darker around here after you left." She paused and said, "I don't believe we're through. You know that, right? However long it takes, until you tell me we're through—"

"We're not through," Gillian said.

"Well. That settles that, I guess."

Gillian smiled. "I'm sorry. Part of my anxiety has been from thinking I gave you up when I left. I wouldn't have blamed you if you moved on and found someone new."

"There's no one else, Jill."

Gillian closed her eyes and another tear rolled down her cheek.

"Are you okay?"

"Yeah. Yes." She wiped her face and sat on the edge of the bed. "Riley..."

After a long wait, Riley said, "Gillian? Are you still there?"

"I'm here. I just... I don't know what I was going to say." She sniffled. "It's really good to hear your voice. I was so lost when you found me."

"When?"

"That night..." Gillian remembered stumbling through her dark apartment, groggy from a lack of sleep, angry at the person sharing her bed, confused when she heard the voice of the person waking her up. Then fear when she saw how much blood was coming out of Riley, the horrible cut running down her side. She pressed her fist against her lips and said, "I had a crush on you for a long time, but I didn't realize how deep it was until I saw you that night. When I thought there was maybe a chance you may not..." She bit her bottom lip as her voice trailed off. "That's when I knew I was in love with you. I thank God that you figured it out at the same time."

"Yeah. Mysterious ways," Riley said.

Gillian smiled.

"Come home."

Gillian closed her eyes. She knew the reasons for leaving well enough by now that she could recite them. Her presence was Riley's vulnerability. As long as she was there, she had a target on her back. And Riley's enemies wouldn't hesitate to use her as leverage. They had already used her once, and it was only due to divine intervention that she escaped. Next time she might not be so lucky.

"Riley..."

"I shouldn't have asked. I'm sorry, Jill."

"No." She chewed her bottom lip and looked out the window. "I don't know. I can't give you any promises. But hearing your voice... God, Riley, I've missed you. I have missed you every minute of the day, I just didn't realize how much until right now. I think that's why I didn't call you. I was afraid that if I heard your voice, I wouldn't be able to say no if you told me to come back."

"I don't want to pressure you."

"I know. I know I can tell you I'm staying. I can't go back there. Not yet."

Riley hesitantly said, "But soon?"

"Yeah. I think I can say soon."

Riley made a sound that was half a chuckle and half a sob. "Well. You be sure to let me know when you nail down a date."

"I'll do that. And Riley... maybe... you could call me tomorrow."

"Yeah. Yes."

"And the next day?"

Riley laughed. "Yeah. What about the day after that?"

Gillian smiled. "Use your own judgment."

Riley laughed again. "I'm done being a martyr, Jill. I love you, and I miss you, and I'm not going to let you go. I've lost too much. I won't lose something as precious as you without a hell of a fight."

Gillian was now crying openly. She looked out the window and said, "That's very good to hear." She checked her watch and saw that it was later than she thought. "God, you must be exhausted. I'm going to let you go to sleep..."

"No," Riley said. "I'm awake."

"Are you sure?"

"What did I just say?" Riley said. "I'm not letting you go easy."

Gillian lay back on the bed and looked at the sloping ceiling above her. "How about this. We can talk until you fall asleep."

"I'm—"

"I know when you're tired, Riley Parra. Don't argue with me."

She could practically hear Riley's smile over the phone. "Yes, doctor."

"Now, tell me about your day, dear."

Gillian listened to Riley's story with equal parts shock, horror, and dread. But the dread wasn't debilitating, and the fear was easily assuaged by the knowledge Riley was still in one piece. Gillian ran because she thought distance would make it easier to deal with the hell Riley faced day in and day out, but that was wrong. What she needed was Riley, at the end of the day, in her arms, in one piece. Safe and warm. That was what she needed to get through the day. And she knew Riley needed her just as badly.

Gillian knew she wasn't ready to go home yet, but she knew it was only a matter of time before she started packing her bags.

My Empire of Dirt

Chapter One

"That's not the point," Riley said as she slammed her car door. "It's about the camaraderie. The friendship between the two leads."

Priest adjusted her coat as she got out of the car and shook her head. "They fought over a woman, and the film ended with a suicidal dash against the Bolivian army. They were thieves. And you revere them?"

"Butch Cassidy and the Sundance Kid are heroes," Riley said. "That doesn't necessarily mean they're perfect or role models. They saw that there was no hope, but they still went out with guns blazing. Despite the odds, despite the fact there was no chance they would win, they didn't hesitate. That's heroic."

"I will admit, knowing your admiration of them explains a lot about you. Not everyone would go up against Marchosias."

"Butch and Sundance would."

Priest smiled. "Indeed they would. I'll bring the DVD back tomorrow."

"No rush. Watch the commentary. It'll enlighten you." She looked down the slope to where the body lay and said, "By the way, they didn't fight over Etta James. They shared her."

Priest frowned.

Riley held up the crime scene tape and Priest ducked underneath it to enter the vacant lot. Odd-shaped stones were piled in the corner, remnants of the building that once occupied the space. A group of uniformed officers stood near the far wall, surrounding a crouching person in a dark blue windbreaker. Riley said, "Tell me there's a confession pinned to the victim's jacket."

"No such luck, Detective," Dr. Mill Herron said. Riley was surprised to find she still expected Gillian to be at her crime scenes. Hopefully before too much longer, things would be back to normal. Herron stood, rubbed his hands on the thighs of his slacks, and said, "Looks to be a body dump, naturally."

Riley and Priest approached. The woman was curled in the fetal position, hands clasped against her stomach. Her eyes were wide in her too-pale face, her mouth hanging slack. She wore a black party dress, which made it hard to see the dried blood on her hips. Riley looked up at the surrounding buildings. She supposed someone could have dropped the woman from one of the windows.

"Are the injuries consistent with a fall?"

"No," Herron said. "She was stabbed. Judging from the lack of blood in the area, and the lividity, she was definitely killed somewhere else and dumped here."

Riley nodded. "Any idea how long she was here?"

"Based on body temp, I would say she's been dead for about seven hours."

Riley moved closer to the woman's body and crouched, craning her neck to examine the rubble next to her. "No purse, wallet, ID?"

Herron shook his head. "You see how she's dressed. Even if she had a purse, it was probably one of them little ones that you can't actually store anything in."

"Sure you can," Riley said. "They're the perfect size to hold a cell phone and a puppy."

"My mistake," Herron said. "Crime scene techs will go through the scene with a fine-tooth comb, let you know what they find." He looked at the scattered garbage and said, "Well. The pertinent things, anyway."

"Much appreciated," Riley said. She motioned one of the uniformed officers over. "I want a canvas of the building across the street and the neighbors here. See if anyone noticed someone parked at the curb, or anything suspicious last night."

The uniform nodded and hurried off. Riley motioned for Priest to follow her back to the car. Riley ducked under the crime scene tape and examined the crowd on the other side of the sawhorses. "All these buildings around here are businesses. If the body was dumped at, what, two this morning? No one would have been here to see anything."

"Doesn't hurt to ask."

"Nope," Riley said. She got into the car just as the crime scene unit arrived. She pulled out and let them have her spot, weaving through the field of cop cars and spectators. "If nobody saw anything, we can look for security cameras. Maybe someone in one of the neighboring buildings happened to be looking out their window."

"At the exact right time?" Priest said. "Kind of a long shot."

"I'm feeling optimistic."

Priest smiled. "I've noticed. I guess Kenzie's visit a couple weeks ago really cleared your mind."

"No. Well... maybe that had something to do with it. But that's not why I'm so..."

"Chipper?"

Riley chuckled. "I've been talking with Gillian."

"Really? Is she coming back?"

"Not yet. We've been talking for three weeks. I think she's getting closer."

Priest smiled. "That's fantastic, Riley. I'm very happy for you both."

"Is that the official line from upstairs?" Riley said. "Two women being in love, isn't that an abomination?"

"True love in any form is always encouraged," Priest said. She looked at Riley. "You're in love with her?"

Riley said, "Yeah. Head over heels."

Priest smiled. "I'm happy to hear it. You deserve some happiness."

Riley was uncomfortable with talking about herself, and changed the subject by nodding toward a coffee shop coming up on the right. "You want something for breakfast? I'm buying."

"Sure."

She found a parking spot not far from the shop. As they got out of the car, Riley's phone rang. "Crime scene guys. Maybe they found something." She reached for her wallet as she answered the phone, but Priest waved her off. "If you say so. Blueberry muffin, coffee black." She put the phone to her ear and leaned against the back of the car. "Detective Parra."

"Detective, this is Officer Davis. I'm still at the crime scene on Ninth."

"Have you found something?"

"Yes, ma'am. The owner of a coin shop across the street was in his front room last night around the time the body was dumped. He said he saw a black sedan pull up, and a man dumped something in the vacant lot. When he came back, he put the black trash bag in his trunk, looked around, and walked away."

Riley looked across the street and saw a black sedan pulling up to the curb. She smirked; that would be nice and easy. "Any license plate number, description?"

"Guy said it was too dark for details, but he said the man was on the young side, and he was wearing a tuxedo."

The driver's side door of the sedan opened, and a man in a tuxedo climbed out. Riley blinked and watched as he walked around to the back of the car.

"Thanks, Davis. Keep me informed, all right?"

Riley flipped the phone shut and watched the man in the tuxedo approach her. She looked past him to the car, then looked over her shoulder to see if Priest was coming back yet. Her badge was fastened to her belt in plain sight, but she still shifted her hips to make sure the man saw it as he approached. He was an older man with jowls starting to form on his jaw line. He wore his gray hair cropped short, and when he smiled, wrinkles framed his mouth and eyes.

"Morning."

He inclined his chin. "Good morning, Detective Parra."

She tensed.

"Before you jump to conclusions, I will put all my cards down on the table. I am a demon. My name is Crocell. But I am not here to cause you any harm. I know of your latest assignment. The unfortunate woman in the vacant lot. My employer would like to help you with your investigation."

"Your employer. That wouldn't happen to be Marchosias, would it?"

Crocell smiled and reached into his suit jacket. "No." Riley's hand went to her gun, but he revealed a business card before she could draw it. He held the card out between two fingers, and Riley took it from him. The raised letters on the front read "Andrea Silver - Ann/Dras Properties and Development." There was an address and a phone number, nothing else. Riley recognized the name; there were signs for Ann/Dras all over town.

"Okay. So what can your boss tell me about this murder?"

Crocell held his hands out palm-up. "I am afraid that is for her to tell you, Detective."

"Is she a demon, too?"

"Yes. Madame was originally called Andras."

Riley looked at the card. Andrea Silver, Ann/Dras Development. Clever. She flicked the corner of the card with her middle finger and said, "Let your boss know we'll be getting in touch."

Crocell bowed his head. "Madame looks forward to it, Detective." He glanced toward the coffee shop, and his expression soured ever so slightly. Riley knew Priest was approaching without having to look. She held up her hand to stop Priest from overreacting. Crocell squared his shoulders. "Leave the angel at home, if you would. She would find Madame's residence... uncomfortable."

"I can't imagine."

"Leave this place," Priest said from behind Riley.

Crocell touched two fingers to his forehead and stepped back. "I was just about to do that, Zerachiel. Always a pleasure. Detective Parra." He spun on his heel and walked quickly back to his car. Riley made a note of the license plate before she faced Priest. The angel's face was glowing, awash with light, her fingers wrinkling the bag with their muffins.

"Priest... I need you to calm down."

Priest closed her eyes. She rolled his shoulders, and Riley felt a wave of heat wash over her. Up and down the street, everyone paused for just a moment as they felt the same wave. It seemed to roll across the sidewalk in gentle, undulating waves before dissipating completely. A few people shook their heads and walked on, while others appeared faintly ill. Riley felt loose in the joints, as if she had just stretched after sitting for a couple of hours. She blinked and said, "Feel better?"

"Slightly. What did that thing want?"

Riley passed the business card over the roof of the car. Priest put down the coffee carrier and took the card. "Andras. Figures. He is a great sower of discord."

"She, actually," Riley said. "Guess you're not the only supernatural being who got a sex change when you joined this mortal coil."

Priest quirked her lips and got into the car. She handed Riley her coffee and said, "Andras, or Andrea Silver, claims to have information on the body in the lot. She wants to talk to me alone. Give me what she knows."

"Do you believe her?"

"A witness saw a car a car at the scene. The description matched Crocell's car. I think it's worth seeing what she has to say." She peeled away part of the muffin's paper and took a bite. "What do you know about Crocell and Andras?"

"Andras is a prince underneath Marchosias. Or I suppose princess would be more apt. She commands her own legions. Andras is highly volatile. If she sees a chance to destroy you, she will take it. I don't understand her requesting your presence. The standard procedure would be to con you into conjuring her, and then tricking you into making yourself vulnerable so she could destroy you. Requesting your presence in her home gives you the power. It doesn't make sense."

"Maybe she really has information about the murder and just wants to be a good citizen."

Priest stared at Riley.

"It could happen," Riley said. She took another bite of her muffin and started the car. "Even if she doesn't, that car has been placed at the crime scene. I need to check it out regardless of who owns it."

Priest didn't look happy about the situation, but she nodded. "I understand. I assume Crocell told you to come alone."

"Yeah. He seems to think you wouldn't like Andrea's house."

Priest snorted. "All right. Just promise me you'll be careful, Riley."

Riley smiled. "Of course. I'm always careful."

"And yet you keep getting hurt."

"Hazards of the job. Besides. I have my guardian angel watching my back. What could go wrong?" As soon as the words were out of her mouth, she shook her head and muttered, "I know, I know. I'll knock on wood when we get to the station."

Chapter Two

On the way to the station, Riley called Officer Davis and confirmed the witness statement. Black car, tuxedo, young man. So it wasn't Crocell, but the car was too big of a coincidence. Andrea Silver, Andras, whatever the thing was called, was involved. And if she wanted to spill her guts to Riley, then more power to her. Riley pulled up in front of the station, the glass in the doors finally replaced after the shooting. "I might as well head out to see Andras. No point in putting off the inevitable."

"Right. It could be helpful."

Riley shrugged. "We can hope. Call me if Dr. Herron gets anything on the body, or if there are any other developments."

Priest nodded. She paused as she was getting out of the car, and bent down to look back into the car. "Be safe, Riley."

Riley saluted and waited until Priest was on the steps before she drove off. The address on the card Crocell provided was in Cobblestone Square, the one truly nice neighborhood remaining in the city. It was located nearly dead center in the "good" part of town, marked at the corners by large estates. The streets were cobblestone, as the name suggested, and Riley felt the change in the tires as she drove onto the first street.

The battered old trucks on either side of the street belonged to landscapers or gardeners, sweaty men in old T-shirts and baseball caps who were next to invisible to the people who lived in the houses. In neighborhoods like this, people like that tended to be invisible. Riley drove past them to a cul-de-sac. Andrea Silver's home stood at the apex of the street, the two houses on either side of her property blocked by a tall security wall. There was a wrought iron gate at every driveway emblazoned with the initials "AS." Apparently Andras owned the entire cul-de-sac and decided to make it into a compound. "Always a pleasure to see a fortress when you show up without back-up," she muttered.

Riley parked at the mouth of the cul-de-sac and quickly surveyed the area. She could see two black sedans parked in one of the appropriated driveways. She checked to make sure her cell phone was receiving a signal and fully charged as she walked down the middle of the street. People appeared at the iron gates, careful not to touch the bars with their skin as they watched her progress. The way they avoided it made her think the bars may be electrocuted. *Could be good to know if I end up being held prisoner here.* That thought was followed by the realization of what a screwed-up world she was living in.

The lawn of the main house was artificially green, perfectly landscaped with a flurry of white and purple flowers in beds around the base of the house. A brick walkway cut across the grass. Crocell opened the door before she arrived, greeting her with a smile. "Good morning, Detective Parra. We're pleased you could arrange a meeting so quickly."

"You know me. Always willing to help a concerned citizen."

Crocell stepped aside and said, "Please, come in. Ms. Silver is expecting you."

Riley took off her sunglasses as she stepped inside. The entryway was a raised platform, two steps leading directly into a sunken living room ready for a magazine photo shoot. Crocell closed the door behind her and said, "Madame is expecting you in the upstairs sitting room." He gestured at a flight of stairs curling away from the main room like a wisp of smoke.

"Out of the frying pan," Riley muttered. She led the way upstairs, Crocell a few steps behind her.

The stairs led directly to an open sitting room. Two sets of French doors stood on the wall to the right, the curtains pulled back to let in the sun. To the left was a railing, looking down into the living room. From this room, Andras could probably monitor all the comings and goings without any of her guests spotting her. A mahogany desk fronted a tall bookshelf filled with what she was sure were many quaint volumes of forgotten lore. Andras sat at the desk, waiting patiently while Riley examined the room.

"I like what you've done with the place," Riley said. "Marchosias had an office kind of like this. Yours has more in the way of... walls."

Andras smiled. "Thank you, Ms. Parra. Crocell, you may go." Her voice was tinged with an accent; Australian or New Zealand, Riley could never tell the difference.

Once Crocell was gone, Andras stood. Riley was impressed in spite of herself. Dazzling blue eyes, dirty blonde hair, strong shoulders. Her lips were curled in a smile that promised she knew more than you did, and dared you to ask her what it was. She wore a black skirt and a blue blouse, unbuttoned at the throat to reveal an onyx gem set in a gold necklace. She rested her hip against the corner of her desk and looked Riley over.

Andras crossed her arms over her chest. "I thought you would be taller."

"I thought you would be older."

Andras smiled and looked down at herself. "Yes, I'm rather fond of it myself. I saw it in a shop downtown and I simply had to have it."

"So you just hopped from your body to this one?"

"Not exactly that simple. But basically. I spent so many years as a man, I decided to see how the other half lived." She brushed her hand along the collar of her blouse, her fingers brushing her throat. "The changes are quite, ah... distinct."

Riley winced. "If you could wait until I'm gone to molest yourself..."

Andras smiled and dropped her hand.

"Your man Crocus said that you had information about a murder I'm looking into."

"To the point. That's what I like about you, Riley. May I call you Riley?"

"No."

Andras shrugged. "I'm afraid I won't be able to give you a name, address, photograph, all that. But I do know the woman who was found murdered. Her name was Heather Cassidy. And I believe you have a witness placing one of my cars at the scene? I will allow your crime scene technicians to examine the entire fleet at their leisure, but anyone could have taken any car. There is no rental agreement to be signed. If someone in my employ needs a vehicle, they know where the keys are."

"What is that, honor among demons?"

Andras raised an eyebrow. "Something like that. Would you like to have a seat?"

"No."

"Something to drink, then..."

Riley gestured at the door. "I should call the CSU about those cars."

Andras pushed away from the desk and crossed the room. "There was a party last night. I have them every so often; houses this big tend to get lonely. Ms. Cassidy was a guest at the party. I spoke with her around midnight, but I don't know when she left or who she left with. You are welcome to a copy of the guest list, but I'm afraid it won't be comprehensive. Some people brought friends and others didn't show up."

"That will be very helpful. If that's all you have..."

"It's not. I called you here for a reason, Riley. I have wanted to talk with you for a very long time. My information regarding this investigation was simply the impetus I needed to bring you here." She walked to the bar at the back of the room. "You see, Riley, I've been keeping an eye on you. Most all of us have, since you rose up and brought the fight to us. And once you killed Alistair Call..." She whistled and shook her head. "Are you sure you wouldn't like a drink?"

"You have five minutes, Ms. Silver, and I'm gone."

Andras sighed. She poured herself a glass of brandy and carried it back to the middle of the room. "History is written by the victors. Winston Churchill said that. I'm sure you've heard it. Hell, I'm sure you've seen it in action. Imagine, for a moment, that there is a ship on the ocean. And the captain of this ship is an egotistical, narcissistic bastard. He requires total loyalty from the crew. The first mate sees that this is no way to run a vessel and attempts to take over for the good of everyone; the crew, the passengers, even the captain himself will benefit from being shown the error of his ways.

"There is a battle aboard the ship. In the end, the first mate is defeated. He, and all who followed his mutiny, are sentenced to walk the plank. Thrown overboard and forgotten. Those who remain on the ship have seen how dissention is treated. Do you think any of them will rise against the captain ever again? And how do you think the first mate will be remembered? A troublemaker. Too full of himself to see that the captain knew best. He would be pitied at best, vilified at worst."

Riley nodded. "Right. I take it God is the captain, and Lucifer is the first mate."

"Very good, Riley." She winked. "Knew you were a detective."

"The poor misunderstood demons. I can see that. You guys have just been trying to do what's good for everyone else."

Andras laughed. "Try having everyone on the planet belittle and malign you for centuries. Let everyone on the planet spit on you and call you evil. It won't take very long before you start to believe it. Demons are simply angels who were cut off from the love of their Lord. I'm sure you know how it feels, Riley. To be torn away from your love. It's as if a part of your soul is missing."

Riley thought of the first few weeks after Gillian left and turned away.

"The pain is unbearable. We became what we are through torture. Plain and simple."

"Is there a point to this, or did I just happen to show up at story time?"

Andras sipped her brandy and touched the corner of her lip with her tongue. "You've only heard one side of the argument. One version of the truth. You were recruited by Samael, an angel destined to fall. The very murderer you were pursuing. Has it ever crossed your mind that you were deceived? You were never given a choice which side you would follow. And since then, they have been able to dictate the rules without consequence. I've decided the time has come to level the playing field."

Riley sighed. "Look, I may not have gone to Sunday school very often, but I think I'll take my chances on the side of angels." She turned and walked back to the stairs. "I'll let myself out, thanks."

"They are lying to you."

Riley hesitated on the top step.

"They believe there is no way you will join us, so they feel free to give you whatever rules they see fit, no negotiation. You are their prisoner, Riley. It is my intention to free you."

"Definitely out of the frying pan," Riley said. She turned to face Andras. "All right, what exactly are they lying about?"

"Your tattoo, for one. It can be removed, relatively painlessly. The hold it has over you will fail. You will no longer be bound to this city as its protector. You will be free to go where you choose, when you choose." She finished her brandy and let the glass hang from her fingers.

Riley said, "I thought the tattoo just granted protection."

Andras nodded slowly. "Yes. But the act of removing it would be a sign to the powers that be. Like taking off your badge and laying it upon your boss' desk. The badge itself has no power, but the act of taking it off speaks for itself." She touched her tongue to her lips, apparently searching for the remnants of her brandy. "I am not telling you this out of charity. I want you gone just as badly as Marchosias does. However, I believe he is going about it wrong. He wants to destroy you. I believe I can get the same results by offering you what you desire.

"I want to invite you to stay here during the course of your investigation. You will have free rein of the grounds, any information you feel will assist you in the case. During that time, you will allow me to show you our side of this battle. I will attempt to sway you to join us. Not through intimidation or mind control. If you decide to join us, it will be of your own free will."

Riley said, "And if I say no, you kill me?"

"No, of course not. At the end of your investigation, the time will come for you to make a choice. There are three options, as I see it." She held up one finger. "You will decide to keep things the way they are. Fighting on the side of angels, as you call it. If that's your decision, I won't stop you. But we will be enemies next time we meet."

"You'll just let me walk out."

Andras shrugged. "I'll have done my part. I have no interest in forcing you to follow me. Your loyalty must be true."

"Okay, and if I decide to join your team?"

"You will be welcomed into my home as a confidant, as a friend, hopefully. You will be protected from retaliation by your former friends among the angels. And Gillian will be safe as well. We'll extend our protection to her, if you wish."

Riley hadn't expected that. She swallowed hard and looked out the windows at Andras' backyard.

"You will not have to fight. Your sole responsibility will be the protection of this estate."

"You said there were three options."

"Correct. The third option... if I'm not convincing enough to bring you to my side, but I successfully show you the error of following the angels, you will be released."

Riley frowned. "What do you mean?"

"The tattoo will be removed, your obligation to this city will be released, and you will be free to leave and go wherever you wish."

Riley was stunned. "And what do you get out of this?"

"The same thing Marchosias gets from killing you," Andras said. "Two options out of three, you are removed from the fight. That is all we demons want. Some of us believe you have to be dead to accomplish that. I don't believe that's true." She walked to the bar and refreshed her glass. "That's all I had to tell you, Riley. You will have full access to my grounds during the course of your investigation. I want to find Ms. Cassidy's murderer. And if I can achieve that while taking you from the battlefield, then all the better."

Riley didn't know what to say to that, so she turned to leave.

"Detective Parra." Riley stopped. "Be sure to discuss this with your partner. I would hate for her to think we were keeping secrets from her." She smiled and sipped her drink. "Thank you for hearing me out, Detective. I'm sure it's going to be an interesting couple of days."

Chapter Three

Crocell was waiting at the bottom of the stairs. He had removed his outer jacket, leaving him in a tuxedo shirt and vest. He had a leather-bound book tucked under his arm, and he presented it to her as she approached. "Detective Parra, a list of the attendees at last night's party. Madame told me to give you a copy."

Riley took the book and flipped it open. It was a typical sign in sheet, with a multitude of different handwriting styles. She had a headache just thinking about translating everyone's name. She closed the book, Andras' offer still ringing in her ears. "Thank you, Freecell. How many people were dressed like you at the party last night? You know, the whole tuxedo route."

"There were six servers, all dressed alike. Myself, of course. And a few of the attendees decided to make it a truly formal affair. I'm afraid I can't give you an exact number."

"If I got you a description, would you be able to match it to a guest?"

"I would do my best."

"Thanks. You're not so bad, for a demon."

His eager to please smile wavered. "And you are not as maddening as other mortals I've met. You should consider yourself fortunate for that, Detective Parra."

"Oh, I'm the luckiest girl in the world, Jeeves."

He ignored the jibe and walked her to the door. "I'm told you'll be staying with us. I want you to know that if it was Madame's intention to harm you... well, I'm sure you know what would happen."

Riley looked toward the landing and saw Andras standing with one hand on the railing. She held a fresh glass of brandy, which she used to toast Riley.

"Yeah," Riley said. "I have a pretty fair idea. Thanks for the guest list."

"My pleasure."

She walked down the brick path to the street, checking her periphery for movement. There was a chance, however small, that the intention of the meeting was to get her to drop her guard. But she reached the street without incident. The real test was the car. There were only so many precautions she could take without Priest there before she bit the bullet and just got inside. She walked around it twice and checked underneath for any obvious signs of tampering. There were no curses painted in blood on the door, or any unholy symbols etched into the sidewalk underneath. She checked the wheel wells for any tracking devices or bugs.

While she looked, she thought about the offer Andras made. Freedom. If the demon was telling the truth - and really, what were the odds there? - then this whole mess could be put behind her. She could forget this town, forget angels and demons existed, let them deal with their own crap like they had been doing for millennia before she came along. All she was going to accomplish was discovering new ways to get herself killed. And if she was released, demons would have no reason to come after her, or Gillian.

Gillian could be safe.

Riley looked out the window at the Andras compound. She felt eyes on her, but couldn't spot anyone in any of the windows. Of course, demons didn't necessarily need to be physically present to spy on someone. She started the car and tossed the guest list onto the passenger seat. She would check it when she got back to the station. For the moment, she wanted to get as far away from Andras and her promises as possible.

Riley arrived to find Priest taking the statement of a slight, bald man with thick glasses. She draped her jacket over the back of her chair and put the guest list on the top of her blotter. Lieutenant Briggs was still holding fort in the interrogation room, the actual lieutenant's office still "under construction." Riley had seen a few contractors wandering through the room, but the door was currently still crossed by crime scene tape.

She went to the interrogation room and knocked on the door. The setup was the same as it had always been, but a file cabinet stood in one corner, and the table in the middle of the room now held a computer monitor and a sea of papers. Briggs glanced up and then went back to what she was writing. "Detective Parra. What can I do for you?"

"I just wanted to give you an update on the Jane Doe we found this morning. We have a name, Heather Cassidy. Apparently she was a guest at a party thrown by Andra—Andrea Silver last night. I have the guest list, and

I believe Detective Priest is interviewing a witness right now. Hopefully we'll be able to narrow down a suspect list without too much trouble."

"Nice work," Briggs said.

"Has Dr. Herron had a chance to examine the body?"

Briggs closed the file. "I think he's just beginning, if you would like to go down and have a look." Riley nodded and started to leave. "Detective, do you have a moment?"

"Sure."

"Close the door."

Riley closed the door and waited.

Briggs folded her hands on top of the desk. "When I took this job, I was told you were a lone wolf. You did things your way, and damn the consequences. I told you I wouldn't put up with that the minute we met. In the short time I've been here, you've done a commendable job of doing things my way. Keeping me in the loop in regards to your investigations. I wanted you to know that I appreciate the effort you're going to."

Riley nodded. "It's my pleasure, ma'am."

"I'm still going to keep my eye on you."

"I understand."

Briggs smiled and relaxed her posture. "All right. You can go now."

Riley left the interrogation room door open and caught Priest's eye. She pointed toward the elevators and mouthed, "Morgue." Priest nodded and turned her attention back to the witness. The elevator doors were just closing as Riley arrived, and she slipped between them and pressed the button for the lowest floor in the building. Allegedly, the morgue was placed next to the garage to facilitate dropping off and picking up bodies. But the truth was, it was stuck in the basement because people were freaked out by the idea of sharing space with bodies that were being dissected.

Going into the morgue felt like seeing someone else in her apartment. It was the same space, but different, victim to the new occupant's tastes and preferences. Dr. Herron hadn't changed very much of Gillian's set-up, but the room still felt utterly alien as Riley entered. The body of Heather Cassidy lay on the center table, modestly covered by two blue sheets. Dr. Herron stood by the feet, preparing an instrument. Her midriff was exposed and Riley could see the now clean cut in her stomach. She had looked young in the vacant lot, but now she looked prepubescent. It was hard to see her lying lifeless on the table.

"Doc, we have an ID for her, in case you want to introduce yourself before you start cutting."

"Couldn't hurt, I suppose. Hello, Detective."

"Hey. Her name is Heather Cassidy."

Herron straightened and looked at the girl's face. "Ooh, yes. I recognize her now. Her father was Reginald Cassidy." He smiled down at her. "Hello, Heather Cassidy. I'm Millard Herron. I'll try to make this as painless as possible."

"Did you know her?"

Herron shook his head. "Not personally. She's in the newspapers a lot. Kind of a party girl. Kind of sad, really. I knew she looked familiar." He clicked his tongue and bent over the body again. "Shame."

"Yeah," Riley said. She felt cheated; the information Andras gave her was starting to look less than helpful if the ME would be able to tell her everything anyway.

"Do you think it's hotter in New Mexico or Florida?"

Riley blinked at the sudden change of subject. "Uh... I don't know. Florida? You wouldn't have to worry about hurricanes in New Mexico."

"True!" He pursed his lips and then focused on the body again. "She was stabbed twice. I thought it was just once, but taking a closer look... she was stabbed twice in almost the exact same place. The cut is slightly mirrored, you see?" He pointed at the wound and Riley saw a slight deviation in the line of the cut. "To hit that exactly, it would have to be two very quick jabs." He demonstrated by thrusting his hand forward.

"Crime of passion, you think?"

"Mm, yes. If it was something else, I believe we would see more injuries. Someone acted impulsively and then tried to cover it up by dumping the body." He rested his hands on the edge of the table. "I like baseball. Florida has the... Marlins? New Mexico... does New Mexico have a professional team?"

"I don't know. I don't think so. What does that have to do with the case?"

"This case? Absolutely nothing." He pushed away from the table and walked to the light board. "I took X-Rays. She has a small fracture on her cheekbone. It wouldn't have been much trouble if she had lived, painful, but not horribly so. I figure someone hit her not long before she died. Bolsters your crime of passion theory. She got into a fight and the stabbing was incidental."

"What kind of blade was it? A knife, a letter opener?"

"A knife, definitely," Herron said. "Single-edged, not terribly long. Long enough to do the job, naturally. But something that could have easily been concealed." He rested his fingers on his chin and drummed them slowly. "Humidity."

Riley glanced at him.

"It affects bodies. Lying out in the heat."

"It rained last night," Riley said. "The temperature was... what, in the sixties at most? If the body was affected by a heat source, then—"

Herron waved his hands. "No, no, not her. I was just thinking out loud. New Mexico and Florida are both so... warm. I'm sure it would affect decomposition."

"What the hell are you talking about?"

He looked at her and said, "Oh. Sorry. I have such a habit of thinking out loud, and it's usually to dead bodies, I just assume people know what I'm talking about." He smiled brightly and walked back to the table. "My time here is almost up. There are offers from two other coroner's offices, but I'm not sure which I should take. New Mexico or Florida. To be honest, it feels like a choice between two evils."

Riley couldn't muster up interest in Herron's story. If he was leaving, that meant she would have to get used to someone else in Gillian's rightful place. "Any idea who your replacement will be?"

"I'm not getting a replacement." He picked up a file and made a note about something he saw on the body.

"What do you mean?"

"I only took this job on a temporary basis. I didn't want to be permanent here. No offense. I'm just not exactly a 'stay in one place' kind of person." He bent down over the body and said, "Bruises on the arm. See?" He pointed with his pinky and Riley put her curiosity aside to examine the dark splotch.

"Someone grabbed her."

"Looks like it. It seems the little lady had a harrowing last night. Unfortunate." He straightened up and walked toward his office.

Riley said, "Wait a minute. If you're not going to get a replacement, who is going to take care of the bodies that come in? The city coroner?"

Herron paused at the door. "No, I heard something about the former medical examiner wanting her job back. Jill something." He waved and turned his back to her. "Nice talking with you, Detective."

Riley couldn't summon up the mental capacity to form a response.

Chapter Four

Riley took the stairs back to her desk, too buzzed to consider the elevator. She would have just bounced off the walls. She reached the stairwell door just as it opened, revealing Priest. They both startled at the sight of the other, and then Riley smiled and grabbed Priest's face. "Hey, Caitlin." She kissed her hard, on the lips, and Priest yelped as Riley released her. "How did the interview with the witness go?"

"Fine," Priest said. She wiped her mouth on her sleeve and said, "I think I enjoyed your company more when you were depressed."

Riley chuckled and leaned against the wall. "Gillian is coming back."

Priest's eyebrows shot up. "Really? Riley, that's fantastic. When?"

"I don't know. Dr. Herron just told me that he's looking at other jobs and, when he leaves, Gillian is getting her old position back. It's just a matter of time, I guess."

Priest leaned against the opposite wall. "It's great news. Truly. But... are you ready for her to come back?"

"I've been ready since the minute she left."

"The reasons she left are still here, Riley. The danger to you, the vulnerability she presents to your enemies... this battle hasn't ended yet."

Riley looked down at her feet. "Maybe I have a way to end it."

"What?"

"I said maybe there's a way." She sighed. "Andras made me an offer. If I agree to it, she'll give me the option of walking away free and clear. No more albatross around my neck. I can 'resign,' and Gillian will be safe. She's willing to take steps to come home, so maybe I should be willing to make some sacrifices myself."

Priest was fuming. "Sacrifices like your soul?"

"Caitlin..."

"This is Zerachiel talking, okay? Any deal you make with a demon is a bad one. My Lord. Riley, I shouldn't have to tell you that. They lie, they trick, they create loopholes that you cannot escape. Whatever she is offering you is not as appealing as it sounds."

"First of all, what they're offering me is freedom. They're giving me a choice, which is more than you guys have done. My God, Samael just waltzes in and dumps all this responsibility on my lap without so much as a how-do-you-do. You don't tell me anything. You refuse to answer my questions, or you answer them so goddamn cryptically that I'm more confused than before I asked."

Priest stepped forward. "Riley, I'm begging you. Stay away from Andras."

Riley advanced as well, closing the distance between them. "Or what?"

Priest's expression softened. "Look at what they've done to us."

After a moment, Riley realized what Priest meant. Her anger dissipated enough to realize her fists were clenched, and she was a heartbeat away from slugging her partner. She backed off a step and relaxed her fingers. "It's frustrating, Priest. Okay? Andras may be a demon, but she's offering me answers."

"Think of what the cost will be."

Riley held her hands out. "Where else am I going to get them, Zerachiel? You? God? Am I supposed to go pray and wait for divine inspiration? I'm not an idiot. I didn't just join this fight yesterday. It's been a couple of months, and I'm not a newbie. I won't go in there blind. But I have to go in there to close this case, anyway. Might as well do a little scouting while I'm at it." She opened the stairwell door and said, "Don't worry, Caitlin. I'll make the right choice."

"I hope so," Priest said as she followed Riley from the stairs. "I hope Andras really lets you make a choice at all."

Riley led the way back to their desks. "What did the witness tell you?"

"He didn't have much. Like he said, it was dark and he was half asleep, so he can't give much of a description. But the body-dumper was wearing a tuxedo, just like Crocell. He arrived in a black sedan..."

"Of which Andras has an entire fleet. She had a party last night when, at a conservative estimate, a dozen people were dressed in tuxedos." Riley opened the book Andras offered her. "This is a list of everyone who was at the party. Or at least those who signed in." She ran her thumb down the page, estimated how many names were on one sheet, then thumbed through to see how many pages were filled. "We've got about forty names here. If we figure each of them brought a date, that's about eighty people who could have done it."

Priest stood behind Riley's seat and looked at the list. She pointed to one name. "Phil N. DeBlanc?"

"Okay, eighty suspects give or take. We'll also eliminate the women. We may not have a description, but the coin dealer did say it was a man." She turned the page so Priest could see it better. "Recognize any names?"

Priest nodded. "Several. Valefar, Gamigin, Shax and Sitri. Not to mention mortal celebrities. Looks like Andras throws quite the shindig."

Riley straightened in her seat. "Shit."

"What?"

Riley pointed to a name at the bottom of the page and then looked across the office. Lieutenant Briggs was still in her office with the door open, but Riley couldn't see her from where she sat. "Do you think we can trust her with this?"

"I don't know," Priest said. "I don't feel anything hanging around her, evil or otherwise. But she's still an unknown agent."

"She is our boss." Riley looked down at the sign in sheet, the last name on the first page of signatures. She could see the man's face perfectly. He was standing on the other side of her detective's badge when she earned it, and he was the man in the newspaper whenever there was an outcry about the crime rate. His autograph said Preston A. Benedict, but she knew him better as the commissioner of the police department.

"Andras isn't necessarily a criminal," Priest said. "We can't take this to Briggs until we know for a fact he did something wrong. Ann/Dras is a big development company. They have projects going all over the city. Maybe the commissioner was just glad-handing."

Riley raised an eyebrow. "Slow down with the lingo, Starsky."

"Who?"

Riley shook her head and continued through the list. "Some big names on this list. A mayor's aide, a newspaper reporter, a couple of vice cops. Andras chooses her friends well."

"She's wily," Priest said. "I hope you keep that in mind."

Riley pressed her lips together and ignored the insinuation.

"How do you want to play this?"

"We can't just randomly walk up to these people and ask them where they were the night of the murder. We need to find out who among them knew Heather Cassidy."

"Heather...?"

"The victim," Riley said. "Sorry. I got her name from Andras."

Priest nodded. "I hope you don't plan on asking Andras for a list of Heather's friends."

"No," Riley said. She opened the bottom drawer of her desk and pulled out a phone book and did a quick search for Cassidy. "I don't turn the newspaper over to get the answers for the crossword, either."

"What does that mean?"

"It means I'm a detective." She stood up and grabbed her coat. "Let's go."

Heather Cassidy lived in a loft downtown, far seedier than her parent's money could have afforded. Riley and Priest rode up in an ancient freight elevator, listening to the clanging of gears and chains over their heads. Riley looked up at the rusted roof of the car and said, "If this thing falls, you'll grab me and fly, right?"

"Fly where? We're locked in a rusted metal box."

Riley grunted. "You have a point."

Heather's loft was on the third floor, and Riley was grateful that they made it without incident. "How about I bust open the window and you fly me down when we're done here?"

"Sounds good to me."

The elevator opened in the middle of the loft, and seemed to serve as a dividing point of the space. To their left were the bedroom and bathroom, both lit by a huge window the size of the TV in Andras' living room. To the right was the spacious living room and kitchen. The furniture was straight out of a thrift store, but it had a certain eclectic charm. A large canvas hung on the far wall, covered with finger-painted portraits, names signed in dripping watercolors, and a sea of handprints in every color of the rainbow.

"I thought her father was some kind of big deal," Priest said. "Why would she live here?"

"Rebellion. Kid who has always had everything resents it, decides to see how the other half life. It usually lasts a couple of years before she comes to her senses and runs home to her silver spoon." She picked up a brown paper bag, looked inside, and wadded it up.

"Sounds like you're speaking from experience."

Riley snorted. "The only experience I have is from busting the spoiled brats for possession. Then I have to hear their sniveling calls to Daddy to come bail 'em out." She carried the bag across the kitchen and scanned the floor for a trash can. There was a tall, narrow cabinet next to the fridge, and she hooked her index finger under the handle. "That's when they didn't overdose before we—"

Riley barely registered the man, her focus locked on the glint of light off the thing in his hand. When he lunged out of the closet at her, she swung her left arm up, ducked down, and used the guy's forward momentum to roll him across her back. When she stood, he tumbled to the ground, clipping the center island with his hip before he sprawled on the tile. Riley pivoted, pulled her gun, and aimed it at the back of the man's head. "Don't move, don't twitch a finger." She kicked the drywall knife away from his hand and said, "Who are you?"

"Calvin. Calvin Coley. Please don't kill me."

Riley growled and bent down to grab the collar of his shirt. "I'm not going to kill you. If you're lucky, I'll just arrest you for assaulting a police officer." She hauled him to his feet and pressed him against the island as she patted him down. The kid trembled throughout the frisking, his eyes darting around the room until her words registered.

Coley tried to look over his shoulder at her. "You're cops? Oh, thank God." He sagged against the edge of the island. "Listen, you gotta help me. My girlfriend..."

"Heather Cassidy?"

"Yeah. She, she's missing. She's been missing since last night. Or, I guess this morning. I don't really... know. I haven't felt... really right since last night. Nothing's right anymore. I can't think. But she's gone, I know that, okay? She went to some party, and I haven't seen her since."

Riley glanced at Priest, whose eyes were filled with compassion. Riley, however, was still seeing the knife coming at her. "Hands behind your back."

"Detective Parra, perhaps we could show a bit of compassion."

Riley hated good cop, bad cop. She hesitated and then released his hands. "Step over there." Coley did as requested. "Mr. Coley, I'm sorry to be the one to inform you, but Heather Cassidy was found murdered this morning."

Coley stared at her for a moment, and then glanced at Priest as if for confirmation. When she nodded, he seemed to deflate. He caught the edge of the fridge and hung his head. "I should have gone with her. I should... have gone."

Priest crossed the room and helped Coley stand. "It's all right. Take your time. Let's go have a seat in the living room, okay?"

"Do you know where Heather was going last night?" Riley asked as she followed them from the kitchen.

"To a party at that developer's house. Andrea Silver." Riley nodded. "Heather said that she was going to get some money from Silver. A couple hundred dollars."

Priest said, "Why did she need money?"

"Her father cut her off. Because of me." He sniffled. "He said his daughter would never get married to some nobody. Guess he was right." He looked at his bare left hand and curled his hand into a fist.

Riley couldn't help feeling sorry for the guy. She sighed and finally took a seat. "How did Heather know Andrea Silver?"

"Heather's dad hired Silver's company all the time. New projects and stuff. I guess they were old family friends. Heather heard about the party and decided to see if she could get an invitation."

"What time did she leave?"

"Around one in the morning."

Riley glanced at Priest, who met her gaze with a frown. "Are you positive about that?"

Coley nodded. "She said that she didn't want to be a party crasher. She planned to get there as things were dying down."

Priest said, "Calvin, would you excuse us for a moment?"

He nodded and Riley walked back toward the elevator. When she turned around, Priest was right behind her. Priest said, "Dr. Herron put the time of death at two in the morning," Riley said. "If she left here at one..."

"She had time to get to the party." She looked at her watch. "But she wouldn't have been there very long at all. Maybe half an hour?"

Priest said, "Someone had to have grabbed her and killed her almost immediately after she got to the party. How does your suspect list look now?"

Riley said, "Down to one." She looked over at Coley, who was rocking back and forth with his head in his hands. "I'm going to have another talk with Andrea Silver."

Chapter Five

Riley expected a wave of energy, a flash of light, some indication that Priest was infusing her old Nova with some kind of special power. But Priest finally dropped her hands from the roof without any fireworks. "It won't turn this thing into a tank, but it should keep any demons from being too interested in it." She put her hands on her hips. "I really wish you would let me go with you."

Riley patted Priest on the shoulder. "I think you would have a hard time keeping your cool there. I know, I know. I'm hardly the level headed one in this relationship. But I think it's best if I go in alone."

"That's exactly what Andras wants."

"Yeah, well... if I pretend to play by her rules, maybe she'll give me more information." Not to mention maybe she'll answer some of my questions about my tattoo. She opened the car door and said, "As soon as we close this case and Heather Cassidy's killer is behind bars, I'm going to cut ties with Andras. Do you need me to drop you off at the station?"

"No. It's a nice day; I think I'll walk."

"If you're sure." Priest started to turn away, and Riley said, "Priest. I do a lot of stupid things, and I make a lot of hair trigger decisions. But a demon is a demon. I'm not going to go dark side on you, Yoda."

Priest didn't turn around, but she said. "Still. Careful, you should be."

Riley grinned. "You rented the DVD?"

Priest smiled over her shoulder. "It's actually not bad. Stay safe, Riley."

"There is hope for you yet, Priest." Riley suddenly remembered something she wanted to ask. "Hey, Priest. Why would the demons at Andrea Silver's place be afraid to touch the gates?"

"Are they iron?"

"I assume so."

Priest nodded. "Iron is anathema to demons. It burns them. It's like putting salt on a slug. It won't kill them, but it'll send them back to the depths of Hell."

Riley raised an eyebrow. "Good to know."

"Riley, if you're close enough to use iron against a demon, it may already be too late."

She shrugged. "Sometimes it's nice to have the option of a last-moment attack."

The compound was a bit more active when Riley arrived the second time. She spotted a few people behind the gates, tending the yards and doing various things with gardening tools. She walked past them and wondered what happened to the original owners of the houses. Andras had the money to buy them out, Riley was sure, but demons rarely got what they wanted by throwing cash around.

The front door of the main house opened as Riley approached. Crocell smiled and said, "Detective Parra. Do you require assistance with your bags?"

"I'm not staying, D-cell. I need to talk to your boss. Where is she?"

"Madame is indisposed at the moment. However..."

"You'll go get her for me."

Crocell's smile wavered. "I was going to say—"

"I don't care." She snapped her fingers and shooed him away. "Chop-chop."

Crocell stepped forward and fixed her with a level stare. "You are a base life form. You are so far below me, that it sickens me to show you even a modicum of respect. Can you imagine bowing to vermin? Such as it is for me. If I were given the order, I would eviscerate you where you stood. I would keep you alive as I tore your—"

"Can I have a glass of water while you're at it? I'm a bit parched."

His eyes widened and Riley saw a flash of fire behind them. Riley didn't budge despite the fact her brain was screaming at her to run.

"You want to tear me apart so bad? Fine. The feeling is mutual. But someone has ordered you to keep your hands off. Someone you're obviously scared to death of. So here's the deal. You stop making empty threats, and I won't make you kiss my feet when I enter a room. Got it?"

Crocell worked his jaw, glared at Riley without blinking, and then forced a smile. "As you wish, Detective Parra. If you'll wait in the sitting room, I'll get Madame for you."

Riley walked into the living room while Crocell went up the stairs. Riley put her hands in her pockets as she scanned the living room. The space flowed directly into the kitchen, and Riley assumed this was where the party happened the night before. She glanced at the coffee table and frowned when she spotted the objects sitting on the corner.

A hammer and a nail, placed at right angles to each other. Riley walked around and looked more closely at the tools. There was no evidence of carpentry, no dust or damage that she could see. She wondered if it was some kind of crucifixion reference, but that didn't make any sense. The nail was more of a spike, anyway, the sort of thing used for railroads and very old construction. Riley was reaching for the hammer when Andras said her name from the top of the stairs.

"Riley. I didn't expect to see you again so soon."

Andras wore a coral-colored robe, her hair held up by a jade pin. The robe ended mid-thigh, and Riley couldn't tear her gaze from the woman's toned, lithe legs as she descended the stairs. That was probably the whole purpose of calling to her from the landing, a forced ogling designed to throw Riley off. Riley was determined not to let such blatant manipulation work; she had seen plenty of legs, the majority of them nicer than these. Well. Half of them nicer, maybe. A good percentage. Damn.

Andras stepped into the living room and Riley saw that the front of the robe was gapped enough to reveal her cleavage. "I was just taking a bath." She lifted her arm and ran her fingers along the skin, dragging her robe sleeve up. "It's one of the indulgences I found myself addicted to after I took human form. The way your skin feels after a bath... there's nothing like it." She brushed her hand down Riley's cheek, and Riley was too startled by the contact to realize how close Andras had gotten to her. "Feel?"

"Yeah. Soft."

Andras' lips parted in a smile. "I'm glad you came back, Riley." Her hand rested on Riley's shoulder and she stepped even closer.

"Andras..."

"Yes, Riley?" Her voice was barely a breath, a puff of warm air that washed over Riley and seemed to rattle her thoughts like leaves on a tree. She closed her eyes and tried to force them back into order, but suddenly Andras' lips were on hers. Riley gasped, and Andras slipped her tongue into Riley's mouth. A fog seemed to fill her mind, flooding across reason and common sense so all she could focus on was how good it felt to be kissing someone. Such a tender touch, sweet lips that tasted of brandy, a flash of a tongue against hers. She desperately wanted to touch the skin she had glimpsed when Andras descended the stairs, wanted to kiss every inch, but something... something was...

Riley pulled back, hands firm against Andras' shoulders and pushing her away. "Stop," she gasped.

Andras moved her hand down Riley's side. "Yes. Perhaps we should take this upstairs."

Riley squirmed away from Andras, the fog clearing the further she got from the demon. "Holy hell." She swallowed hard and licked her lips. She took a few steadying breaths before she risked facing Andras again. "Don't... do that." The words sounded hollow in her own ears, but it was the best she could do under the circumstances.

"As you wish," Andras said. "I merely assumed your return... well." She smiled and held her hands out. "I have desires like anyone else. And you are a very attractive woman."

Riley decided to ignore that. "What's with the tools?"

Andras looked down at the hammer and smiled. "Consider it a visual aid."

"For?"

"It's not important." She tugged the two halves of her robe together, a modest move that actually drew more attention to her breasts. And the fact she was naked underneath the silk. "If you didn't come here to take me up on my offer, why have you come?"

"I have some questions about Heather Cassidy. According to her boyfriend, she didn't leave home until about one this morning. Our medical examiner estimates she was killed around an hour later. Not much time to get here and mingle. Plus, you lied to me. You told me you saw her around midnight."

Andras shook her head. "No, I said I spoke with her at midnight. We spoke on the phone."

"Was she ever at the party? Can you confirm she made it to the house?"

"I'm not sure. I never saw her."

Riley started for the door. "Thanks, Ms. Silver. I think I can see just how much help you'll be. I'll contact you if I have any further questions."

"Your tattoo was given to you after a night of passion with the first woman you ever loved. Christine Lee. You thought the tattoo was a gift, but it was truly a curse. She cursed you to this battle, Riley, by branding you. Marked you for the angels to take notice. When she died, all that weight dropped on you. What I'm offering you is freedom."

Riley faced Andras. "You lied about Heather Cassidy. Or, fine, you screwed with the facts so I'd draw the wrong conclusions. When you kissed me, I couldn't think or reason... so I hope you won't be offended when I say I plan to stay the hell away from you."

Andras raised an eyebrow. "Does your head remain clear when you kissed Gillian? How reasonable are you when she touched your bare stomach and then slid her hand higher?" Andras slowly approached. "Perhaps you are too quick to blame my nature." She brought her hand up to touch Riley's hair. "Perhaps you are merely lonely. Ah, I know the feeling all too well."

Riley twisted her head and Andras touched air. "I wish I could say it was nice talking to you, Andras. I'll come back if I want any more lies or cryptic clues."

Andras smiled. "I'll hold you to that promise, Detective."

Riley left the house without spotting Crocell, still trying to shake the haze caused by Andras' kiss. It had nothing to do with feelings. *She's a demon. So why is my heart still pounding? Why are my hands shaking?* She shook her head. "Because you realize how damned close that was." If she hadn't stopped it, she had no doubt she would have ended up in Andras' bed. Naked, vulnerable, and... She pushed the image out of her head. She would have been putty in Andras' hands. And then, well, there's no telling what might have happened or how she would have ended up. An image of her bloody corpse decorating the front of Marchosias' building eradicated any remnants of the spell Andras cast on her.

Riley got into her car and stared at the wheel for a long moment. She was safe here. Priest's blessing wasn't the strongest weapon against demonic interference, but it would do the trick. It was like taking an antacid to quell the stirrings of heartburn. Preventative measures to keep her from unnecessary pain. She gripped the steering wheel and thought back to the tableau in the living room.

Andras smiling down at the hammer and the nail. What did that mean? Heather Cassidy was murdered by a knife. Calvin Coley had attacked Riley with a knife in the apartment, but that didn't mean anything. Anyone who hears an intruder breaking in would grab a handy weapon, and nine times out of ten, that was a knife.

Riley looked back at the house and saw Andras standing in the upstairs window. She was still in the robe, her hair down around her shoulders. Her smile widened when she realized Riley was watching her, and she lifted her hand in greeting. It was only after Riley waved back that she realized the sun was shining on her car's window. The glass would have been a mirror, and she should have been invisible to the demon.

The thought made her shudder and drop her hand. She turned to face the street and saw Crocell standing on the corner of the cul-de-sac. His hands were in his pockets, eyes locked on her car. Riley was suddenly very aware that she hadn't given the car a check before she got in, but she wasn't going to let Crocell know he had shaken her with just his presence. She gripped the key and twisted, biting the inside of her cheek when the engine roared to life.

She refused to look at Crocell as she drove past him, but she did look in her rearview mirror as she turned the corner. He had moved to the middle of the street to watch her leave.

"I actually considered taking her invitation to move in," Riley muttered. "I must be out of my goddamn mind..."

She was glad she was alone in the car, because she couldn't think of anyone who would disagree with that statement.

Chapter Six

"What does a hammer and nail mean to you?"

Priest looked up as Riley passed her desk. She rested her hands on her desk blotter and thought for a moment. "Construction work?"

"Not visibly. Maybe there were some renovations and the carpenter left them behind. Although I didn't notice them this morning." Riley shrugged and sat down. "Not that I was looking for them when I was there the first time."

"I wish I had been present for the start of this conversation."

Riley smiled. "Sorry. Andras had a hammer and a nail sitting on the coffee table. She said it was a visual aid."

"To help with the case?"

"I don't know. I assume so."

Priest watched Riley carefully. "What else happened while you were there?"

"Nothing," Riley muttered. She ran her thumb over her bottom lip and said, "She also changed her story. She said she spoke with Heather Cassidy at around midnight. She never actually saw her at the party."

"The dump vehicle and the tuxedoed man place her at the property, however briefly."

"I timed the distance between Heather's loft and the Andras compound. It took just over half an hour to get there, with just a little traffic. Figure about twenty minutes in the dead of night. How far is the Silver compound from the dump site?"

"At that time of night, ten minutes. Give or take."

Riley nodded. "Sounds right. So Heather arrives at the party at one-twenty. She must have been killed by one-forty-five at the latest. Not a lot of time to piss someone off. Unless she was going there to confront someone."

"Blackmail?"

"Coley did say that she expected to get some cash. She wasn't going to the party as a guest; she was going because she knew someone would be there."

Priest gestured at the guest list. "Coley said that she only expected a couple hundred dollars. The people on that list, you could blackmail them for thousands and they wouldn't miss it. Some of them could afford millions in order to save face. So why such a low payday?"

"Maybe it was a bluff. Or maybe she decided to ask for a low amount and increase the odds the people will pay. If you can afford to pay a blackmailer two million dollars, think of how fast you would run to an ATM if they only asked for five hundred."

Priest said, "An economical thief? And you say I'm naïve."

Riley smirked. "I've been corrupting you with too many bad movies. Let's say she was blackmailing someone. They agreed to pay, and set up the meeting at Andras' party. She said herself that the guest list was fluid. No one really knew for sure who was there and who wasn't. It was about as anonymous as you could get. She shows up, maybe she decides to ask for more money after seeing rich people amusing themselves. Target gets angry, grabs a knife, stabs her."

"The party was still going at the time. It may have been slowing down, but people would have been around. You think the guests will cover up a murder?"

"Maybe Heather and her killer met outside by the cars. But even if it happened in the middle of the living room, there's no guarantee anyone would come forward. You know how these rich people are. They think they can buy anything, even an alibi for murder. They get attacked, they throw money at the problem. Before long, it's their go-to solution to everything. It's just the way they think." She sighed. "When you're..." She blinked.

"What is it?"

Riley straightened in her chair. "When you're a hammer, you tend to see every problem as a nail. That's what Andras was trying to tell me with her little visual aid."

"Okay. What does it mean?"

Riley shook her head. "I don't have a clue."

"Are you the hammer or the nail?"

Riley rubbed her chin. She obviously hoped Andras considered her a hammer; being a nail was too dangerous. Hammers attacked. Hammers... solved problems. "I'm a hammer."

"Good. What's the nail?"

"This case?" Riley said. "Heather Cassidy." She scanned the room. "Andras?" She put the pieces together, amazed to find out they fit. "You and I are both hammers. We found out there was a demon involved and, because of who we are, we immediately focused on her."

"Naturally."

"Maybe we need to take the demons out of the equation. If anyone else had taken this case, they would have put Andrea Silver to one side as soon as they interviewed her. She doesn't have anything to add; she didn't even see Heather the night she died. The only connection is Heather driving to Andras' place in the middle of the night to get some money."

"A couple hundred dollars. Are we still on the blackmail theory?"

Riley heard Andras in her head, a whisper of a voice breaking through the fog. "I have desires like anyone else. And you are a very attractive woman."

"Heather was a call girl."

"What?"

Riley counted off the reasons on her fingers. "Andras told me that she has desires just like anyone else. But Andrea Silver is a prominent businesswoman; she can't exactly go out to clubs hoping to pick up a one night stand. Maybe that's what the whole party was about; she was trying to get laid. But either she didn't get any takers, or she didn't like the potential conquests who were there, so she called in professional help. I'll bet she had used Heather in the past. She calls Heather up as the party is winding down, asks her to come over for a little fun."

"Our earlier timeline only gives them a twenty-five minute window for sexual relations."

Riley shrugged. "Yeah."

"That's nowhere near enough time."

Riley laughed, and then realized Priest was serious. "Good lord, woman."

"What?"

Riley waved her off. "Okay, let's not assume they had sex. What happened? She ran into someone she knew downstairs."

"Why would they kill her? And it seems that if Andras called someone for sex, she would be aware when they arrived. Hell, Crocell met me at the door both times I visited." She chewed her bottom lip. "Someone in that house saw something."

"Good luck getting it out of them."

"I'm not even going to ask."

"Oh, right. You're a detective."

Riley said, "Sarcasm is not becoming on you, Caitlin."

Priest shrugged and leaned back in her chair. Riley watched her, surprised at how comfortable they were with each other. She would never have dreamed about replacing Sweet Kara, but necessity and happenstance and a horrid chain of events... she supposed she could have ended up with a worse partner. She rested her elbows on the arms of her chair and looked up at the ceiling as she rattled the facts of the case in her brain.

The rattle of the chains in Heather's loft elevator came to mind. It would drive her crazy if she had to live next to something that damn noisy. You could probably hear it from every apartment, all day long. Riley furrowed her brow and said, "Coley knew we were coming."

"Mmm?"

"He wasn't hiding in the kitchen closet all day. He heard us coming. He must have heard us talking when we were in the apartment, too. He didn't attack until I found him."

"So?"

"He thought someone was coming after him. The elevator was a cue to get the knife and find a hiding place. He thought we were there to kill him. But he claimed he didn't know Heather was dead."

"His surprise seemed genuine."

"But he knew someone wanted him and Heather dead. Maybe his surprise was just because he didn't realize Heather had been caught."

Priest nodded. "So we need to find out who he was so afraid of."

Riley stood and grabbed her jacket off the back of her chair. "And we better hope we get to him before Heather's killers do."

"We're not going to be able to ride up in the elevator," Riley said. "We're going to want the element of surprise this time. Did you see any stairs last time we were there?"

"Just the fire escape."

Riley winced. "Probably make just as much noise as the elevator did."

"I'm not going to fly you through the window."

"One of these days, you're going to fly me."

"It's not a parlor trick."

Riley smiled. "I know. It's better than a parlor trick. It kicks ass."

Priest rolled her eyes as they pulled into the parking lot of the building. Riley slowed to a crawl and scanned the building. The fire escape looked hazardous; she wouldn't trust it to perform its true purpose, let alone provide them with a stealthy way to enter the building. She tried to determine if there were any new cars parked outside the building, but it was impossible to tell.

She parked near the doors and got out, walking around to the trunk of the car. She handed Priest a Kevlar vest before donning her own. She fastened the Velcro on the shoulders, checked her guns ammo, and said, "Okay. Let's hope this is all pointless and we're actually ahead of the game for once."

They entered the building and Riley started across the lobby toward the elevator. She was almost there when Priest said, "Riley." She turned and saw Priest standing at a door marked Maintenance Only. Riley walked back and tested the knob. The door was unlocked and revealed an incredibly narrow staircase. Priest said, "I saw better craftsmanship when we were in the Underground."

"But hey, it's rent-controlled," Riley said. "Come on."

They moved quickly up the stairs, passing doors that gave maintenance men, landlords, and other various entities access to the apartments. Riley thought it was ironic that anyone could reach any loft via the elevator, but the worker's entrance seemed to have more security than anything else in the building.

When they reached the apartment where Heather and Coley lived, Riley tested the knob. The door was unlocked, and she leaned her shoulder against it. The door opened a crack, and she pulled on the knob as she leaned on the door to keep it from opening too far. She peered into the apartment, scanning for movement or signs of a struggle. She spotted Calvin Coley sitting at the kitchen table, one bare foot bouncing on the floor as he stared at the elevator. A rifle was propped against the table next to him.

Riley was imminently grateful Priest had found the alternate entrance. She turned to Priest, nodded once, and pushed the door open far enough that she could walk through. "Mr. Coley, this is the police. Stay right where you are."

Coley nearly jumped out of his skin, his hands going for the gun.

"Don't touch that gun, Mr. Coley. That's your last warning."

He froze, eyes wide as he moved his head slightly to look at her. "It's you again."

"Yes, sir, Mr. Coley." Riley was even with the table, and she reached out to take the gun away. She handed it to Priest before she relaxed. "Expecting visitors?"

Coley swallowed hard.

"Let me guess. Heather's pimp?"

He blinked, looked at Priest and then said, "Wha... n-no, Heather wasn't a prostitute."

"We know what she was going over to Andrea Silver's house, Calvin. We're not vice, so we could care less about how Heather got her money."

Coley wrapped his hands together in tight fists and held them between his knees. He shifted uncomfortably on his chair, and said, "She wasn't some streetwalker. She was a call girl."

"Much more respectable," Riley said.

"It was," Coley insisted. He shook his head and said, "It's not like she planned it. Some woman came up to her in the supermarket and said she could earn a lot of money. Hundreds of bucks for one night."

Riley remembered what Andras said about her host body: "I saw it in a shop downtown and I simply had to have it." Riley said, "You didn't mind loaning your girlfriend out?"

"Heather said she would only work for women. It cut down on her income, but, you know, it wasn't like she was cheating on me."

Riley rolled her eyes.

"So who wants to kill her, and why?"

"Her boss. The guy who runs the escort company. Heather... had been skimming. She would take jobs off the books. We were trying to save some money so we could move somewhere nicer. Maybe get a nest egg so she wouldn't have to keep doing this shit. She started giving her home number to some of her regulars, so they could call her without going through the agency. She gave them a discount, but she still got more money because the agency didn't get the cut."

Riley said, "I guess the boss didn't take kindly to her becoming a free agent."

The elevator behind them started to rattle. Priest looked at the metal grate that covered the door and said, "Looks like we're about to have company."

Riley said, "Mr. Coley, the maintenance stairs. Get there. Now."

"He's not messing around. He'll..."

"Now, Mr. Coley."

He looked at them for a long minute, then hurried into the safety of the closet. Riley went to one side of the elevator and checked her ammo again. She glanced at Priest. "How much ammo do you have left?"

Priest lowered her voice to a drawl and quoted the movie. "We're going to run out unless we can get to that mule and get some more."

Riley chuckled at the movie quote. "Whoever is coming up in this elevator, I doubt it's as bad as the Bolivian army."

"Are you sure?"

Riley sighed. "Why take chances." She pressed her back against the wall and waited for the elevator to arrive.

Chapter Seven

The elevator reached the apartment with a heavy thud. Priest met Riley's eye and nodded, and Riley winked. When the heavy door slid up, Riley pressed herself back and attempted to blend into the cracked drywall. A man exited the elevator and paused, standing just a few feet in front of Riley as he scanned the room. "Mr. Coley," he said, his voice echoing off the empty apartment walls. "We just want to talk."

The man stepped forward and Riley scanned him for weapons. He carried a gun in his left hand as he crossed toward the maintenance door. He was wide in the shoulders, tapered at the waist. Riley didn't want to try him in a hand to hand fight. Of course, if it got to that, she would just fight dirty. "Sonny, head down to the lobby and make sure our friend isn't trying to escape."

Riley stepped forward while Priest swung around and aimed her weapon into the elevator. "I've got a better idea," Riley said. "Why don't you all just put your guns down and we'll have a nice friendly conversation?"

The man turned slowly, casually, and eyed her vest. "You're the police?"

"Now we know you can read. I feel like we've bonded. Lose the gun. Priest?"

"Two in the elevator. Both armed."

"Can you handle them?"

Priest said, "Yeah."

"I'm Detective Parra. That's Detective Priest."

The man seemed to debate whether or not to give his real name, and then finally said, "Steven Linder."

"A pleasure." She gestured at the seat Coley had just vacated. "Sit a spell."

Linder walked to the chair and sat down. He put the gun on the table and then pushed it just out of easy reach. "Sonny, Kevin, why don't you give the detective your weapons and join us in here." He opened his jacket and showed Riley that he was unarmed. Riley stepped to one side and looked over her shoulder. The two men in the elevator, carbon copies of Linder in cheaper suits, handed their guns to Priest and entered the room with their hands out and their fingers splayed.

"Nice and polite," Linder said. "We wouldn't want the detectives to get the wrong idea."

The men took seats around the table. Riley waited until Priest retrieved Linder's gun before she relaxed her stance. "Now, Mr. Linder. Want to explain to us why you were entering this private residence with a loaded weapon?"

"On the contrary, Detective. Have your partner check the weapon."

Riley watched as Priest took out the clip. Priest raised an eyebrow. "Empty."

"Ms. Cassidy and her boyfriend owed me some money. I find that with most debtors, all you have to do is make the threat. Sometimes you just need to show them the gun, and their minds fill in the blanks." He smiled. "Besides. A dead man can't exactly pay his debts, right?"

"No, but he can serve as an example to others," Riley said. She looked at the two men sitting next to him, Sonny and Kevin. They were both wearing suits that looked like they'd been pulled randomly off the rack. "Your boys always dress like that? Maybe some nights they decide to dress to the nines and wear a tux?"

Linder chuckled. "No, Detective. You are looking at the extent of their wardrobe, I'm afraid. I've tried to improve their fashion sense, but..."

"Did you try to get your money out of Heather Cassidy last night? Maybe you tried to intimidate her with a knife and things got out of hand. You and your boys started to rough her up a little, next thing you know Sonny-Boy had stabbed her."

Linder's smile seemed more forced now. "We had a conversation with Heather last night, yes. We knew she was taking jobs off the books, so I had Kevin keep an eye on her apartment. He followed her when she left, and I met him at that woman's house."

"Andrea Silver."

"Yes, I believe so. Things did get heated, Detective, I'll admit that freely. But we did not kill her. When I left, she was alive."

Riley glanced at the two goons again. "When *you* left?"

"I decided Kevin and Sonny could have a conversation with Heather for me. There was no need for my presence."

"Meaning you didn't want the people at Andrea Silver's party to see you arguing with a prostitute in the street."

Linder leaned forward. "She was not a prostitute, she was—"

"A woman who had sex for money. Call 'em like I see them."

Linder rolled his eyes. "How very closed-minded of you. But fine, whatever you wish to call her. I have a reputation in this town. I would prefer not be associated with that kind of engagement."

"So really, your alibi just covers yourself."

Kevin and Sonny stared at her without malice. Innocence or stupidity, she couldn't tell.

"You boys want to take a shot at defending yourselves?"

One of the goons said, "Mr. Linder left when the old man came outta the house. He asked us what we was doing on his property and we explained we were just trying to get payment from the whore."

"Kevin," Linder snapped.

Kevin shifted and looked down at his lap. "Sorry, Mr. Linder. Anyways, the old guy told us to get off the property. Sonny and me, we told him we weren't on his property. We was on the street, right? Public grounds. I tol' the old guy we weren't leavin' without the who—without Ms. Cassidy. He said that we should talk about it in private, so we went into the house."

"Did you see the owner?"

"Don't know who the owner is."

"Andrea Silver. She's about five foot ten, thick blonde hair, eyes like ice. Gorgeous. Golden skin. Strong hands." She caught movement out of the corner of her eye and realized Priest was staring at her. She thought back over her description and wondered where it had come from. She cleared her throat and focused on Kevin. "Ring a bell?"

"Nah. We all went in this back office, me and the old guy and the girl. Sonny stayed with the car."

Riley waited for him to continue. When he didn't, she said, "And?"

"We had a nice talk."

Riley blinked. "About what?"

"Things."

Linder and Sonny both looked confused at Kevin's sudden reticence. "Are you all right, Kevin?"

"Just fine, Mr. L."

"Answer the detective's question. What happened in the office?"

"We had a nice talk."

"We covered that," Riley said. "What did you talk about?"

"Things."

Priest held up a hand to stop Riley's next question. "Kevin, what color was the carpet in the room?" He turned to look at her, frowning as if he didn't understand the question. "Did you sit or stand? Were the overhead lights on? Just a lamp? Could you hear the sounds of the party going on outside?"

"We had a nice talk."

Riley said, "What is he, hypnotized?"

Priest pressed her lips together and looked at Riley. "Duchess Gillian."

Riley's eyes widened and looked at Kevin. The eyewitness said a young man driving a black sedan had dumped Heather's body in the vacant lot. Riley had excluded Crocell because of his age. But if demons could jump into someone's body...

"Mr. Linder, how long was Kevin inside the house?"

"About forty-five minutes," Linder said, still looking at his flunky.

Priest said, "What happened when he came back?"

Linder thought about it. "He had cash. He said that Heather saw the error of her ways and gave him some money. We were supposed to pick up the rest today. It's the whole reason we're here. He was out of breath, though. Sweaty. I thought he'd just roughed her up."

Riley could picture it in perfect, horrible clarity. Crocell, Kevin and Heather all in a private room together. Crocell, for one reason or another, possessed Kevin. Whether he had done so before or after he killed Heather, they would probably never know. He had changed clothes, carried Heather to one of the sedans, and left the complex without Linder or Sonny noticing. Dumped the body, swapped outfits and bodies, and went on with his evening. The money was probably a sick joke on the demon's part.

Riley holstered her weapon and nodded toward the elevator. "Take the next one down. You're done with this apartment. Calvin Coley's already lost enough."

"As you wish, Detective Parra," Linder said.

Riley pulled down the grate of the elevator and stepped back, jabbing the ground floor button with two fingers. "It was Crocell," Priest said. "He possessed that kid up there. Probably used his body to kill. He's going to have nightmares. Phantasms. Just because he wasn't in control of his body doesn't mean his soul will forget."

Riley, not for the first time, thought of what horrors Gillian had been subject to. What nightmares had driven her to retreat across the country? She said, "Is there any hope for him?"

"Not by himself. He'll need help. Long-term."

"Yeah," Riley said. She scratched her forehead and said, "Damn. I should have realized. Crocell was right there in my face the whole time."

"He was a demon. You expected animosity from him."

"Right," Riley muttered. "Doesn't make me feel any better about missing him." She realized Priest was choosing her words carefully. "What?"

"Perhaps you weren't in your right mind. Gorgeous and golden skin? Riley, you were speaking about Andras like a lover."

Riley shook her head. "No."

"Did she get to you?"

Riley pressed her lips together. "Yes. A little. But I got past it." She looked at Priest. "Trust me?"

"I do."

"Andras doesn't have a hold on me."

The elevator reached the ground floor and Priest said, "You don't have to keep assuring me you're on the right side, Riley. If there's anything in this mortal world I trust, it's that you are a good person. I believe that with all my heart."

Riley shrugged as she stepped off the elevator. "Glad one of us has that much faith in me. C'mon. Let's go try to arrest a demon."

Chapter Eight

Riley called in back-up on the way to Andras' compound. When she hung up, Priest said, "Do you think that's wise? Involving people who have no idea what they're walking into?"

"Maybe Andras and Crocell will be on their best behavior because of their presence," Riley said. She waited a moment and then said, "Yeah, I don't buy that, either. But we can't walk in by ourselves."

Priest raised her eyebrows. "You're growing."

Riley smirked.

She parked at the mouth of the cul-de-sac and looked toward the building. "You know, there's a chance Andras doesn't know anything about the murder. Maybe she'll sacrifice Crocell and this whole thing will end peacefully." She looked at Priest, who was smiling at her like a parent humoring a child. "It could happen."

"Yes, I suppose it could."

Riley settled back in her seat. "So this is playing by the rules. It's dull."

"Keeps you alive."

"But is this really a life worth living?"

Priest shrugged. "It gets you home to Gillian."

Riley smiled. "Okay. By the rules it is."

"I'm very happy she's coming home, Riley. I've been praying for it."

"God reunites lesbian lovers? What would Pat Robertson think?"

Priest shook her head. "He's not one of ours."

Riley snorted. She watched the front door of the house open, and Crocell stepped out onto the porch. He stood with his arms across over his chest, staring at Riley's car. "I think we've been made."

"Sorry. That's my fault. They probably felt me coming from two miles away."

"Should we have stopped by a church first? Recharged the batteries, topped off the tank?"

Priest chuckled. "No, I'll be fine."

They could hear sirens rising in the distance. Riley checked her watch and said, "Looks like they're making good time. What do you say we get a little head start?"

"You call that playing by the rules?"

Riley shrugged. "Nothing wrong with bending the rules a little bit." She opened the car door and climbed out, forcing Priest to climb out as well to follow her. Riley had her badge on her hip, the Kevlar hanging from her shoulders, gun in a hip holster where she could easily grab it. With their sunglasses, she knew she probably looked like something out of a John Woo movie. If only there were a couple of doves to fly slow-motion across her path, it would be perfect. When Priest got up next to her, Riley said, "On the way home, I'll rent you a copy of The Good, the Bad and the Ugly."

"Angels are good, demons are the bad and that would make humans..."

"Watch it, wing girl."

Priest smirked.

"I liked you better when you were ignorant."

They got to the center of the cul-de-sac before Crocell left his post. He stood on the sidewalk and said, "The angel is not welcome here."

"I am here under the protection of this badge, Crocell. I am a police officer in this city, and you will afford me the respect of one regardless of my nature. Is that understood?"

Crocell glared at her.

Riley leaned toward Gillian. "Does it have a first name?"

"State your name for the record, demon."

Crocell said, "Go to hell, Zerachiel. I would be happy to give you a guided tour once you get there."

Riley pulled her handcuffs off her belt. "Fine. The hard way. Crocell, you are under arrest for the murder of Heather Cassidy. You—"

The street behind them exploded.

Riley and Priest both ducked, scattering to avoid the raining bits of cobblestone that rained down on their backs. Riley looked up in time to see Crocell running toward the house. "Priest, you okay?"

"Fine," Priest said. She was watching the smoke settle.

Riley got to her feet and raced toward the house. The door was already closed when she reached it, so she ran onto the grass and aimed herself for a window. She stopped her advance long enough to slam the butt of her gun against the glass, hitting it in all four corners of the pane until it cracked.

The concussion of the bomb blast had weakened it, so the shards fell apart easily. Riley reached inside and unlatched the window, and she was inside a moment later.

Crocell was nowhere to be seen, but the house felt much different. Darker, deeper. Riley felt a moment of vertigo when she tried to focus on the far wall. She closed her eyes, centered herself, and counted to ten. When she opened her eyes, the effect was diminished but still there. It was like she was drunk and standing on the edge of a tall staircase; gravity seemed to be tugging her in every direction at once. She scanned the ground floor and, determining Crocell was most likely heading for higher ground, took the stairs two at a time.

When Riley got to the landing, she spotted Crocell hunched next to a window that looked down on the front walk. Riley aimed at the middle of his back and picked up where she left off. "Have the right to remain silent." The sirens sounded like they were right outside the front door, echoing off every surface of the house. "Anything you say can and will be used against you in a court of law. You have the right to have an attorney present during questioning. If you cannot afford an attorney, one will be appointed for you." She was standing right behind him then, gun aimed at the back of his head. "Do you understand each of these rights I have explained to you, you son of a bitch?"

"He won't be able to answer you."

Riley kept her gun where it was, but looked over her shoulder. Andras was standing between Riley and the stairs. She wore a strapless red sheath dress, her shoulders bare. The material clung to every curve, and for a moment Riley thought she was completely naked. Her hair was down, but seemed caught on a breeze that Riley couldn't feel. Riley took her attention from Crocell, realizing the body was nothing more than a shell now.

"The police are so sexist. Assuming that it must have been Crocell who possessed the young thug's body."

Riley raised her gun. "Why?"

"To get you here," Andras said as she walked forward. "To make you my offer. The body was dumped in your jurisdiction, during your shift. I didn't lie about my motives, however. I do have the answers you're looking for. If you want them." She reached up and wrapped her fingers around the barrel of Riley's gun. "Do you want to let this go for me?"

Riley's fingers went limp and Andras took the gun from her. She smiled and held the gun by her side. "Such a good girl. Why don't you take off your shirt for me?"

Riley frowned.

"I just want to see that lovely tattoo of yours."

Riley tugged the Velcro holding her vest up. It was just so damn heavy. She let it fall to the ground with a heavy thump. Like a dead body, she thought. She felt something plucking at the top button of her shirt. She looked down and saw it was her own fingers. She undid one, then moved to the next. Andras chuckled and said, "Do you realize when you were chosen, Riley? What exact moment you became this city's sovereign protector?"

"The... tattoo?"

"No. That just lit you like a beacon. The angels were giving you protection, you owed them service." Andras put her hands on Riley's chest and spread them out, pushing the blouse off her shoulders and letting it fall to the floor. Riley hadn't even realized she had finished undoing the buttons.

"Then the roof. Samael fell."

Andras shook her head. "Not then, either. *You were chosen the night you died.*"

Riley frowned.

Andras whispered, "Turn around. Let me see that beautiful artwork." Riley hesitated. "Riley, please. Don't you want me to remove it for you? Don't you want to be free?" Andras stepped forward, her body pressed tight against Riley's. When she spoke, her lips brushed against Riley's and made her shiver. "Ask me. Please, Riley. I want to do it for you. Perhaps afterward we can find other ways to spend your time." She licked Riley's bottom lip.

Riley brushed her hand down Andras' arm.

"Mm," Andras said, shivering. "I like it when you touch me."

Riley took Andras' hand in her own, her fingers twisting around the gun that Andras still held. They both looked down, and Andras said, "Oh. Let me get rid of that for you."

Riley took the gun from Andras and, her voice slurred, said, "No." She brought the gun up and fired twice. Andras howled in pain as she was pushed back by the shots. Riley put her free hand to her forehead as Andras' shrieks echoed through her skull. It was as if every nerve ending in her brain was set on fire. The world around her tilted and spun, the walls seeming to expand and contract like she was inside of a giant lung.

"Everything I've done for you, everything I've offered you!" Andras howled, her voice ugly and wretched. Blood poured down her dress.

"This tattoo is protection," Riley said. "That's what Christine Lee said to me the night she put it on my back. What would you have done once I was unprotected?"

Andras stared at her for a long moment, and then smiled. "I would have torn your mind asunder as my brethren rode your soul to Hell."

The entire front wall of the house imploded and the concussion threw Riley and Andras over the railing like confetti caught on a gust of wind. Riley landed on the couch, while Andras had a rougher landing on the floor. Riley rolled to the floor, hitting her hands and knees and trying to figure out which way was up. She heard Priest's voice outside, a wordless shout of anger, and prayed she was okay. Riley started to get to her feet, but she had only moved her right foot when Andras was on top of her again, arms wrapped around Riley in a fierce embrace. They twisted and Andras threw Riley to the floor and pinned her there.

Andras' face was hideous in her fury, eyes ablaze and teeth bared. The beautiful woman whose body the demon inhabited was nowhere in evidence. When she spoke, she spit a mixture of saliva and blood. "No holy water, no blessed bullets," Andras said. "You're not prepared this time, Riley Parra. This will be your final stand."

Riley closed her eyes and pictured Gillian. She pressed the gun against Andras' chest and pulled the trigger. Andras growled, "You will fail, Riley. I told you this would end in death. You will not be so fortunate. When you die, you will be dropped into Hell and the torment will last for eons. You cannot imagine the anguish." Riley fired twice more and Andras reared back to swat the gun away.

Riley took advantage of the demon's awkward position and bucked her off. Andras tumbled, and Riley threw herself at the coffee table. She had one hope... and there it was. She grabbed the nail Andras used for her earlier 'visual aid,' and just barely had time to grab the hammer before Andras swiped at her back. Riley howled as fingernails sharper than they should have been rent through the skin like a razor blade through wrapping paper.

Andras then pressed against Riley from behind. "This could have gone so much easier," Andras said, her voice again a low, seductive purr. "You could have been destroyed writhing in ecstasy. Instead you will know, oh, so much pain before I finally release you."

Riley twisted at the waist and pressed the tip of the nail against Andras' temple. Andras had time to gasp before Riley swung the hammer.

Andras fell back, her arms and legs limp, and hit the floor with a lifeless 'thud.' Riley said, "Cold iron... bitch. You should pick your visual aids better."

Riley felt blood dripping down her back as she got to her feet. The floor continued to shift under her feet, but she made it to the gaping maw that had once been the front of the house. Priest was on the front lawn, wings fully displayed, facing toward the street. Riley thought of everything she had ever described as a war zone - bad No Man's Land streets, a junkie's apartment, her own apartment - and realized how utterly wrong she had been. Dead bodies, presumably hosts to demons, littered the destroyed street. Smoke and flame still rose from the pit that blocked the mouth of the cul-de-sac.

Riley coughed and put her hand on Priest's shoulder to steady herself. "Priest. Got this covered?"

"Holding my own," Priest said. She lowered her wings and moved to Riley's side. "Are you... where is Andras?"

"She had a headache. We postponed the fight until she was feeling better." She put her arm around Priest's shoulder and winced as the move pulled at the torn skin on her back. The wind changed and a smell of sulfur washed over her. "How are we going to explain this one?"

"Booby traps in the Silver homestead. We came to arrest Crocell, and he set them off. Wanted to go out in a blaze of glory. You and I got caught in the blast, but we were far enough away that we weren't too badly injured."

"Speak for yourself," Riley scoffed. She frowned and said, "There's a problem with your story."

"No," Priest said. "There's isn't."

Riley was about to argue when the house exploded behind them. They were thrown off their feet, and Riley braced for the inevitable concussion of the blast to hit them. Suddenly, she was gently lowered to the ground face first, cool wind blowing across her exposed back. Priest dropped to the grass next to her, arms draped over bent knees, head bowed as she caught her breath. Riley looked back at the street and saw how far away from the house they were. "You flew me."

"Desperate times."

"You're going to have to do that again sometime I can appreciate it."

Priest sighed. "You're never satisfied."

Riley laughed.

Priest looked at her and said, "Riley, there is blood on your face, but no wounds. Did Andras bleed on you? Did any of it get into your mouth or eyes?"

"I don't know."

Priest looked out at the street. Riley heard the scream of sirens.

"Why?"

Priest shook her head. "It's probably nothing."

Riley grunted and said, "Oh, yeah. That's always a good thing to hear." She wanted to argue more, but it took every ounce of strength she had not to pass out. She finally decided that she might need that strength later and sagged against the grass. It was so nice and cool, she might as well take advantage of it. Priest would wake her when the cavalry arrived.

Epilogue

Riley took the tray from the counter, thanked the clerk, and carried it back to the table where Priest was waiting. They hadn't gotten released from the scene until almost eleven, forced to explain the situation to the SWAT team, the firefighters, Lieutenant Briggs, and then the reporters who were clamoring over each other for their exclusive. The latter was punishment, Riley thought, for going in before their back-up arrived. Riley dutifully explained what happened to the sea of microphones, squinting at their impossibly bright spotlights, and silenced further inquiries with a terse 'no comment.'

She lowered herself into the wooden seat, amazed she could even stand up. "So while I was out, my back seemed to get healed a little."

"I didn't have anything else to do," Priest said. She took her meal off the tray and placed it in front of herself.

"Thanks. I know you're reluctant to do the healing thing."

Priest shrugged. "I was busy wiping out Andras' second string. I couldn't even take a moment to think about helping you until it was too late. Healing your wounds was the least I could do to make up for leaving you alone."

"What blew up the front of the house?"

"I was swarmed by the damn reinforcements. I gave them a light show."

"Wish I could have seen that."

Priest said, "You would have been permanently blinded."

"Oh." She shrugged. "That's fine. Burn my eyes and I'll just have my superhero partner heal them."

"It's not a get out of jail free card, you know."

Riley whistled. "Look at you, with the pop culture references."

Priest winked and poured ketchup onto her plate.

Riley opened her sandwich and dismantled it, putting the pickles, lettuce and tomato aside. She closed the sandwich, then ate one of the pickles by itself. She chewed slowly and then said, "I was tempted. What Andras offered me, the freedom, the answers. I wanted to say yes. It took everything in my power to say no."

"I understand. You've grown."

"Don't give me that bullshit. A demon is a demon. And I'm sure that Andras told everyone she could find about her little plan. She may even have told them how close it came to working. There are going to be others who come after me with the same promise. Answers, explanations. One of these days... I'm going to cave."

Priest was staring at her sandwich.

"Of course, it won't be much of a temptation if you answered some of my damn questions."

Priest exhaled and placed her hands on the table. "Riley. I want to tell you. Honestly, I do. But there are..." She licked her bottom lip and then looked away. "There are angels who have seen the face of God. They never speak again. They never blink again. One glimpse of His visage is enough to stun them for eternity. There are some things that are just not necessary to know. There is knowledge that can be fatal. When it is time, your questions will be answered."

Riley stared at her sandwich and leaned back in her chair. "Yeah."

"That is a solemn vow, Riley."

Riley nodded. "I understand, Priest. I do. Just... go back to your sandwich. I still need to take you by the video store before I head home."

Priest winced at the lack of emotion in Riley's voice. "I'm sorr—"

"I get it."

Priest leaned forward and picked up her sandwich. They finished eating their meal in a not-quite comfortable silence.

Priest begged off of the trip to the video store when they finished eating. It was late, and she could tell Riley's heart wasn't in it. They left the diner and Priest stood on the sidewalk to button her jacket. The night was surprisingly cold, and there was a smell of rain in the air. "Need a ride home?" Riley asked.

"No. I'll walk. Thank you."

Riley nodded.

Priest said, "Are you going to speak to Gillian tonight?"

"Yeah."

"Give her my love."

Riley nodded. "Got plans?"

"I'm going to find Linder's man, Kevin. He needs help understanding what happened to him, and what he did while under Andras' influence."

Riley said, "Good luck. Let me know how it goes." She started to walk away and then stopped. "We'll be okay tomorrow, Caitlin. But... I just need to be pissed off at you for a while, okay?"

"I understand."

Riley looked at Priest in the glow of the streetlight for a moment and then nodded. "Okay. See you tomorrow."

"Sleep well, Riley. Pleasant dreams."

Riley lifted her hand in a lazy wave as she crossed the street to her car. Priest watched her unlock the door and then slide inside, her body still stiff from the fight with Andras. Priest hadn't healed every ache and pain, but she couldn't sit idly by. She had no independent confirmation, but she was fairly sure the lowest cut on Riley's back would have proven fatal.

Priest was aware of someone beside her. She didn't have to look; she knew his presence anywhere. "Michael. Good to see you again."

Michael wore, as always, the "armor of God." It changed with the times, and now resembled a desert camo uniform. He looked like a soldier just air-dropped from Afghanistan, his hands clasped behind him as he settled into a parade rest. "Quite the battle. I heard Detective Parra took down the demon on her own."

"Just like Alistair Call," Priest reminded him.

"Mm."

Priest had been dreading the next question, but she still cringed when he asked it.

"Did she ingest the demon's blood?"

"There's no way to know."

Michael was silent for a long time as Riley finally pulled away from the curb and drove away. "She won't be silenced. She wants the answers to her questions."

Priest whispered, "Yes."

"And damn the consequences."

"She is not..."

"She is strong enough. She has felled two demons and an angel, Zerachiel. She is strong enough. And if there is the slightest chance she ingested the demon blood..." He sighed. "This is the time. She must undergo the trial."

Priest closed her eyes and a tear broke free. She pressed her lips together and said, "And if she dies? If the damned trial kills her?"

Michael stepped in front of Priest and said, "Being down here has changed you, Zerachiel. You know what happens if the trial kills her. It means she wasn't worthy for the position in the first place. As it has been for millennia, as it will be now. Riley Parra will face the trial, and she will either be successful, or we will find someone to replace her." He started to walk away and spoke over his shoulder. "The trial should begin sooner rather than later, Zerachiel. We will let you choose the time and the place."

Priest watched him go, and then looked in the direction Riley had driven. She was sobbing openly now, dreading what lay ahead for Riley. Riley was Zerachiel's charge, Zerachiel's responsibility. But she was Caitlin Priest's friend.

Priest started walking, but she wasn't going to find Linder and his men. She was going to spend as much time as possible in as many churches as she could find. Riley would need all the help she could get.

The Life of Riley

Chapter One

Caitlin Priest went to the roof well before dawn, already dressed for the day. She needed very little sleep, but she found she enjoyed the ritual; bathing, brushing her teeth, undressing and crawling under the blankets with all the lights off. The joy of waking was enough to make up for the inconvenience of being asleep. But she didn't give in that night. She wanted to be sure she was awake when the time came.

She wore a white collarless blouse and a pair of black suspenders. Her slacks appeared tailored, even though they were off the rack, and her shoes shone as if they had just received a layer of fresh polish. When she stepped onto the roof, her short blonde hair was pushed away from her forehead. It was still dark, the ambient glow of the city bleeding into the night sky.

Her shoes made quiet shushing sounds as she crossed the roof. She could hear sirens in the distance, and heavy engines of garbage trucks beginning their rounds. It wouldn't be long. She rested her hands on the edge of the roof and looked down at the street. Her shoulders ached. Her ears were still ringing from the explosion at Andras' compound. Such a strange thing, human frailty. She wasn't quite used to it yet.

She didn't know the exact moment of sunrise, but she felt it. She looked east and watched the sky gradually brighten, like the beam of a flashlight moving ever closer. After a few seconds of incremental improvement, suddenly the sky was awash in brilliant colors. Brighter, brighter still. Windows began to shine like molten lava, buildings tossed their lanky shadows across the street. Finally, the sun peeked around the edge of a building and Priest felt its warmth on her face.

Priest squinted into the light and straightened her back, facing the dawn with her head held high. The moment of the day's beginning, its birth. She wondered how many people were watching the same sunrise. People who were on their way home from bad dates or overnight shifts at wherever they worked, people who woke up early to catch the train, mothers preparing their family's day...

Riley was out there, somewhere. Hopefully sleeping. Hopefully blissfully unaware of what the coming day would bring.

Priest heard footsteps on the roof behind her.

"Are you ready?"

Priest looked over her shoulder. Michael was already in his armor; she doubted he ever took it off.

"Yes," Priest said. She pushed away from the edge of the building and her wings unfurled behind her. The feathers caught the breeze, wafting gently before they curved with the movement of the wind. She lifted one foot and rested it against the brick for a moment before she shoved away. Michael followed her, his shorter wings moving faster to keep up with her. Priest led Michael into the rising sun, both of them glowing brighter as the beams wrapped around them. Priest closed her eyes and felt the city fade away beneath her as the day began.

Riley barely slept that night. She took a long shower to soothe the aches she received from the fight with Andras, and then prepared for bed. Instead of sleeping she stripped the blankets and sheets and put them aside for laundry. She found fresh linens in the closet and dressed the bed with them, making sure everything was perfect. The new blanket was royal blue, the pillowcases white. It looked like something out of a magazine, and it made the floor and nightstands look more cluttered than they actually were, so she tidied them up.

By the time she gathered all the dirty laundry and put it in a hamper by the door, it was almost three in the morning. She decided that the bedroom was fine, but the living room was the first thing Gillian would see when she got back. She grabbed a trash bag from the kitchen and began picking up the empty take-out containers, shocked at her own ability to be a slob. She nearly vacuumed, but decided not to risk the anger of her neighbors.

Finally, at five in the morning, Riley stretched out on the couch to avoid wrinkling the bed she took so long to make. She dozed, tossing and turning to find a position that didn't hurt, and finally fell asleep twenty minutes before her alarm went off.

She showered again, dressed for work, and called Gillian as she searched the fridge for breakfast. She let the phone ring ten times before she hung up. She figured Gillian was out for a run, eating breakfast, or maybe still asleep. She slipped the phone into her pocket and left the apartment. The newsstand at her corner was still closed, so she got bagels and coffee from a local deli before she drove to Priest's apartment.

The storefront church Priest lived over was in the middle of a service, and Riley heard the hymns even through the foyer and the front windows. The stairwell reverberated with the sounds, and Riley prepared herself to find Priest sprawled on the floor naked again. She knocked and went into the room. "Priest. I told you to lock this door." She looked down the hall, catching the living room in her peripheral vision. A TV with a DVD player built in sat on a milk crate, the sole piece of furniture in the apartment. Riley didn't see Priest on the floor, so she went down the hall to the bedroom.

"Priest, you down here? Did you oversleep? Can you oversleep?" She knocked on the bedroom door before she peeked inside.

To her surprise, Priest had a bed. Actual box springs, headboard, sheets and blankets, the works. It was odd to see in such a spartan place, but she was glad to see Priest had someplace comfortable to go at the end of the day. But she wasn't in bed, or in the bathroom. Riley stood in the hall for a long minute and finally decided Priest had just gone into work early. They hadn't parted on the best of terms following the Andras thing, so maybe she was just trying to avoid awkward moments.

Riley left the apartment, making sure to lock the door behind her, and went downstairs to the church. She drove to the station thinking about her argument with Priest the night before. All she wanted was a clear, honest conversation about her role in this apparently eternal battle. Was she supposed to fight until she died and then... what? She'd never believed in an afterlife, Heaven or Hell or Purgatory. So what was her reward for giving her life to this fight?

It wasn't Priest's fault that she wasn't "allowed" to know the answers. She would apologize, and they would be fine. She would just learn to live with the fact that she was going to have to fight for the answers she wanted.

Riley parked in the underground garage and rode the elevator up to the bullpen. She was surprised to see that the lieutenant's office lacked the cross of yellow crime scene tape that had covered the door for months. She remembered the firestorm within, the demon she and Priest had destroyed by dousing him with holy water from the sprinklers. She was grateful the crime scene techs and the department brass apparently bought their ridiculous cover story. It was easier than accepting the truth of the situation.

Priest's desk was empty, and Riley eyed it as she walked past.

She knocked on the brand new door, the fresh black lettering on the glass declaring it to be Lieutenant Zoe Briggs' office. She heard a muffled acknowledgement and stepped inside. Briggs was still in the process of moving in, but there was enough memorabilia on the walls to reveal Briggs was a baseball fan. She was currently trying to center a framed print of Yankee Stadium on the wall behind her desk when Riley came in. "Detective Parra. Does that look straight to you?"

"Um... raise it up a little on the left. Up. There."

Briggs stepped back with a satisfied sigh. "Thank you, Detective. Everything else can wait, but I wanted to get this up as soon as possible. It doesn't feel like home without it." She smiled at Riley as she took a seat. "What can I do for you?"

"Have you seen Detective Priest?"

Briggs furrowed her brow and shuffled some papers on her desk. "Detective Priest was transferred, wasn't she?"

A series of emotions ran through Riley. Fear, surprise, shock, apprehension, worry. "Transferred, ma'am?"

"To Burglary. They've been a few men short, so Detective Priest offered to fill in for a week or two."

"Why wasn't I told about this?"

"I assumed she spoke with you about it."

Riley shook her head. "When did all this happen?"

"Last week."

Well before the incident at Andrea Silver's house. Before Heather Cassidy was murdered, even. This couldn't have anything to do with their argument about the answers Riley wanted. Of course, angels didn't necessarily work linearly. Maybe she knew the argument was coming and set up an escape plan. It's the only explanation for why she hadn't mentioned the temporary reassignment.

"Thanks, Lieutenant," Riley muttered as she left the office. She walked to her desk and sat down, staring at the window across the room. She drummed her fingers on the edge of the desk for a moment before she finally decided to call Priest's cell phone. It rang twice before the call went directly to voicemail.

"This is Caitlin Priest. I'm not with my phone right now. Please leave your name and number and I'll try to call you back as soon as I can. It may be a while, Riley."

Riley frowned as the tone sounded in her ear. "Priest, what the hell is going on? Where are you?" She stared at Priest's empty desk as if she expected an answer. "All right. Call me back." She closed the phone and tapped the corner of it against her chin as she stared at Priest's empty chair. She didn't know what the game was supposed to be, but she wasn't going to take it lying down.

She stood up and grabbed her coat as Lieutenant Briggs came out of her office. "Detective Parra. Mind taking a case on your own?"

Riley considered saying no, but she decided it would be better to occupy her mind with a case. "Sure."

"It's in No Man's Land."

"That's not a problem," Riley said, holding her hand out for the memo slip.

Briggs handed it over and glanced at Priest's desk. "She's coming back, you know. The two of you make quite a team. I wouldn't let her waste her talents in Burglary forever."

"Good to know," Riley said. She shrugged into her jacket and checked the address of the murder. It seemed vaguely familiar to her, but she'd spent most of her formative years running through those streets. She folded the paper in half and put it in her pocket. "ME and uniforms on the scene?"

"Uniforms, yes. Dr. Herron is still working on a body, so he'll be there as soon as he can."

Riley nodded. "Will do, boss."

On the way downstairs, Riley stopped on the third floor. Burglary occupied a space identical to Homicide's, but the room seemed infinitely smaller. Rows of file cabinets, cluttered desks, overflowing garbage cans, and the stink of a coffee machine pushed into service past its prime gave the place the feel of a squatter's paradise. Riley didn't even try to find Priest in the labyrinth of desks; she went directly to the lieutenant's office and knocked on the glass. "Excuse me, lieutenant. Detective Riley Parra, Homicide."

The man looked warily at her. He was muscular, with a military haircut and broad shoulders. His tie hung loose, as if he'd been tugging at it every five minutes. He gave her a full three seconds of his attention before he turned back to his paperwork. "Hope you're not here on business. We're swamped as it is."

"Not..." Riley cleared her throat. "I'm looking for my partner, Caitlin Priest. I heard she was loaned to you guys. I just need to speak with her about an on-going case."

"Sorry, no can do. Priest and her new partner, Doyle, already left for the day." He tapped a stack of manila envelopes on the desk next to him. "We've got eighteen cases going cold as we speak. That's not to mention the ones currently being investigated. Your friend Priest is somewhere out there going from one scene to the next. We're doing our best to give people the impression we're doing our best. You know?"

Riley nodded. "So no clue where Priest is? No way to contact her?"

"You could try her cell, but I'm sure you already tried that. She and Doyle took about twelve case files when they left, so they could be at any one of those locations, or in transit between them. I could try and find the list, if you like."

Riley stopped him before he could start digging in his pile again. Hadn't these people heard of computers? "No, that's fine."

"You sure you're busy enough up there in Homicide? We could always use another body down here."

"Sorry. Always people willing to kill someone else."

The lieutenant sighed and looked at his stack. "Yeah, same with stealing. Thanks anyway, Detective Parra. Wish I could have been a bigger help."

"You did you best, Lieutenant Archer."

He smiled and waved as she left the room. "You can call me Michael."

Riley drove through No Man's Land, thinking about Priest. At a stoplight, she drummed her fingers on the steering wheel. The radio was playing, but she was only vaguely aware of the music as she waited for the traffic to let her pass. She saw her reflection in the side mirror and scoffed at it. She shook her head. "I did just fine for years before Caitlin Zerachiel Priest showed up. I don't need her watching my back. If she wants to take a breather for a week, then more power to her." She chewed the inside of her cheek and said, "Of course, if she was here, I wouldn't be talking to myself like a moron."

She sighed and jabbed the radio to change the stations. All By Myself was playing on a station that usually played country. She wondered if the singer had died, and then wondered who the singer was. She changed stations and found Alone Again, Naturally.

"Thought this crap only happened in movies..." she muttered.

The next station, country, was playing Patsy Cline singing Have You Ever Been Lonely? Riley glared at the radio as the light turned green. She accelerated just as the radio signal died in a burst of static. Patsy Cline's voice faded out, replaced by a screeching male voice. Riley reached down and twisted the knob for the radio, turning it off. Still, the voice continued.

"You're all alone, Riley Parra. No angels on your shoulders this time. Hope you're ready for the end."

Riley felt a chill as the car fell silent. The radio looked normal when she glanced down at it, but the voice still echoed in her head. She fished her cell phone out of her pocket and tried calling Priest again. She got the voicemail message again, but she cut the call off before she could hear Priest's lame apology again. On a whim, she dialed Gillian's number. Her heart pounded as she listened to the unending tones of an unanswered phone.

"Come on, Jill..."

The call finally cut off, and the soothing voice of the operator came through. Riley tossed the phone into the empty passenger seat as she crossed over the imaginary border of No Man's Land. She was all by herself. Alone again. Naturally.

Chapter Two

The address Briggs gave her belonged to an ancient tenement. Riley parked behind a patrol car, one of the last remaining older models in the city apparently. She stopped and ran her hand over the top of the cruiser. It was just like the kind she had once patrolled in. She didn't mind the new, sleeker cars the department got a couple years back, but they definitely lacked the character of the old sedans. She dropped her hand and glanced up and down the street.

The car wasn't the only thing tickling her memory. There was something uncomfortably familiar about the entire area, like seeing somebody after a few years and knowing she should know their name. She tried to ignore the added decay, replacing broken windows and trying to mentally fill the empty lots with various buildings in an attempt to jog her memory.

When she saw the faded ads in the liquor store window, recognition shook her hard enough that she had to grab the car door to steady herself. The liquor store had once been one half of a convenience store, Gilbert's, if she remembered correctly. She could see the tall racks of candy and chips, the magazines carefully alphabetized by the front door. There was a seating area across from the cash register where old men sat to read newspapers and play chess.

Riley could see a sixteen year old delinquent sidling down one of the aisles and placing a bottle of Jack Daniel's under her jacket. Her hair was covered by a hoodie, and she wore big sunglasses that she hoped covered enough of her face that the clerk wouldn't recognize her. She played it cool as she made her way toward the door, but calm turned to panic when she spotted the white and blue cop car parked outside. There was nothing for the punk thief to do but try to run. It wasn't like the cops gave enough of a shit to chase a thief.

Riley could almost hear the thief's pounding footsteps on the pavement as the ghosts moved in front of her. A little slip of nothing, dressed head to toe in a dark blue uniform, pursued the kid. It wasn't a long chase, and the kid was thrown facedown onto the ground in front of the cop's car. Her sunglasses broke, and her dark hair spilled out from under her hoodie as the cop handcuffed her. The girl shouted and cursed, called the cop every name in the book and tried to kick her as she was hauled to the back of the car.

The ghosts faded and the liquor store came back into full relief. She licked her suddenly dry lips. She could still feel the handcuffs snap closed around her wrist. Her first arrest, her first trip down to the police station. Even then, she knew the sound of that ratcheting metal signaled the end of life as she knew it. And, as it turned out, she was right. Just not in the way she expected.

If anyone else had grabbed her, delinquent Riley Parra probably would have been processed and tossed back out onto the streets until her next arrest. The vicious cycle would have started right there. But Officer Christine Lee wasn't willing to give up on her. Lee saw Riley's first arrest as a wake-up call. She went through the ballet of processing but, when it was over, unlocked the cuffs and asked if Riley wanted a ride home. "I don't want to do this for real," Lee said as she led Riley down the steps. "You can be anything you want, and this city already has too many fucking has-beens."

And Riley cried. Something inside of her, something she thought was too hard to ever be overcome broke. She poured out all of her pain and regrets. And Christine Lee listened. They sat in her cop car, and Riley wept for everything she'd lost and everything she might lose if she continued down the same path.

Riley bit back the memory, the surge of emotions threatening to push her over the edge. She looked at the decrepit building and wondered if she should go inside and pay for the whiskey she tried to steal. Probably too little too late. Now that she thought about it, the patrol car she'd parked behind was also from the era when Christine busted her.

She cleared her throat, straightened her shirt collar, and looked around to make sure no one had seen her flashback. A man was standing on the corner, looking away from her. Riley almost ignored him until she noticed his trenchcoat was just slightly out of season. Her eyes were drawn to the tail of the coat, hanging near the man's ankles. She just barely saw the tips of two furled wings. She sucked in a breath and looked at the opposite corner. Another angel stood guard there. His hands were clasped behind his back, his eyes locked on her.

"Hope you guys are on my side."

The Life of Riley

Neither of them answered, or even acknowledged she had spoken. She closed the door and secured her badge on her belt as she stepped onto the curb. The front door of the tenement was open, and she walked into the foyer. The building had obviously been abandoned for a while, with trash that had blown in from outside blown into the corner. The tile floor was water damaged, and half the windows on the ground floor were covered by plywood. As Riley started up the stairs, a uniformed officer was coming down. He was holding a handkerchief against his mouth and nose, breathing deeply.

"Take it easy, officer," Riley said as he passed. "It gets easier with time. Is your partner upstairs?"

The officer half-turned and said, "Top floor." His voice was muffled through the hanky, but Riley thought she recognized it from somewhere. Probably one of the newbies who stood guard at her crime scenes. She watched him leave before she ascended the stairs.

The top floor turned out to be the fifth. Doors were missing from the majority of rooms, bare mattresses and paraphernalia on the floor indicating the building was a junkie hangout. The sight depressed Riley. The neighborhood hadn't been terrific when she lived here, but at least it wasn't this hopeless. She heard the static of a police radio from the room at the end of the hall and aimed herself toward that room.

When she reached the doorway, she stopped and took in the scene. Old furniture was crammed against the far wall, leaving a wide open space in the middle of the room. Judging by the scorch mark on the floor, some kind of fire had been started there. Maybe deliberate, to cook a meal, and it got a bit out of hand. A cop was standing at the picture window, looking out at the street below. Maybe taking some kind of sick amusement in his partner's weak stomach.

"Heard you had a body for me."

"Yeah," the guy said. He seemed young, but his voice was already rough from cigarettes. He gestured at one of the couches without turning around. "Real sad. Woman, Hispanic, mid thirties. Looks like someone roughed her up real good before she died."

Riley crossed toward the couch. "Any ID?"

"No, but there's a distinguishing mark."

"Oh, yeah?" Riley looked over the back of the couch and saw it was empty.

"Bitch has a tattoo on her right shoulder."

Riley turned just as the cop swung his baton at her head. She twisted, but it still glanced painfully off her chin. Riley twisted with the blow, turning her back to her attacker. When he stepped forward for another swipe, Riley straightened and let her arm swing with the momentum of her movement. She backhanded the cop across the face, her nail raking across his cheek. She doubted it would draw blood, but it might distract him.

Riley tried to slip past him, but the cop put his hand in the middle of her chest and shoved her back toward the couch. His strength was unbelievable, but she didn't have time to think about it before his fingers closed in the material of her shirt. He dropped his baton, his other hand grabbing the waistband of her jeans. Riley's feet left the ground as the cop lifted her like she was a rag doll, her body arcing through the air until she was parallel with the ground. She went limp, but it didn't help as she was hurled into the floor. Every bone in her body vibrated with the impact, her diaphragm, lungs and heart temporarily shocked into inactivity.

The cop stepped over her, one foot on either side of her torso, and bent down so she could see his face. His eyes were pure black, bruised and sunken as if he hadn't slept in years. When he grinned, she could smell the decay of his teeth and the reek of his breath washing over her like fog settling on water. She coughed, eyes watering, and finally recognized the face under the ruin.

"Samael," she rasped.

He grabbed a handful of hair and hauled Riley to her feet. She kicked at him, her foot glancing off his shin, but Samael hardly noticed. He dipped her, as if they were in the middle of a ballroom dancing demonstration, one hand in the small of her back with the fingers splayed. "This is going to hurt," he warned, his voice still raw and broken. He shoved with all his might, which was considerable, and Riley was hurled across the small room like a major league pitch. She twisted during the point-six seconds she was in the air, trying to protect her internal organs. She didn't know if the bones of the back were stronger than the ribs, but it couldn't hurt.

Riley hit the wall and felt, for a moment, as if she was going to continue through the drywall. The initial impact was jarring, and then there was a sickening moment of release. Whether the wall cratered, or her bones cracked, she wasn't sure. The pain radiated away from her in waves, coming back over her in mind-numbing, throbbing beats. She didn't even have the strength to drop down to her knees; the wall cradled her as Samael approached.

"You're—"

"No talking," Samael growled. He punched her once, in the face, and the pain exploded into darkness.

Chapter Three

The world seemed red behind her eyelids, and Riley was reluctant to open them and face whatever was out there. Her arms were stretched out to either side, her back against the wall. She tried to move her right hand and cried out as a sharp, piercing pain shot down her arm. The shock forced her eyes open, and she looked to see what had caused such an immediate injury.

A string of barbed wire was wrapped loosely around her wrist, holding it to the wall. There were four loops, each with barbs pressed warningly against the tender part of her wrist. She turned her head and saw an identical restraint on her other wrist. She looked down and saw an X of the wire crossing her chest. Several barbs had snagged on her blouse and given the material several small tears. She was on her knees, with her feet flat against the wall. She tested the limits of the bindings and discovered she could move about a quarter inch in any direction before the barbs cut her flesh. "Aha. A quarter inch. I got you right where I want you, Sammy."

She was still in the room where Samael ambushed her, but anything that might help her escape was on the opposite wall. The window was covered by a black tarp, but sunlight was still visible at the edges. As far as she could tell, it was still early morning. She hadn't been unconscious for very long, unless she had lost an entire day. No, she would be able to tell. And the pain wouldn't be so intense after twenty-four hours. Her right side felt tight, and she assumed several ribs were broken.

Riley could hear movement outside and turned to face the door just as Samael entered. He was still wearing his police uniform, but the shirt was unbuttoned to reveal a white undershirt. Blood spotted the cotton, and Riley wondered if the gunshot wounds she inflicted on him so long ago were still bleeding. "Probably should have killed you when I had the chance," she said. "I'll make a note for next time."

Samael went to the pile of old furniture without comment. He lifted two floodlights, the kind used for night crime scenes, and placed them a few feet in front of her. He ran the cords to the wall, plugged them in, and switched them on. Riley squinted and turned her head away, the heat from the lights already noticeable on her face. Samael stepped between the lights, now just a blurry shape against the glow.

"I didn't ask for this assignment. It was a gift."

"Did I miss your birthday? That makes me feel bad."

Samael sighed. "So glib, even now. Detective, you must realize there is no rescue in the offing. No back-up. No magic bullets. No angels on your shoulders." The repeated phrase made Riley realize Samael had been the voice on her radio. "It's just you and me. Do you realize time passes differently in Hell? Or maybe it just seems that way. It's not like there are clocks around. And do you realize what it's like to be an angel there? Imagine being a cop in prison. I was surrounded by creatures who took delight in causing pain. It was their only talent, but they did it well. They took especial pride in causing me anguish. It was a game to them. Each wanted to ensure that every day was worse than the day before. Each wanted to cause me more pain that the demon that came before. I learned new and unique ways that I could hurt. And in Hell, there are no rules. I cannot count the number of times I should have died. The things they did to me... Even angels should not be able to withstand that."

Riley said, "Sorry. There was nothing about that in the brochures. Next time I recommend a vacation for you, I'll be sure to check it out better."

Samael stepped out of the penumbra of the lights and swung his hand toward her face. He didn't slap her, and it took a moment before she felt the sting and the warm blood trickling down her cheek. She saw the blade in his hand only after she realized she'd been cut.

"I can't repay you even a fraction of what you condemned me to endure. But I can make your death long and painful. I can have you begging for Hell. But once you get there... once you see what I have seen..." He laughed. "You can't even beg for death, because it won't come. Wounds don't heal in quite the same way down there. Healing requires life force. Regeneration. You will be tortured to death, without the reward of dying. Over and over again."

Riley felt the blood dripping off her chin. "Can't be worse than listening to you babble."

Samael turned and walked out of the light. When he returned, he placed an old-fashioned boom box between the two lights. He knelt down and said, "You thought yourself capable of going against demons. You thought you were only risking your own life. You walked into the den of Alistair Call with the sin of pride, and so you will pay for that sin by hearing the pain you caused." He pressed Play and the speakers emitted a quiet, humming static. Samael rose. "You will hear the cries of Gillian Hunt as the Duchess raped her mind and violated her body."

"Stop..." Gillian suddenly gasped, her voice sounding loud enough to fill the room.

"No," Riley said. Everything in her seized and she pulled against the restraints. The barbs didn't matter, she just wanted to get to the radio and silence it. "Don't..."

Samael walked away as Gillian began to scream.

Riley closed her eyes tightly, biting down on the inside of her cheeks as she tried to block the sounds of Gillian's torture.

The tape had faded into white noise by the time Samael returned. Blood dripped from Riley's wrists to the floor, the barbed wire tight against her chest from repeated efforts to cross the room and shut off the tape player. She could feel the pinpricks in her chest, the sick trickle of blood running along her stomach. She would have pushed the damn wire straight through her body if it meant shutting off that damn tape.

"Which was the worst part?" Samael asked. "The screams? I didn't know human beings could make that kind of noise. Of course, it's nothing compared to what I heard in Hell. But it was close. Very similar." He knelt down and turned off the tape. "But I know you, Riley. I'm sure the worst part for you was the crying."

"Stop it," Riley said. Her voice was rough from screaming, from shouting as she cried, imagining every horror that had been visited on Gillian. She stared at a spot on the wall, her eyes wide and twitching. The tape may have stopped, but the sounds still filled her ears.

"Such sobbing. Resignation to death. It's heartbreaking. Did she tell you that she gave up?"

"Shut up," Riley said.

"Gillian succumbed to the demon. I cannot imagine anyone recovering from that, no matter how far from you they run—"

Riley lunged forward, howling in pain as the barbs dug into his skin and seemed to twist. Samael watched her with detached interest until she sagged back against the wall.

"Ask me for some water."

"Go to Hell."

"Been there," Samael shouted. "Ask me for some water. I am sure you must be parched. Your throat is dry. No one can hear you, by the way. The sentries you saw before you came into the building have blocked this building off."

"More Fallen?"

"No. They're the good guys. They want this to happen to you."

Riley shook her head. "They would never..."

"It was Zerachiel's idea." Riley looked up at Samael, trying to find a hint of deception in his voice. To her horror, she couldn't hear any. "She set it up. She scheduled it. She left you so that this could happen. If you want to curse someone's name, curse hers. Condemn your beloved Priest for what she has done to you. Perhaps if you send another angel to Hell in your place, you will be set free. Worth a try, isn't it?"

Riley grunted as she relaxed, the twisting barbs pulling out of her flesh.

"May I have some water?"

"Say 'please, Samael.'"

Riley closed her eyes. "Please. Samael. May I have some water?"

Samael bent down and picked something up. He walked forward and Riley parted her lips in anticipation of a drink. A bucket of water was poured over her head, leaving her sputtering. She shook her head, sending droplets flying like a wet dog, and realized belatedly that none of the water had entered her mouth. She licked her lips, trying to get as much as she could into her dry mouth. Samael laughed and returned to his position behind the lights.

"What would you do to make me stop?"

Riley grunted.

"I'm being sincere, Riley. I can be reasoned with. You can be spared this pain, this torture."

"At what cost," Riley muttered. She hung her head and saw the blood staining her shirt. How much blood had she lost? How much more could she risk losing? She shook her head and said, "I'm not selling my soul to you. If I die, fine. Fine. It's about damn time."

Samael said, "It won't be quite that easy, Riley." He walked forward and grabbed a handful of her hair. He forced her to straighten her spine, and wrapped something around her throat and then fastened it to the wall. When he released her hair, Riley sagged forward slightly and felt more barbed wire press into her throat. This loop was tighter than the others; she had no leeway whatsoever. If she relaxed her spine or changed posture, the barbs would cut into her.

Samael stepped back and said, "I'll come by and check on you soon, Riley. I hope you're comfortable."

Riley closed her eyes and listened to his retreating footsteps. It hadn't even been a full minute, and already she was straining to keep in the correct position. How deep could this damn necklace pierce her? Would Samael really risk ending his little game just because she relaxed? Could it be that easy? Just go limp and let the cord cut her open. Let Samael return to find a corpse. It was one way to win. Of course, Samael would also win.

The only way to win, while making Samael lose, was to keep position until he returned. No matter how hard it might be. She braced her feet against the wall and settled in to the position Samael had forced on her. The muscles between her shoulder blades were starting to protest. She didn't know how long she could hold the position, but she would be damned if she gave up before every ounce of strength was gone.

The heat from the lights was starting to get to her. She closed her eyes against them, but still they burned. She was sweating, dehydrated, tired. She licked her dry lips and shifted her weight from one knee to the other. The movement caused the barbed wire around her neck to bite into the thin flesh. She could feel one barb resting on her pulse point. That's how easy it would be to end this torture. Just shake your head and boom, you're out.

She silenced the voice and closed off her mind. She refused to think of how her shoulders burned, how heavy her arms felt, how much blood must have dripped out of her already. She was lightheaded, but not enough to pass out. God, if she did pass out, even for a second, it was over. She tried moving slowly and felt the barbs glide over her raw flesh without tearing. But there was no way to use the slight freedom this gave her to escape. When she relaxed her shoulders, the barbs pressed against her throat without cutting. The wire still pressed against her windpipe, however, and made breathing dangerous.

She could hear Samael outside, moving around in other rooms. She wondered if he was gathering more toys. How long was this little game supposed to last? Until she gave in? Until she succumbed to blood loss and dehydration? There was no way she could know what the finish line was, but she vowed that she wasn't going to give Samael an easy victory.

Chapter Four

The movie played in her head for the third time. She watched Samael, bleeding from bullet wounds in his chest, get engulfed by a pillar of fire. He was gone in an instant, and Riley was left to recuperate on her own. She remembered kneeling on the roof, utterly spent, waiting for the arrival of either death or the strength to get to her feet and leave the building. Either would have been welcomed.

Riley knew this day was coming. She had just been hoping it would take longer to arrive. Her arms were numb, dead weight hanging from the wall. But she didn't dare relax the muscles. Even if she couldn't feel her hands, she still wanted them in one piece. She opened and closed her fingers for the painful pins and needles sensation that told her that her hand was, indeed, still attached to her body.

Samael finally returned and released her noose. Riley was careful not to relax too much; the straps around her chest were still in place. But having the noose gone was such a relief. She dropped her chin and let her tired muscles relax. The muscles twitched and sent a series of spasms through her body, and she realized they were locked in place. Terrific.

Samael dropped the noose to the ground and said, "Ask me for water."

"May I have a drink of water?"

"Milord."

"Oh, fuck you," Riley grunted.

Samael stood with his back to her. "I have been ordered to give you a gift."

"Hope you kept the receipt."

Samael said, "The gift is knowledge. And I was ordered by Zerachiel to bestow it upon you." He stepped forward. "You wish to know why you were chosen. Why you are the human who must undergo these trials and face this torture. You want to know why you above all others are condemned to this fight. It is because you cheated, Riley Parra. You broke the natural order. You asked for this."

"I didn't," Riley said.

Samael leaned down so that his face was directly in front of hers. She tried to meet his gaze, but the eyes were too horrible to focus on. She finally focused on his forehead.

"Remember your sin, Riley Parra."

"Police! Freeze!" The voice, her voice, echoed through the room from unseen speakers. She heard shoes pounding on pavement, kicking through split-open garbage bags. She could see the alley and the back of the man she was pursuing as clearly as if she were watching it on a screen. "Freeze! I will shoot!"

And then a vice grip around her throat, inhumanly strong fingers lifting her off the roof. Holding her in the air and, oh, God, her first look at a demon. Her first encounter with Marchosias. She was still in uniform, looking like a toddler even though the memory was barely five years old now. She remembered her mind racing when Marchosias attacked her, thinking about how she had joined the police academy at the earlier possible time, growing up as a punk and growing mature with a badge on her chest. And now to have it end in such a pathetic way, thrown off the roof by some asshole in a fright mask. He walked to the edge of the building with her. She squeaked out a plea before Marchosias hurled her off the building.

"You were chosen the night you died."

That voice belonged to Andras. Riley remembered now, the fall, the unending fall through the air. It was almost five years since that night, and she remembered everything about it. Except for what happened after the fall. The knowledge came back to her with alarming clarity. She died. What else could happen when someone was thrown off the roof of a building with nothing to break their fall?

She watched from afar, Samael's gift to her. She watched herself hit the pavement. Her body half-skidded and bounced slightly, landing on the sidewalk. Her hips were twisted, one arm draped across her stomach. Her eyes were open, staring sightlessly across the street. There was no blood, surprisingly, but there was no doubt that her death had been instantaneous. Riley looked at her corpse with horror, unable to process the sight.

"What have you done?"

"She was in my way."

Riley only barely recognized the man in the leather trenchcoat. She had only seen him alive once, their other meetings occurring in the morgue. He was Ridwan, the angel whose murder had awakened Riley to what was really going on in the city. The other man haunted her nightmares; Marchosias. They stood in the mouth of the alley, looking down at her body. Ridwan looked irritated, Marchosias looked like a man waiting for a late bus.

"The tattoo..."

"Didn't do much of a job, did it?" Marchosias said. "I suppose technically, I just threw her. The street killed her." He chuckled at his own joke.

Ridwan glared at the demon. "This must be made right."

"Just another cop."

"No," Ridwan said. "She was the former lover of Christine Lee."

Marchosias laughed.

"Silence," Ridwan said. "When Christine died, this city was left unprotected."

"And high times for my boys. It's been a good run."

Ridwan knelt next to Riley's body and tenderly touched her forehead. "Balance, Marchosias. Is that not what you and I agreed to? You can destroy a protector, but only if they are aware of the battle. Riley Parra did not have that benefit."

Marchosias sighed. "Well, it's a little late now."

"No. It's not." He brushed Riley's hair out of her face and covered her eyes with his hand. "Riley, can you hear me?"

His voice made Riley tremble, as if her body was a wire and his voice was a current from far away. She realized he was speaking to her soul, and she suddenly felt utterly small. "Do you wish to wake up?"

Riley remembered the night. She remembered patrolling No Man's Land because no one else would do it. Someone needed to be there. Someone needed to protect them when everyone else wrote them off. And if she died, who would take her place? She knew what her answer to Ridwan was. She knew what it would always be.

"You can't be serious," Marchosias said. "Doing this sacrifices your divinity. It will leave you defenseless. You would make yourself vulnerable for... this?"

"Being vulnerable doesn't necessarily mean that I will be killed, Marchosias. You can't do anything about it, after all." He smiled patronizingly and then looked down at Riley's body again. "This one is worth it. She will make a difference, I'm certain."

Marchosias shook his head and started to walk away. "Your sentimentality will get you killed one of these days, Ridwan. Mark my words."

Ridwan watched the demon leave, then carefully lifted Riley off the ground. She stirred, eyes swimming into focus as he moved her. "What happened?" she asked.

"Rest a while longer," Ridwan said. "You still need to heal. You will wake in a moment."

Riley saw her eyes close as Ridwan carried her to the spot where she remembered waking all those years ago. The vision faded and she was left staring into the bright lights of her torture den, her muscles remembering their various aches and pains as she returned to the present. "Ridwan used something to bring me back to life, and that left him vulnerable to you. Did you know he had done it? Did you realize you were killing him when you swung that sword?"

"Yes," Samael said. "And so did he. He bowed his head and waited for the end to come. He accepted it. For you."

"So what is the tattoo?"

"Protection. Christine Lee was given the tattoo when she chose to become the city's sentinel. It would have protected her from being murdered by a demon, if not for her sacrifice. She feared for you, Riley, and she bestowed part of that protection to you. She inked your shoulder and gave away a portion of what kept her safe. As soon as we realized what had happened, we sent out demons to remove her from the equation. It was embarrassingly easy. A car accident." He laughed and shook his head.

Riley bowed her head, tears burning her eyes.

"How many other good people sacrificed themselves to save you, Riley? How many more will have to die before you simply give up?" He moved forward and she felt his breath on her face. "Will you destroy Zerachiel on this quest? Will Gillian Hunt be the next to fall? Mackenzie Crowe decided to stay in the city because of you. Perhaps we will deliver her corpse to your door as a prize." He grabbed her chin and forward her to look at him. "Give up. Save them by sacrificing yourself like so many sacrificed for you."

"They didn't die so I could give up," Riley said. "Take your lame threats and rotten breath somewhere else."

Samael placed two fingers against the soft flesh above Riley's collarbone and pressed down. Riley grunted and squeezed her eyes shut as her body instinctively moved down and away from the touch. The inadvertent retreat caused her wrists to pull the barbed wire, cutting her wrists at a new angle. He stood up, increasing the pressure as he moved, until Riley was sure one barb was embedded under the flesh. She gasped with relief when he released her. He was backlit by the floodlights and she thought she could see charred wings hanging behind him like ragged curtains.

"Your tattoo will not help you, Riley. There is no rescue coming. There is no escape. The sooner you realize that and accept your fate, the better."

"I just realized," Riley said, her voice filled with wonder. She looked up at Samael. "You called in a false police report. Oh, man, are you in trouble now. That's a misdemeanor charge. You're going to have to pay a fine and everything."

Samael turned and walked from the room.

"Hey, get back here. I need to read you your rights. You have the right to remain silent... and some... other stuff." She dropped her head to her chest and exhaled sharply, watching her chest rise and fall underneath the barbed wire. The floor around her was dotted with blood, some pools larger than others. It stained the wallpaper and the baseboard, with streaks and pools on her jeans and probably on her shoes and socks as well. Laundry was going to be a bitch.

She took a deep breath, testing to see how far she could stretch the harness around her torso. She could breathe in to a certain point before the barbs found flesh, and then a little more until the pain became unbearable and forced her to exhale. She carefully twisted and looked toward the roof. Her vision was blurred and unaccustomed to the darkness thanks to Samael's lighting, but she could see that the barbed wire stretched up along the wall to a socket in the ceiling. She wouldn't have to break the wire or cut through her body to escape, she just had to get that socket broken. How hard could that be?

Riley twisted her wrists until her hands were palm-up. The skin on the edges of her wrist was thinner, but the bone was thicker. She hoped she would be able to apply more strength in that position. She moved her body up and down, watching as the barbs moved her blouse with her motion. After a few forward thrusts, she had a bit of padding between her flesh and the barbed wire. She exhaled, braced her feet against the wall, and lunged forward.

The barbs cut, and she felt the wire tightening around her torso. Something above her creaked, and Riley dug her fingernails into her palms. It hurt, but it was a pain she could control. She could stop that pain at any time, and it distracted from the myriad other pains she was inflicting upon herself. "Come on," she grunted. "Come on... how strong do they make these fucking buildings...?"

There was a crack, a crumbling noise, and Riley fell forward. She threw out her hands to break her fall at the last moment, sure that the barbed wire would embed itself in her chest if she fell on it. Her arms and legs were both asleep, and pieces of the ceiling tile rained down on her back, but she hardly ignored those minor pains. She examined the barbed wire wrapped around her wrists and figured out a way to gingerly remove it. She pricked her fingers and palms more than a few times, but that was no matter.

The X across her chest was harder to remove, but she found a way to get one loop undone and then ducked under the other as she pulled it over her head. It snagged her hair, pulling a few strands free in the process, but she dropped it to the floor with a sense of utter victory. She got to her feet, wobbling on uncertain legs, and moved past the blinding lights to search the room for a weapon.

She had scanned the couch before she realized something was wrong. She turned and frowned at the ceiling, then stared at the piece of it that lay in the spot she had just been imprisoned. The pool of blood was alarming. How could she have bled that much without being lightheaded? But that wasn't the main thing that caught her interest.

Small words were written on the wallpaper behind her back. She approached cautiously until she was close enough to read it.

What do you suppose you were chained to?

It was then that she heard the beeping.

Riley turned and ran for the door, but it was too late.

The building shook with the force of the explosion.

Chapter Five

Her heart was pounding. That was good. That meant it was still beating.

Then she wondered if the pounding was causing more blood to pump out of her body. That would be less good. She opened her eyes and tried to assess her situation. She remembered the concussion of the blast, being picked up off her feet and thrown like debris. The shock when she realized the floor wasn't where she expected it to be, the pain when she finally reached the floor a few seconds later. She passed out after that.

Riley lay completely still for a few moments, waiting to see how stable the building was. Something heavy lay across her legs. Something sharp pressed against her back. But she was out of the bindings, so wherever she was now had to be an improvement. She just hoped Samael had been caught in the explosion. Damn booby trapping bastard. She finally opened her eyes and tried to figure out just how screwed she was.

Her right leg was pinned underneath a slab of concrete. The edge crumbled when she tried to push it away, but it didn't budge an inch. Tall support beams towered over her on all sides, like ribs of a giant whale that had swallowed her. She examined her wrists and saw that the bleeding had slowed to a trickle. She unbuttoned her shirt, pulling down the collar of her tank top to examine her chest. Not terrible, but she would have to put her swimsuit modeling career on hold for a while.

She tore strips from her blouse, the holes made by the barbed wire making it easy, and wrapped them around her wrists. She then daubed at the blood on her face. She hoped the cut Samael made was shallow; she would hate to walk around with a permanent scar on her face. "Off the Titanic and into the freezing North Atlantic," she muttered. Her holster was missing, but her badge was still hooked on her belt. She supposed that counted for something.

"Detective Parra."

Samael's voice echoed off the remnants of the building, bouncing off so many formerly flat surfaces that she wasn't sure where it originated. She became still, trying to listen for tell-tale movement. She heard shifting debris, broken slabs of concrete scraping against the floor as they were moved. If she didn't speak, there was a chance that he wouldn't find her.

"All the blood you've lost. Surely you're becoming a bit lightheaded. Not to mention the thirst. How long has it been since you had something to drink, Riley? How long do you think you can survive without a glass of water? Hell, how long do you think you'll last without a blood transfusion?" She could hear him moving behind her. She lay down on the rubble, moving as quietly as possible. The concrete floor next to her was bowed, two halves folded like leaves of an open book, and she pressed herself into the crevasse. She shifted, twisting her pinned leg painfully, and tried to use the shadow to conceal herself as his voice came nearer.

"There are angels who believe you are a lost cause. They believe they should cut their losses and appoint a new keeper for this city. Either that, or pull out completely. This city is not the war, it's a battle. Some fronts have to be sacrificed for the better of the campaign. But with all the effort put into this city..." He sighed. "They're starting to think it's not worth it. Zerachiel could be monumentally helpful elsewhere. But she is stuck here, babysitting an obstinate mortal with an inflated sense of self-importance."

Samael came over a pile of debris above Riley's hiding place. He scanned the area and moved away to her right.

"There will come a point, Riley. How long have you known your true purpose? Almost a year now? And what have you done to protect this city? You've eliminated a few demons, sure. But Marchosias is as strong as ever. He views you as a plaything. An amusement. Do you think you actually scare him? When he tires of you, or the moment you pose a real threat, he was squash you like the bug you are."

Samael disappeared behind a slab, and Riley reached down to her leg. The piece of concrete was resting on her leg just below the knee. She hooked her fingers on the bottom edge on either side of her leg and lifted. She didn't think she could move the entire thing, but she prayed she would be able to give herself a little wiggle room. *Come on, give me back that quarter inch I had earlier. I could really use it now.*

Her lips pulled back over her teeth, Riley strained already tired muscles as she tried to move the rock. "Just that quarter inch I had earlier. Come on, I can work with that now. Give me a quarter inch."

Riley pushed, then twisted her leg to the side. She pulled her leg back as the slab fell, missing the toe of her shoe by a hair. She fell back against the stone, exhausted, and glanced to make sure Samael hadn't backtracked. She rolled onto her front and tried to stand. Her leg protested with a loud shock of pain, but she bit the inside of her cheek and ignored it. She had to figure out where the entrance was, and hope that Samael wasn't between her and it. She moved in the direction opposite of Samael and tried to get her bearings.

Straight ahead was north, as near as she could tell. The entrance to the building was on the south face. Samael had been moving to the east. Riley used the debris as cover, moving as quietly as she could across the destroyed building. She swept aside chunks of concrete and saw the faded tile of the lobby floor.

"Riley? Is that you?"

She stopped in her tracks and ducked down, trying to blend into the new rocky landscape of the building. She could hear girders overhead groaning under stress, and the entire structure seemed to move slightly starboard with the breeze. There were no sirens in the distance; divine intervention or just shoddy response time? Surely a building collapse registered with the police, no matter where it happened. Riley heard Samael's footsteps on stone, like a rat skittering inside the walls, and moved in the opposite direction.

"If you fail, Riley, they'll just start over again. They don't trust you. They don't believe in you. They want you to fail."

Priest believes in me. She wouldn't have put me in this situation if she didn't think I could survive it. She paused and added, *I'm still going to punch her in the face next time I see her, though. How dare she have this much faith in me?* She scanned the ground for any weapons she could find; palm sized chunks of concrete, broken furniture, anything. She was sure if she had a half hour and a MacGyver handbook she would be able to put something together, but on the fly, she was feeling useless.

"You're not worthy, Riley. You've never been worthy. Christine Lee made a grave mistake when she chose you."

Riley's jaw tightened and she had to bite back a retort. *Never badmouth a woman's first love, you son of a bitch.* She spotted something in the rubble and moved toward it, making a bit more noise than she intended. She heard Samael closing in as she cleared away the broken concrete from her prize. She nearly cheered when she discovered the object was loose, and she wrapped both hands around it as Samael's shadow fell over her.

"We can finish this somewhere else," Samael said. "We did have a Plan B."

Riley turned to face him, swinging the length of rebar like a baseball bat. She hit Samael in the side and knocked him off his feet. He crumpled in on himself, groping for something to keep him from falling completely and grabbing air. Riley didn't wait to fight; she knew she didn't stand a chance against him hand to hand, especially in this condition. She heard him get back to his feet and prayed she would make it to the door.

And then what? You saw the angels standing guard out there.

"Anywhere is better than in here," she panted. Samael shouted her name and she turned to see him spreading horrifically burnt wings. He flew in two short hops, then launched himself at her with a howl. Riley spun on her heel, dropped down to one knee, and lifted the rebar like a spear. Samael didn't have time to change his course; he slammed into the rebar and kept going, impaling himself on the steel. Riley let the bar fall, and Samael went with it.

Riley didn't stand around to gloat. She ran through the maze of the destroyed building, coughing as she inhaled the dust floating around the site. *Come on, I just need a man-shaped hole. I just need sunshine.* She squeezed between two slabs and saw the answer to her prayer. A broken window, empty except for a splintered frame, led out to the main street. She ran across the room and ducked through to the outside, taking deep breaths of fresh, clean air.

The building where she'd been held captive looked like a crushed soda can, collapsed in on itself with the outer walls of the bottom two floors standing up like the sides of a shoebox. Riley ran across the street, hoping the meager distance would offer some protection, and examined her surroundings. She was on the eastern side of the building, and the sun wasn't visible over the buildings. Sometime after noon, then. She glanced in the direction of her car, and doubted the angels standing guard would let her anywhere near it. But would they hand her back over to Samael for more torture?

She had no idea. The thought terrified her. If she couldn't even trust the angels, then she was truly alone for the first time since this whole battle began.

Sometimes, she decided, when you weren't sure who your friends were, you needed to go deeper into enemy territory. At least there you knew where people stood, and you knew they wanted you dead. She looked over her shoulder to make sure Samael wasn't following her, but the interior of the building was silent. She coughed up another lungful of concrete dust, checked to make sure her bandages were secure, and ducked down an alley. The tricks and secrets of her childhood came flooding back to her as she sidestepped an overflowing dumpster and leapt halfway up a chain link fence.

If there was one place where Riley Parra knew how to disappear, it was in the warrens of No Man's Land.

Chapter Six

Bruce Springsteen expounded about his glory days through speakers that blasted through the open door of the Original Bar pool hall. Riley moved inside and tried to fade into the shadows, moving her badge to the pocket of her jeans before she moved deeper into the room. Cigar smoke, stale beer and body odor filled the air, riding on a fog that draped from the ceiling like an old sheet. Riley waved off the bartender's grunt of inquiry and found a phone booth at the back of the room. It was actually semi-enclosed, offering her a bit of privacy from the rest of the room. She closed the door behind her and searched her pockets for money. "Great. Figures."

She picked up the receiver anyway and dialed zero, hoping to get someone to accept collect call charges. After a moment, an operator answered. "Nine-one-one, what is your emergency?"

Riley frowned. "What? No, I didn't—"

"What's that, ma'am? A potential assault victim staggering around in the Original Bar? We have officers en route. Don't let the victim leave, whatever you do."

Riley slammed the phone down and backed out of the booth. The bartender was staring at her, and a few of the men behind the curtain of smoke seemed much more interested in her as well. She shrugged and said, "Getting to where I can't even go out on laundry day, people think I got hit by a car." She moved toward the bar's front door, but one of the patrons moved to intercept her.

Riley shifted her weight to her left foot, leaning back as the man grabbed for her. She ducked under his outstretched arms, put a hand on his back, and shoved. His momentum carried him straight into the bar, where he sprawled. Riley swung her legs and kicked his feet out from underneath him, and he hit his chin on the bar as he fell. Two more men came at her from behind and she grabbed a bar stool to defend herself with.

"We're just trying to help you, miss. The cops will be here soon, just..."

Riley fished in her pocket for her badge and held it up for them to see. "I am a cop. I don't know who is supposedly coming to get me, but my guess is they won't be my friends and I don't want to see them. So I'm going to walk out the door, you guys are going to stay in here and get plastered, and everything will be fine. All right?" She eased toward the door, relieved when they didn't follow her.

As she stepped out into the daylight, she heard sirens dangerously close. Maybe that was why the barflies hadn't pursued her; they didn't think she had time to get away. But Riley had grown up running from the cops in No Man's Land. She turned and darted down the street, taking the first alley she found.

Long in the past, when the city government still cared about No Man's Land, the main road had been widened to four lanes. It was an unnecessary improvement, and it played havoc with the property lines along the project. Some buildings were demolished, only to be rebuilt farther back on their plots. Others simply lost half their parking lot. The buildings that moved were brought uncomfortably close to their neighbors, forming a tight meandering passageway. This practically inaccessible alley had been closed off by a tall fence, but that hadn't even hindered a ten year old Riley Parra.

She worked her fingers under the edge of the fence and pulled, forming a gap just wide enough for her to slip through when she was six. Now that a few decades were under her belt, she pulled harder and tried to improve the gap with little luck. She turned sideways, sucked in a breath, and wormed through the opening. The brick wall scraped her back, and she nearly got pinned at one point, but she made it through. The fence fell back into place with a solid slap, and Riley was alone in the tight space.

At least she hoped she was alone. It was hard to tell in the darkness.

The passageway was so tight that she had to turn sideways, and the brick still scraped against her shoulders.

When she was ten, these secret passages were ways out. Ways to escape her father and his friends. She never really cared where she was going back then, just as long as it was out. She would wander during most of the night, just trying to stay warm and keep her stomach full. She was around eleven when she realized how easy it was to just grab something off a shelf and duck out of a store. The majority of clerks wouldn't run very far over a candy bar. Losing one dollar wasn't worth huffing and puffing down the street in pursuit of a preteen thief.

Once Riley discovered how to pick her victims, stealing became easier and the prizes became bigger. She would wait until the clerks were distracted by a larger group - usually punks with shiny guns tucked in their sweaters, waiting for a chance to break open the cash register - before she started loading her own pockets with food. Potential armed robbers were the perfect decoy for a young, harmless girl in a dirty T-shirt.

She moved up to books, cassette tapes, the occasional outfit from a department store with bored teenage saleswomen popping their gum and reading their magazines as she made her way out of the store with her loot. People who thought thieves were lazy or unwilling to work didn't understand how difficult it was to steal without getting caught. It was a job in and of itself and, by the time Riley got home with the things she'd stolen, she felt like she had earned every single thing she now owned.

As she got older, stealing got easier. It also got easier to worm out of trouble when she got caught. When she became a teenager, lanky but with curves in the right places, she learned that a lot of business owners were lonely men who were afraid of their wives. When one caught her, all she had to do was rub against them a little, coo for forgiveness, maybe thrust her chest out toward them. Then when they took the bait, she jumped away and screamed rape. It was easier for them to let her go than to explain what their hands were doing on her ass.

She would be there still, she thought. She didn't have any motive for getting a real job. Why would she? Who needed money when the stores were practically giving her the stuff free of charge? And when she did need money, people were so stupid about their wallets and purses. She used other people like portable ATMs. It was going so well until that stupid cop wouldn't overlook one stinking bottle of whiskey.

What right did that stupid cop have? Tackling her like that, handcuffing her and tossing her into the back of the squad car. Riley still remembered the kaleidoscope of feelings washing over her as they sat there. Fear, anger, embarrassment, humiliation, shame. She was fingerprinted, photographed, and for the first time, she felt like a true criminal. And then that cop took her out to the car, sat her in the backseat, and just watched her in the rearview mirror. When she finally spoke, she turned to face Riley. Looked her right in the eyes. And all she said was, "So did you enjoy how this felt?"

Riley didn't know how close to the edge she was until she started crying. And once she started, she couldn't stop. The cop came around to the back of the car and opened the door, sliding in next to Riley. She pushed her forward, undid the handcuffs, and sat next to her in the back of the cruiser until the tears dried up. Riley wiped her face on the sleeves of her sweater, sniffling and blinking rapidly to clear her vision.

Christine put her hand on Riley's shoulder and rubbed gently. "In that case... what do you want to do about it?"

They set up a regular meeting in a coffee shop. Christine would buy Riley dinner if she could prove she had been in school that day. Before long, they were talking about Riley's father and her home life. When Christine started to talk about Riley's future, Riley realized she had never thought that far ahead. Christine told her that people who ran without a destination in mind ended up falling flat on their faces.

Riley didn't know she was falling in love with Christine. She didn't recognize the feeling, and didn't understand why she was having such strong feelings for another woman. When the high school's prom came around, Riley was surprised to find she wasn't interested in mocking the venture. She instead thought of ways she could ask Christine to go with her. She came up with a noncommittal way of breaking the ice, and felt her heart constrict when Christine said no.

"It's not that I don't want to, Riley," Christine said. She put her hand on Riley's back, both of them sitting on the same side of the booth. "I'm flattered you asked. But it... wouldn't look right. I'm a lot older than you."

"Not that much," Riley said, fighting back tears. God, why could this woman always make her feel like a little kid?

"You're seventeen," Christine said. "Even a little bit older is a... a lot of problems."

Christine drove her home as always, in the front seat of the cruiser instead of the back. When she parked at the curb, Riley turned in her seat and said, "I don't want to go up there. I want to go home with you."

"Riley..."

She didn't give time to finish the statement. She leaned across the console and kissed Christine's lips. Her heart soared, slamming against her chest as Christine relented and then began to kiss her back.

Riley had been with men before, but she counted that as the night she lost her virginity. It was that moment she realized that making love and fucking were two very different things. As she lay in bed next to Christine that night, struggling to stay awake to remember every minute detail of their first night together.

Riley reached the end of the alley, her reverie broken by the apparent renovation of the area. She doubted any official construction projects had destroyed her exit; more likely some tenant took it upon himself to make an improvement at the detriment of his neighbors. Riley could just barely make out the shape of a wooden fence fronted with chicken wire. She hooked her fingers in the wire and hauled herself up, the sagging barrier making her feel like she was trying to climb a rope ladder.

When she reached the top, she saw a dizzying drop to the ground on the other side. She looked for alternative exits and saw a lead pipe attached to one of the buildings. "Well, no one will be looking up." She tested the strength of the pipe and, content it would hold her weight, moved from the fence to the pipe.

It wasn't an easy climb, and she thought she was going to fall more than once, but she finally got to the roof. She hauled herself over the edge, lying flat against the hot tar for a moment to catch her breath. She rolled onto her back and stared up at the sun, letting it warm her face as she took stock of her sorry state.

Her clothes were torn and bloody. She had wounds on her wrists, chest and throat that could open up at any time. How much blood had she lost already? How much more could she spare to lose? She remembered having the same debate while she was imprisoned, but that had been hours ago. Hadn't it? Didn't the body regenerate blood? No, why would hospitals need blood donors all the time if blood just fixed itself? Oh, God, she would need a transfusion. That meant hospitals. She hated hospitals.

It would all be a moot point if she stayed here a little longer. Let the sun bake her into the tar. Let the demons find her and realize they were too late. It would be the easiest thing in the world. Just close her eyes, fall asleep... she wouldn't even realize she hadn't woken up. No more battles, no more wars. No angels, no demons.

No Gillian.

It always went back to that. She opened her eyes and grunted as she pushed herself up. She took a moment, standing under her own power and trying to decide which direction to run.

Chapter Seven

Riley leaned against the brick wall and listened to Warren Zevon shout his way through a song. He wanted to feel bad, because it was better than not feeling anything at all. She understood that. She didn't mind; he was getting her state of mind pretty accurately. She might feel like hell warmed over, a hundred miles of bad road, and something the cat dragged in all wrapped up in one, but it was better than not feeling anything.

She cradled her hand to her stomach, eyeing the scrapes and tears from the barbed wire. She didn't even want to think about what her neck looked like. Her blouse was in tatters, her undershirt red with streaks and drips of dried blood. She was weak. Thank God for brick walls to lean against.

The worn-out sneaker next to the boom box scuffed the sidewalk as its owner moved back toward the alley. He leaned against the wall and pretended to listen to the music as he waited for another customer. "So what exactly is it you need?" Muse asked.

"Gun. Something with stopping power."

"Correct me if I'm wrong, and I never am, don't they give you one of those when you become a cop?"

Riley said, "I don't have time to explain right now, Muse. Can you get me a gun?"

"Yeah, I think I could hook you up with something. Give me an hour or two."

"Can't do it, Muse. I need a gun right now. I know you're carrying."

He laughed. "Shit, that's my security blanket. You want to leave me naked out here? You know how much fire would rain down on me if people knew I was unarmed?"

"I'm unarmed, too, Muse. I've got enemies on my ass right now."

Muse hesitated. He reached under his oversized Seattle Seahawks jersey and pulled a gun from the small of his back. He looked down the street to make sure no one was watching and then ducked into the alley. "You best...

hoh-holy..." The street patter dissipated and Muse said, "What happened to you?"

"You should see the other guy." She held out her hand for the gun.

"You don't need this gun, you need a bazooka. You need an army. Give me twenty minutes and I'll put one together for you."

Riley shook her head. "This is my war."

Muse handed over the gun and said, "Yeah, just make sure you survive it, hear me?"

"Yeah." Riley checked the ammunition before sticking the gun into her belt. "Thanks, Muse."

"I was serious about that army. You need back-up?"

Riley smiled. "I appreciate the offer. But I'd be more likely to get whoever followed me killed."

He nodded. "Where you planning to go?"

Riley looked out into the street and shook her head. "I don't know. I'm probably going somewhere I shouldn't and do things that are ill-advised."

"Sounds like the Detective Parra I know," Muse said. He pulled a cell phone from his jeans and held it out. "There. You're leaving me totally naked, but I think you need it worse than I do. Go on, just make sure I get it back. Put a note on there for the medical examiner if you have to. It's got all my contacts on it."

"Legal contacts?"

Muse shook his head. "I cannot believe... I'm doing the woman a favor, and she goes and gets all 'cop' on me. Talk about gratitude."

Riley smiled and took the phone. She doubted it would give her anything but static, or a hotline straight to the demons chasing her, but it was comforting to have it in her pocket. It was amazing how quickly she had gone from never having a cell phone to being utterly dependant on having one nearby. She pushed away from the wall and gathered her strength for another dash.

"Muse," Riley said. "You've always been a good friend. I appreciate you always being here for me."

"Stop, you're going to get me misty. Hold on." He went back out onto the street and returned with a bottle of water. "It's a little warm, but—"

Riley snatched the bottle away from him, twisted off the top, and took a long swig. She wiped her lips on her sleeve, gasping as the water revitalized her. "Thanks for the spinach."

"No problem, Popeye," Muse said.

Riley slapped him on the shoulder as she left the alley. She knew he was watching her go, just as she knew that his offer of an army was sincere. Muse had a lot more power than even she knew, and she was lucky enough to be considered his friend. Maybe if she survived, she would take him up on the offer someday. She could use an army when the time came to take Marchosias down once and for all.

She stopped at the corner and thought about that for a moment. She came to No Man's Land because it was the one place she knew angels feared to tread. It was demon territory. But at the moment, angel territory was far more hazardous to her health. She flipped open Muse's phone and stared at the keypad. Did it matter who she tried to call? Would Samael and his cronies intercept the call? She dialed Priest's cell phone and waited.

"You've reached Caitlin Priest's phone. She's not going to help you, but if you leave your name and location, we'll come and finish destroying you."

Riley looked at the street sign. "I'm at the corner of Harding and Sixth Avenue, in No Man's Land. I'm heading south. You want to finish what you started before I blew up your toy box? Come and get me, you son of a bitch." She snapped the phone shut, but left it on. She figured the angels could track her without the cell signal, now that they had an idea where she was, but she didn't want to make it difficult for them. She wanted them to come now.

She found an abandoned car nearby and checked the handle. Locked, naturally. That was no problem for someone with a No Man's Land education. Riley grabbed the car antenna and snapped it off with a flick of the wrist. She held it by the bottom and swung the antenna at the car window with a wide sweep of her arm. The ball at the end hit the glass, and it shattered instantly. Riley dropped the antenna and opened the door, carefully sweeping the pieces of glass off the seat before she climbed behind her wheel.

The steering column came off easily, and Riley twisted the appropriate wires. She had never "stolen" a car, but she had gone on her share of joyrides. The engine roared in less than thirty seconds, and she pulled the door shut behind her. She glanced down the street and saw Muse watching her. He shook his head and wagged a finger at her. Riley winked, even though he was probably too far away to catch it, and pulled away from the curb.

She had barely made it one block before she spotted a shadow on the sidewalk. It was too big to be a bird, and she didn't have to look to see what it was. "Careful, showboat," she said. "You'll blow your cover. Then where will you be?" She didn't change direction or try to evade the angel; she just sped up to give the impression she wanted to lose him. She wondered if it was Samael or one of the guards she spotted outside the building. Either way, it didn't matter. Samael would get there eventually, if he was still in the fight. And if he was out of the fight, well, she didn't care where he was.

Riley waited at the stoplight, trying to get her bearings. She knew where she wanted to go, but she wasn't entirely sure how to get there from where she currently was. Her attempt at navigation was disturbed by the angel dropping to the road next to her car. He landed gently, a tap of wingtip shoes on the asphalt, and Riley calmly turned her head to look at him. He wore a green V-neck sweater, his hair hanging sloppy over his forehead as he leaned down to look into the broken window.

"Who are you? Angel of the morning, baby?"

"I am Puriel. I am the one who set these events into motion. You will cease your flight and return to the trial at once."

Riley frowned at his extended wings. "You want to hand me over to Samael, knowing what he did to me? He had your permission for that, did he?"

Puriel said, "It was for the greater good."

Riley pursed her lips. "You know, as attractive as that sounds, Purell, I think I'm going to pass. But thanks for the offer. I'll mention your service to my sadomasochistic friends."

Puriel reached into the car and Riley twisted to evade his grasp. She turned in the seat so that she was facing the door and wrapped both hands around his forearm. She twisted, and then swung the arm against the edge of the door. Puriel howled as she repeated the move until his arm bent back at an unnatural angle. He withdrew his arm and Riley stepped on the gas, peeling away from the stop sign in front of an oncoming car.

Riley heard a horn honk and waved an apology through the back window. The other driver flipped her off, but his attention was diverted when Puriel launched himself onto the trunk of her car. His wings were unfurled and waved with the breeze. He extended his wings, maybe in an attempt to slow her down, but it failed. Riley picked up the speed, wondering what her tailgater thought of her new passenger.

"Kind of blew your cover, didn't you?" Riley called out the window.

Three more shadows crossed the road in front of her. She craned her neck, swerving to avoid a parked car as she counted the angels filling the sky above her. "There's four," she muttered. She took a sharp corner and heard Puriel's weight thudding against the trunk as he tried to keep his grip. "Come on, buddy," she muttered. "Give it up. Eat some asphalt."

One of the other angels landed on her roof. The car seemed to slow a bit, and Riley knew the other angel was extending her wings to increase the drag. Riley pressed her lips together and said, "All right, you guys want me to stop so bad..." She pushed the accelerator up just a little faster, pushing it into the red, and then stood on the brakes and twisted the wheel. The car fishtailed, almost standing on its front tires as it laid down twin rows of burnt rubber.

Puriel and his cohort were thrown from the car like buckshot, twisting in midair as they tried to catch a breeze on their wings. Riley threw the car into reverse and backed away from them as fast as she could. "Come on, guys. You can't be that easy to get rid of."

Sure enough, Puriel and the other angel were already in pursuit of her again. Riley stopped, put the car into drive, and revved the engine. Puriel motioned for his partner to head up, in case she meant to ram them. Riley didn't plan anything of the sort; she just had somewhere she needed to be. She turned down a side street and watched the sidewalk for signs the angels were still following her lead.

"How many now," she muttered as she tried to count the interweaving shadows. Maybe six? Seven? Riley gave up trying to count. She looked in the rearview mirror and saw Puriel had settled for flying not far behind her. She wondered how many people were watching the spectacle out their apartment windows, how it would be explained away if anyone happened to get video footage. Not her problem.

Riley started seeing familiar landmarks and knew that she was nearing her destination. Judging from the expression on Puriel's face, he knew where they were, too. He fell back slightly, as if debating whether to continue the pursuit or retreat. It was the moment of truth, and Riley watched him very carefully for a decision.

Finally, he flexed his wings and closed the distance between them. He flew alongside the car, trailing just behind the broken driver's side window. "I suppose you think you're clever."

"I have my moments," Riley shouted back to him.

"What do you hope to accomplish?"

Riley shrugged. "Hopefully enough confusion that I can slip away unnoticed."

"You'll only get yourself killed!"

Riley laughed. "This day is going to end with me dead no matter what happens. You guys have pissed me off enough that I just want to take a couple of you with me." She twitched the wheel and the car lurched to one side. She clipped Puriel and sent him tumbling to the street. Riley saw him getting to his feet as she rounded the last corner.

Marchosias' building, where Samael fell and Riley nearly died on two different occasions, loomed ahead of her. It looked innocent, but she could feel the evil radiating from the brick even as the distance between the front of her car and the wide double doors shrank. The shadows of angels scattered, unsure whether to proceed or retreat. It was too late to turn back now, and Riley belatedly wondered if her stolen car had airbags.

The car leapfrogged the curb and went up the front steps of the building like a ramp. Riley went limp, hoping to spare herself broken bones, and closed her eyes as the car shattered the front doors of the building. An airbag did indeed explode, slamming her back into her seat and suffocating her before she managed to fight it out of the way. She kicked the door open and stumbled out into the foyer of Marchosias' building. Demons lined the edges of the room, staring at her car with shock.

Marchosias stood on the first floor landing, eyes flaming as he shouted, "What in blazes do you think you're doing?"

"Cutting out the middle man," Riley said. She covered her head and moved forward as the front of the building cracked. She took cover in front of the car's hood as a hole was blown in the wall and angels began to pour into the hotel.

Chapter Eight

The chaos was like something out of a Renaissance painting. Demons leapt from the upper levels, howling as they locked onto angelic targets. The angels seemed to glow as they engaged their enemy. What followed was a cacophony of howls and bells, metal sliding against metal, bloody husks falling to the tile floor as another player was taken from the game. Riley held Muse's gun like a totem, knuckles white as she watched the battle raging above her head.

Puriel had launched from the hood of her car, grappling with two demons in torn jeans. A demon grabbed Riley by the collar and tried to pull her to the ground. She planted her foot on his face and said, "I am really not in the mood." She put all her weight on that foot and pushed off the demon's face as she crossed the lobby to the base of the stairs. She had memories, horrible memories that were too scarring for even nightmares, about these stairs. Demons overpowering her, whispering ghastly things in her ear. But there was no other way to Marchosias, so that was the way she would have to go.

A clawed hand grabbed the back of her shirt and Riley twisted away, tearing the material. She turned and saw a hideous creature with an exposed skull of a face and wickedly curved claws for hands. Riley swung her gun around, holding it by the barrel as she smashed the butt into the demons face. His exposed skull cracked and caved in on itself and he fell back, blind and defenseless.

Puriel was hurled against the front wall of the building and the foundation seemed to tremble under Riley's feet. A few of the angels had produced swords and were hacking at the demons with blades of yellow flame. The demons weren't defenseless, however. Black swarms of flame assaulted the angels and pushed them back, the entire lobby of Marchosias' building crackling with unspent energy. It looked like the worst electrical storm in history, Riley's nostrils burning with the scent of charred flesh and clothing.

Riley knocked back another demon that wanted to take her on and ran up the stairs. Marchosias was watching the mayhem unfold with the slightly irritated expression of a man who discovers his neighbor's dog on his lawn. He spotted Riley's approach and flashed a smile before he retreated into one of the apartments. A blast of pure white light blinded Riley for a moment, and she turned to see a handful of demons falling dead to the floor.

She wasn't dumb enough to run blindly into the room where Marchosias fled, but she knew that nothing she could do would protect her from his attack. She lowered her gun and stepped into the doorway. Marchosias stood at the opposite end of the room, smiling broadly. He was standing in front of an open window, the breeze blowing past him and ruffling his shirt. He applauded in a slow, mocking way and said, "Very impressive, Detective Parra. Two armies want you dead, so you push them together in the hopes they... what? Kill each other? Do you truly want the angels dead?"

"Hey, do unto others. That's in the book they all love so much. Live by the sword, die by the sword. I think that's in the book, too."

"What did you hope to accomplish? Eliminating me in one fell swoop?"

Riley smiled. "More like if I have to go down, I'm taking everyone with me." She brought the gun up and said, "Mind if I empty this into you?"

"It won't do anything."

"It'll make me feel better." She fired once, hitting Marchosias in the shoulder. He jerked with the impact and slowly straightened, looking down at the wound. He touched the torn shirt and Riley said, "Sorry. Would you have preferred a head shot?"

Marchosias shrugged. "Whatever makes you happy, Detective Parra."

Riley stepped forward. "I heard you and Ridwan talking the night I... got this job." Marchosias smiled. "You said there had to be balance. Good and evil. If I'm the champion for the angels, does that mean you have a champion as well?"

"It would stand to reason, wouldn't it?"

"Who?"

Marchosias smiled. "Oh, that would make it far too easy for you, Detective Parra."

She shot him in the other shoulder. He grunted and shook his head, like a prizewinning boxer shaking off the blow of a lesser opponent. "They won't be distracted forever, you know. Perhaps you should use this clash to your advantage."

Riley looked past him to the window. "Fire escape?"

"Hmm?"

The angels would be occupied for a while, taking down the legions of Marchosias' followers. It would be a good time to lose them. She stuck the gun back into her belt and crossed the room. Marchosias moved out of her way as she leaned out the window and eyed the fire escape. It was well secured, looked sturdy, and it was the one way out of the building that wouldn't make her lose any more blood. She looked back at Marchosias. "I'll be back, you know."

"I would be offended if you weren't, Detective. Besides, you owe me a new front door."

Riley smirked and said, "Yeah, I'll get right on that." She brought her gun up and fired one last time for good measure. The bullet caught Marchosias in his forehead and knocked him off his feet. Even if the shot didn't kill him, she was sure it would cause a bit of a headache. She turned and threw herself down the fire escape, her feet barely touching the steps as she moved toward the street.

Her childhood bedroom had led to the fire escape, and she had many memories of pushing open the window and carefully moving down the metal steps to the street. She did it barefoot, so as not to wake her father. Not that he would have cared that she was leaving. She was just worried that, if he knew she was outside, he would lock the window so she wouldn't be able to get back in. Her nights on the streets were spent learning how to drink and smoke, how to act tough when she was scared out of her mind.

Riley remembered her first lover, a boy who worked the graveyard shift at the corner store. He caught her stealing, and threatened to call the cops. She convinced him to let her off with a warning by taking him into the back room and undressing. The resulting few minutes weren't very fun, but it was better than being taken downtown and fingerprinted. It was over quicker, too. When she discovered the clerk would let her steal more and more stuff as long as she let him do things with her, it was like being handed the keys to the candy store.

It wasn't until she spent the night with Christine that she realized what sex was supposed to be like.

She ran down the street, the sounds of Armageddon inside the apartment building curiously muted. Her mind was foggy, her head throbbing from either dehydration or exertion or both. She ignored the pain and moved down the sidewalk, turning to look into the sky. It was nearly dusk; she simultaneously wondered how the day had disappeared so quickly and how it could possibly be any longer.

Riley got to the corner before her legs gave out. She put her hand out to the wall, stopping herself from crumbling to the pavement, and breathed deeply. Her body was shaking, pushed to the limit. She pressed her shoulder to the wall and used it to keep herself from falling over, her chest heaving with the effort of drawing breath.

She heard cars on parallel streets. People shouting at their kids from apartment windows. She heard the incessant beeping of a garbage truck making its rounds and the rumble of the el train snaking through the sky. Tires screeched on another street and the banshee wails of police sirens were carried on the breeze. After the explosion, she knew she was alive because she heard her heartbeat. The same was true of No Man's Land. This was the heartbeat, the pulse, and it was still strong. That was why she was chosen; because she cared about No Man's Land. She cared about the people there and, even though she may be alone in the belief, she knew it could be saved. It just needed someone to fight.

Someone was approaching her from the direction of the apartment building, but she was too tired to care or to run. She opened her eyes and watched Puriel approach with detached indifference. The sun was now out of sight and the shadows stretched long across the ground. He was unarmed, but his clothing had been torn and burned away in several places. His hair was mussed, his left arm hanging uselessly by his side. Riley sighed and held her arms out to either side.

"All right. You got me. What now, you take me back to Samael and he shoves bamboo shoots under my fingernails? Waterboarding? Maybe force me to watch reruns of Hee Haw? Shall I lay prostate before you, or whatever it's called?"

Puriel stood in front of her and said, "The sun has set. The daylight of your trial has ended. It's time for the judgment."

"What happens if I don't pass that?"

Puriel's face had no emotion. "Then you will not live to see the sun rise again."

Riley looked at the sky. It was purple, a few clouds still capturing the sun's rays and glowing golden. She knew she wouldn't be able to survive No Man's Land in the dark, not in her condition. Angels to the left of her, demons to the right, and the most dangerous creature of all: mortals who hadn't gotten had the benefit of being saved from a life of crime. Even if she found a semi-safe place to bunk, she would never find the strength to do it all over again tomorrow. It had to end.

She held out Muse's gun by the barrel, and Puriel took it from her. She sagged against the wall and said, "I'm going to need a hand."

Puriel stepped forward and ducked under Riley's arm. He put his hand around her waist and helped her stand. "You're certain?" he asked. "There is no going back. And this part of the trial will not be easy."

"Good. Because the first part was kind of a cakewalk." She grunted as her position put pressure on her ribs. "Lay on, MacDuff."

Chapter Nine

Riley wasn't sure exactly where she was taken. Puriel loaded her into the backseat of a car and someone else fastened her seatbelt. Two angels sat on either side of her in case she tried to make a break for it. They shouldn't have bothered. With the setting of the sun, her last bit of energy had dried up. She was far too tired to try anything clever. She rested against the back of the seat and closed her eyes, letting them take her wherever they wanted.

She didn't recognize the building Puriel led her into, which caused a moment of alarm. She thought she knew most of the city, and the parts she didn't know at least had a recognizable skyline. "I'm not in Kansas anymore, am I?" she asked.

"Just relax, Detective Parra," Puriel said.

The front door of the building led to a long hallway, the walls draped with blue velvet. Riley resisted the urge to sing, but she did chuckle to herself as Puriel guided her into a large loading area. Lanterns formed a square in the middle of the space, surrounding a metal folding chair. Puriel pointed to the chair and said, "Have a seat, Riley Parra."

"Don't mind if I do," Riley said. She started toward the chair and noticed people standing in the shadows watching her. "Hey, guys. Wouldn't happen to have a La-Z-Boy or something like that, would you? A recliner would really hit the spot right about now." She sat on the chair and realized just how tired she had to be; the simple act of sitting and relaxing was like a gift from the gods. She sagged against the back of the chair and closed her eyes, afraid she would fall asleep given just a little incentive. Her head started to loll before Puriel spoke.

"Now is your judgment, Riley Parra."

"Great. Can't wait. Hope I win." She looked at the silhouettes in the darkness. "I doubt that's a jury of my peers."

Puriel walked along the edge of the lit area, still bearing the wounds of his battle in the demon-infested building. "That was a very wrathful thing you did this afternoon, Riley. Leading us into a battle with demons."

"You poked the bear," Riley said. "Got you out of my hair for a while."

"The battle still rages. Now that we have engaged the enemy, it will be difficult to retreat without allowing them a great victory."

Riley shrugged. "Hey, great. That means you're doing something. I've kind of been waiting for that."

"Protecting this city is your responsibility, Riley."

"And I used the tools at my disposal. I had a half dozen pissed off angels looking for a fight, and a building full of demons that wanted to kill the first thing they saw. So I figured I would take care of you both at the same time."

Puriel nodded slowly. "Regardless, you are charged with the cardinal sin of wrath. How do you plead?"

Riley held her hands out. "Guilty, I suppose."

Puriel nodded and a murmur flowed through the spectators. He held up a hand, and they quieted. "To the cardinal sin of pride. How do you plead?"

Riley considered the question. "I worked hard to get where I am. To be a detective, to have a life of my own." She thought of her time in No Man's Land, the criminal she would be now if she hadn't been pulled up by Christine Lee. "I'm proud of who I've become, yes. If that's a sin, then fine. So be it. Guilty."

Puriel clasped his hands behind his back, and Riley realized his wounds were considerably less serious than a few minutes ago. "You do not lie to increase your stature. You do not accept accolades for achievements you have made. You do not flaunt your victories in the face of your enemies. You are therefore found not guilty of the sin of pride."

"Well, how about that. Things are looking up for me."

"And to the cardinal charge of lust?"

Riley laughed out loud. "Oh, and things were going so well. Guilty."

"You have committed adultery."

"I've caused adultery to be committed, yes," Riley said. She remembered the blonde woman in the back of her squad car, the wedding ring catching the streetlight as they grappled for buttons and zippers. It was a moment of weakness, but Riley was a young cop enamored with the power her new badge provided. The woman offered a deal in order to get out of a fine, and Riley was more than willing to sully the uniform a little bit.

"You have lusted for others."

"Yeah," Riley said. "Lusted, and consummated that lust on several occasions."

"But not since your devotion to Gillian Hunt?"

Riley frowned. "No."

"Given the opportunity to give in to lust with Mackenzie Crowe, you did not yield to temptation."

"No, I didn't."

Puriel said, "To the charge of lust, you have been found guilty. To the cardinal virtue of chastity, you are also found guilty."

"Virtue?" Riley said. She chuckled. "No one's ever accused me of that before. So, what, do those two kind of cancel each other out?"

Puriel didn't answer. "To the cardinal sin of envy, how do you plead?"

"Envy?" Riley said. She looked down at the ground and thought about it. "I don't envy anyone or anything."

"Really."

She shook her head. "I accepted my lot in life when I was a kid. I thought I would be a No Man's Land rat until the day I died. When I was offered a way out, I took it. I worked hard to become a detective, but I would say that was out of personal pride, and you've already charged me with that. So no. Not guilty."

Another murmur went up around her and Puriel slowly nodded. "Very well. The corresponding virtue is kindness. How do you plead?"

Riley shook her head. "I've never been exceptionally kind, either."

"You are wrong, Riley. You have always been kind to your friends, to your coworkers, and to your partners. You have gone above and beyond the responsibilities of a friend."

"I didn't do anything special."

"Do you think we don't know about the money?"

Riley blinked. "I... I don't..."

"You will not break a confidence you made to yourself? Not even to save your life?"

Riley looked away. "The money isn't... anything special."

"One hundred dollars from every paycheck. How long will your penance last? How much do you believe you owe Kara Sweet's niece?"

Riley shook her head. "I'm only giving her the money Kara would have given her if... I hadn't..."

"Kara Sweet had been corrupted by a fallen angel. Her soul was tarnished. Your execution gave her a fighting chance to save her soul when she stood before her Judge."

Riley hung her head. "It's still a sin on my record."

"Perhaps." Puriel nodded. "You are now found guilty of the cardinal virtue of humility. As well as kindness."

"What's that? Three sins to three virtues? I'm doing better than I thought. What's next? Keep 'em coming."

Puriel actually smiled a bit at that. "Sloth."

"I've been known to hit the snooze button once or twice."

"That is not the same. You are charged with a failure to utilize your talent and your gift. How do you plead?"

Riley shook her head. "Not guilty. I've been busting my ass trying to save this city. I put this badge to use every single day."

"Wrong." Puriel stopped pacing and turned to face her. "There was one moment. A time when you could have helped but you chose not to. The consequences of that action were immense. So much could have changed with one word, one helping hand. You were a patrol officer in No Man's Land. It was dusk, and you had worked for two shifts. It was winter, and it was cold. You were eager to return to your car for the warmth. Your shift was nearly over. All you wanted was a warm bed and sleep."

Riley didn't doubt his words. He could have been describing any number of nights during her patrol days.

"She called out to you."

"Who?"

"The snow was just beginning to fall and you were worried about the roads. You saw her, but did not slow. The woman had blankets, after all, and a coat. Surely she would find someplace warmer before anything bad happened to her. Right?"

Riley vaguely remembered the street woman. She had been bundled in frayed blankets with a knit hat pulled down over her ears. Her eyes looked so desperate. But there was a homeless shelter not far away, and they had cots and warm meals. It was walking distance; she didn't have the time or the energy to deal with it. So she just said, "There's a shelter about two blocks to the east. They'll take care of you," and continued on.

That night, the temperature dropped below freezing. Riley had a passing thought about the homeless woman, but she was sure she'd made it to the shelter. She was more concerned about the warm body curled against hers - the conquest of the week - and the cocoa warming on the stove to think too hard about it.

"She died," Riley said, surprised to find how much that information hurt. "I didn't... the shelter was just around the corner."

"The woman was weak. Ill. She would have required your assistance to get into the patrol car; two blocks would have been impossible. A hospital may have pulled her back from the precipice, and maybe she would have had the opportunity to speak with you."

"What could she have possibly told me?"

Puriel said, "The woman was your mother, Riley. Jacqueline Inez Parra."

Riley recoiled as if she had been punched. "That's a damn lie."

"She was watching you. She knew your patrol. Your mother was very sick, Riley. She heard voices. She took medication, but that only aggravated her symptoms. Do you even remember why she left?" Riley shook her head slowly. "She left to protect you. She was afraid that she was going to harm you. The night she left, she held you under the bathwater for nearly twenty seconds before she realized what she was doing."

"Mom... was schizophrenic," Riley muttered. She'd wrapped her arms around her stomach, rocking slowly as she remembered the few facts her father had given her.

"Your mother was tormented by demons. Demons who knew what you would grow up to be, and wanted you dead. She was strong enough to escape, save your life, but she never recovered. She lived on the streets and did whatever she could to follow your life. But she never dared reach out to you. Until the moment when you could have saved her life, and you did nothing. Riley Parra, to the cardinal sin of sloth, how—"

"Guilty," Riley said.

Puriel nodded. "To the cardinal virtue of patience, how do you plead?"

"I don't... uh, I-I don't know."

"Endurance against adversity. Resolving conflicts without violence, and to show mercy to those who sin against you."

Riley scoffed. "Like when I shot Kara in the head?"

"Like when you applied pressure to the wounds of the one who violated your body. You showed compassion to Nina Hathaway."

"She was bleeding to death because of me."

"Regardless."

Riley closed her eyes. "All right, fine, mark me down for that one. What is the purpose of this? Do I get merit badges on the way to Hell or something?"

"The balance is necessary, Riley. If we are to accept you as this city's champion, we must believe you are a good person at heart. We must know we are entrusting this battlefield to the right person. We must determine whether you are virtuous at heart, or if your soul is overburdened by the mark of sin."

"I eat in moderation and I don't throw away money on extravagances. Gluttony, not guilty. As long as I have money for rent and food, I'm happy. As long as I have a little extra cash to take my girlfriend out to dinner a couple times a month, I'm happy. Greed, not guilty. Is that seven?"

"Three virtues remain."

Riley thought about it and said, "Can't think of 'em. Says something about a society that focuses more on the sins than the virtues."

"Temperance, Charity and Diligence. You are charitable to Kara Sweet's family, as I have noted before. You are moderate with your money and time. You are exceptional at your job, despite a willingness to break the rules when you deem it necessary."

"Three for three," Riley said. "So what's the verdict, guys? Is my soul heavier than a feather, or is there some other test to run?"

"The judgment has been passed, Riley. You have been found virtuous."

Riley was surprised to feel a surge of pride at his words. She pressed her lips together and scanned the shadows, looking for a familiar shape. She doubted she had met any of the angels watching her trial, but she was hoping... "Listen, do you know if Zerach—God." She clutched her side and lurched forward, falling out of the chair. "What..."

"Your body is failing. We tempered your pain as much as we could, but now that your trial has ended..."

Riley clenched her jaw against the pain suddenly shooting through her body. She hadn't realized when they stopped her from hurting, but now that it was back, she could barely stand it. She tried to stand and fell hard to her knees. "You sons of bitches... you can't just..." Her words faded into an incoherent shout of anguish. She crawled forward a few steps before her arm gave out. She could no longer support her weight on it.

"Things will change now, Riley Parra," Puriel said. "I hope you are prepared."

"You can't just leave me here," she grunted. But the sound of shoes on concrete echoed through the space, the sound of angels leaving her to fate. Riley spit blood onto the floor and said, "Oh, you pious assholes." She fell to the floor, panting. She rolled onto her back, surprised to see the sky overhead.

It was daybreak. The sun was rising in the east, making the windows shine like liquid gold. Riley panted, blinking into the growing light. The spirits did it all in one night, Riley thought, then closed her eyes to the pain. She heard tires screech on the pavement and running footsteps coming up next to her. A woman leaned down and looked at her face. "Oh, God."

The woman wore a Kangol cap and a nice blouse. Riley thought she looked like something out of a novel about Old New York. Or would it have been New Amsterdam back then? She turned her head and saw the curved bumper of a Checker cab. That, plus the woman's attire, made Riley wonder if the angels had tossed her back to the turn of the century to atone for her sins. Might be nice. No Man's Land wasn't nearly as large then as it is now.

Riley squeezed her eyes shut as the woman called for an ambulance on her cell phone. She didn't hear the actual words, and she doubted an ambulance would get there in time to save her.

The good thing about the trial was that now she was fairly sure she was going to Heaven. She just didn't realize she was due to arrive so soon.

Chapter Ten

She could hear her heartbeat. In her head, and in a loud mechanical beep coming from over her right shoulder. She turned toward it and looked at the peaks and valleys that was evidence of her survival. She had bulky bandages on her wrist, and she felt another around her neck. She looked down, but her chest was hidden by a white hospital gown. There were blue checks on the material, and she could tell she was naked underneath it. The indignity of being a patient. She rested her head on what must have been the softest pillow she had ever had the honor to use and closed her eyes.

"...some cabbie brought her in."

Riley opened her eyes. She wondered how a doctor and nurse could have gotten into her room so quickly. She was sure she hadn't fallen asleep. The doctor noticed she was awake and offered her a smile. "Well, good morning, Detective. Glad to see you're back with us." He pulled something from his pocket and leaned over the bed to look into her eyes. "We were starting to get a little..."

Riley refused to believe she had drifted off in mid-sentence, so she decided to believe the doctor had merely vanished into thin air. She turned her head toward the window and watched rain streaking down the glass. She could hear thunder, but there was no lightning to go along with it. She listened to the music of raindrops for a while, hoping it would push her back into rest. She didn't know how long it had been since she was left in the street, but she could use another couple weeks worth of sleep.

"Hello, Riley."

She turned slowly toward the door and saw Priest standing just outside the room. She was drenched from the rain, her dress shirt wrinkled and her tie loose. She had her hands clasped in front of her, as if in prayer.

"I won't ask to come in..."

"Can I tell you to come in?"

Priest looked up and, after a moment, entered the room. She walked up to the bed and laid her hand on top of Riley's. "I am so sorry."

"Don't be," Riley said.

"I arranged the test to give you the answers you sought. I knew it would be bad, but..." She shook her head. "I did not know they were recruiting Samael. If I had known..." She swallowed hard. "Perhaps that is why Michael forced me to leave."

"Michael?" Riley said. "Lieutenant Archer, from Burglary."

Priest smiled. "He did have a hand in getting me 'transferred' at the last minute." She brushed Riley's hand with the tips of her fingers. "I am in awe of your strength. So many others failed their trials in the first hours. The few who actually finish..."

"Yeah. Well. I'm stubborn." She swallowed and winced. "So, I go through all that to get a couple of questions answered. Is there a plaque or something, at least?"

"The answers weren't your only reward, Riley. You've changed things. You have been deemed a worthy champion. You will have the full support you require. You're no longer alone in this fight. Of course... that may not be readily apparent. The angels will be occupied with the war you began. You may be called upon to clean up some of their messes."

Riley closed her eyes, surprised to find they were wet with tears. "Well. What else is new?"

"Everything, Riley. The battle has taken a dramatic shift. You effectively called in the cavalry. Demons are frightened, the angels are inspired in a way they haven't been in ages... your trial has changed everything. There is real hope for No Man's Land."

Riley smiled. "Stop it. You'll make me blush and I can't spare the blood. So... how long do I have to be in here?"

"They gave you a blood transfusion yesterday..."

"Yesterday?"

"You were unconscious for nearly thirty-six hours, Riley."

Riley winced. "Ow."

"Yes. They want to keep you for another few days, just to be certain you're healing properly. You had four broken ribs, a broken leg, two broken fingers..."

Riley looked at her hands and saw that the last two fingers on her right hand were splinted. "Huh. Wonder when I did that."

"And that's just the beginning of the list. Riley, if I had known..."

"Hey. Every job has a little hazing, right? And now I have some muscle on my side... it was worth it, I guess." She relaxed against the mattress and groaned. "I'm going to steal this pillow. Will that affect my sin-to-virtue ratio?"

Priest smiled. "You're not angry at me?"

"No," Riley said. "You were only doing what I asked you to do. Next time just punch me in the nose and tell me it's a million times worse than that. I'll let it go, trust me."

"Duly noted." She looked down at Riley's legs and said, "Is there anything else I can do for you? I feel the need to serve a penance for my part in what happened."

Riley started to say no, but she hesitated. She looked at the heart monitor and said, "Yeah. There is one thing you could do for me."

Kenzie Crowe had never been much of a sentimental person. She toyed with the pink flowers, trying to arrange them so that they were evenly spaced with the yellow ones. The bouquet was a grossly overpriced gift shop variant, but she hadn't thought about flowers until she was already in the hospital. She and Riley were both anti-flowers, but she felt that they would be a nice ironic gesture. Riley would appreciate that. And the bigger they were, the bigger the irony.

The teddy bear tucked under her arm was maybe a bit over the top. But damn it, this was Riley. And the gift shop didn't exactly have a huge selection.

The elevator dinged, and she stepped out of the car. She hated hospitals, with their counterintuitive feel of a quiet rush. Everything was so hushed and muted, but every nurse and doctor seemed to be moving at double-speed. Kenzie had spent far too long in them after she came home, and she was reluctant to set foot in one even as a visitor. But, as previously stated... this was Riley.

The note from Lieutenant Briggs said that Riley was in Room 242, at the end of the hall. Kenzie checked her hair in the glass of a picture frame as she walked past, wanting to make a good impression on her former partner. She knocked on the door frame and said, "Rye, get your hand out from under your gown, you got company." She pushed the curtain out of the way and saw the bed was empty.

"Rye. Come on out." She knocked on the bathroom door and then peeked inside.

"Riley?"

She stepped into the hallway and hesitated before she moved to the nurse's station. "Excuse me," she said. Lieutenant Briggs came around the corner at that moment and spotted Kenzie as the nurse looked up from her computer monitor. "Was Detective Riley Parra taken anywhere? For tests, or an X-Ray, maybe?"

"Just a moment." The nurse tapped on the keyboard.

Briggs said, "What's wrong?"

"Riley's not in her room."

"She's gone."

Briggs and Kenzie both turned and saw Priest walking toward them from Riley's room. Kenzie frowned. "I was just... where did you...? What do you mean 'gone'?"

"She left the hospital."

"Not according to our records," the nurse said. She stood up and placed her hands on her hips. "Where, exactly, did Ms. Parra go?"

"That's not important," Priest said. "She's safe."

The nurse shook her head. "Ms. Parra was a very sick woman. She needs to be in a hospital under the care of a trained physician..."

Priest smiled. "Don't worry. She has a doctor with her."

Epilogue

Riley kissed the dip of Gillian's spine and shifted her weight on the bed. She stretched out next to Gillian, covering the left side of her body with her own. She put her hand on Gillian's right hip, covering the tattoo Riley had given her the night before. It was a smaller version of the one on Riley's right shoulder, granting a portion of Riley's protection to her. She kissed Gillian's shoulder, and Gillian twisted to kiss Riley's lips. "Mm. I've missed that," Riley whispered.

"Better get your fill in. In case we have to go back early."

Riley smiled and kissed Gillian harder, sliding her hand down Gillian's bare hip. Gillian shifted on the mattress and Riley moved closer to her. Gillian's legs slid between hers easily, their bodies moving together like they had never been apart.

"Will your tattoo be less effective now?"

Riley brushed Gillian's hair out of her face. "If the supernatural shits in town really want to hurt me, they can. I know that now. The tattoo was a security blanket for me. Giving it to you... it will make the difference. I know that, too. So yes, it will probably be a little less effective. But I would give up all the protection for you."

"I wouldn't want that."

"I know."

Gillian kissed the flat of Riley's chest. Riley kissed her way from Gillian's mouth to her ear. There were two piercings, even though she only ever wore one in each ear. She wanted to remember every inch of Gillian in case they were ever apart again.

Gillian brushed her thumb over the bandage on Riley's neck. "You must have been in such pain."

"I can cope," Riley said. "Priest healed me a little bit before she brought me here. Enough that I could... appreciate being with you again." Her hand slipped and Gillian's chuckle turned into a groan of pleasure. Riley kissed her neck.

"Remind me to thank that woman next time I see her."

"So you're definitely coming back with me?"

"Yes."

Riley moved her hand and Gillian whimpered. "Say it."

"This is torture, Detective," Gillian moaned.

"I got an education in that recently. I'm a product of my environment." She bent down and nibbled Gillian's ear. "Say it. I need to hear you say it."

Gillian said, "When you fly home... I'm coming with you."

"And now?"

Gillian whimpered. "What...?"

"Are you coming now?" Riley asked.

"Oh," Gillian said. She exhaled sharply. "Yes, Riley."

Riley kissed Gillian's lips and said, "I love you."

Gillian put her arms around Riley. She pulled her close and said, "I love you, too." Her hands slid across Riley's back, over already-healing wounds from her trial. "You have to get back to the city, don't you? Rejoin the fight. Demons versus angels."

"Yeah. Only at the moment the angels and demons are kicking each other's asses without my help. The war won't be short, but I'm not fighting it alone anymore. Still, I think I'll give them a little time to settle down before I go back."

"A vacation? You?"

"I think I've earned it."

Gillian smiled and moved her hands along Riley's flank. "Got any plans for your free time?"

"Some," Riley said. She bent down and kissed Gillian's bottom lip. "But I'm open to suggestions."

Outside the bedroom, a rain had begun to fall. It was a quiet, southern United States kind of rain without the threat of severe weather. A steady downpour that turned the world gray-blue and washed away the heat of the world. It beat against the glass, keeping the world inside isolated from the world outside. The light provided by the meager glow of the bedside lamp barely allowed the two women to see each other, but it was enough for the moment. Later, they would turn on the overhead lights and explore one another again. Later, they would take the time to appreciate being together again.

Right now, they had more pressing things to attend to.

Ride Along

Set Before the Beginning of the Series

One moment she wasn't, the next moment she was. Angels didn't have a bullpen, a batting cage where they waited to be called on-deck. Most of the time, he existed in what they thought of as a "null" state. Inchoate, but present, aware. One moment Zerachiel was at rest, and the next she was in the backseat of a familiar car. A bag rustled as the passenger dug for something within. Three French fries, which were promptly consumed. The driver ignored the feast and kept her eyes on the building across the street.

"He's not coming back tonight," the passenger said. Her name was Kara Sweet, known as Sweet Kara to all who knew her. She was peripheral to Zerachiel's interest; her true focus was on the driver, Detective Riley Parra. Sweet Kara's partner and friend, Riley was slumped in her seat to make less of a silhouette in the window, her dark hair hiding her face from Kara's examination. But Zerachiel could feel the frustration rising from Riley in waves.

"Did you hear me?" Kara asked.

"Yeah, I heard you," Riley said. "I'm just ignoring you."

"Not nice," Kara said. She dug for more fries and came up empty. "Shit. Okay, I'm calling it. Ten more minutes and we're out of here."

Riley checked her watch and then looked back across the street. "He'll be here. His brother said he would be here."

Kara scoffed. "Real reliable source of information there."

"Fifteen more minutes, and then we'll go," Riley said. "Happy?"

Kara grinned. "Fifteen will do."

"You have a hot date tonight or something?"

Kara said, "Me myself and I, along with a couple of double-As. You?"

Riley shook her head. "Might go down to the bar. See what's going on."

"That's your problem. Always picking up skanks for a one night stand. You need to find a nice girl and settle down. Maybe Lieutenant Hathaway."

Riley laughed. "Yeah, that would solve all my problems, wouldn't it? Tell her I didn't finish my paperwork because I was too busy banging her in the break room."

Kara grinned, but it faded quickly. "Aw, shit. I was so close to a boring night in front of the TV. Check out the corner." She nodded toward the broken streetlight, illuminated by the flickering light coming from a nearby window. A broad-shouldered man was limping down the street, his head ducked and his hands stuffed into his pockets. His elbows stuck out to either side, making him look like a teacup. The limp was the clincher; the dead clerk had gunshot residue on his hands, indicating he'd gotten a shot off. The blood trail showed he'd hit his mark, and the security camera indicated it was his lower right leg.

Riley said, "That's our boy."

They waited until he was past them before Kara got out of the car. She jogged across the street, ignoring the suspect's progress. Riley got out of the car a few seconds later. The suspect was focused on Kara, making sure she wasn't doubling back on him, and didn't hear her as she approached. He ducked into his building and Riley followed him.

Zerachiel didn't leave the car; she didn't have to. She simply changed her perspective to Riley's. She went directly from the backseat to the lobby of the suspect's apartment building. Half the lights were out, giving just enough of a glow to keep people from falling down the stairs. The man at the front desk opened his mouth to speak, but he shut up when Riley pulled up the tail of her shirt to show her badge.

"Douglas Wright."

He didn't even turn to look before he started running. Riley said, "You're going to regret making me run. Freeze right now, Mr. Wright."

Douglas ignored her. When he reached the landing, he dropped to one knee and spun to face her. Zerachiel put her hands in the middle of Riley's chest and pushed her to the side. Riley credited her instincts as she hit the wall and dropped to one knee, avoiding the bullet by a hair. She moved into the small alcove for the light fixture and cursed. A second bullet hit the plaster near Riley's head; Zerachiel placed the side of her hand against the wall and the bullet deflected toward the ground.

"It's clear. You have three seconds," Zerachiel whispered.

Riley leaned out and took her shot. The bullet grabbed Douglas Wright's shoulder and twisted him back, knocking him flat on the ground. Riley came out of hiding and hurried up the stairs. Zerachiel reached Douglas before Riley did, and she pinched her fingers together where his trigger finger attached to his hand. He tried and failed to fire it as Riley approached.

She pulled the gun from his hand and tucked it into her belt.

"Riley?"

"Got him," Riley said. She flipped him over onto his stomach and pulled his arms together. "Douglas Wright, you are under arrest..."

Kara came up the stairs with her gun still drawn. "Jesus, Riley."

"It's fine," Riley said. "Didn't even come close." She patted Douglas on the shoulder before she cuffed him. "Don't worry, Mr. Wright. We're still gonna charge you with assault on a police officer, attempted murder of a police officer. Lots of fun stuff. We'll keep you busy for a good long while until we get you on the grocery store robbery. You have the right to remain silent..."

Lieutenant Hathaway came out of her office as Riley and Kara returned. "Riley. Dr. Hunt wants to see the two of you. Something about the Watson case."

"We'll head down once we're done with this paperwork," Riley said.

Hathaway nodded. "Douglas Wright?"

Kara said, "Downstairs in a nice set of new bracelets."

"Nice work, you two. You might want to check with Dr. Hunt before the paperwork. I had a feeling she was kind of swamped, so you may not get a chance later."

Riley said, "Anything to put off paperwork." She draped her jacket over the back of her chair before she turned and went back to the stairs.

Kara followed her and, unseen, Zerachiel joined them as they headed down the stairs. Kara waited until the door was closed before she spoke. "So you'd really do her?"

"Who?" Riley said.

"Hathaway. I mean, God knows she's interested, but—"

"God, no," Riley said. "The woman is a sexual harassment lawsuit waiting to happen. I don't need to get involved with that." They arrived at the morgue level. The hallway leading to the coolers was dark, as usual, and shadows hung on either side of the corridor like tapestries.

"I've always been kind of terrified of the morgue. I've had nightmares about this place."

"It's not so bad," Riley said. She led the way to the examination room doors, but she paused with her hand poised to push the door open. Through the glass, she could see Dr. Gillian Hunt pushing an empty bed toward the coolers.

"What's wrong?" Kara said. "Squeamish all of a sudden?"

"No," Riley said. Zerachiel moved closer to Riley. There was something ailing her, but she couldn't quite put her finger on it. Riley stepped away from the door and said, "Listen, you find out what she wants, and I'll go up and take care of Douglas Wright's paperwork. We don't both have to be here for this."

"You'll take all the paperwork? That's a deal." She looked past Riley to the window. Gillian still had her back to the doors, her red hair bundled in a sloppy ponytail to expose her neck. "You know what's odd? You'll joke about having sex with anyone. I mean, you joke about going down on Lieutenant Hathaway, banging a suspect, you've even joked about having sex with me."

"What's your point?" Riley said.

Kara brushed past Riley and flashed a knowing smile at her as she gestured at Gillian. "You never, ever joke about her."

The door swung shut on Riley as her face started to flush. Zerachiel felt the distress again, and identified it this time. It was a difficult thing to label. There was loss, but not loss of something that had ever been acquired. There was pain of something yet to happen, and shame at being unworthy of something. Zerachiel held onto these feelings until they became something slightly more identifiable.

Desire.

Riley watched as Gillian and Kara spoke, and then turned away. Zerachiel followed. It was strange to feel desire - a good thing - grown to the point where it was pain. She didn't understand it. If desire caused pain, why wouldn't Riley just put an end to it? Why didn't she simply attempt to acquire what she wanted? Either the desire would be fulfilled or, in the case of rejection, the desire would fade and she would move on.

Then it made sense. The joy of desire was conflicting with the pain of possible loss. If Riley never tried to get Gillian, then Gillian could never reject her.

Zerachiel put out her hand and brushed it over Riley's shoulder. Riley paused as if she felt the touch, shook her head, and left the stairwell.

Zerachiel left Riley that night. The important people in Riley's life were like beacons to her, and she followed the trail of each one until she found who she was looking for. Dr. Gillian Hunt was asleep in her bed, her hair covering most of her face. She was tangled in her blankets, one leg stretched out across the empty mattress. Zerachiel crouched next to the bed and felt Gillian's thoughts. It was like sorting a crowded closet with both eyes closed and thick gloves on both hands; mostly guesswork and intuition.

Zerachiel found Riley. She occupied a small but protected corner of Gillian's consciousness. It was a stronger section than the one set aside for other colleagues. Zerachiel pushed harder and found an image.

Riley standing by an exam bed in the morgue, her hair up. There was a loose strand of hair on her neck, and Gillian seemed obsessed by it. They were talking, but the words were lost to Gillian's memory. There was a quiet hum, white noise as Gillian lifted one gloved hand. She used the back to brush the hair away, her fingertips brushing Riley's neck. Riley shuddered at the touch and Gillian withdrew her hand with a quick, "Sorry, I was just..."

"It's okay," Riley said, but she didn't look at Gillian.

Zerachiel retreated. Her exploration had brought the memory to the forefront of Gillian's mind, and she stirred in her sleep. She rolled her shoulders and made a quiet noise of contentment. She shifted under the blankets. Zerachiel watched and then, with only a thought, returned to Riley.

Riley was asleep on her couch in a pair of jeans and an old T-shirt. The television was on, the remote on the floor by Riley's outstretched hand. Zerachiel touched Riley's temple and then focused on Gillian's apartment. The two connected, and Riley tensed in her sleep. Gillian rolled onto her back, the shoulder strap of her nightgown falling down as she tried to find a more comfortable spot. Her arm dropped, her hand resting on her thigh before her fingers brushed aside the lace hem of her nightgown.

Riley moved a hand between her legs, pressing against the crotch of her jeans. Riley had her other arm tucked under her head, and she turned her face against it as she began to rub with two fingers. Zerachiel knew that she was seeing Gillian in her bed, picturing the plain white nightgown with perfect clarity. And she knew that Gillian had a crystal-clear image of Riley touching herself on the couch.

After a few seconds, Riley woke up enough to get her jeans undone, pushing them low on her hips and then pushing her hand into her underwear. Gillian bit her lip at the sight and slipped her hand under her nightgown. Riley whimpered and gently nipped the flesh of her arm.

Neither of them lasted very long before orgasm. Riley groaned to prevent herself from saying the name of her fantasy, but Gillian said, "Oh, Riley, you're beautiful." She licked her lips and pressed her thighs together, rocking her hips against her hand until she was finished.

Zerachiel withdrew her hand, and Riley's eyes opened. She sat up, pulled her jeans back up, and ran her fingers through her hair. "God. Damn it." She sighed, rubbed her eyes, and picked up the remote control to turn the TV off. In the silence of the apartment, Riley sat with her head in her hands for a long time, breathing slowly, trying to ignore the remnants of what she thought was just a dream. Finally, she got up and walked to the bedroom, shutting the door behind her.

Zerachiel watched her go before she moved to the bedroom. Riley took off her jeans and crawled into bed with her T-shirt on. Zerachiel moved to the far corner of the room and let her presence slowly dissipate. She returned to the place she had started, the place that was there while being insubstantial.

Riley would need her again, she was sure. Until then, she was content to watch and wait.

Maintenance

Set Before "Losing My Religion"

Caitlin Priest had several things to learn about being human.

She figured out how to fake it well enough in public. She had actually fooled Riley into believing she was just another cop until she was forced to expose herself as an angel. But she wasn't prepared for all the tiny little things that having a mortal body required. There was certain maintenance required that Michael hadn't mentioned when he gave her the assignment of moving to the mortal coil. She hadn't realized that toenails needed to be trimmed. Hair sometimes seemed to grow everywhere if she didn't keep track of it. Her breath could become atrocious without brushing at least twice a day.

She considered herself lucky that she didn't have to sleep; she spent most of her evenings trying to figure out personal hygiene. How long was necessary in the shower? She assumed a half hour was too much, but was five minutes enough?

Priest was in the middle of a makeup experiment when Riley arrived one morning. Riley blinked at her, furrowed her brow, and said, "What the hell happened to you?"

"Makeup."

"Take it down to a single coat, Tammy Faye." She checked her watch and guided Priest back into the apartment. "Come on, I'll help you scrape some of that stuff off."

In the bathroom, Priest removed her blouse and stood in her undershirt while Riley removed the most garish of the cosmetics. "You're a gorgeous woman, Priest. Literally angelic. When it comes to embellishing that, less is more."

"Like you."

Riley scoffed. "Not exactly. All right, you're presentable. Let's get to work."

Priest put her blouse back on and followed Riley through the apartment.

"You know, you shouldn't consider your body as just a way to get around. You should enjoy it. You wear suits to work and you wear pajamas the rest of the time. No reason you can't enjoy the body God literally gave to you."

After work, Priest considered Riley's comment. She went shopping and examined the racks upon racks of clothing for sale. It didn't make sense to her. Like the strings of restaurants on every block. Italian food, Mexican, burgers, pizza, sushi, sandwich shops, fast food places, chicken. Food was sustenance. It was necessary to survive, like breathing and using the restroom. Yet mortals somehow made eating one of life's pleasures. She would eat, but she couldn't get the same pleasure from a meal as humans seemed to. Fish, chicken, meat... it all tasted the same to her.

The same with clothing. All that was required was something to protect you from the elements. Colors and designs and outfits and layers... it made no sense to her.

Still, she picked out some casual clothes to help her blend in with the rest of her neighborhood. She was on her way to the cashier to pay when she passed a section labeled "intimates." Priest hesitated, eyeing the sea of colorful lace. She looked around, as if someone might consider her perverted for her interest, and stepped into the section. This was another aspect of humanity that she didn't quite understand, but it did make more sense than food and clothing. Underwear was a necessity, but this was meant to seduce and entice.

She picked several colors, hid them under her other purchases, and moved quickly to the cashier to pay and get out of the store.

When she got home, she removed the tags and placed her new outfits on hangers. She took a shower, this time trying for twelve minutes, and toweled off before she looked at the small white bag she'd left on the counter. She bit her bottom lip, looked at her reflection in the mirror, and decided it was all part of the human experience. She took out a black bra and matching panties, putting them on before she stepped back and looked at herself. Her stomach was flat, athletically muscled. Her breasts were small, but well-proportioned to her frame. She dragged her fingers down her stomach to her hips and turned sideways.

Priest had to admit that it was a good body, compared to some of the bodies she'd seen during her time on Earth. She rested her shoulders against the wall and ran her hands down her stomach, over her navel. Her body responded to the gentle touch, and she shivered as goosebumps rose under her fingertips. She moved her hand up to her breasts and touched them through the thin lace of her new brassiere. Her nipples responded to her touch, becoming tight and erect.

Her other hand strayed to the waistband of her panties. Riley had told her to enjoy her new body; she supposed there were worse ways she could do that. She could go down to the pizza parlor and eat an entire large pepperoni by herself. She could pierce herself, get tattoos... sexual gratification was as much a part of the human experience as eating. It was a necessary biological urge and, like eating, Priest had found herself fighting easily urges from time to time, but what if she gave in?

She pushed two fingers into her underwear, through the thin patch of pubic hair she had only recently decided to cut. It felt soft against the pads of her fingers and she stroked it, closing her eyes as she let the feeling wash through her. She moved her feet further apart and moved her fingers lower. She'd ignored this part of her anatomy for the most part; there was no real purpose to it beyond using the restroom, and the idea of exploration had never really occurred to her until now.

Two fingers moved between her legs, and her other hand ran up along her torso. Somehow touching herself there made her entire torso tingle, made her skin hypersensitive, and she took advantage of it by brushing her hand over her ribs and up to the underside of her breasts. She closed her eyes and wondered if she should fantasize. Was it necessary? Could she climax with just a touch, or was there a mental aspect to it as well?

Her fingers explored the folds between her legs. She wished Riley could be there to answer the questions she had.

The idea of Riley sitting on the sink, watching her, made Priest suck in a breath between clenched teeth. She didn't try to determine which thought caused the reaction, being watched or being watched by Riley, she just held on to the feeling as she stroked the pad of her finger over the wet flesh of her mound. She alternated fingers, stroking with her index finger before using the middle finger to tease herself with penetration. She ran her other hand across her chest, under the cup of her bra to squeeze her breast.

Priest used the tip of her index finger to spread the gathering moisture over her folds, her breath catching in her throat. She crossed her fingers together and, after a moment of teasing herself, let her fingers push inside. She groaned and sagged against the wall, bending her knees as she rocked her hips forward. She started a gentle rhythm, rocking her hips in time with the movement of her fingers, running her thumb over her hard nipple.

With two fingers inside of herself, Priest pressed the heel of her hand against her mound. She slipped her middle finger out and ran it along her folds, stroking until she found the hard bud of her clitoris. Her lips parted in a silent moan as she ran her wet fingertip over it, and the pleasure seemed to wash out across her body in waves. She touched her tongue to her top lip, tasted sweat, and moved her hips to increase the pressure between her legs.

She looked at her reflection in the mirror. Sweat beaded on her forehead, glistened on her chest. Her eyes were hooded, her lips parted, and for the first time she could see herself as Caitlin Priest. A mortal. She rested her head against the wall and touched her clitoris with more pressure, her finger slick with her own juices. She pinched her nipple and moaned loudly, arching her back as she balanced on the balls of her feet. She could feel something happening, could feel the pleasure branching out from the spot she was touching. It spread through her body like a warmth, her heart beating a staccato rhythm against her ribs.

"Oh, my," she gasped, her voice weak. "Oh... feels so good..."

Her toes curled against the tile of her bathroom and her eyes rolled back in her head. She groaned loudly and her fingers clutched her breast hard enough to leave red marks as she pressed her hips forward and her hand inward. "Yes... yes..."

Her entire body convulsed with her climax, and her wings spontaneously expanded from her shoulder blades. They barely fit in the confines of the bathroom, curling out and around her like a curtain. The gossamer feathers flexed as if with their own breath, casting a pale white-gold glow on every reflective surface in the bathroom.

Priest's skin felt hypersensitive, as if any touch would trigger a second convulsion. She kept still, eyes closed, wings trembling around her as she sagged against the wall. She dropped her free hand between her legs, cupping her other hand through the lace of her panties. A shock of blonde hair fell into her eyes, and she found herself chuckling, her skin flushed, her teeth working her bottom lip as her feet sank flat to the floor.

She would move eventually. Put on her regular pajamas and go to bed. But she just wanted to bask in the feeling for a little while longer before she went back to her regular life. She sank to the floor, folded her wings around herself like a shawl, and waited for the shockwaves of pleasure to stop.

Riley arrived a few minutes later than usual the next morning, but Priest was ready to go. She adjusted her suit jacket, made sure the knot in her tie was sitting just so against her collarbone, ran her hand down the material of her vest. She was wearing her new, special underwear beneath the suit. She wasn't sure why; there was no real point to it. No one would ever see it. But the knowledge that she had it on gave her a thrill.

She answered the door and smiled. "Good morning, Riley."

Riley raised her eyebrows and dipped her chin in greeting. "You ready to go?"

"I am." She took her jacket off the hook and closed her apartment door before following Riley down the stairs. "I masturbated last night."

Riley nearly tripped over the bottom stair. She turned and looked at Priest for a long moment before she decided to just shake her head and let it go. "Really? Me too. How was yours?"

Priest grinned. "It was awesome. I look forward to doing it again."

"Just try to contain yourself in the car. I need to keep my attention on the road."

"I'm sure I'll be able to restrain myself." She glanced back toward her apartment and mentally added, *At least until I get home tonight.* She chuckled and got into Riley's car.

About the Author

Geonn Cannon is from Oklahoma. He writes the things he would like to read and reads things he wishes he had written. In his spare time he writes the occasional review for the online publication Geek Speak Magazine.

www.ingramcontent.com/pod-product-compliance
Lightning Source LLC
LaVergne TN
LVHW091527060526
838200LV00036B/508